No Mayday! No Mayday!

A Novel by Terry Stanton.

"There are only two emotions in a plane: boredom and terror." Orson Welles.

No Mayday! No Mayday!

First Printing 2019
Second Edition January 2020

ISBN: 978-0-6485470-0-6

For more information contact tez_stanton@hotmail.com

Bookcover artwork by Ron Hindmarsh.

Note: Some of this novel is technical with regard to aircraft communications. To avoid including too much of that sort of thing in the story, I have put an Annexe at the end in which I have endeavoured to explain the technicalities in what I hope is a correct and simple fashion.

List of Characters

Mustafa Sirigur. 1st Officer Pilot.
Muhamed Subrama. Flight Captain.
Lynn Galloway. Investigative Journalist, Exposure TV.
Detective Sergeant Simpson, Hampshire CID.
Zane Pretorius III. CIA Agent (aka Adam Dennis).
Reza Ali Bukhari. Iranian Scientist. (aka Ove Larsen).
Ho Chang. Chinese Scientist.
Jamie Stallard. Meteorologist. Lynn's boyfriend.
Shaw Bradford. Executive at Noga Corporation (CIA).
Chief (Ethel Hardwick) at Noga Corporation (CIA).
Selim Abdullah. Iranian Scientist (aka Leopold Reicha).
Peck, Jacobs, Donarski, and Hurt. CIA ('Company') men.
Karen Macauley. Lynn's best friend and sister of her solicitor.
Kadijha Subrama. Captain Subrama's wife.
Nancy Koh. His mistress.
Nick Carter. Lynn's pilot friend.
Liz Carter. Nick's wife.
Spencer Bunder. Lynn's cousin, and a Flight Captain.
Marion Gorman. Editor, Exposure TV.
Julian Prentis. In-house solicitor at Exposure TV.
Malcolm Broadbridge. Producer at Exposure TV.
Niall Merrylees. Lynn's solicitor; Karen Macauley's brother.

Gavin Johnson. Former Royal Marine.
Matt Gordon. TV cameraman with Exposure TV.
Nicola (Nic) Stark. Assistant Producer at Exposure TV.
Greg Armstrong. Ex paratrooper. Bodyguard with Harrington Security.
Clint Esterhazy. United States Navy Sailor.
Bernardo O'Higgins. Argentinean Private Investigator.
Grant Young. Washington DC journalist.
Jane Morgan. Petersfield Teacher.
Detective Inspector Colin Lacey. Metropolitan Police, SO15.
Dr Graham Phillips, Coroner's pathologist for Portsmouth.
British Foreign Secretary.
Sir Arthur Napier, Permanent Secretary, Foreign Office.

Prologue

9th March, 2013.

Just before Captain Muhamed Subrama headed to the runway, Air Traffic Control (ATC) gave him the Squawk Code for secondary radar identification of the plane by the authorities. He entered the code into the transponder equipment.

Having reached the runway he was given clearance for take-off. Then the green and gold South East Asia Airways plane, with its beautiful frangipani blossom logo on the tail fin, took off from Kuala Lumpur Airport at 1.42 am bound for Beijing. The Captain was assisted by First Officer Mustafa Sirigur who was flying the plane. The world standard time, known as Greenwich Mean Time (GMT), or UTC, was 17.42. Soon after that, as the plane continued to climb, First Officer Sirigur turned off the seat-belt sign. At 18.12 UTC the Captain informed ATC in Kuala Lumpur they had reached their allotted cruising height of 35,000 feet.

At 2.23am Malaysia time (18.23 pm UTC) ATC radioed the plane:
"Please contact Ho Chi Minh City. Goodnight."
People on the ground thought it was First Officer Sirigur who replied, "Goodnight South East Asia 439."
After that, apart from some brief old-style WW2 defence radar contact, and other technical electronic communications, the plane was never heard from again. As far as could reliably be ascertained at the time by people on the ground, it

was never seen again either. It started the biggest mystery in the history of aviation.

Lynn, 9th March, 2014.

I saw a statuesque coloured woman come through the doors into the airport Departure concourse in a brisk and business-like manner. She looked very serious despite her gay multi-coloured Nigerian style dress. I was in the concourse with my cameraman making a film and doing a piece to camera.

"I've just been interviewing the head of security here in Sydney's Kingsford Smith Airport – and he's ..."

Suddenly I noticed that the lady in the African outfit was heading for me. She was running, knocking into and even knocking over one or two of the people milling about. My focus changed immediately as she careered across the huge space. I could see she was angry. I stopped talking and as I did so she grabbed my arm hard, saying in a clearly Australian accent, "My husband died on that plane, and I godda find out why."

Restraining the urge to punch the woman, I did my best to smile: "I'm sorry to hear about your husband, but I've really no idea what you're talking about. Please let go of my arm."

She did so. "Your TV station's been making enquiries; their application to the Transport Safety Bureau's been turned down by the Chief Commissioner."

I shook my head. "Are you talking about the Australian ABC, ma'am? I'm with a British TV company."

The coloured woman seized up for a moment. "Fair dinkum? I should have noticed your pommie accent. Sorry." She started to cry. "I'm so upset; no-one tells us anything. I was talking about SEA439."

"Now I get it," I said, nodding in understanding. "I'm Lynn Galloway. I'm with Exposure TV based in London." We shook hands. "No need to apologise. So your husband is missing with the plane which vanished a year ago?" I decided against signalling the cameraman to stop filming. I try not to take advantage of the distraught but this looked like a new story as well as a news story. I like to think my programmes are more serious than simply exploiting the emotions of the bereaved. "You mentioned an application?"

"Yeah. The ABC has asked for a copy of the report of the ATSB ..."

"That's the Transport Safety Board for Australia?"

"That's the one. They asked for a copy of the report which went to the Malaysian Investigators, but they won't tell us, the relatives, the widows and kids. They say it's all down to the Malaysian Government to tell us what happened. I came in here looking for someone who might have more information."

"Have you got children?" I asked, fishing in the pocket of my black jeans for a hanky and handing it to the woman.

"Thanks. I've got three little-uns." She dried her eyes, then blew her nose on it loudly, and offered it back to me.

I waved it away as politely as I could. "You keep it; you might need it." I felt I had to do something for her. "I can't help you, I'm afraid. I'm here making a documentary about

3

airport security and crime in Sydney and around the world. I think you'd do well to go to the ABC and ask them how their Freedom of Information request is doing. That's what it's called, isn't it?"

"That's exactly what I mean. Lynn, did you say? I'm Kiralee. I want a copy of the report that's been kept secret. It's a year today since the plane disappeared from Kuala Lumpur, I know nothing about it, and my own government don't help me. Whose side are they on? Who are they protecting? Themselves for searching in the wrong bloody place? Or the airline? Or the Malaysians? Or someone else?"

"Someone else, Kiralee?" That sounded intriguing.

"I thought the airport people here might know something."

"They might." I pointed down the concourse. "I've just interviewed the head of security. His office is down there. You turn left after that kiosk, and his door will be right in front of you."

She took hold of my hand. "You've been very kind. I'd been married ten years when he disappeared last year. It's a year ago today. You've been very kind - yeah - I said that already. I hope I haven't messed up your filming too much."

I told her not to worry, pointed to her dress and asked: "Have you been to Nigeria?"

The woman looked down at her bright clothes and smiled. "No, Lynn. I'm a native Australian. What you call an aborigine. I just love these colours." She wandered off, very subdued again. The camera man turned off his video and said: "Poor soul."

"Definitely, Matt. Looks like a great story, though. Well, we'd better try to get the show on the road again. Ready?" Matt switched back on and gave a thumbs up. 'This is Lynn Galloway in Sydney's Kingston Smith Airport. I've been talking with the Head of ....'"

10th August, 2015.

Detective Sergeant Simpson from Hampshire CID stood on the lip of the gulley, staring down at the corpse of the red-headed woman lying in the mud at the bottom. A Police photographer had taken pictures of her as she'd been found, face down. Once he'd examined the immediate surroundings the pathologist had turned her over onto a sheet of plastic so he could study the wound that had killed her. There was enough mud on her face. He didn't want it in her hair too.

Simpson had thought he'd never seen her before. He thought it unlikely she was part of the local underworld, even from Portsmouth; he knew most of them, having put many behind bars. Still, it looked like a gangland killing. That's what the neat bullet hole in the middle of her forehead told him. The slug had exited from the back of her skull, leaving a huge clot of blood in her thick hair.

"Can you wipe the mud off her face, Graham?"

The pathologist looked up. He was crouching by the woman's head. "Should be OK. It's obviously this mud here, so we know what it is." He pointed at the puddle. "You want to take a photo?"

"Yeah. No clue who she is. I better circulate the picture through the force asap. Misspers and all that."

"Doubt anyone's reported her missing yet. I'm sure she only died in the last 14 or 15 hours. She hasn't been here that long."

Simpson summoned the photographer over, but turned back to Graham Phillips. "Before you clean her up, what about gunpowder traces? Don't want to destroy evidence."

Dr Phillips chuckled. "No need to worry about that. I can tell at a glance, even through the dirt, she was shot at point blank range. The powder burns are all round the entry wound." He mimed firing a pistol. "Someone put that gun right up against her forehead, pulled the trigger. Curtains for whoever she was."

Simpson actually shuddered. "Not suicide, was it."

"Not a chance. It's hard to hold a gun straight to your own forehead at 90 degrees, and then pull the trigger. And when you drop down dead, how d'you hide the weapon? Hasn't been found, has it?"

Simpson shook his head. "No. So she must have been shot somewhere else and dumped here. We won't find the bullet either."

"Well, with a hole that size in the back of her skull it would be almost impossible to find round here even if she was shot here. But if she was, where's the blood? Hardly a drop on the ground, is there?"

Part 1. The Background.

October 1988.

Muhamed Subrama had noticed several times that a tall man who didn't seem to have anything much to do with the flying school dined in the canteen quite often. When he did so, he always seemed to find a seat fairly close to Muhamed. On one occasion Muhamed was eating out cheaply with a friend in a Chinese restaurant when the man came in, said 'hello' to him, and then sat at a table nearby.

The man was very elegantly dressed in a cream linen suit, white shirt, and a paisley patterned green tie, and highly polished brown shoes. He had well-groomed dark hair, and a slim moustache the width of his top lip. He had a dark complexion, and looked like a fifties film star. Muhamed thought of Gregory Peck or David Niven. He sounded American. He read a book while he waited for his food, and while eating. He put a small black object on the table. Muhamed thought it looked like a camera.

He noticed the same man quite a few times after that; he often had the camera with him. His lofty elegance contrasted sharply with Muhamed's casual attire, thick black curly hair, homely round face, and medium height.

Muhamed was in Manila training to be a commercial pilot. He had been sent there six months earlier by South East Asia Airways, the Malaysian company he'd joined as a cadet that year. He wasn't getting much money to live on, but the company was paying for his course. He thought that was great. He was very keen and making good progress. All his reports were excellent or marked 'distinction'.

He could afford a small, cheap, and rather dingy flat in the city. He could even afford to eat out some of the time, but he preferred to save his cash by eating as well as he could in the flying school canteen. This school was owned by some Americans, and the Instructors were mostly American too. The chance of learning to fly big Boeings or Airbuses was what appealed to Muhamed. He had a lovely girlfriend back home and hoped to marry her in due course, so he wanted to save. Her name was Kadijha.

Towards the end of October, at about 6 o'clock in the evening, Muhamed was getting his dinner ready when there was a knock at the door. When he opened it a crack he found himself looking up at the moustachioed man standing there.

"May I come in?" he said.

"What for? I not really know you."

"That's true, but I've called so that we can get to know each other better."

"Should I want to? Very unhappy about this."

"No need to be unhappy, Muhamed. I hope what I have to say will make you a good bit happier. May I come in please?"

Muhamed was hesitant. How did this man know his name? He did not want to be rude in case the man was important at the flying school or the airline. After thinking about it for a few seconds, he opened the door reluctantly, and stood back for the man to pass.

He left off getting his meal and made them both green tea. They sat at the small table. The American smiled and held out his hand.

"My name is Dennis. Mr Adam Dennis."

"How you know my name is Muhamed?"

"Ah well, that's not important. Just say that it's my business to know things, and I've been keeping an eye on you lately."

Muhamed looked worried. "I know. I see you lots of times. You watch me in canteen. I not like it. I do no wrong thing."

"I know that, Muhamed. The directors of the flying school tell me you're a very bright young man, and are doing exceptionally well." Dennis looked around. "But you do not live well here."

"I ver' well. Not ill. I have flat, money, food."

Adam Dennis chuckled at that, and looked around again somewhat contemptuously. "I know, but it's not much of a flat, is it? And you have to be careful about the cost of things."

"What you want, Mr Dennis? I am happy here."

"Yes, I know. But I can make you happier. That photo on the shelf, that's your girlfriend, isn't it? Lovely girl. I know you want to get married. I can help you save up."

Muhamed was getting cross. "You want something, Mr Dennis. You tell."

"OK, Muhamed." Mr Dennis took off his jacket and hung it on the back of his chair and sat down again. Muhamed was scared stiff when he saw Dennis was carrying

9

a pistol in a shoulder holster. "I've heard you talking to your friends and people on the course. I know you're going to be a good pilot. I know you want to earn good money, but it'll be a while. I work for the Noga Corporation. It's a sort of American government thing."

"Sort of thing?" Muhamed was trembling and his voice shook.

"Don't worry about that or what we do, Muhamed. The thing is we look for clever people like you who may be able to do something to help us one day. You want good money, and that is something the USA likes. You sound like you're right wing, not a socialist or communist. That's how you talk to your friends."

Muhamed was getting anxious again. "How you know what we say?"

The man took the small black object from his pocket. "Have you seen this?"

"Yes. Is camera?"

"Well, it can be a camera, but it also has a very sensitive microphone. It does this." The man pressed a button and a voice was heard speaking Bahasa Malay. "Now, I've got a friend who told me what that says."

"Is my voice. I say I want to earn good money flying Boeings. That not bad thing to say."

"Not at all bad. Very good, in fact. These recordings tell me you think like most Americans, and if you help us we can help you."

"How I help you?"

"Muhamed, I don't have a definite thing the Noga Corporation wants you to do right now. We just like to get clever guys like you to be on our side and say they'll do something to help us one day if we need them to. You're only twenty-one, so there's plenty of time for something to crop up ..."

"Crop up? What is crop up?"

"Something will happen, OK? At the moment it's more about what we can do to help you, like we could pay the rent on this flat, and then when you've finished the flying course, we'll go on paying the same amount into a bank account so you can save up to get married." The man paused for some seconds. "Look, you don't need to decide this now. Think about it for a few days, and next time you see me in the canteen, say 'Hello Mr Dennis', and I'll know you're interested. Then we'll start giving you the money for your rent. If you don't speak to me, I know you don't want anything to do with it."

"How I know when you want me to help you?"

"Oh, I'll be in touch, maybe ask you to find out something about a pilot or crew member, or a passenger, or where someone is going; perhaps what's in the cargo hold. Maybe something more serious, but if I do that, we'll pay you a lot of money."

"How much is lot?"

"Well, it depends what the job is, but you'd never need to work again, OK? I gotta go now. Last thing is, don't talk to anyone about this, and I mean anyone. This is serious stuff, just between you and me. Here's a little something to be going on with." He threw 500 dollars in dollar bills onto the table, and as Muhamed picked it up and looked at him, Dennis was taking his photo.

Two weeks later Mr Dennis was sitting in the canteen, and Muhamed Subrama said: "Hello, Mr Dennis."

Dennis held out his hand, and Muhamed took it, thinking they were going to shake hands. Dennis squeezed the knuckles of the Malaysian's hand in a grip like a vice, and drew him down until they were face to face. "Just remember, Muhamed, I shall be relying on you. Don't ever let me down."

***

Adam Dennis's real name was Zane Pretorius III. Dennis was his covert name. He was the son of an Iranian American father whose grandparents had emigrated from Tehran to the USA in the 1930s. They had brought up their children, including Zane's father, to be bilingual, had converted to Christianity, and joined the Episcopal Church in Detroit. Grandfather changed his name to Zane Pretorius, and named his elder son after himself. The whole family became model American citizens. Zane Pretorius II joined the army as a radio engineer. When posted to Alabama he married a local girl, Marcia, a pretty mixed race Afro-American. He had been a top language student at Columbus and spoke excellent French and Spanish with hardly a trace of accent. French was also spoken at home, as it was one of the languages used in Iran, and Marcia had learned it at school to a high standard. He continued his parents' policy, and he and Marcia brought up their son and daughter to speak perfect Farsi, and good

French. The third Zane Pretorius thus had the dark looks and speech necessary to pass as Iranian, or from many places in the Middle East and North Africa.

Zane had joined an officer recruitment programme at University, and had passed with distinction. His ambition was to have an Army career, just like his father. His swarthy appearance and knowledge of languages made him perfect material for the CIA. He was recruited, and began to climb the ladder. He knew the Chief of the Noga Corporation, an off-shoot of the Central Intelligence Agency in Washington. His seniority was such that he even knew her name was Ethel Hardwick. Chief was her code name, although it was also a nick-name for the Presidents of the USA. Ethel would have had no objection to being that Chief.

Putting it very mildly indeed, Zane Pretorius III was not a nice man. He was an excellent shot, and had assassinated a Russian discovered with false identity papers working in a factory making parts for the latest fighter jets. There was nothing he was not prepared to undertake.

January, 2003.

The restaurant stood on a large wooden jetty protruding over the water on the West Bank of the St Lawrence River in Montreal, Province of Quebec, Canada. It was evening and the moon seemed to be suspended a foot above the horizon. Two young men sat at a table near the windows. It was freezing out, but very warm inside. The man with his back to the water was tall and slim, with a full beard of the kind many Muslims wear. That was not surprising, because a

Muslim was what he was. His name was Reza Ali Bukhari. Like his hair, the beard was black and neatly trimmed.

The other man, facing the water and the Muslim across the table, could see the moon. He was clearly from the Far East. In fact he was Chinese. His name was Ho Chang, an honours graduate of the Nuclear Physics Faculty of a top University in Beijing. He was thirty, a year or two younger than his Iranian companion, who had a PhD in the same science from Cambridge University. Chang was sponsored by the People's Republic Government to undertake postgraduate study in the West to see how, if at all, the subject of atomic science was taught and learned differently from the Chinese methods. He had been a conscientious student of English throughout his schooling, and had continued that course to degree level at University. His French was adequate but not as good as his English. Like many Far Eastern English speakers he had an American accent, which, with his Chinese accent, affected his French, too. Still, it was good enough to get him by in Montreal, where many French Canadians prefer people who speak their language. Chang was short, stocky, looked fit, and clean shaven.

Reza's route to Montreal was rather different. He had been sent to England to study at Cambridge on an Iranian Government grant. He considered himself to have been extremely lucky to have gone there. In fact, he believed himself lucky to have survived childhood. Born in 1971, Reza was the son of Ali, a high ranking Iranian Police officer, who had been of similar rank under the government of Muhammad Reza Shah Pahlavi, the Shah of Iran. The Shah came to power backed by the USA in 1953, and was forced by demonstrators to leave the country in 1979. Many of his father's colleagues simply disappeared when Ayatollah Khomeini returned from his exile in France, and the Shah fled into his own, taking a fortune with him, abandoning the Peacock Throne. He stayed for a while in Egypt, and then in Morrocco. Extremely ill with cancer, the Shah was admitted recluctantly by President Carter to the USA for medical treatment. He died in Egypt and was buried there.

Ali Bukhari had named his son after the then ruling Shah, and this could have been the most unlucky thing to have done by 1979 when the Shah had to flee. However, father had good contacts on both sides of the political chasm. Like most senior police officers everywhere, Ali possessed much dirt on the main players in both camps. He negotiated his survival and that of his family by undertaking to the incoming powers that he would not reveal what he knew about them, and would share with them what he knew about the heads of the former regime. Unknown to young Reza, this largely explained why a number of his father's old friends had disappeared. He had traded their secrets to the Ayatollah's henchmen, resulting in their arrest, or had warned real friends that they ought to say goodbye to Iran. He had retained his Police Rank under the new system, and been promoted for his zeal in hunting down as criminals former members of the Shah's government. Criminal thugs and torturers is exactly what some of them were.

Bukhari Senior had gone in his youth from Tehran to Birmingham University as part of an Anglo-Iranian exchange, and had met and married Reza's mother there. They were a very happy family, notwithstanding the virtual double life Ali was forced to live. Reza had grown up bi-lingual, speaking idiomatic and colloquial English with an educated upper class accent. He also spoke fluent French. It was no secret that Iran wanted to develop nuclear power. As Reza put it, whether that was for peaceful or warlike purposes depended on whose secret service propaganda you listened to. In pursuit of that development the government had sponsored Reza to fly to Canada to further his knowledge there.

The Chinese and the Iranian had met by chance two weeks earlier. They had gone to the same lecture in the Ernest Rutherford Physics Building of McGill University, and fortuitously sat next to each other, exchanging only polite greetings. At the next lecture they chose to sit in the same seats, and exchanged a few remarks about the lecture and the lecturer. At the finish, Chang asked Reza if he would like to go for coffee, which they did. They found they had much in common. Both had learned to play classical music as children. Chang's instrument was the violin, which made him laugh. He said so many kids were learning the violin in China, it was a certainty that few of them would make it into an orchestra, let alone to the concert platform as a virtuoso. Reza had obtained his taste for Beethoven and Mozart from his mother, who was an accomplished pianist, had attended the Royal College of Music in Kensington as a student, and

16

given recitals in Wigmore Hall and other venues. He played almost as well as his mother. He hated a day to go by when he did not play, and had hired a keyboard for the lounge of the small flat he had rented off Rue St Denis in the suburbs of Montreal.

Chang suggested he should come to the Iranian's flat the following week with his violin, so they could try a Mozart Sonata he just happened to have brought from home. Reza thought that a delightful idea. They had a most enjoyable afternoon; they played then so as not to disturb Reza's neighbours, who were out at work all day.

They agreed to play again the next week and afterwards have dinner together. That was why they were now sitting in the very French looking river-bank restaurant in the St Gabriel district of the city. They talked about what they might play next. Reza offered to go to a music shop and buy something suitable, and Chang said he'd go to the University music library and see what he could borrow.

Fewer than half of the tables in the restaurant were occupied, but Reza noticed the couple behind Chang and to his left. This table was occupied by a young man and the most enormously fat woman he had ever seen. He was a well-mannered man, and did not like to stare, but found it difficult not to do so. The lady was so wide she occupied almost all of her side of a table for four, and her friend, being of normal proportions, took up only half of his.

It seemed as though he gazed for ages, but in fact it was only a few seconds before he returned his attention to Chang. He could hear the couple talking about the moon and the lights of yachts, fishing vessels, and small ships to be seen in the river. He and Chang finished discussing music, turned to the course they were on, and the practical difficulties of the science which interested them.

"The trouble is Iran has a tough time getting hold of uranium at all, let alone enriched uranium of weapons grade."

Chang nodded his head. "So we hear in China, if what we are told is to be believed. Of course, the acquisition of the basic ore is not a problem for us. The Australians have loads of it, and will sell anything to anyone if the price is right and you know who to talk to. And we have our own."

"Maybe, but the Australians won't sell to us. The Americans don't want them to, and they always do what they're told by the USA."

Chang was puzzled. "Do you want Iran to have nuclear weapons, then?"

"Well, you have them, don't you?"

"Yes, we do."

Reza laughed. "Frankly, I don't understand why anyone wants them. They all say they're for defence, but you don't need to defend yourself with them unless you're being attacked with them. If you are, and retaliate accordingly, you just end up with two uninhabitable countries, so any victory is completely hollow. On top of that you may poison the rest of the planet with radiation, and there may be no-one left to celebrate the end of such a ghastly idiotic war."

"So, Reza, are you saying the only real purpose of nuclear weapons is to attack?"

"I don't know what I'm saying, or at least I have no idea what the answer might be, but it's worth recalling that the only time the bomb has been dropped on an enemy was in 1945 when only the Yanks had it. That was an attack."

Chang shook his head again. "Well, on that gloomy note perhaps we'd better get a bit lighter. How's it going with finding a girlfriend?"

Reza laughed again, and that was what they chatted about.

Reza was absorbed in this much more interesting topic, and failed to notice the obese woman struggle to her feet. She held her mobile phone in her right hand. She took a photo as she pushed herself up from her chair with her left hand on the top of the table.

She leaned over the table and then moved surprisingly lightly on her feet to the door, and went outside to dial. When her call was answered she heard: "Noga Corporation, Montreal Office."

"I've just heard a strange conversation between an Arab - I think Iranian from what I heard - and some sort of Asian guy. It was about uranium and ....."

"Not over the phone. Come in at ten tomorrow and tell me then."

"Fine. I've got a photo too."

She took another shot as she went back in and sat down.

Lynn, May 2005.

I came out of the Regency door of Exposure TV in a state of high excitement, looking at my mobile phone. The

TV company occupied a couple of elegant buildings in a corner of an equally elegant square behind the Bayswater Road. I skipped down the steps, turned left and collided with someone, and nearly hit the ground. I'd walked straight into the path of a tall good looking man with wavy chestnut hair, who was walking towards me reading the early evening paper. He dropped the paper, and fell to his knees. I dropped my phone, and staggered back. He picked up the phone and his paper.

I was a bit shocked, but still too happy to be cross. When I laughed, he did too. I held my hand out to help him up, but he put the phone into it, and stayed on his knees. I smiled. "Are you going to propose?"

He laughed again, giving me a brief appraising and appreciative scrutiny. "Might not be a bad idea. Bit soon for that though, don't you think? I've a better idea. Why don't we go to the pub near the station and have a drink and get over our dreadful accident?"

"Station?"

"Lancaster Gate Underground."

This was a bit sudden and I was minded to refuse. But he was good looking, and his bright blue eyes held no threat, just good humour. "I don't know the pub. I live in Fulham; don't often get over here."

He rose to his feet, and held out his hand. "I'm Jamie Stallard. I live round the corner in the Square. "You seem very happy; had some good news?"

I introduced myself. "Let's talk about it over our drink – just one drink!"

That's what we did. I felt a bit out of place in the pub. I'd dressed carefully for the interview in a cream blouse under a suit I'd had made in a blue pin-stripe. A modest gold chain round my neck was my only adornment. The skirt ended just above the knee, and my tights disappeared into black patent leather shoes with four inch heels. Jamie clearly thought I was very attractive indeed. I didn't object to that at all.

He told me he worked at the Meteorological Office and was passionate about the weather. I thought that sounded pretty boring, but he made me laugh so much about almost everything that I thought perhaps he was more fun than his job suggested. I told him I wasn't just happy today; I was ecstatic. I'd been with the BBC since doing journalism at City University, London, eight years ago, and was an investigative reporter for police and criminal matters. I'd applied to a relatively new TV production company, Exposure, for a new position. It involved doing much deeper investigations - more serious stuff involving police corruption, powerful gangs, drugs, murders, and even some international involvement. A slight drop in pay was the price I had to pay for now, but this job was exactly what I wanted.

"Let me guess. You got the job."

"I did, Jamie. I can hardly believe it."

"Well I can believe it, just to look at you. If you were any happier you'd explode."

"I need to celebrate."

Jamie smiled again. "One drink in this pub is hardly a celebration, but I tell you what." He pulled an envelope out of the pocket of his rather expensive looking tweed jacket.

"Here are two tickets for 'Phantom of the Opera' tomorrow at Her Majesty's Theatre. I'll be honest. I didn't buy them hoping to bump into you. My mother was supposed to come up from the village, but she's got the flu. Can I celebrate with you, please? Can I take you out to dinner and to the show?"

"Are you always that romantic?"

He pretended to look worried: "What, talking about Mum, you mean?"

I laughed again: "No, I'm glad you're a man who loves his Mum. I mean you wooing a girl with one of the most romantic musicals ever, on the first date too."

"Speaking for myself, I hope it's the first of many. In any case, for real romance I'd take you to 'La Traviata', but maybe you don't like opera."

If only you knew, I thought, but didn't say; a woman has to keep some sense of mystery, doesn't she? Violetta was my favourite operatic heroine; I'd give anything to be able to sing her arias. Jamie smiled as he gave me another look showing just how attractive he found me. There's such a difference between men who leer and those who adore.

July 2007.

Chang and Reza walked along together in Shuangxiu Park in Beijing.

"I shouldn't really say this, Reza, but when I was in Canada I saw freedom of speech in the press, and on TV, and I heard Canadians saying just whatever they fancied. They don't seem to worry about what the government or anyone else thinks. I'm worried that your views on nuclear weapons will get me into very big trouble here. After all, I work in the nuclear industry."

Reza nodded. "I know, and I have to tell you I haven't been entirely up front with you. When the government nuclear people at home knew I was coming here – I had to tell them – they ordered me to find out if there was any way China would sell weapons grade uranium to us."

Chang's jaw dropped, and it was a moment before he could speak. "Jesus, Reza ...."

"Hey, Ho, that's a pretty peculiar expletive for a communist to use to a Muslim, isn't it? Anyway, you must come to Iran, and see what we are doing, and we can share more of our ideas. Meanwhile, you may be able to talk to someone who knows how our requirements could be met."

Chang became very intense. "I didn't think Iran had much money because of the US and UN sanctions."

"I'm not well up on that, but we have plenty of oil, and I'm sure ways can be found to get a lot of it over to China. After all, it only has to go about 1000 miles through Afghanistan, or a little bit more through Pakistan, and probably less through Turkmenistan, Uzbekistan, and Tajikistan. There are corrupt officials and politicians in all those countries. They'll do almost anything for a fistful of dollars."

"OK, Reza. We'll have to be very careful - get as much information as we can." He was whispering. "We should pretend the last thing we are doing is to get weapons grade uranium for Iran. We get some of our uranium from Kazakhstan. Maybe we can divert some material to Iran as

23

trucks go back and forth. If our government is prepared to do it, I'm sure we can find a way."

Reza nodded again and laughed. "That's the last time we'll even say it. We'd have to be pretty careful about that. What you'll come to Iran for is to discuss the import of our dates and dried fruit into China. Iran is in enough trouble with the USA and the UN and sanctions because they think Iran wants to make atom bombs. We don't want any more of that!"

"Absolutely." Chang thought for a moment. "I've made arrangements for you to see some of our plant. On Wednesday we'll go to the China Institute of Atomic Energy. They built the 60 Megawatt China Advanced Research Reactor, and the 65 Megawatt Experimental Fast Reactor. With a bit of luck we'll get permission for you to see those too."

"Fantastic. I can't wait." Reza skipped like a boy a couple of times then turned to Chang with a big smile. "We need some good music to celebrate."

"We certainly do. You remember I wrote and told you I'd started learning the viola instead of the violin?"

"I do. You said there aren't so many viola players so it's easier to get people to play with, and find groups which need a violist."

"That's just it. Well, I have a friend who plays the clarinet well, and she wants to play a trio by Mozart."

"You mean the Kegellstadt. It's great. Really happy stuff. Just right for a celebration."

"Her name's Marcelle. Her Dad's French – works at the Embassy. She's coming round tomorrow afternoon."

"I'll be there. Try and stop me!"

July, 2007.

Shaw Bradford walked into his supervisor's office at Noga Corporation in Washington DC. He carried a file.

"Don't you know you're supposed to knock before you come in here?"

"Sorry, Chief. I just forgot. I thought you ought to know about this stuff immediately. I was too excited. That's all I could think about." Shaw could not get on with this woman. She was about fifty-five, very tall and slim, with a beehive hairdo that was out of fashion when she started wearing her pale brown hair like that thirty years ago. She always dressed in a dark grey business suit, which matched her hair - greying these days - with a black scarf tied round her neck and tucked into the top of a white blouse, the top button of which was undone. She never dressed any differently. Shaw wondered whether she wore five sets of identical clothes on weekdays, as they were always clean and looked freshly pressed. They couldn't actually be the same ones she wore the day before. To him she was maybe like Einstein, who was said to have seven sets of identical suits, shirts, ties and shoes so that he didn't have to spend any time thinking about what to wear each day. Shaw didn't know what she wore at weekends. He didn't even know her name; everyone at his level at Noga called her Chief.

She spoke: "You're here now, so sit down and tell me this momentous 'stuff', as you call it." Her Brahmin Boston Harvard accent made a strong contrast with Shaw's small town Wyoming twang.

"One of my tasks is to keep an eye on the monitoring of an Iranian called Reza Bukhari." He made a gesture with a manila folder. This file says in 2003 an agent called Marcia phoned in to the Montreal office with a report on this guy Bukhari. She said he was in Montreal talking to a Chinese guy about uranium and nuclear science."

"I recall that. I sent out a memo asking for him to be monitored. So you landed that job?"

"Yes, Chief. Well, you know ..."

"If I know, don't tell me. And if I don't know you need to tell me, so don't say 'you know', because that's why you're telling me."

Shaw wriggled with embarrassment in his seat, thinking that she had to be the world's worst control freak. "Sure. This guy Bukhari has kept in touch with the Chinaman. His name is Ho Chang. We've had a report from one of our people in Beijing that last week Reza Bukhari landed at Beijing airport, and was met by Chang. They went to stay at Chang's apartment in some sort of classy Chinese Condominium ..."

"I'm sure they don't call them that."

"Well, whatever a Chinese Condo is. This Chinese agent of ours is pretty smart, and succeeded ...."

"He needs to be smart to get the kind of money we pay them over there. And not get caught, but stay alive."

"... in following them about a lot. He says they talked about going to a nuclear facility near Beijing together, but he didn't follow them there, as security would be very tight. Our agent reported this after he got to sit near them in a restaurant. He didn't want to risk being watched or caught, as then the whole operation could be compromised. He got as close as he could to them in more restaurants and other places without being recognised. He overheard some of their conversations. All this smells fishy to me, but he reports that we may be wasting our time on these two."

"Why is that?"

Shaw took a deep breath. "Well, a lot of their talk indicates they don't think nuclear should be used for weapons, especially the Iranian guy. It might just be some sort of cover, I suppose. If China wants to look as though it's prepared to use them, it would be silly for Chang to say he doesn't agree with the use of those weapons."

"He might just say that to get a reaction from Bukhari."

"Maybe, Chief, but if that's what he wanted he didn't get it. They spend a lot of time talking about selling dates and stuff to China. Fact is, the report doesn't say Chang said what he thinks about it. The Iranian said he was not in favour of nuclear weapons. He just wants the peaceful application for power generation."

The Chief leant back in her chair. "That could be so, but I think we still have to keep an eye on these two." She linked her fingers together, and leaned forward on her elbows. "Get our people in Iran keep an eye on Bukhari and let you know when he gets back to Tehran. The next thing we know

Chang'll pay a return visit to Iran. If he does, I want to know about it straight away."

"That's about it, Chief. Chang talked about paying a return visit to Iran, just like you said."

Ethel Hardwick simply snorted. She had no time for sycophants.

Lynn, August 2007.

"So how long have you been with the new TV outfit now, Lynn?"

Karen Macauley and I were sitting in a small select bistro in New King's Road. We could see the grass and trees on Parson's Green across the road to our right. Karen is my oldest and best friend. We've known each other since we were babies, although we did not know we knew each other at the time. Our mothers got to know each other when they took us in our strollers for walks in the local parks in Fulham. Both families lived in Perrymead Street then, and our mums started talking babies whilst sitting on the same park benches.

After a while our fathers became friends too, and they all used to dine together now and again.

"Can you believe it, Karen? It's over two years since I started with Exposure. I still can't quite get hold of how exciting this move has been for me."

"You've certainly come up in the world. I've noticed a lot of the BBC and Channel 4 programmes Scott and I watch are made by your company – even a few on ITV sometimes."

I could imagine the TV shows that Karen and her husband found interesting would come from Exposure. I'm pretty serious myself, but Karen is much more intellectual. We both went to the same Primary School, and then to Lady Margaret School For Girls on Parson's Green. We could just see it from where we sat in the bistro. After A levels I went to work at the local rag, the Fulham Chronicle, not knowing then, but quickly realising, that journalism was what I really wanted. Karen was the brightest girl in our year, and I was third, but she got a scholarship to Girton College, Cambridge. She studied Politics and International Relations, with Music. She was so good on classical guitar she could easily have gone professional when she left university.

"How is Scott, by the way? Here's to him." We both raised our glasses of a very good Verdelho, clinked them, and sipped. "We'd better look at the menu."

Karen said: "I don't think I need to. The special looks good to me." I looked up at the blackboard. Boeuf Bourguignon would suit me too. Karen continued: "Scott's fine. The engineering side of his business is really taking off now, and that makes him happy. So does the other thing."

"What's that, Karen?"

She ran her hand around her stomach the way women do when ... "I've got it! You're having another baby, aren't you? Doesn't show yet, though."

"Number three on the way, Lynn, but I've only just found out for sure."

"So Niall's going to be an Uncle for the third time."

"He's going to be a Godfather to this one. It's about time he had some kids of his own, if you ask me."

Niall Merrylees is Karen's brother. He's also my solicitor. Karen married Scott Macauley 6 years ago and got into the family production business straight away. I said: "Well, some people like to take their time. He's only been married for what – six months?"

"Nine actually." She started twiddling a lock of her dark blond hair the way she always did. "What about you? Jamie still around?"

"I hope for ever. He hasn't said, but I'm fairly sure he wants to pop the question."

"And?"

"He's ideal, but I keep letting my job get in the way. Don't really want to talk about it; makes me feel guilty".

"OK; I'm not going to cross-examine you, even if I think you're silly. So what are you doing at Exposure?"

I told her the company was only three years old when I joined, and the stories I've worked on are bigger and more challenging than anything I'd been given at the BBC. That's ironic as the BBC are now paying for a lot of what I investigate. I've had assignments in Italy connected with the Mafia and British police cooperation with the Italian force in dealing with Mafia links in London and Glasgow.

The waiter came to take our order. I asked for a glass of red to go with it, but Karen declined, saying one wine was enough for the mother-to-be.

"Do you go abroad a lot?"

"Absolutely. That's why we don't get to do lunch much anymore. I'm always away. I've been to Germany and the USA looking into terrorist links between Islamists in both countries, and the way the security forces handle the problems involved. I'm still only thirty-two!"

"I know that, Lynn. We're the same age, remember?"

I told myself to stop short of boasting. As an investigative journalist with Exposure TV my reputation has grown enormously. My reports have been sold internationally, especially in Commonwealth countries such as Australia, New Zealand and Canada. Some have gone to America.

Exposure is now a leading English television production company, still based in London, with rather an anti-establishment reputation, deserved or not. Karen must have read my mind; she went on: "Political corruption and cover-ups, miscarriages of justice, controversial police and intelligence investigations, prejudicial links between government departments and big business on one side of politics, and trade unions on the other – it's just the sort of thing I relish."

"Of course you do. It's what you got your honours degree for, isn't it?"

"You're right. Maybe I should have been a journalist too. D'you ever need help?"

"Quite possibly. One day I may get a political case and need a new independent expert to talk to. The old ones tend to get trotted out all the time."

Conversation ceased when our food arrived, though Karen managed to up-date me on Kerry, 6, and Naomi, 2. I was Godmother to both of them.

Over coffee I told Karen about a section of the company which makes programmes of a serious nature with a message, and another department that films plays and series commissioned by the broadcasters.

Along with my rising repute (modest Lynn!) and that of the company, I've had excellent pay-rises, and I'm now a kind of star in my field. Jamie and I bought a house a year ago.

Lynn, May 2010.

The first thing I noticed as I walked in was a huge bunch of roses, beautifully arranged in a cut-glass vase on the small Pembroke table in the entrance hall. We'd been living in this house for the best part of three years, having dated for about four months after 'Phantom', finding so much in common and to laugh about. One evening after a rather expensive meal in a great restaurant in the King's Road, we'd laughed our way into bed in Jamie's Bayswater flat, and after that could not keep our hands off each other. A week later I moved in with him, and stayed two years.

Jamie now had a senior position in Meteorology, and my career had taken off to an even higher level. We decided to buy the house in Doneraile Street together. It was just round the corner from Craven Cottage, the Fulham Football Ground. Between us we had a big deposit, and Niall Merrylees, Karen's brother, found us a good mortgage with a building society. He was a solicitor at the other end of Fulham, up near Chelsea Football Ground.

When I walked into the lounge I could see through to the dining area where the table was already laid as though royalty were coming to dinner. What was Jamie up to? We shared the cooking most of the time, and he could more than hold his own in the kitchen.

I heard him coming down the stairs and called out: "Have we got company tonight?"

"No, love, only you and me. The dinner's in the oven; should be ready in an hour. I thought we'd go for a walk in the park by the river and come back and eat." Jamie put his arms around me, drew me close, and kissed me with that hint of controlled passion which always aroused me.

"You're up to something, you naughty boy. What's with all those flowers in the hall? It's not my birthday, you know."

"Of course I know, Lynn. But today's a bit special so I thought I'd make something of it. I'll tell you in the park."

We walked hand in hand through Bishop's Park, past the old Palace, to the River. We stood by the railings watching some people from the rowing clubs on the other side sculling up and down. Jamie put his arm round me again, kissed me, and then led me to a seat. He was still on his feet as I sat down.

"The first time I met you, I was on my knees." He sank to his left knee. "That was five years ago today. I've been in love with you ever since." He put his hand in his jacket pocket and brought out a small blue leather box. "Lynn Galloway, will you please marry me?"

An elderly couple walking towards us about fifty yards away stopped to watch, looking much amused.

"I love you too, Jamie, you know I do. And this sapphire and diamond ring is beautiful, so beautiful." I paused and put my hand to Jamie's cheek. "But I have to think about this. We've talked about it before. I'm still not sure I'm ready for it. You know how much my career means to me." I took his hand to pull him up. "Sit here. Put your arm round me again. We'll marry one day, love, and I'm not going anywhere else or with anyone else."

The old people walked past and the lady said, smiling: 'I hope she accepted".

Jamie told her I was thinking about it. I felt rotten.

Jamie looked resentful and a bit sullen, but sat beside me, as I asked, and put his arm round my shoulders. "Well, that's something, I suppose. I half expected this. We're both rather independent, so ...."

"That's the odd thing, Jamie. I'm not independent of you. I couldn't live without you, but I'm just not ready to get wedded yet. Do you hate me now?"

He kissed me again. "How could I?" He ran his fingers through my auburn hair, down to my shoulder. "You're the most beautiful, intelligent, brave woman I've ever met. No-one could come close." He stood. "Let's go home and have dinner."

When we were through the front door I said: "Forget the dinner. Take me to bed."

2011

When the China Airways flight touched down at Tehran airport, Reza Bukhari was waiting for Chang at the exit barrier. They shook hands and gave a high five. Reza was wearing a light blue linen suit. Chang wore a black tracksuit, saying it was more comfortable on the plane. "I have a suit for visits to official places."

"Great, Ho. I've fixed up some good places to show you, and some visits to date farms and dried fruit warehouses and dealers."

"Must create the right impression, mustn't we?" Ho laughed.

They got into Reza's Audi and drove to his home in a prosperous suburb of the city. Reza cooked dinner. Ho went to bed early as He was very tired. The next day they went sightseeing in Tehran, visited two warehouses and the Golestan Palace, had a late lunch in the Tehran Bazaar, and spent the afternoon wandering round it. They ate out that evening, and went to bed early again, but Reza rose early to pray to Allah facing Mecca. When Ho got up he claimed he was much refreshed from two good nights' sleep.

"That's good." Reza was pleased. "I fixed up the first visit, and we have to start today. We've got a long way to go. We're off to see Bushehr Nuclear Power Plant. It's near the city of Bushehr, which is about ten miles from the Gulf Coast and the power plant. We'll have to stay the night in Bushehr, where we'll see a date farm, and go to the plant the next morning."

"That's fantastic. Will we stop to see any sights on the way? We don't want to appear to be anything but friends having a look around, and doing the fruit business. You know what they say: the CIA has agents and spies everywhere."

"Absolutely. I thought about that and we can stop in Esfahan and see the marvellous Music Museum there. The collection includes all the kinds of instruments Persian classical and folk music is played on. We can stay in the town for the night. Next day we can go Persepolis which ...."

"Is near Shiraz. I've looked it up. It is one of the oldest and most historic sights in the world. I've wanted to go there ever since I read about it." Ho was really excited about that, and said as much.

Reza smiled. "That's great. We'll be driving and take a day to get to each place, see a farm or warehouse on the way, and can stop for anything else you fancy. It's almost 600 miles to Bushehr, which is not far from Shiraz either. On the way back from seeing the plant there, we'll take a couple of days, and go to Qum. There's a uranium enrichment plant there."

Chang was excited. "Isn't there one at Natanz as well?"

"There is, and Fordu too. The government is very keen to be completely self sufficient. You better get packed for a five day trip. We'll do more tourist stuff after we get back to Tehran. I want you to see what a great historic country this is and Persia was."

Ho responded: "OK. Almost as historic as China." Reza gave him a serious look, and then they both laughed. Chang went on: "You can tell me more in the car. And tell me the history of nuclear in Iran."

***

They were fairly quiet for an hour or so as Reza negotiated the Tehran traffic. They started chatting when they emerged into the countryside.

"You were going to tell me about nuclear in Iran."

Reza nodded. "Yes, I was. Well, it goes back a bit further than people think, or further than they are usually told in the West. Mostly people in the US and UK and so on are led to think that it's only under the Ayatollahs that Iran has been looking for nuclear power.

"It goes back ten years before that. In about 1970, the USA intended to help the Shah develop nuclear power. That was because he ran a pro-America government. He shafted the British – the Anglo-Iranian Oil Company – by nationalising the oil fields.

"The nuclear power was slow in coming, and in 1979 the Shah was thrown out because he was a brutal dictator, and Ayatollah Khomeini took over, creating an Islamic state but it remained a more or less secular government, with elections, a Prime Minister, and a Parliament."

Ho chimed in. "Yes, and the Yanks hated it. They'll support any dictatorial regime that sucks up to them. Batista in Cuba, the Army in South Vietnam, Marcos in the Philippines. They dislike any government or party that wants to help the poor, because they don't want poor Americans to think that any of their rich ones would pay tax to help them.

"Yeah, and then they impose sanctions on countries they don't like, such as Cuba and Russia, and Iran, so they can't sell things, their economy goes to pot, and then the Yanks say 'Look, socialism and communism don't work'."

Reza laughed. "Right, but they and the UK still sell arms to almost anyone. It's hypocrisy, yet there's more where that came from! When the Shah ran off to America, the US government cancelled the Iranian nuclear programme. We looked around for another helper, and some years later Russia stepped forward. They helped build the Bushehr 1 Reactor, and it was officially opened earlier this year."

"Is that it?"

"Not by a long way," Reza said. "We're working on a new 360 megawatt plant at Darkhoyen in western Khuzestan Province, and I've already told you about the Qum, Fordu, and Natanz enrichment sites."

"Western politicians probably think that the fuel is enriched just to make bombs, but you don't have to go that far. You can get better results for peaceful nuclear energy with enriched uranium which is not such a high grade as weapons grade," Ho said in a disgusted tone.

"Probably. That's certainly what they want their peoples to think, but the politicians should know better. After all they've got a group called P5+1 which monitors Iran's nuclear developments. It consists of China, Russia – OK, they're not the West – France, the UK and the USA, and the plus 1 is Germany. The first five all have the bomb, and so do India and Pakistan, but no-one does anything about it. Israel has it too, and is happy to attack anybody any time."

"They just haven't used nuclear weapons – yet!" Ho pauses: "So is Iran trying to make its own weapons grade uranium, Reza?"

"Not that I know of, but that's why we should like to get some from you, if we can."

"Well, we're working on that, aren't we? You haven't yet told me about Iran and Persia's great past."

"Well, let's start with Cyrus the Great. He lived 2500 years ago. He took over Nebuchadnezzar's empire, and let the Jews who wanted to, go back to Palestine. Then we come to ....."

**

They stopped a couple of times for coffee and toilets, and arrived in Esfahan before lunch. They were both fascinated by the instruments in the Music Museum, Ho especially so. He speculated that many of these musical ideas had travelled back and forth along the Silk Road for hundreds of years. Later they found a hotel and dinner.

Next day they drove on to Marvdasht and booked into a hotel before going on to the ruins at Persepolis. Reza had not been there before, so the wonder and excitement was mutual. They could barely drag themselves away, and stayed until the sun went down.

They dined in the hotel restaurant at the hotel in Marvdasht.

**

A few tables away a bearded Iranian gentleman wearing a grey suit and an Arab head-dress was eating. He seemed to be an Iranian because he was dark and bearded, and spoke fluent Farsi to the waiter, and into his mobile phone. He came into the cafe shortly after Reza and his friend sat down. When he was not on the phone he was reading a newspaper and appeared totally uninterested in the two scientists.

When they left the restaurant, the man with the phone took a photograph from his jacket pocket, studied it to compare it with the faces of the two men, and immediately keyed in a number, and began speaking in perfect American English. "I tracked the consignment you told me about. It has just arrived in Marvdasht, and is now going on to the depot, where it will be for a day or two."

He listened for a moment. "Yes. I was able to recognise that package from the Montreal manifests you supplied."

He listened again. "OK. I'll get Joe keep an eye on it. He'll let me know if it arrives safely at the plant, and what happens next."

***

The next day the friends went to Bushehr, checked in at another hotel, met the directors of a dried fruit company, and went to the Nuclear reactor. Reza presented the entry permits he had already obtained, and they were there all day.

The following day they drove back to Esfahan, stayed the night, and went on to the nuclear plant at Qum on the morrow. Then they drove back to Reza's apartment.

After a day's rest, and another day looking around the Sadabaad Palace and its collections of different artefacts and historical and artistic objects, Reza proposed another tourist trip for the following day. They went out to dinner, and Reza

40

introduced Chang to a friend of his, Selim Abdullah, a scientist, also from Tehran, who dined with them.

Reza explained that Selim was involved in the planning of the acquisition of the additional product. If Chang had no objection, he would accompany them on tomorrow's journey, which would be to the far east of the country, close to the border with Turkmenistan, where they would see the Iman Reza Holy Shrine. "It is one of the most remarkable creations in the Middle East," Selim added.

"I should be very glad to have you with us," rejoined Chang.

***

The Imam Reza Holy Shrine impressed Chang greatly. "It is so beautiful. Very different from the Forbidden City, but just as incredibly beautiful in its way."

Reza added: "It's the largest mosque in the world, and even has a university in it."

Selim spoke to the same effect, that Allah was great, and mosques and other structures dedicated to him had to be the best that human ingenuity could do to reflect that greatness. Chang commented that Europeans had much the same point of view about Cathedrals. That drew rather contemptuous glances from the Iranians, who asked: "What about your reverence for Mao Dse Dong?"

They all laughed at each other.

***

While the Iranians and the Chinaman were in the Holy Shrine, Pretorius fixed a listening and tracking device in their Audi, using his special electronic key and a code the CIA had obtained from the makers via the German Secret Service, the Bundesnachrichtendienst.

After an exhausting day touring the site, the three companions dined in a restaurant near their hotel. A clean shaven man in a blue suit with glasses came and sat at a nearby table to eat. He ordered his food in French, and seemed uninterested in the three scientists. He was still drinking his coffee with a brandy when they went back to their hotel.

He took out his phone, and went into the lobby. He spoke English. "The two consignments have now been united with a third. They've been at the depot in Mashhad all day. I believe one of them will be shipped to China shortly. The man in charge of the goods seems to think that arrangements can be made for the exchange with the other product the customers are interested in. Yes, Chief, I'll keep you informed."

Another faultless disguise for the previously bearded American from the cafe in Marvdasht, Zane Pretorius III.

***

For another two weeks Reza Bukhari and Ho Chang found time for some Mozart and Haydn, went sightseeing, looked into dried fruit exports, and met some of Reza's friends, including young women, Iran being fairly relaxed in that respect. They also dined with Selim a number of times, and then the three went back to Reza's flat to talk about their uranium project.

At the end of that fortnight Reza put Chang on the plane back to Beijing. They thought they were unobserved, but standing in full Arab dress and sun-glasses in the crowd of families seeing their relatives fly away, Zane Pretorius III was all but invisible, and certainly not recognisable.

He waited in the airport until the plane took off, and then waited another half hour to ensure that Chang had indeed gone on his way to China. Then he walked out of the terminal, got in his car, and used his car phone.

"Hello, Chief. You'll be pleased to know that the goods are on route. They'll be picked up when they arrive?" A pause. "That's great. Keep me in the picture." Another pause. "No, the radio in the car picked up nothing worth listening to."

The reason the device had recorded nothing interesting was that none of the three men mentioned the project in the car during the rest of Chang's 'holiday'.

Pretorius terminated the call, and started up the engine.

October 2012.

Reza was called in to the office of the Head Administrator of the Qum Plant, where he now worked. He was introduced to two extremely fit men of about thirty, both clean shaven with good dark blue suits, silk ties, and shoes so shiny they looked like patent leather. They were quietly spoken, but there was an undisguised air of menace about them. The Administrator left the room. Reza felt apprehensive.

The taller one spoke. "Your reports of your dealings with Ho Chang have met with approval. You are to send him an email using this laptop, which cannot be traced to you." He handed Reza a lap-top and a piece of paper. "You are to use this email address, which belongs to no-one except us. You will ask him if the goods you want are now ready, as the dried fruit he wants to buy will shortly be available. Don't say anything else, and sign off with the name Bashir Muktas. Have you got that?"

"I have." Reza's mouth was as dry as old leather.

"In due course you will fly to China with Selim Abdullah. You will be taking a roundabout route through other countries to Beijing. You'll have extra tickets for destinations beyond Beijing to which you will not fly. They are to lay a false trail. You will be given false passports with new identities. You will be told more about that in time. Do you understand?"

Reza swallowed. "I do."

"Any questions?"

"No. I expect I'll be told everything I need to know when the time comes." Reza paused. "Sorry. Yes, I have one question. Why Selim and me? We're not very old. No-one would take us for experienced diplomats or politicians, or even top flight nuclear boffins. Why should the Chinese Government have faith in us?"

The tall man smiled. "That's just the point. No-one would think you two had the authority, but all this has been cleared with Beijing. The important consideration is that the US, Britain, Russia, Israel, they'll suspect nothing."

"If we're lucky," Reza thought.

The tall man went on: "The Ambassador had all the authority he needed to negotiate with the nuclear people over there. All the 'trade' details are fine. You two may not be top-flight nuclear boffins, as you call it, but you are both extremely knowledgeable. Your job is to check with your friend Ho Chang that all the right safety precautions and transport are in place, and that the nuclear material being supplied to us is of the grade we want. Another senior diplomat at the Embassy will oversee the paperwork and the commercial side.

"Right, that's it! The names you were given by your Boss are not our names. You do not need to know them. Don't talk to anyone about this, not even Selim. We shall tell him what he needs to know, and he won't talk to you about it either until you are on the way to Beijing."

December, 2012

The phone rang in Pretorius's small house in Tehran. He could tell at once it was a scrambled call. "Yes, Ethel."

"There is odd movement in Beijing. The Chinese guy has been going to military places, and also to the Ministry of Defence. We think something's cooking, so you must keep a closer eye on your Iranian friend. Whatever he gets up to may be significant."

Pretorius thought about Selim Abdullah. "Should I have someone watch his friend too?"

"Yes, but neither of them must get suspicious."

A week later Pretorius put a call through to Washington. "Nothing seems to be happening here. The Iranian feller goes to his work at the plant, and the other one, his friend, goes to the University where he teaches. Sometimes they go out together, but nothing unusual happens and they never talk about anything but work, films they've seen or are going to see, and girls."

"Sound like regular guys, don't they?"

"If you discount wanting nukes, I'd say that's just what they are."

"We're pretty certain they're not, so be as vigilant as you can. Did you fix a tracking signal to the Audi?"

"Yep, but it's not been anywhere his mother wouldn't go."

Pretorius's problem was that Reza only saw 'the two men from the Ministry', as he called them, in the office of the Administrator. No-one else knew what these meetings were for. Similarly, Selim was being called into his Head of Faculties office from time to time, usually within a few hours before or after the two men had seen Reza. They were gradually being given more information about their trip to China.

After what Pretorius called Christmas, which meant nothing to most Iranians, he put through another call, and had no more to report than the last time. He was told that Chang was still seeing Military and Defence Department officials, but why was not known. However, the CIA's belief was that it was still to do with getting weapons grade uranium to Iran, and the importance of strict surveillance was emphasised.

February, 2013

Many nations' secret services and big mafia-type groups have a horde of stolen passports. Using stolen British and Australian passports the Israelis' Mossad assassinated a man they believed to be a Hamas leader in the lift of a hotel in Dubai in January 2010. Iran was no exception to the possession of this type of document.

In early February Reza was called into the office again, and Selim into the professor's sanctum. Both men were given airline tickets to Kuala Lumpur and then to Beijing, and then to Oslo for Reza and Prague for Selim. Those last two were the ones they would not need. They were to use their own passports to leave Iran, and land in Malaysia with the stolen ones. Both were given a fair amount of Malaysian currency, and had to stay in separate hotels for two nights before getting on the China Flight. Credit cards were not to be used as they could be traced. They were to leave Tehran on 6th March, land in Kuala Lumpur on the 7th, and take off for China on the 9th.

They were both handed stolen passports the owners of which bore a reasonably close resemblance to them. Reza's was Norwegian, and Selim's Czech. They were instructed that no-one would be likely to speak either of those languages at the airport in Kuala Lumpur unless they got into serious trouble, so they should speak English, and brush up their knowledge of it. Reza said that wasn't a problem for him, and he would use the remaining month to help Selim improve his English before they left.

They met daily for English lessons, and once for dinner and the cinema, but the only relevant thing they ever said in public was: "You all fixed up for the holidays?"

Pretorius was going frantic keeping them in his sights or those of some colleagues. He had different people keeping watch on Reza's flat and the house where Selim Abdullah lived, but they did nothing odd, and he was learning nothing.

1st March, 2013.

Zane Pretorius III was fast asleep at 3.30am when his phone rang. It was a scrambled call.

"Zane, we've had a breakthrough. We've been monitoring flight bookings from Tehran. We had a bit of luck. We noticed that tickets for Reza Bukhari and Selim Abdullah to fly to Kuala Lumpur were booked on the same day from the same travel agent. The same agent made another couple of bookings for a Norwegian and a Czech to fly from Kuala Lumpur to Beijing and then on to Oslo for the Norwegian guy and Prague for the Czech. The Norwegian's Ove Larsen. The Czech is Leopold Reicha. Those bookings were all made with the same call, which looks odd. Added to that, the agency is one used by the Iranian government for most of its international travel arrangements."

"So where do I come in?"

"You have to get to Kuala Lumpur, make enquiries of the airline, and keep an eye on things, including the take-off. It's vital we know it leaves. The Captain on the flight to

Beijing will be Muhamed Subrama. Our computer freaks got into the Airline's rosters, and he's one of our Malaysian assets. We may be able to make use of him."

"Now hold your horses, Chief. Sure, we can't just pull these guys off the street in Iran, much too risky, but you could take them in Kuala Lumpur. The authorities in Malaysia are pretty cooperative, aren't they?"

"Won't work. Contacts in China think there are some Chinese in Malaysia who're involved in this thing, and will be on the plane too. Maybe it's Ho Chang. We need to take them all together, but we won't know who they are until they get on the plane."

"Hell, Ethel, if you're planning what I think you've got in mind, it'll damage Uncle Sam's reputation for ever. We've never truly got over the torture and rendition allegations."

"I'm not about to tell you anything over the phone, even if it is scrambled. Keep your opinions to yourself; remember what I told you before. You just get on a plane to Kuala Lumpur yesterday, if not sooner, Zane. If you doubt it, that's an order."

Pretorius thought about that. He'd had an argument with Hardwick some time ago about the way to handle this mission. He'd taken the view that it would be better to seize these men on the street somewhere rather than take the plane and all its passengers and crew. She'd pointed out that it was essential they were all taken together. Not only that, but the chances of finding the three of them together on the street and capturing them all simultaneously would be pretty remote. In addition, the three spent most of their time in Iran

49

on the one hand and China on the other, and a botched attempt in either country could lead to disastrous diplomatic and political consequences. Besides, enormous obstacles would make it impossible to smuggle all of them out of either of those countries.

Zane recalled Ethel saying it was bad enough when Jimmy Carter sent in Special Forces to rescue the hostages from the US Embassy in Teheran. Fucking up another operation there would be a huge gift to the Ayatollah. The same would apply in China. Neither nation was of no consequence. All American citizens in either country would be placed at risk. The CIA's freedom to act would be examined by Congress, criticised by the President, and perhaps curtailed. He would obey her orders.

5th March, 2013.

Pretorius went straight from Kuala Lumpur Airport arrivals to the American Embassy, and asked to see Security urgently. He showed his ID to the lady who came out to greet him, and she took him straight to her office. "Leave me here on my own for a while, please. I want to make a call to Washington. I can't tell you what it's about."

"No problem, Mr Pretorius. If you want a scrambled call, use the green phone." She left the room at once, switching on a red light outside the door warning 'No Entry'.

"Hello, Chief, it's Pretorius. I'm in the Embassy. Have the hackers been keeping an eye on the crew and passenger manifests for the Beijing Flights?"

"Sure they have, Zane. Muhamed Subrama is still the Captain. The First Officer is Mustafa Sirigur. What's the problem?"

"No problem. I just want to make sure that Subrama is the pilot on the day, the 9th. The whole scheme falls apart if he's rostered on a different flight, or calls in sick or there's some other cock-up. Mind you, what I'll threaten him with if he craps on us, he'll make sure he's there unless he's already with the funeral home."

"Don't worry. I've got someone sitting on the SEA flight crew data 24/7. We've checked out all the passengers, too, and there's no-one who's likely to mess things up for us. If anything changes, I'll let you know at once. You phone in on the 9th before the flight leaves and I'll up-date you in any event. There are only 243 passengers booked on the flight so far, so the plane is far from full. There will be twelve crew."

Fifty minutes later Pretorius knocked at the door of Subrama's house in a street off Jalan Cochrane. Subrama himself came to open it, and let him in. The pilot took him into his study, and shut the door. Pretorius showed him his cover ID, and asked to see his. Subrama produced his pilot's licence and passport.

"You were contacted recently and told that at last you have a job to do for us."

"That is so, Mr Dennis. It's twenty years since you recruited me in the Philippines; I've received a small retainer ever since. What am I to do?"

"Let's look at something else first. We've been keeping an eye on you, particularly recently."

Subrama smiled: "I expected that. You told me it would happen back in the Philippines when I learning to fly."

Pretorius had noticed over the years, that the Captain's English had improved considerably. No doubt this was due to contact with many people from English speaking countries, attending courses, learning to fly new planes, and using new technology. "So we know you and your wife are living apart, and that you have a girlfriend, but you've had a bust-up and ..."

"Burstup? I do not know this word."

"You and the girl have had a big quarrel."

"Yes, is true. I do not see her, three weeks, or four."

"Five actually. So there's nothing to keep you here now, except your job, the children ..."

"And that I cannot afford to leave!"

"Well, there we are. So if you had a million dollars in a bank account no-one knows about, and went to live abroad, would that help?"

Subrama laughed, smiled, and then looked shocked. "But I love flying, and I have no reason to stop."

"Look, buddy, I don't want to come all heavy with you ..."

"What is this 'heavy'? You're not fat. Not me, either."

"OK, Captain Subrama, let's be clear. If we tell the airline that you've been on our payroll all this time and working for us, your flying days are numbered. But we don't want to do that. And a million dollars and a new identity in another country would solve all your problems, wouldn't they?"

Subrama looked very sad. "They would, but I miss my kids then."

"We can't do much about that, but we can find a way to look after them financially - through a charity or something."

"Do I have a choice? I suppose I do not."

"If you don't do what we want, we may have to kill your wife and children, as well as you, so do I take that as a yes?"

Muhamed looked down at his knees, and his shoulders slumped in despair. "Yes," he whispered.

Then Zane Pretorius III told him exactly what he had to do on 9th March, and what else would happen that day. He also gave him what looked like a fountain pen, and told him how to use it. After that he called on four men at the American Embassy, and told them what to do on the 9th. They were all of medium build, looking extremely fit. They were CIA 'minders', all former Navy Seals, experts in martial arts and methods of killing people. They had recently been on a three day training course with Boeing learning all about the pressurisation and emergency oxygen supply systems on planes.

At the end of it they flew out to Malaysia, seconded temporarily to Embassy staff; very temporarily.

9th March, 2013.

Just before Captain Muhamed Subrama taxied to the runway, the Air Traffic Controller gave him the transponder code for secondary radar identification of the plane by Air Traffic Control, and the military. The code is known as the 'Squawk Code'. The pilot can turn the transponder off, and then there is no positive way of identifying the aircraft. He entered that code into the transponder equipment.

He did not have to switch on another system which identifies an aircraft. The Aircraft Communications Addressing and Reporting System (ACARS for short), which sends messages about the aircraft's performance and position via satellite to receiving stations on the ground is automatic. Having reached the runway he was given clearance for take-off. Then the green and gold South East Asia Airways plane, with its beautiful frangipani blossom logo on the tail fin, bound for Beijing, took off from Kuala Lumpur Airport at 1.42am. Captain Subrama was assisted by 2nd Officer Mustafa Sirigur who was actually flying the plane. The world standard time, known as Greenwich Mean Time, or UTC, was 17.42. At 18.12 UTC Subrama informed ATC in Kuala Lumpur they had reached their allotted cruising height of 35,000 feet. A few minutes before that, when the plane had reached that altitude, Sirigur turned off the seat-belt sign.

At 2.23am Malaysia time (18.23 pm UTC) the ATC radioed the Captain: "Please contact Ho Chi Minh City. Goodnight." People on the ground thought it was First Officer Sirigur who replied: "Goodnight South East Asia 439."

After that, apart from some primary radar contact, and Inmarsat's electronic communications, the plane was never heard from again. As far as could reliably be ascertained at the time by people on the ground, it was never seen again either. It started the biggest mystery in the history of aviation.

***

In the passenger cabin, as soon as the seat-belts could be unfastened, the four men from the Embassy left their seats and made their way to the toilets. One man had to wait as that toilet was already occupied, but the other three entered theirs immediately. Having kept their hand luggage at their feet under the seats in front, they took those bags into the toilets with them. Swiftly they stripped to their underpants, removed from the bags full-body thermal underwear with long sleeves and long legs, which they donned. They put very warm sweat-shirts with hoods over woollen shirts, and stuck balaclavas in their pockets along with sheepskin gloves.

All of these men were armed with Special Forces knives which had been left with life-jackets in the compartments under their seats where a financially desperate Malay cleaner had put them for a bribe. To him this cash was a fortune, but to the Americans it was a mere two weeks salary. Finding a corrupt employee at the airline was not unusual. Regardless of their qualifications or experience for the job, they were often given such posts by equally corrupt politicians. South East Asia Airways was, after all, a government company. 'Jobs for the boys' is a way of life for politicians everywhere.

They returned to their seats. One was sitting next to an Australian woman who asked him if he was expecting to get cold in the plane. He answered in Russian that he did not understand. She did not speak to him again.

Within two minutes after Subrama said 'Goodnight' to ATC the passengers heard Captain Subrama announce that they had been allotted a new cruising altitude and the plane would be ascending again shortly. When the plane began to rise, it also began a gentle bank to the left. At this the four Embassy men rose from their seats and moved rapidly to the rear of the plane. The Captain announced that seat belts should be fastened again and put the seat belt sign on.

The Embassy men were Americans: Ronald Donarski, flying on a CIA 'forged' Russian passport as Nikolai Brodscovitch; Alan Peck, flying on an Estonian passport of similar origin under the name Oleg Chustrahk; the third and fourth were Jerry Jacobs on a Georgian passport, as Sergei Deineka, and Nicolas Hurt, as Alexei Gornakov. They could each get by in the language of the country they purported to hail from.

The passports were not truly forged, but valid passports issued in the countries in question, procured for cash from corrupt officials in the passport offices, and issued in fictitious names. Consequently on any check by immigration or airline officials they would show up as genuine.

Facing the back of the plane, Donarski and Hurt moved down the left aisle, Peck and Jacobs down the right. Donarski went straight past a galley opening, with Hurt following. A stewardess stepped out of the galley between them and started to tell Hurt to go back to his seat but before she could finish her instruction he pushed her back into the kitchen area, killing her instantly and silently with a brutal chop across the throat. A steward who tried to stop Jacobs met the same fate. Peck slipped through a door at the side of the toilet into a crew rest area, where he found two members of the cabin staff relaxing. He hit one with the same sort of blow, and grabbed the other round the head, twisting it violently to the left and snapping her spine.

The other three had hastened to the back of the plane, dragging with them a stewardess who was going up the aisle towards them checking that seat belts were done up. Hurt sliced her carotid artery and windpipe with his knife as soon as they got into the rear galley. The flood of blood all over the galley did not worry Hurt; he'd seen plenty of it before, and anyone who wandered in there would die the same way as the stewardess. Another steward and two hostesses were there and were disposed of rapidly by the same brutality as all the others had been. There were another five to be eliminated. They were in the galley between First and Business Class. The three men came back up the aisle, and Jacobs joined them as he exited the rest area. A male passenger came out of the next set of toilets as they raced past, and Donarski kicked him in the groin, pushed him back into the toilet, and, out of sight of any other passengers, stabbed him directly into the heart. He died instantly. In the forward galley area the four CIA men killed the four crew who worked there, and a fifth who had gone there from Economy to confer with her colleagues about serving the first meal. Their actions were as cold-blooded and unemotional as those of Mafia hit-men, reflecting the way they were trained, and the kind of men they were.

The Company was now in control of the passenger cabin and the people in it. Hurt and Donarski ran back to seats 34B and C, and pulled the two Iranians, Bukhari and Abdullah, out of their seats, and marched them with painful arm locks down to the rear kitchen. Simultaneously Jacobs and Peck grabbed Ho Chang out of seat 20C, and manhandled him with a half nelson to the same kitchen. There, they took seven oxygen bottles with masks from a cupboard, and gave one to each of their prisoners. At knife point they told the captives to don the masks and turn the bottles on, and immediately did the same with their own.

The four men and their three prisoners sat in the very back seats of the plane. The CIA men covered the prisoners with blankets, and did the same to each other. The whole of this operation took about three minutes. Peck took the chief steward's microphone and announced to the passengers, three of whom had begun to get out of their seats, that all was well, and that the man who had been pushed into the toilet had been drunk and making a nuisance of himself. Under no circumstances were passengers to get out of their seats again until the seat belt sign was switched off.

During that short period the plane had been climbing steadily, passing 36,500 feet. The air pressure was falling steadily as the height increased, and the oxygen content of the air with it. The passengers felt more and more drowsy every passing second. Consequently they did not notice that this was happening, nor that the oxygen masks had not dropped down for their use. At 38,000 feet most of them were asleep, and after another thirty seconds all but one man were. As a result they were in no condition to notice that the temperature was also falling quite rapidly. Even so that one man seemed to be struggling to keep awake. He stood up in his seat and shouted: "Why the fuck haven't the masks come down? There's no fucking air!" He reached up to the overhead panel from which the masks should dangle, and appeared to be trying to force it open with a door key. Jacobs ran to the man and chopped him down with a well-practised unarmed combat stroke. Those sitting around this passenger were in no state to do anything; they were already unconscious.

After another two minutes they were nearly all dead, the plane was at 40,000 feet, and the temperature had dropped to ten degrees below freezing. At 41,000 feet there was hardly any oxygen left in the cabin air, and the cabin temperature was 40 degrees below and falling. Whatever oxygen was left in the passengers' bodies was leaking fast out of every pore and orifice, as there was not enough pressure at this high altitude for the body to retain it. The passengers had all passed into the world beyond.

Even if the passengers' oxygen masks had deployed they were only intended for emergencies, last about 20 minutes, and the quality of oxygen provided is questionable. If a pilot has deliberately created the emergency and is in control of the plane and wants to keep its altitude high, the passengers are doomed.

At this point the aircraft began a rapid descent, and the air pressure came back on with the air conditioning, warming the cabin. The plane went down to 30,000 feet, travelling at 7,000 feet a minute, and levelled off. The minders took off their masks and turned their oxygen bottles off. Hurt and Jacobs made the three prisoners do the same, collected all seven masks and bottles, and returned them to the cupboard in the kitchen.

The plane flew on in the darkness.

Part 2. Suspicion.

7th May, 2014.

I'd got back from Sydney a couple of weeks after the incident with Kiralee, the indigenous Australian woman. When I got over the jetlag Jamie took me out to celebrate. We went to dinner at the Waldorf and then to the Royal Opera house in Covent Garden to see Gounod's "Faust." That was on 22nd April. It was wonderful and Bryn Terfel as Mephistopheles was just amazing. I won't describe our additional celebratory activity when we got home.

The documentary about global airport security and links with drugs and criminals was still a work in progress. Some trips to European airports were filmed, and others to places further away were needed. It would take time to put it all together. Since then I'd been in the office working on another story, but I could not clear my mind of what the Australian had told me about the aeroplane her husband was on when it vanished. Of course, I knew the story after a fashion. Most people did as it had been huge news for weeks and revived every time someone thought they'd seen wreckage or another search was instituted or abandoned.

Something ought to be done by someone to solve the mystery, and maybe that someone was me. The something would be a story. I'd have to look into it. I could do some research today working at home.

I opened the lap-top this morning as soon as I'd had a cup of tea and a bit of toast. I wanted to look into whatever was known about the missing plane, the pilot, the passengers, and everything else I could find. I decided to start with the pilot, the Captain of the plane. There was a lot of stuff in newspaper articles and more from TV and Radio stations, but I found a more official source.

This was a report of the Malaysian Safety Investigating Team. It said that Muhamed Subrama was 47 when the plane took off on 9th March 2013. He had joined the airline as a cadet in 1986, and was sent to train in Manila in the Philippines. My news-hound's antennae quivered when I read that, but I could not work out why.

The Captain stayed with that airline throughout his career. He became a First Officer in 1988, and Captain of Boeing 737-400s in 1994. He moved up to Captain of Airbus A330-300s three years later, and to Chief Pilot of Boeing 777-200s in 2000. He qualified to be an instructor and examiner in many aspects of commercial flying. He had clocked up over 15,000 hours of flying, so he was a very experienced pilot.

Many pundits and experts postulated that he might have committed suicide. According to news reports it seemed that most of his friends thought that very unlikely, but said that he had left his wife, Kadijha, and that he had had a bust-up with his girlfriend, Nancy Koh. Could that have pushed him over the edge? I felt suicide was plain wrong. It would pay me to visit the wife and the girlfriend at some stage.

I read that Subrama had a social media presence which showed he disliked the government, but that hardly seemed to be a cause for him to kill himself, nor for the Malaysian authorities to take him out and kill 243 passengers and eleven innocent members of the crew in the process. Surely that couldn't be true, either.

There were a number of photos of Subrama in reports and newspaper articles, and I thought I recognised him. It was about four or five years ago. I was in Berlin visiting my friends Nick and Liz Carter. Nick was a pilot flying out of Berlin for EasyJet, and they were living in Berlin whilst this job lasted, and had rented out their house in Breechwood Green. Nick arrived home from a flight and brought a friend with him. He was also a pilot and they had met by chance at the airport when the man flew in from Kuala Lumpur in Malaysia, where he lived and was based. I recalled he flew for an Asian Airline.

The man Subrama had not been fat, but not slim either, more of a middling build, as though he ate well, but moderately. He was about five foot six. The chap in the photos looked much the same shape and size. There was an unusual feature about him which I saw at the Carter's dining table. He had a line of thick marks running down the centre of each thumbnail, which he told Liz, who asked about it, was due to a lack of some mineral or vitamin in his system.

He also had a large ruby in an unusual setting. Liz had asked him where he got it. He explained it was a rare

Burmese ruby which had been his grandfather's, and he'd inherited it years ago. "I've put on a little weight so my finger has grown around it a bit, and I can't get it off. I wouldn't want to, either. I loved my grandfather, and I'm so proud to have his ring."

Whilst at this research, I thought I'd check out the First Officer too, Pilot Mustafa Sirigur. He was much younger, and somewhat less experienced, but still well qualified for the job, and with no record of anything ever having gone wrong on his watch that he had been unable to handle. He had been trained at Langkawi Aerospace Centre in Malaysia. He'd had special training for Boeing 777s, including several sessions on flight simulators, some of which were rehearsals for mid-air mishaps. He'd done a number of supervised flights in the aircraft themselves. This was to be his first flight where he would be able to take control if the Captain so desired.

I found no suggestions at all that Sirigur might be vulnerable to depression or suicide attempts, though there was some speculation that he could have been responsible for the plane's disappearance. I recalled from what I had read and heard at the time it went missing that both pilots were suspected of being terrorists. There was no evidence to support that apart from the fact, I read today, that Subrama was supposed to have cleared all his social dates out of his diary. I felt that was a pretty feeble basis on which to blame a man for mass murder of the crew and passengers, as well as his own suicide.

My next task was to look at the plane and the facts of the flight, so far as they were known. The plane was a Boeing 777-200ER. ER means extended range. These could fly over 7,000 miles non-stop. This one had two Rolls Royce Trent 875 engines which can cruise at about 540 miles an hour and fly at higher speeds if necessary. These planes can stay airborne for around 16 hours, if full of fuel.

Captain Subrama was going to fly this one from Kuala Lumpur to Beijing; that's only 2,700 miles. At a cruising speed of, say, 540 miles an hour, that's five to six hours flying. I found out from my cousin, Spencer Bunder, himself a long haul pilot, that it's the pilot's job to order up the fuel he needs. Malaysian authorities said he loaded up 49,100 kg of fuel, but I saw some speculation that as Malaysia is rather corrupt, it would be easy to bribe ground-staff to load more. A pilot of Boeing 747s posted a comment that flight times to Beijing are completely unreliable because the Chinese military interfere, delaying landings and organising diversions to other airports. Spencer said long periods of stacking above the airport may then be needed. That means extra fuel. He'd have to load more still to avoid storms or other risks, so he would have a safety margin. If there were no emergency, he could fly further if he wanted to. In any case, 49,100 kg of fuel would be more than enough to get to Beijing, with a good safety margin.

I saw that there were at least 1,000 of these planes in use on the planet, and they had a very good safety record: nine mishaps in two decades of flight, resulting in only three passengers dying until SEA439 came along.

At first I thought that dealing with the details of the flight would be a problem, as there was so much information. I decided, having given it some thought, that the type of people who might be interested in this would have read most of it before, or could look it up now. The best thing for this purpose would be to simplify it down to the basics.

I felt hungry, went out for a walk, and called in at a snack bar in Fulham Palace Road for an avocado and cheese sandwich, a coffee, and a glass of water. I'd been on the computer for hours without a break or a drink. I was gasping. When I got back, I phoned the office and asked someone to tell Marion Gorman I'd be there the day after tomorrow. Then I went back to the lap-top.

***

It appeared that Captain Subrama might have told Sirigur to assume control of the plane for take-off and the initial stages of the flight. This left communication with ATC in the Captain's lap. That explained why it was the Captain's voice which said "Goodnight South East Asia 439."

The plane took off at 01.42 Malaysia Time on Sunday 9th March 2013, which was 17.42 Greenwich Mean Time (GMT) on Saturday the 8th in England, where Greenwich is. Arrival was supposed to be at 07.30 Beijing local time on the 9th; Beijing is one hour ahead of Kuala Lumpur, so with about a six hour flight, landing at Beijing should have been at about 00.30 GMT that day. The plane's VHF radio system was sending messages on the ACARS system until 02.08 Malaysia time (18.08 GMT). That was the last one. The ACARS system is 'Aircraft Communications Addressing and

Reporting System'. Its main function is to send periodic messages about the position and condition of the plane and the engines at regular intervals to a databank on the ground.

SEA439 had reached cruising height of 35,000 feet in 20 minutes from leaving the ground, and a few moments later reported this to Air Traffic Control (ATC). At 02.21 Malaysia time it was approaching the changeover area between Kuala Lumpur ATC and the one for Ho Chi Minh City in Vietnam. The Malaysian ATC then instructed Subrama to notify Ho Chi Minh of his approach. It seems that there can be a gap between the two zones operated by different ATCs, and I read that if the pilot wants the plane to vanish, this is a good place to do it. There was some controversy for a while about whether it was Subrama or Sirigur who replied "Goodnight South East Asia 439," but Mrs Subrama had identified the voice as her husband's.

Local Malaysian radar picked the plane up for the last time at about 02.30 (18.30 GMT). A few minutes later, out of range of primary radar, the secondary radar transponder was switched off. The plane was then believed to have turned slightly south of west, and flew back across Malaysia, where it would be visible on the old radar, but not identifiable. Its route was more or less along the border with Thailand, close to the island of Penang. Then it veered north-west, fairly close to Phuket Island, Thailand, flying across the Andaman Sea and the Indian Ocean. It seemed that these route changes were picked up by Malaysian Radar, but I could not work out how they knew it was SEA439, as the secondary radar transponder was switched off. They might see it as blips on the old-fashioned primary radar, but that would not tell anyone exactly which plane it was.

Perhaps they had had it in their sights all the time, somehow, but no-one was saying how that could be done. The trouble seemed to be, as one commentator put it, that the military do not want to admit it if they have done something wrong or omitted to do what they are supposed to do. Even less do they want to give away information that may betray the strength or the weakness of their defence installations, including radar.

What puzzled a lot of experts was that when the plane apparently turned back in the middle of the Gulf of Thailand, and started crossing Malaysian air space unidentified and without a flight plan, the Malaysian Air Force didn't send up fighters to intercept it. What Malaysian authorities and politicians said about that was odd. It seemed that the Military knew from their radar exactly what was going on and did not think that the plane was a threat. They said they knew it was a commercial flight. How could they tell, unless they had positively identified it as SEA439? And if they had, how was it that a huge search for it took place in the South China Sea? Are politicians to be believed? Or could there be some dark explanation? I was getting more and more sceptical about the whole business.

Another aspect of that was puzzling, too. My cousin Spencer Bunder, a very experienced airline Flight Captain, told me that the pilot has to file a flight plan before take-off. Subrama's would have shown destination Beijing. Once he turned round over the sea, his plan would no longer apply. At that point would he have filed an amended plan to show he had no intention of going to Beijing? Not if he wanted to keep his landing place a secret. Again I was forced to ask: "Why were the Malaysian Military so uninterested in this apparently unidentified plane flying in the wrong direction?"

I was also getting confused. As I have said, there are two types of radar: primary and secondary. Primary is the oldest type, which relies on radio signals being reflected back from the plane. A target plane does not have to cooperate. If it is in the range of the transmitter the signal will bounce back. This system does not identify the plane.

That is where the secondary radar type comes in. The transponder on the plane sends out signals to Air Traffic Control and the military, giving information about the aircraft's position, altitude and other matters. That's why I was confused. If the transponder was turned off when the plane turned west, how could anyone identify it from then on? Nobody seemed to be asking that question, or commenting on this apparent oddity.

Another search disclosed a speech made on 18th March 2013 by a Minister in the Malaysian Government. After saying that at first the Malaysian Airforce thought the plane had turned back after its ACARS system and transponder were turned off, but could not be certain of that, he continued: "Now we know from satellite data that the plane picked up by the primary radar was Flight SEA439. Scientific analysis by the FAA, the NTSB, and the AAIB reveal this, and we Malaysians agree." Did this make sense? If the equipment that identified the plane to ACARS, Air

Traffic Control and the military had all been switched off, or just ceased to function, what made it possible to identify the plane? The cynic in me took note of the fact that all three of those acronyms relate to US air traffic authorities. Could their analysis be relied on if the CIA, for example had hijacked the plane?

From Penang the plane (assuming it was SEA439) made another change of course, turning north-west towards the tiny island of Perak, which is at the top of the Malacca Strait, and heading past Phuket in the direction of the Andaman Islands. It was somewhere along that stretch that another change of course took the plane more westerly, and primary radar contact ended on 9th March at 03.24 Malaysian time (19.24 GMT on the 8th). The plane was not then on anybody's radar. Not only that, but by then the ACARS and SATCOM systems had also stopped working; there was apparently no solution to the question: "How did that happen?"

After passing over Perak Island, it veered slightly north-west, towards the Nicobar Islands, which lie south of the Andaman chain. At that point there had been four, possibly five, changes of direction.

Before all the information about the changes of course had emerged, the Malaysians acted as though the aircraft had ditched in the South China Sea or Gulf of Thailand. Search planes took off from Malaysia, China, Singapore, the Philippines, and Vietnam, but that did not happen for almost three hours after the plane had disappeared. I was puzzled when I read that the USA also 'volunteered to assist with the search'.

Soon after the change of direction became known there were about 75 ships from eight nations, including the USA and Australia, searching the Northern part of the Indian Ocean, and finding nothing.

For months different calculations were being reported in the media about the likely place the plane crashed into the sea. There were no landing places for it in the Andaman Islands, and no wreckage had been found. Some people on the Maldives Islands in the Indian Ocean reported seeing a plane heading west at about the right time that SEA439 would have been passing them, if it were going that way. One said its lights were very bright, but I thought it unlikely that a pilot who wanted his plane to be undetectable would fly with his landing lights on. They may have meant the flashing lights on the wing-tips, but cousin Spencer told me that the pilot can turn off all the lights, including these 'collision prevention' lights.

It emerged that there was another system keeping tabs on the plane. This is a satellite tracking method for ships and planes called SATCOM. It receives signals from planes and sends them to a firm called Inmarsat in London. These signals are generated by a device on the plane. If that device isn't working, the ground station sends signals, known as 'heartbeats', to the plane. If these heartbeats bounce back to the satellites they are known as 'handshakes'. When the ACARS and SATCOM went off, the handshakes started. Inmarsat received one at 03.12 (19.12 GMT). Inmarsat reported that they had last had contact with the plane at 09.12 Malaysia time (04.12 GMT) on the Saturday. That was almost seven and a half hours after take-off, or a flight of around 4,500 to 4,600 miles. That would be much further than the scheduled flight to Beijing.

The thing that confounded all the experts whose opinions I read was one simple fact: if there had been no sudden cataclysmic event - like the plane blowing up as the terrorist-bombed Pan Am Flight 103 over Lockerbie did in December 1988 - why was there no 'Mayday' call? The conversations with ATC in Kuala Lumpur showed the radio systems worked well and clearly. All the experts believed that if something like a fault had developed, then at 35,000 feet the plane could have glided for miles even if both engines packed up. The pilots would have had plenty of time to shout 'Mayday! Mayday!' What this story cried out was 'No Mayday! No Mayday!' In fact I found that cry was a Daily Mirror headline a couple of days after the plane vanished.

One thing kept escaping me, and I still do not understand it. The big powers, like America, China, and Russia, have powerful spy satellites with extremely precise cameras which can film an object as small as an 18 inch baguette on the ground from miles and miles above the Earth. How could they miss an airliner body over 20 feet wide and nearly 300 feet long, with large wings sticking out the sides? Some experts commented that satellites do not cover every square foot of the Earth's surface, but with a big American presence in the Red Sea and Persian Gulf, and a Fleet of the US Navy in the Pacific, with Al Qaida having blown a hole in the USS Cole a few years before, with Israel watching everyone in the Middle East, and India and Pakistan having their own satellites, I found it inconceivable that the Indian Ocean went unobserved by someone.

Then I came across what might be the explanation for all this: it was reported that a very high-ranking official of the aircraft section of the US National Transportation Safety Board said: "We would hate it if anyone thought that the USA was trying to control this search, but in fact that's exactly what is happening." That quotation was in 'The Washington Post'. It tied in nicely with what the Malaysian Minister had said on 18th March. The Americans were controlling all of it.

Why on earth would they want to be covertly in charge of an investigation which was the duty of the Malaysians? Was it because they wanted to supply inaccurate information? One explanation was that if they looked as though they were in control it would show how much better the American equipment, knowledge and resources were than anyone else's. Since when was the US noted for modesty? It wanted the world to know it was now the only superpower. In my experience it boasted about everything, even the alleged superiority of its game of so-called 'football' as compared with the England's national sport of the same name, five or six hundred years older, and now called 'the beautiful game' all over the world. I had to tell Jamie that; he'd love it.

The downside of concealing that they were 'in charge' was that the cynics (like me) would suspect the Americans knew more than they wanted to tell anyone else, even if that secrecy rendered the search hopeless. "Deliberately or negligently hopeless?" I asked myself. Another possibility was that there might be some defence tie between the USA and Malaysia. I had found a vague connection; nothing definite, of course, but who can tell in the world of the military and secret services? I discovered that there was a Status of Forces Agreement between Australia and the Malaysians from July 1999. This agreement was about stationing forces in each other's country.

Australia seemed to be quite influential in southern Asian defence circles. So was the USA. The Australians also have a Status of Forces Agreement with America from 1992. The Australians do almost anything the US wants them to, so if they wanted Canberra to tell Kuala Lumpur not to release certain information, they might well comply. This could be the 'dark explanation' I thought about earlier.

I also discovered that a 'spy base' called Pine Gap in Australia, not very far from Alice Springs, is a US and Australian facility. It can monitor electronic communications of any type anywhere, apparently. Its tasks include monitoring missile strikes and nuclear weapons all over the world too. It belongs to the USA, and is operated jointly (really? jointly? equal partners?) with the Australian Defence Forces. Didn't it see or hear the plane on any of its systems?

What else can it do? If it could intercept signals emanating from aircraft, could it stop them reaching their intended recipient, or even distort them to create a completely false location for the plane? Could it create totally false signals? No-one outside the US Defence and Intelligence Departments and the CIA really knows, and they won't be telling anyone anytime soon. Pine Gap's been there since the 1960s.

I had spent hours on this; it was about 8 o'clock; I needed food. I went out to eat in a Chinese, got home at nine o'clock, listened to my favourite Brahms's Symphony, his 3rd, had a glass of wine, and went to bed.

31st May, 2014.

I awoke thinking about Captain Subrama and the fact he was trained in the Philippines. I knew a bit about Philippine history.

In about 2000 I'd gone to the Imperial War Museum in South London. The thing that fascinated - and appalled me - most was an exhibition on the top floor about 20th Century Genocide. The first entry started at the end of the previous century. According to that, the first genocidal campaign of those times was one carried out by the Americans in the Philippines. Those islands were then part of the Spanish Empire, and the USA wanted the Spanish out of the Caribbean and the Pacific.

Emilio Aguinaldo was a revolutionary who started a revolt against the Spanish in 1896 in a bid for freedom. The Americans promised him and his supporters that in return for their help, America would give the islands their independence once the Spanish had been driven out. The Spanish were driven out in 1898 after the US Navy destroyed the Spanish Fleet in Manila Bay. Aguinaldo declared the Philippines independent, but Spain ceded the country to the USA with other islands in the Caribbean for $20 million.

Like most nations occupied by a foreign armed force, the Filipinos did not care to be an American colony and revolted. Looking back to 1770 or so, the Americans didn't like being a bunch of colonies, so they fought the English and drove them out. They just don't seem to see the hypocrisy in taking over other countries in the same way, even if they don't call them colonies. The Filipino revolt lasted three years, with the USA slaughtering massive numbers of them. The Imperial War Museum Exhibition estimated 100,000 or so, but in encyclopaedias I have seen a figure of 200,000. Wikipedia even quotes up to 250,000, giving various authorities, including one chillingly called "Final Solutions," giving a nod and a wink to Hitler and the gas chambers.

Maybe these islanders would have thrown off all contact with the USA after that, but even when they achieved independence in 1946, the USA remained with military bases and economic aid. Was this an environment in which our pilot, Captain Subrama, could be recruited by the CIA? After all, he wasn't a Filipino, and a great deal of the world's flying education and the planes themselves are American. Is it likely that the CIA recruit skilled (and unskilled) people abroad to serve them for reward? It must be so. Is a white or black American likely to be taken at face value trying to infiltrate Russian government bodies or Armed Forces, let alone Chinese, Indian, or Pakistani ones? Or a Malaysian one?

Why did I feel that America might have something to do with the missing plane?

What I had been researching, after looking at Subrama,

were all the promising entries on the internet about the missing plane. Many of them suggested that the aircraft had caught alight and crashed, but no wreckage that could definitely be from the plane in question had ever been found. There were some reports of debris being found in scattered places from Madagascar to Reunion Island in the Indian Ocean, and even off the coast of Western Australia. Others said perhaps SEA439 had simply crashed into the sea and sunk without trace. Locations for this varied from the middle of the Gulf of Thailand, east of Malaysia, to far south into the Indian Ocean, and many points in between.

The latter was based on calculations plotting contacts between the plane and radar installations, and signals sent automatically between bases on land and the plane and bounced via satellites to Inmarsat. Apparently the plane was still involuntarily sending back regular handshakes to the satellites. At one time it was thought that these signals meant the plane could have gone north-west towards Turkmenistan, but no wreckage had ever been found, and the crash area, if that was what it was, was more and more certainly put in the southern Indian Ocean.

Then I came across suggestions that the plane had been hijacked (the very first theory); that the pilot Subrama had hijacked it himself to commit suicide; or had flown the plane over 41,000 feet where all on board, including him, had passed out through lack of oxygen. But in that last case, why and how had he turned the plane round from his scheduled course to Beijing and flown west, nearly in the opposite direction? Especially if he were unconscious or dead. That didn't make any sense to me. If he wanted to kill himself, why not plunge the plane into the sea at the earliest opportunity? And if he and everyone else on board were already dead from decompression and lack of oxygen, how did the plane make all the other turns west and south, if it was really SEA439?

If Subrama had flown so high everyone including him, was unconscious or dead, how did he bring the plane back down to normal height and then put it back on automatic pilot? That idea lost traction when authorities said there seemed to be something wrong with the data recording the high altitude flying. But did that mean it was no longer possible? I'd have to investigate that.

I phoned Rolls Royce to find out what they thought about the handshakes. They told me to send a letter or an email to their enquiries desk.

A few people had suggested that the plane's computers had been taken over in the air by some outside device of the sort that flies drones, tapping into the aircraft's systems, and guiding it to some unknown destination. As I looked into that further it became apparent that although this had been done experimentally on flight simulators and model planes, it was still only theoretical for the real thing. I phoned my cousin Spencer for his view. He advised me that if he thought his auto-pilot had been 'taken over' he would simply switch it off, and take control manually.

He also told me that a Flight Captain on 777s had posted on Youtube a small film about a hatch cover in a corridor of the plane which is not locked. I searched for the film. The hatch gives access to the room containing most of the plane's vital electrical equipment, so anyone with the knowledge could mess it up, or perhaps take the plane over. That film was immediately followed by another where a man was in that room filming the equipment and explaining what it does. The space looked large enough to conceal at least four people – enough for a hijack. Is that what it was? So where was the plane, and who were the hijackers or terrorists?

Over dinner I asked Jamie if he'd heard or seen anything about the plane. To my surprise he said he did have something, but it wasn't new. He uses his lap-top looking at the global weather a great deal. It seems a very nerdy hobby for a fellow who is a meteorologist for a living, but he always said it wasn't just a job to him, but a passion.

"I was looking at different web-sites round the world, and came across some old entries in an Australian chat-room specialising in the weather. Guess what? They call it Weatherzone! These posts were in April last year - only a month after the plane disappeared - speculating that it must have gone to Diego Garcia somehow. Seems unlikely to me. I mean, why would the US not say they had the plane? After all, there were some Americans on it, too."

I did not want to give anything away, not even to Jamie, and managed to hide my surprise. "Yes, it does look odd. And most of the effort of searching for it is nowhere near that island."

"Why do you ask, love?"

"Just fascinated that a huge plane with all those people can simply disappear, and no-one knows anything about it?"

Jamie smiled. "It's a story for Sherlock Galloway!"

My turn to smile. "Maybe you're right.

Weatherzone website chat-room!! Yes, Jamie's job was also one of his hobbies! I'd read a few theories to the same effect, that the plane had been deliberately flown to Diego Garcia. This small Indian Ocean paradise atoll lies between Sri Lanka and the African coast, roughly speaking. I realised this resolved the problem about fuel. The distance from Kuala Lumpur to Beijing and Diego Garcia are about the same, so if Subrama loaded enough fuel to avoid trouble over China, he could easily have enough to cover going back and forth over Malaysia and part of the South China Sea, and land on Diego Garcia.

None of the theories I read about seemed conclusive; most of them had a flaw, as I've already explained. For example, if it had been a hijack, why hadn't Al Qaida or other terrorist outfits claimed the credit – if you can call it that – for this outrage, which had stunned the world? If one of the pilots wanted to commit suicide by plunging the plane into the sea, why wait all those extra hours? If he had passed out and died with everyone else when the cabin depressurised, how did the plane manage to change direction several times after that if it was on automatic pilot? My friend Nick Carter - a very experienced but now retired pilot and Flight Captain - told me that the pilot can re-route the autopilot after take-off. This might be done if there is sudden unexpected bad weather, or something similar. But why would he bother to do that in order to kill himself? According to both Nick and Spencer he would do it if he wanted to go somewhere specific whether dead or alive, as they said it is very difficult indeed to fly a large plane by hand without a co-pilot; thus the autopilot would be reprogrammed, and in any case, they said, it is illegal to fly without it at an altitude such as 35,000 feet.

So why not Diego Garcia for a secret destination of the plane?

It is home to a large contingent of American Forces and civilians. That was when I began to wonder about the possible involvement of the USA in the 'disappearance' of the plane. It might be worth looking into. No-one else seemed to be doing that seriously. Before I went to bed I phoned Karen and asked her if I could come round for coffee in the morning. I wanted her input on US foreign relations, to test whether there were any likelihood from earlier precedents why they might have hijacked SEA439.

1st June, 2014.

I arrived at Karen's at 10.30. The aroma of good coffee greeted me as soon as she opened the front door. If I didn't love her to bits I could find her quite aggravating. She's not only a First Class Honours Graduate, attractive, humorous, and elegant, but she took to being a wife and a Mum with gusto. She works at home supplying opinion pieces to MPs and newspapers on matters which concern them, but still keeps the house and the kids spotless, happy, and learning fast. Pictures – mostly watercolours – are tastefully arranged along the hallway and in all the rooms. She still practices the guitar beautifully. Get the idea? She's as near perfect as it's possible to be.

She seated me on the yellow chesterfield sofa in her very comfortably furnished lounge and brought in the coffee. I didn't tell her about the plane. After some family talk, I brought the conversation round to British politics, and Europe, and then led it off on a tangent to the 'special relationship'. Karen laughed. "What special relationship? I looked at that a good deal when I was at university. I concluded it was largely a myth."

"Did you look at US relations with many other countries? I was thinking about the Philippines yesterday, and how the US hung on to them after the war with Spain."

Karen smiled, but became more serious. "America has never lost its grip on the Philippines. It was the major trading partner for these islands." It was a good place to recruit a pilot or other skilled people to help it, I thought. But would the USA get someone to hijack a plane and murder everybody on board apart from the pilot and whoever on board was helping him? I asked Karen about their record with other countries.

"Pretty dreadful really, Lynn. Look at Cuba. America wanted to colonise it before the Spanish War in 1898. After Castro took Cuba away from the American's dictator stooge Batista in the 1950s, they planned a Cuban exile invasion of the island, but when it failed, Kennedy left the invaders on the beach, instead of rescuing them as they had promised. Then the CIA wanted to stage some 'terrorist' attacks in Florida to make it look as though Castro was behind them, thus giving an excuse for a US invasion, but Kennedy vetoed that. He didn't want Americans killed by American bombs, even if it gave him an excuse to invade Cuba."

"Am I right in thinking the US supported dictators all over the world as long as they were subservient to the might of the dollar?"

Karen nodded. "Think Marcos in the Philippines, the Military regime in South Vietnam, the CIA sponsored murder of left-wing President Allende in Chile, and their support of his brutal right-wing replacement, General Pinochet, right?"

I looked down at my hands for a moment, and then back at Karen. "I suppose they acted pretty dreadfully over the shooting of the journalist Namir Noor-Eldeen in Baghdad in July 2007. I guess I'm bound to remember an awful thing like that happening to a fellow newsman."

Karen thumped the arm of her chair with a fist, and leaned right over the coffee table. "What that Apache helicopter did was murderous. They killed him, his driver, plus ten other people, and wounded two children in a van which stopped to help them. The murderers in the helicopter didn't know who they were shooting. They took no steps to identify them. This was no accident. They didn't pull the trigger by accident. They knew when they pulled it that people would die."

"That's murder, alright. It's no use them arguing that this was a war. George Bush called it a 'War on Terror', but it was no longer a war on Iraq, making all who lived there valid targets. It was a war on certain groups and individuals. It didn't confer rights on a soldier to shoot down anyone he didn't like the look of."

I thought about the US practice of awarding medals for almost anything you could think of. Did the Apache pilots get medals for that terribly daring raid, shooting innocent unarmed men from a speck in the sky the victims probably could not see? Do the incredibly brave men and women in concrete bunkers in the desert in Nevada who are never in danger get medals for working computers controlling lethal drones which shoot some terrorists but also kill wedding guests, brides, grooms, school-children, and families they do not know and care less about? And that happens even in countries the Americans are not at war with in any sense, like Pakistan.

Karen laughed ironically. "What would the Irish in Boston, Massachusetts have thought if Britain had used similar tactics around Dublin during The Troubles, or just dropped bombs all over it?

"What about Bradley Manning? If he hadn't had the courage, through Wikileaks, to reveal the truth about that murder in Iraq, and more besides, to the whole world, no-one would know. So what did the USA, the so-called bastion of freedom and free speech, do? It locked him away for it." Karen paused for breath. She was inflamed. "Britain thinks it has a special relationship with the USA, but it was Eisenhower who stopped the invasion of Egypt by Britain and France to keep open the Suez Canal, which they owned. Ike cut off Britain's oil supplies. Closing the canal doubled the length of time ships took to get to India, Pakistan,

Australia, New Zealand, Hong Kong, and many other places in which Britain had serious investments and obligations. America was supposed to be Australia and New Zealand's ally too, but assisting Nasser to keep the Canal closed harmed the trade of those small populations. Was that the act of a special friend? Did it contribute to the trouble in the Middle East ever since? Didn't it damage the British Commonwealth?"

She stopped again. "Boy, I do go off on one, don't I?"

My turn to laugh. "Well, I did ask you to, remember? We can talk about your hairdresser or the kids or other girlie things if you wish."

"God forbid! So come clean. What is this really about?"

"Very well, Karen. But this is entirely in confidence; cross your heart and all that."

She gave a three fingered salute. "OK, Scouts honour, seriously. This is just between you and me; not the gatepost."

"Exactly. I haven't even told Jamie, so you cannot - and I mean cannot - tell even Steve."

She stood up and walked to the bookcase, saying as she went: "Blimey, this is serious." She pulled a Bible out of the shelves and holding it up swore by Almighty God she would tell no-one. I smiled at that.

"You've got the message."

"I'm working on a big story about the plane that ..."

"Do you mean SEA439?"

"Spot on. Now I can't tell you why, but I think it's likely that the Americans hijacked it. What I want to know is, do you think it possible that they might have done it?"

Karen fell back into her chair, closed her eyes and ran her fingers through her hair. She took a deep breath and silence reigned. After a couple of minutes her onyx eyes were staring at me. "It would depend on whether they had a motive. Bearing in mind some of the evil things they've done in the past, and given a motive, they could have perpetrated such a hijack."

I nodded at the sense of that. It followed that if the USA thought it was in its interests to get hold of this plane for some reason, it would not hesitate. Then I shook my head at the question of motive. "I'd be bloody lucky if they told me why they did it. All I can do is try to follow the evidence, if I can find any."

"Well, what about our country, Britain? Remember how in 1991 Customs and Excise charged the directors of a company called Matrix Churchill with supplying arms-making machines to Saddam Hussein before he invaded Kuwait? In fact they'd been given licences to export this stuff to Iraq by the Department of Trade and Industry, which knew all along what the machines were for because it wanted the millions of pounds of exports. Thatcher's government had connived at the prosecution going ahead, so it kept up the pretence that Matrix Churchill had deceived the DTI. The case collapsed because one director was working for MI6 and the former sales manager for MI5."

"Of course I remember. I was in Court covering the story. That cross-examination of the former minister, Alan Clark? Rapier-like, the way that QC elicited the truth. I remember wondering at the time whether Clark may have been straightforward in the witness box because he'd lost his job, considered he'd been libelled in the Daily Telegraph, but was prevented from suing by the Cabinet. Presumably that was because Thatcher's successor, John Major, feared all the paperwork and the truth would emerge in Court."

Karen poured more coffee. "Coming clean in the witness box was a perfect opportunity for Clark to take his revenge, and save the defendants from jail. What the Matrix Churchill case showed was that Ministers and their minions use anything they can think of to cover up what they do, and defend themselves. They lie to the public and to Parliament. Can politicians ever be trusted? Their conduct in this case was what, throughout the Cold War, they used to tell us was so terrible about Communist regimes."

"Well, I've made a note of all that, thanks. Are we off to lunch?"

"Sorry, Lynn. Kerry's class is going on a trip to the Science Museum at lunch time. I'm an escort with the teacher. Steve will be home today for Naomi when she comes in."

"OK, I'll be off then, and thanks again for all your help, Karen." I finished my coffee. "Just one question more. When I said about following the evidence, you didn't ask what I was after or what I'd got so far. Why?"

"I know you well enough to know when I'd be wasting my time." We both laughed.

2nd June, 2014.

I went to Exposure TV's offices. I was lucky. Marion

Gorman, my commissioning editor, was free and agreed to see me immediately. I was luckier still to find that by chance Julian Prentis, the company in-house solicitor, was with her. She asked him politely to leave us.

As he moved to the door I said: "No, Marion. Julian should stay. We both need him to hear this."

She waved him back to his chair and I sat, too. Marion asked what was cooking.

"Perhaps the biggest story Exposure has ever done. Even more shocking than Watergate or the Pentagon Papers! Or Bradley Manning!"

Marion controlled a laugh. She could see I was not joking. In his very restrained upper class way Julian just said: "Good Heavens." If he knows a vulgar four letter word, I doubt any-one has ever heard him utter one.

Marion said: "OK, so let's hear it, Lynn."

I kept the details of my research as brief as possible. Neither of them needed things spelt out much, if at all. "The main thing is I think it possible - just possible - that the plane, SEA 439, ended up on Diego Garcia, didn't crash anywhere, on land or sea. It's a story no-one seems to be doing. I need to do a lot more digging on the internet, and try to find someone, or several someones, who can talk to me about the place, whether the plane turned up there; if it did, how it disappeared."

Julian smiled grimly. "Sounds like a tall order, Lynn. As far as I know only US military personnel get there. It's shrouded in secrecy. Anyone who tells you anything will be seen as another Bradley Manning. Getting someone to talk will be hard even if you find them."

"I understand that alright. I just have to hope and pray for a lot of luck."

Marion was poker-faced. "I don't suppose you've come in here with a budget and a plan, have you?"

"Hardly. You pay me anyway, so the research will cost nothing more, but I need to travel a bit, and maybe a lot. The places I almost certainly have to visit are Malaysia, and maybe the U.S. I may need to interview people here at home, and if I do get lucky and hear of an American or two, I'll have to go there. I'd need a camera-man, and a producer. And a minder some of the time, I expect. Especially in Kuala Lumpur and the States. 250 people and a plane have already disappeared. It's a dangerous story."

"You'd need a fixer in Malaysia, someone who could either be your interpreter or find you one." Julian was serious. A very thorough lawyer, he had been in the business a long time, and seen it all. Tall, with dark wavy hair, always immaculately dressed, he cared about the people at Exposure whom it was his job to advise and protect from a legal stand-point. I'd have to find one for Malaysia. I might even need a fixer in the States.

Marion said: "It seems to me you need an opening budget so we can look at what you get, and see if it's worth spending any more. We need to get onto one of the Channels and get them to commission this story."

"Just what I was thinking," Julian said.

Marion gave him a look which said that wasn't his field,

and continued: "I think we should ask for 50 grand for openers, and I'll speak to Channel 4; it's their kind of thing. You've worked with Malcolm Broadbridge before, haven't you." Marion was making a statement. She rarely forgot a thing.

"Several times. And I like him. He's tough on the surface and good."

Julian smiled. Marion said: "And he delivers excellent programmes."

"Yes, he does," Julian added, "but above all, he can be trusted to say absolutely nothing to anyone. This story is so sensitive if it's true – and I don't doubt what you say, Lynn - that we need to be twice as careful and three times as secretive as usual. God help us if we go public with this and it's false."

Marion nodded her agreement. "Quite. RIP Exposure." She paused. "Clearly this won't take up all your time until you get some leads, Lynn, so keep on with the one about crime in airports for now? We need a code name for this aircraft project for email and phone calls."

"I can, for the first point, and 'The Vulture' for the second." With that the meeting broke up, but as it did, Marion said: "I'll give you a month to find something more."

"Not enough, Marion. This isn't my usual sort of case, where I've got Police and underworld contacts. At the moment I haven't a clue where my leads will come from."

"OK. Make it two months, but keep me informed."

I could only pray I'd have something to inform her about, but I was very excited. I arranged to film the next day, recording my research on camera. Malcolm would illustrate that with film archives of the incidents I'd looked up, old news about Iraq, Matrix Churchill, and so on, for background to my voice. Then I bought a new lap-top on the way home.

In my study I transferred the entire contents of the old computer, including the story so far, onto a USB and then put the story only into the new computer. Having done that I wiped everything off the old lap-top and cleared the Recycle bin. I intended to take it into a computer service I used, get them to remove the hard drive for me, install a new one, move everything but 'The Vulture' from the USB onto the new drive, and then I'd destroy the old one; set light to it or something drastic. If anyone stole or found the old computer they'd never know 'The Vulture' had ever been on it. The new lap-top would never leave my sight from now on.

It was my habit to get down to Mum and Dad's at their old cottage in Shere near Guildford most weeks, usually at weekends. It's on the outskirts of the village, towards the road from Albury to Farley Green. It is a beautiful brick mid-18th Century house in its own grounds, with a hedge of rhododendrons growing along the boundaries. I could print the story off there as it grew and post it, or take it, to Karen Macauley's place. Still thinking, I realised I could get Mum or Dad to post the stuff to Karen.

I phoned Karen to tell her that is what would happen; she could guess what it was about from our last talk, but not to tell anyone. I started a routine of putting a few sheets of story in an envelope marked 'Niall Merrylees, Strictly Private and Confidential, from Lynn Galloway; DO NOT OPEN; keep in safe', and putting that inside another envelope addressed to Karen. Inside the first of the envelopes for Karen I put a note asking her to tell Niall that if anything happened to me he should open them and go to Marion Gorman immediately. I got Mum or Dad to write Karen's name and address on the outer envelopes. If one of them, or even their cleaner, Edna, could then to take it to the Post Office a day or two after I left, it would have even less of an appearance of being anything to do with me.

4th June, 2014.

Marion appeared in front of my desk.

"I've been to Channel 4 with Julian. We had very private - secret in fact – talks with them. They signed one of Julian's non-disclosure agreements. They are very, very interested in the story. We shall have a contract."

"Awesome!"

"They refused to pay 50,000 quid for starters, but we agreed on 45 thousand and the rest of our expenses as we go. The final figure will be in the contract, and we'll get a small percentage of the advertising revenue round the programme. We can have more if we have real progress and need extra to make it a blockbuster. When the story's finished they'll broadcast it and put it out there. Julian pointed out they could be sure to sell it to Malaysian TV, China, Australia, an American TV company or two, and that any country which had passengers or crew on board will want it."

I was speechless, and could barely mutter: "Let's go for a drink. Will Julian come?"

18th June, 2014.

Idle curiosity, but while doing more surfing of the net for gen on Diego Garcia, I wondered about women going to the island. I keyed in: 'Women on Diego Garcia'. I dug up diamonds.

I'd already found out a good bit about the island – well, atoll really. It was a British Empire possession since the Napoleonic Wars. It was a naval base for them, and the native people were called the Chagos. As Britain shed colonies and dependencies in the 1950s and 60s, the USA asked if it could take it over as a military/naval/air-force establishment. In 1967 there was 'an exchange of notes' between the two powers under which the atoll would remain British, the Americans would have a kind of lease of it for about 50 years, and all the natives would be shipped out, lock, stock, and barrel.

What did the locals thinks about that? Not a lot; they weren't even consulted, just told. Mind you, the USA was good at that: just ask any descendant of Red Cloud, Cochese, Geronimo or Sitting Bull how his great-great-grandad felt about being moved onto a reservation when he'd had the whole of the prairie to hunt over. However, the evacuation was down to Britain, so Harold Wilson got on with it. Basically, it doesn't matter what side of politics someone says he's on, left or right, if there's a nasty bit of work to do, they'll find a nasty piece of work to do it for them.

By 1970 all the Chagos had gone, and they weren't allowed back. If they had been working abroad or visiting family overseas, or just away on holiday, they were refused entry, and their belongings just disappeared. I doubt that 'pissed off' would cover how they must have felt.

The USA got weaving. They improved the dock facilities, put up hangars, constructed living quarters, admin buildings, you name it, they built it. The atoll looks a bit like a footprint from the air, so they called it "Freedom's Footprint." That's not what some of the people who were 'renditioned' there after the Twin Towers and 9/11 may have called it, but I'll come to that later.

The US Airforce was not neglected. In the early 80s they got two runways 12,000 feet long. That's about 2.5 miles or 3.75 kilometres. They could take the biggest bombers, cargo planes like C4s, and – how about that – civilian airliners such as a Boeing 747-200ER! Despite all that, it was still an island paradise in many ways, and now it was much easier to get to; but only, I found, if you were in the American Armed Services, or a sworn-to-secrecy-public-servant from the US. If you were on a yacht on a round the world jaunt, or even a cruise liner with 2,000 passengers on board, and got into trouble you could not approach within two miles of the island, but had to await help way off shore – if you were lucky.

I could find no record of anyone landing a plane there in an emergency, either, though on YouTube someone had posted a film taken on a mobile phone or video camera of some sort of jet landing there ordinarily with two pilots and at least one other person in the cockpit. The men wore short-sleeved white shirts with black and gold striped epaulettes, so they might have been civilian or military. I couldn't tell which.

I found a promotional US Navy Recruitment article from 2004 describing this atoll paradise as one of the world's best 'unknown' places, with fantastic beauty and lifestyle.

Quite a number of sites said that DG was used for landing terrorist detainees on their way to a rendition holiday camp. Instead of swimming they'd be given endless water-boarding and other sources of great fun. Some were said to have been detained on the island and tortured. This was routinely denied in Washington to Congressional Committees, and in London to the House of Commons. However, I saw that on 21st February, 2008 David Milliband, one of Tony Blair's Ministers, was forced to admit that two US rendition flights used Diego as a refuelling stop, but insisted the prisoners did not get off the plane.

There was even a joke amongst journalists that the first one to file a story from the atoll would win a case of the most expensive Scotch money could buy. There has yet to be a winner.

Anyway, as I said, I decided to have a look to see if there was anything about ladies on the island. In response to my search up popped 'PROPEOPDEMREPDG', or 'The Provisional People's Democratic Republic of Diego Garcia'. This had nothing to do with the Chagossian people whose island home it used to be. It was not, on the face of it, an official site, but a social diary of events, facilities and more. There were at least 50 pages, in different colours, with photos of one or two buildings, and lots of talk of 'The Brit

94

Club'. Photos of this place, inside and out, were included, and the interior shots showed ladies.

There were many posts about the Club, the wild-life (birds and animals, not the goings on in the Club), and other matters, and the last entry I noticed was dated 2nd January 2014. This was meant to be amusing about what were discreetly called 'provocative post-cards', and a sample showed an Edwardian bathing belle, whose costume left everything to the imagination, it covered so much.

It seemed that there were about 300 women to about 1200 men. Some of the girls were service personnel; others were civil servants. They were all pretty popular, according to some of the features. But what were they doing at The Brit Club? And why was it called The Brit Club? The answer was obvious once you knew about it. There was a section about the history of the island and even what had happened to the natives, and this 'magazine' (for want of a better word) acknowledged that the place was 'British Indian Ocean Territory'. Entries said that this Club was the most relaxed place on the island. In the US parts of the island the sexes weren't supposed to fraternise.

As that's about being brothers I thought that would be OK. Surely what the authorities wanted to stop was heterosexualising!! But that's what you could do in The Brit Club, and there were even photos of the guys and dolls doing just that.

Then I spotted the really big diamond: the UK kept a contingent of its own Service people on the atoll. Where they came from wasn't specified, but it said that about 18 of them were Royal Marines whose job was to police the atoll and surrounding islands.

Bingo! I knew all I needed was to find a Marine who had served on DG. I say 'all', but that would be hard. Getting one of these tough men to open up about it would be damn near impossible. Persuading one to talk about what might have happened there on 9th March 2013 would be absolutely impossible, wouldn't it? I'd just have to try.

23rd June, 2014.

A couple of days ago I emailed the Ministry of Defence press desk in Whitehall. I introduced myself as a journalist wanting to do a TV story about what life was like for a marine or two. I was given an appointment to see a Captain at the Royal Marines base in Lympstone, Devon, and today I drove down there to see him.

He was Captain Archibald, tall, fit, well-spoken, with fair wavy hair that reminded me of the posh bloke on a TV series called 'Cold Feet'. I repeated what I'd said to the telephonist about being a journalist and doing a programme about a couple of his men. I felt I'd better say I'd really like one who'd served on Diego Garcia, as I knew that some Marines went there. I'd like to talk about The Brit Club, and what it was like working with the Americans.

Archibald was extremely polite. "I'm afraid we can't help you, Miss Galloway. A lot of what the Marines do and where they go is classified. I'm surprised the MOD didn't tell you that. As I'm sure you know, whilst it's no secret that

Marines go to Diego, it is not something we're allowed to talk about."

"It may not be a secret, Captain, but it certainly isn't very well known. Most people have never heard of Diego Garcia."

"Well, there we are, Miss Galloway. It's certainly not something I intend to help publicise. I like my job, and I don't want to get thrown out of it, or worse."

"Or worse?

"Yes. Court Martialled for a breach of the Official Secrets Act, or some other beastly charge."

"I wouldn't want to be the cause of that, Captain. It looks as though I've wasted your time and mine coming down here." Captain Archibald said he was afraid so, and had me escorted from his office and off the base to the visitors car park on the other side of the road.

I stopped for lunch in Exmouth, took a stroll along the beach, wondering what to do next, and then drove home along the A303. The countryside was at its verdant best. Passing Stonehenge is always a weird experience for me, imagining folk running around in woad and animal skins clutching clubs and spears. How on earth did they get those huge stones all the way from the Prescelly Mountains in West Wales 3,500 years ago?

Then it came to me: old monuments link up with other old things, which link up with museums. Would any of the ex-marines at their Museum in Southsea be of any help?

Back at the office I Googled 'Royal Marines Museum, Southsea,' noted the opening times. A tourist didn't need an appointment to go to a museum.

24th June, 2014.

I went by train from Waterloo to Southsea and walked to the Museum.

Sam Barton (it was on his lapel badge) appointed himself as my guide. Normally I prefer to go round galleries, museums and stately homes on my own, unless I can get Jamie to come. They're not 'his thing', as they say – one of those modern expressions used by people short of vocabulary, which I try hard to avoid.

He showed me all sorts of weapons, a display of Victoria Crosses, all about them, and who won them. He showed me uniforms and more besides. I was actually enjoying myself. So was Sam. I think he liked having a younger woman to talk to. He was about 65, and my height, his hair thick, strong, grey and cut short. He was very smartly turned out in a dark blazer, pressed grey trousers, and a regimental tie on a sparkling white shirt. I could see he was still pretty fit, admitting proudly in answer to my question that he had been a marine himself, and had seen active service in the Falklands. This was a perfect opening for my real purpose there.

Having told him I was a TV Journalist, I said: "I'm trying to get up a story about a couple of youngish marines who are either still serving, or may have left the force in the last year or two. Do you know anyone who might be able to help me? I'm afraid they wouldn't get paid anything except expenses if they came into the studios."

Sam scratched his head. "Well, I can't say I do. We don't get many blokes currently wearing the uniform coming in here. It's mainly sightseers like you, or old blokes like me coming in to reminisce, or show their wives or grandchildren what it all stood for." He paused for a moment, curling his fingers round his chin in thought. "Tell you what though. There is a young bloke comes in quite regular, like; maybe once every two or three weeks. Don't say much. Just wanders round on his own, and doesn't want any help. I did ask him if he'd been in the Armed Services, and he said he'd been a marine. He applied for discharge about nine months ago, but he never said why."

"How would I get hold of him?"

"I dunno. He's a funny cove. Seems lonely 'n' fed up, to me. I don't think he's got a job." Sam hestitated. Hang on a mo', though. He always signs the visitors' book. I think he writes his name an' address in full. Come back to the office."

That's where we went. Sam got the book out and flicked back a page or two. "Here we are, see." He pointed with a slightly nicotine-stained forefinger to a name. "There you are; why don't you copy that out?"

The name was Gavin Johnson, and the address was in Clarence Parade.

Sam had not finished. "Bloody posh road, that is. Right behind the seafront. Big houses, most of 'em, lawyers and doctors, big business, that sort mostly. Some've been divided into flats. That's where our Gavin is. D'you want a taxi? I can phone one from here if you like?"

"Yes, thanks Sam. But let's have another half hour in here before I go, shall we?" I wanted to see a bit more, and not appear to be too keen to get away. "And I'll take the cab back to the station. I'll try to get hold of Gavin another time."

Sam made the call, and asked for the taxi to come for me in thirty minutes.

***

When it came I told the driver to go to Clarence Parade. I wanted no grass to grow under my feet, but didn't want anyone else to know that. I found Gavin Johnson's flat on the ground floor of a large, beautifully converted 1930s family villa. I got the cab to wait in case he was out, but he answered the door. I told him who I was, and gave him the same spiel I gave Sam. He invited me in, but I didn't want that, so I said we could go for a drink, or lunch if he wanted to.

As with Sam, and I know it sounds vain to say it, I think my appearance and age did the trick, and he agreed to lunch. He appeared taciturn, and I just hoped he would talk when we were in the pub. I asked him where, and he suggested a pub where marines go, so I told him I'd rather it was just us: it would be safer for both of us. He named another pub a bit further away. In fact it was in Old Portsmouth, and turned out to be very nice, with good grub, busy enough that we didn't attract attention, but not so crowded that anyone would overhear us. We got in my cab and off we went.

He was an inch or so taller than my five foot six, with pale brown hair going a bit grey at the sides. He had good but run-down-looking clothes; his very expensive brown shoes were scuffed and down at heel. He told me he was thirty-one.

I could see he was very fit. His shoulders and biceps filled his pale green shirt.

"When did you leave the marines?"

"September last year. I was fed up with it, feeling depressed, but not ill. I couldn't tell them why I wanted out, but I persuaded the doctor I was no longer suited to a marine's life, he signed me off, and I got my discharge."

"What made you fed up? I thought most men, once they were in the marines, never wanted to leave and stayed on as long as they could."

"Well, that's probably the case."

"So what happened to you?"

"That's the thing. Nothing did happen to me. It's what happened to others that got me down."

"Other marines?"

Gavin smiled a ghoulish sort of a smile. "I wish it had been me, or some of the blokes. We expect we may get killed in that business, though that's not the aim. No. These others were civilians, innocent civilians; lots of them."

"When did this happen? And how did you know about it?"

He shook his head. "Look, I've probably said too much already. I could go to prison if I say any more."

"Prison? You're pulling my leg!"

"Wish I were. Coming cleans about our ops is treason."

"OK. When did this happen?

"It was six months before I was discharged. I was there."

"So if you were discharged nine months ago, you were wherever it was in what - March last year?" Did he mean

101

where I hoped he meant? I almost spilt my gin and tonic as he took another swig of his Whitbread Pale. Gavin nodded.

"So where was that?" I held my breath. Was my luck going to hold out, or run out?

It ran out. "Can't tell you; sorry."

"I understand. In my business people have all sorts of reasons for not wanting to talk about things. Makes my job harder; sometimes downright impossible. So I'll tell you what. I'm going to take a risk and come clean with you, but it's in confidence. Then maybe you'll tell me what you can." I was telling him about SEA439 when he said he knew all about it. I told him again that what I was going to say next was confidential, and he promised to tell no-one; it was a risk my story would be blown in other media, but I believed his promise. I told him I was working on a story about the plane, taking a line no-one had taken seriously before. I told him about Diego Garcia, that it had been dismissed as just another conspiracy story, but gave him reasons why it could be true. I appealed to his sense of justice and sympathy for the missing and their relatives. He must have had family die, and seen comrades in arms shot. He agreed with that. I went on: "Shouldn't we speak up for these people? If something so serious happened you had to resign from a job you loved, don't you want to let the poison out?"

He shook his head again, sadly this time. "Very well. You're right. I do want to clear my conscience. I've never talked to anyone about this before. For a start I'm not allowed to. Second, as I say, if I do and the Government find out I'll end up inside. But you know what? I've been churning all this over and over for the last fifteen months and it's driving me mad. I'm still fed up, maybe even truly depressed now. I don't care what happens any more. Maybe I've been praying someone like you would turn up. It's why I don't have a job. I couldn't think straight about work."

"How do you afford to live in Clarence Parade then? Your flat looks expensive."

"It was, but I own it. You don't get to spend all your money in the services if you're careful and don't drink too much. They clothe and feed you. What else do you need? In any case my parents are both dead. Dad died suddenly ten years ago, and Mum three years ago. I had no brothers or sisters, so I got their house in Wiltshire and all the money. Didn't need a house. Sold it and bought the flat. Got plenty in the bank and some shares, even after Inheritance Tax. I'm just living off the income, and a bit of pension from the marines."

"It doesn't sound too bad."

"It's not, but I've no purpose in life. I keep busy, running five or six miles twice a week, karate and judo club three times a week, and for light relief, I play tennis twice a week. I also keep up my shooting at a gun club once a fortnight. I'll lose the Army pension if this story goes ahead, but I've got to get this off my chest. Then maybe I can really find something to do."

"Maybe you should join a security outfit." Gavin laughed, but seemed to like the idea, too.

At that point the barman brought our lunch over, so conversation stopped for a while as we ate. When we had finished I had to make my position clear. "Look Gavin, I told you I'm in TV. If you help me make a programme about whatever it is may be bugging you, everyone will know, not just the government. I'm not in the business of putting my helpers in prison."

"It's like this, Miss Galloway."

For the second time I asked him to call me Lynn.

"OK. Lynn it is. I want to come clean. This thing, although I didn't do it, it's on my conscience. Marines don't just kill people. We're supposed to be fighting for truth and justice, and no-one's telling the truth, and there's no bloody justice in it."

I got my note book out. I told Gavin I was going to make some notes. He told me to record it on my phone if I had one. He swallowed another mouthful of his beer as I moved to a seat closer to him and put the phone on the table between us. I repeated onto it the preamble about who he was, who I am, where we were, and that these were notes for a TV programme. Then he leaned over the phone and said: "She's just bought me lunch. It wasn't a bribe," and he laughed. "I may go to prison for this. I'm not doing that for the price of a lunch I can buy myself."

"We could use an actor to play your part and say whatever it is you have to tell me. Then you can remain anonymous."

"Yes, I've seen that sort of documentary, but now I've decided to go for it, that's not what I want. In for a penny, in for a pound. If you film me then no-one can say that TV made this up. I want everyone to know it's me, and that I was there."

"Prison included?"

"Prison included, if it comes to that."

Then we went over the parts about him wanting to get things off his conscience, that something had occurred in March 2013 which made him seek his discharge from the Royal Marines a few months later. It looked as though I was going to get a pretty good story, even if it wasn't the one I hoped for. "Do you recall the date, Gavin?"

"I should think almost everyone recalls this date. It was 9th March, 2013, the day that SEA 439 went missing."

I nearly choked. This seemed too good to be true. I felt like a panhandler who'd just washed a handful of large gold nuggets out of the river.

He didn't notice my reaction. He was back in the past, staring at the beer mat on the table. "I was on duty patrolling outside the perimeter of the US Airbase on Diego Garcia, in the Indian Ocean. It was early morning, but light. The Royal Marines have the policing of the Island as it's still a British possession, but nearly everyone else there is American.

"An aeroplane came into land. At first I took little notice, since there are lots of flights coming and going all the time. Spy planes, supply planes, flights of troops going home on leave or coming back, cargoes of equipment. However, I did a double take when I saw this green plane with gold lettering, so it was clearly a civil aircraft."

"Is that rare, to see a civilian plane on Diego Garcia?"

"Perhaps not rare, but very unusual. Air Force One has been there with a President on board, I was told, perhaps some other politicians. I used to carry binoculars with me on patrol in case I saw anything odd in the distance, and sometimes I'd use them for a bird I hadn't seen before. Anyway, I took a peek at this green plane and I could see the name of the airline. I moved on, but stopped again when I saw some men come out. I used the binoculars. Four were clearly in charge of three other men, and those three were wearing handcuffs. I watched them disappear into a building, and by then more troops were coming out of the buildings in fatigues."

"Where did they go?"

"They were carrying some stuff but I couldn't see what it was, just big black packets of something. They went up into the plane, and a few minutes later they started coming out carrying these black body bags which obviously had bodies in them. Four blokes to each bag, one at the head and feet and one each side. There were about 20, or maybe a couple of dozen, doing this and I watched for about ten minutes."

I was shocked rigid. "What happened then?"

"I thought I'd better get moving or I'd be in trouble for not finishing the patrol on time, and the next patrol would be waiting for me before they could go out. I was in the canteen having lunch and the radio was on. I was sitting next to a man I'd met in the Club a few times - nice chap - American. I said I'd seen this plane, and he said he'd seen it too. Just then the news came on and the newsman said a plane had gone missing from Kuala Lumpur Airport. It was a jet from South East Asia Airways."

"Was that the one you saw?"

"It was. The American fellow said he'd seen it too. He'd even taken a photo of it. We thought about this for a few minutes. We were both pretty shocked as this plane was clearly not missing if it was there on DG, which meant the officers on the base had not told anyone they knew where it was. They must have known it was missing because there'd be all sorts of radio traffic about sending out search planes and so on before it got on civilian radio. In fact a few took off from Diego for some reason but we weren't told where or why they were going."

"How did you find out?"

"Later we were all called into a lecture and told that we were to say absolutely nothing to anyone about the plane or what we might or might not have observed. It was a state secret of the highest grade, and anyone saying anything to anyone was a traitor.

"Anyway, back at lunch the American said he thought something really serious was going down, and he didn't like it. 'We'll be in deep shit if we even know about this' was what he told me. I said: 'But what about all the men carrying the body bags out of the plane?' 'They won't say anything. They won't know whose bodies they were. They're trained to do as they're told, and they do'."

"What did you say to that?"

Gavin smiled ruefully. "I asked him 'What about you?' He said, very seriously, that he was too sensitive for some of this. He'd never been able to accept any old order without questioning dubious ones, even if only in his own mind. He told me another time the bodies had been taken into a huge freezer at the back of one of the buildings, and he didn't know what had happened to the three prisoners and their guards. He said the pilot was still on the island then, and a few days later a plastic surgeon was flown in from California, but he didn't know what for."

"Did you ever see the pilot?"

"No, I didn't but my American friend told me he'd seen him get out of the plane, and that two or three weeks later, the pilot was supposed to have been flown off to the States with the surgeon."

"What happened next?"

"A month later I was sent home at the end of my tour of duty. I stayed in touch with the American, and he emailed me he'd gone home a couple of months after that."

"What was his name, Gavin?"

Gavin shook his head. "Can't tell you that. Sorry. He may be a friend of mine but I don't know if he wants to go down this path I'm following. I might write to him and see if he'd talk to you. It'd help if you could give me your photo so he can recognise you if you meet him. It'll be a letter; less likely to be monitored than an email. I think they spy on all of us now, since Bradley Manning."

"I'm sure they do. OK. I'll bring you a photo. What happened to the plane and the corpses?"

"I don't know for sure but this friend emailed something about a ship that took them away.'

"Did you see this ship?"

"Afraid not. He had to be careful what he said over the internet so I don't know any more about it."

"OK, I'll go along with that. I have to anyway. Maybe your friend can tell me, when and if I get to see him. Now I really must thank you for letting me record this, but I'd like to take a photo, and come back to see you with my camera man, a sound man - or woman - and my producer soon to film you."

"When?"

"Three days if everyone else is free. Would that be alright?"

Gavin agreed and gave me his landline number, saying he wouldn't be going anywhere. We went outside the pub, the Lord St Vincent, and he posed for a photo. Before we parted in separate taxis I put my hand on his arm. "What you said about prison. Remember? If you get charged you don't necessarily get convicted. Juries can do the right thing no matter what the law says. Don't forget Clive Ponting."

"Clive who?"

"Ponting. He was a civil servant in the Ministry of Defence during the Falklands War. He was charged with breaches of the Official Secrets Act for giving secret documents to the Labour MP Tam Dalyell. They showed that the General Belgrano, an Argentinian battle cruiser, was sailing away from the war, and was not a threat to the British Navy or the troops."

"I don't understand. How does that help me?"

"The judge told the jury they should convict Ponting."

"And?"

"They disobeyed. Those twelve people must have preferred the defence, that it was in the public interest to know the truth and for the secret to be told to Parliament."

"So they acquitted him?"

"Right, and I think they'd acquit you as well if you end up in Court."

27th June, 2014

Back at home three nights ago I sent Marion Gorman and Julian Prentis an email. I headed it 'The Vulture' and marked it 'High Importance'.

Hi Marion and Julian. FOR LEGAL GUIDANCE.

I've struck a gold seam. I need to go back in three days to dig it out. It may disappear. We need an urgent meeting. It's not for me to tell you, Marion, to drop everything, since you're the Boss, but I'm telling you just that. Please get the usual suspects in. Get Julian there too for his angle on this.

Lynn.

Marion had them all there the next day. She announced at the outset that Channel 4 had agreed to take the programme, and the contract was signed.

I told them all about Gavin Johnson, and played them the recording. Everyone there was absolutely shattered by it. The trip to Southsea was approved. We would get one of our drivers to hire a 'people-carrier' to take us. Exposure has its own vehicles, but we didn't want anyone clocking our marked TV van turning up outside any place where we might see Gavin. This Vulture project was still highly confidential.

110

Julian said we must be sure to get the warning to Gavin on the film, and that we were not paying him. I said there wouldn't be any lunch this time and reminded them all of what Gavin had said about contacting his American chum. I wanted to see if that turned anything up.

Marion said she thought if Gavin repeated on the film what he said to my phone, it was time for a trip to meet Gavin's US Navy friend, if he was prepared to cooperate. Greg Armstrong said he'd never been there and would love to go. Exposure TV hires him through a really fine security firm the company uses. He's a bodyguard or minder. I had not expected him to be at the meeting.

I asked why Greg had been called in. Julian said it was his idea. "I consider the USA a dangerous place in any event, but when you're investigating a story that may involve their Government and the CIA you could be a real target."

Marion agreed. I laughed nervously and assured him and the others I should not go without Greg. He was about 40, ex-paratrooper, about five foot eight, stocky, with brown wavy hair, fawn chinos, and an old Parka. He's a bachelor, and has an old Mum he adores somewhere in Pembrokeshire in Wales. Most of the time he looks pretty ordinary, but a look comes into his eyes occasionally that puts me in mind of a tiger that's just spotted its dinner. I've worked with him before. He can be rather dangerous.

Matt Gordon, a great camera man from Wentworth TV I'd worked with in Oz, said he'd love to go to America too.

Malcolm agreed with that, so Marion reluctantly went along with it. "I don't like the length of time this story is

111

taking to come together, but I feel that it's worth pursuing a little further. If it works, it's the biggest story for decades. The shareholders will love it when Channel 4 sells it to all the TV stations around the world."

Typically Greg said: "That's if I can stop them bumping you all off first."

Julian muttered "Precisely," but no-one else made a sound. The real risks we were running were brought home to all. Journalists are murdered. Jill Dando, who presented a crime programme which resulted in villains being convicted, was killed in 2004. Others following stories governments would prefer them to leave alone have been killed (murdered, almost certainly) quite often. No-one doing my job would ever forget Anna Politkovskaya shot dead in Russia on Vladimir Putin's birthday in 2006, those shot by Iaraeli troops, and those killed in Bagdhad.

So today we went to Gavin's flat in Southsea in the mini-bus, and Matt had his camera and tripod in a huge hold-all. We had a sound engineer with us. He had his stuff in another hold-all. Malcolm Broadbridge had hired a young freelance and, he said, very talented Assistant Producer to accompany us, Nic Stark by name. When Nic turned up she was a raven-haired woman about ten years younger than me.

The teams put together by Marion and Malcolm are always 100% trustworthy. The constant fear is that someone will leak the story, and when it involves government, in Britain or elsewhere, the consequences can be dire, killing the story, and even resulting in journalists going to prison for refusing to name their sources, for example. I had never known a leak at Exposure. One of the ways we protect our story when we go out to interviews is never to say who we intend to see, nor what story we are pursuing. A call sheet is sent out to the people involved telling them where to go and when, who is going, and how to get there. In this case most of the people involved knew already, but none of them would talk.

Gavin had suggested having the meeting in his flat for two reasons. First, it lent authenticity, as it was clearly him and his home. Secondly, it was better than hiring somewhere where we might be interrupted, or where others were alerted to what we were up to. He said his neighbours were nearly all out at work during the day, so the chances of anyone being suspicious were remote; he didn't care anyway, but I told him we needed to keep "The Vulture" secret until the tale was ready to tell. Matt said he'd go back in a day or two so it did not look connected to our visit today if anyone did spot us, and film the outside of the flat and Clarence Parade.

Nic Stark had paid close attention to creating a scene and an atmosphere which suited Gavin. She sat the two of us at a mahogany dining table in elegant chairs, with a large picture of Gavin in uniform right behind him, which she asked Matt to zoom onto briefly now and again. The camera was at an angle to the garden past us, which was the first thing Matt filmed, swinging back to Gavin as the interview started. Nic cut some roses from the bushes out there and put them in a vase on the table, with a pile of Gavin's books. These touches created the clear impression he was a tough, sensitive, intelligent man unlikely to doing this for money.

113

Gavin was wearing a pale blue shirt, with his old military tie, a casual striped summer jacket, and grey slacks. He was as good as his word. After we had done a sequence explaining who he was, he put everything he told me in the Lord St Vincent on film. He wanted us to film him full frontal, as it were. He said he was proud of what he was doing, adding that many might say he was a traitor, but he was the patriot in sticking up for what he believed Britain and the Royal Marines stood for – truth and justice and free speech.

I handed him my photo, which he'd requested for his American friend.

I was dropped off at my parents in Shere instead of going back to London. I typed up all the latest instalments and printed them off. I stayed the night. Dad said he would take me to Guildford station in the morning, and mail my notes to Karen on his way home.

2nd July, 2014.

Today 'The Independent' reported that a Malaysian official from the consulate in Tanzania was shot dead three days ago in the streets of the capital of Zanzibar. It was believed that he had been handed some debris which was thought to be from SEA439, which he was to deliver to the Investigating Authority back home in Malaysia. Some suggested that this murder was connected with the disappearance of the plane.

I doubted that. If there had been no ordinary air crash, and if the Americans had done something else with the aircraft, why would they do anything that might cast doubt on the false idea that there had been a crash? If the debris were found in the areas where it would have been washed up by currents from the Southern Indian Ocean, the CIA would do better to leave people thinking that was where the plane went down. The man must have been taken out for other reasons, and by someone else.

14th July, 2014.

I'm typing my notes in my hotel room in Kuala Lumpur. I got here three days ago. I came here to find Captain Subrama's wife and girlfriend if I could. Marion Gorman agreed to the trip, and that I should have Matt and Greg with me. Before we left she sent me and Matt on a 'Hostile Environment Course'. I'd not been on one before. The British Police and even London Criminal Gangs were not considered that high risk, but journalists who worked in Afghanistan, Iraq, most of Africa, were always at risk, so these courses were routine for them. Northern Ireland used to be the same.

We learned what and whom to look out for, how to talk ourselves out of a hole, how to observe surveillance we might be subjected to, and how to dodge it. The instructors also taught us a certain amount of self-defence.

With Greg to rely on I found all this useful but not too worrying. However, there was at least one very significant thing I learned on the course, but not from an instructor. Deborah Lloyd is a very experienced foreign correspondent and investigative journalist. She was there on a refresher course, telling me she had to do one every three or four years. She'd worked in all the dangerous environments I'd mentioned and had even been arrested in the Congo when doing a report on the children lost and orphaned in the tribal strife and civil wars there. When she was arrested her fixer was beaten up by the local Police.

Her work included following up terrorism leads to Al Qaeda in Indonesia and Malaysia. She was able to give me the name of a 'fixer' who would be able to take us anywhere in Malaysia we wished to go, find the women in Subrama's life, and act as translator. Deborah's fixer was Noorida Tiong. Deborah told me that fixers are often totally untrustworthy, and the more dictatorial a government is, the more likely the fixer is to be a government agent or spy.

Noorida is about 38, and small, but told me in excellent English that she was a black belt in judo and could take care of us as well as herself. She took Greg to her gym and they had a work-out, after which he said he was glad she was on his side. Normally she drove a taxi, so she knew her way about, and such is the interest in SEA439 here that she even knows where the wife and the mistress live. Yesterday she took us to see the girlfriend. The day before it was Mrs Subrama.

Kadijha Subrama was plump and pretty, and about five foot two. She saw me and Noorida alone in her sitting room, squatting on rugs and cushions in Moslem fashion. She was very proud of her two small children, a boy and a girl, who were at school. She told me that Muhamed had been a good husband. "I know he had had a girlfriend for a year or more, but he still loved me, his wife, and was kind and generous to me and the children. As a Moslem he could have taken another wife, and I did not want to share my home with another woman; a mistress I could put up with."

He was mad keen on flying and being a good pilot. She showed me a flight simulator he used to help other people, and used himself to plan how to land and take off at different airports. Noorida was translating all this.

"A few days before the plane disappeared he changed. He was very quiet and preoccupied. Then he moved out, and he wasn't with Nancy either."

"Nancy?"

"Yes, she is the mistress, Nancy Koh. He was staying in a hotel. I phoned him, but he wouldn't come home, and he barely spoke to me. Nancy even phoned me. She said he wouldn't talk to her. They had had a row."

"What about?"

"I do not know, and I do not think Nancy understood why he should want to stop seeing her."

"People say your husband committed suicide."

"That is not true. He was quiet, yes, but I know – knew – this man. He was not unhappy like suicide. Something had happened to him but I do not know what it was. He would not kill all the people on the plane even if he wanted to take his own life."

"Is there anything else you can tell me? Any little thing that might help? Anything odd or unusual?"

Kadijha thought for a few seconds. "There was one thing. After we got married I realised he had an extra bit of income so that we had more money than he got from South East Asia Airways. One day I asked him about it. He was very angry and told me never to mention it again, and never to tell anyone about it. Now that he is probably dead I don't think it matters."

I asked if he had any noticeable mannerisms, or distinguishing marks. She made the same eyebrow stroking gesture I had seen at Nick and Liz's, and she laughed and said: "He used to do that."

"Anything else?"

"He wears a heavy gold ring with a big ruby in it, and he has curious marks like train tracks running down his thumb nails." I recalled those too, and said so.

Now she frowned. "Yes, he did. How do you know those things?"

"I met him years ago in England at a friend's house. He was a pilot then, too."

When I asked Mrs Subrama if I could bring Matt in to film an interview she drew a scarf over her head and covered up her colourful dress with a sober hijab. Then she agreed to see Matt and be filmed. She repeated all that she had told me in a very straightforward and credible fashion, Noorida still interpreting. I left feeling Subrama had been a very lucky chap, and matrimonial problems could not possibly have provided a motive for suicide plus the murder of about 250 people, apart from crashing a 250 million pound plane he loved to fly. There had to be something else.

Nancy Koh was quite different from Kadijha. She was very westernised, and not a Moslem, possibly Vietnamese or

Cambodian, slim, about 5 foot 5 with blond hair care of a good hairdresser, manicured nails, and a dress which left precious little to the imagination. For an Asian woman she had fairly large breasts, and I suspected implants. She had 'good-time-girl' writ large all over her. She had no qualms about letting Greg and Matt in, and let Noorida sit in, even though her interpreter skills were superfluous; Nancy spoke American English well.

I told her I wanted to ask about Muhamed Subrama. Nancy laughed, showing beautiful white teeth, expensively cared for. "I've been asked about him so often. Can there be anything left to ask?"

"I'm sorry if this is a bore, but I'm making a TV documentary about SEA439 and Captain Subrama. I have to check as much of the information as I can for myself."

"Is the programme a British one?"

"Yes, for Exposure TV. It'll be broadcast on Channel 4."

"That's OK then. It'll be pretty reliable. So much rubbish has been printed and said on radio and TV about me and Muhamed, I don't want any more of it." She pointed at Matt. "He can start filming if you want."

"Thanks. What I'll do is just put on an intro about me and you and why we're here, and then ask my questions, OK?" Nancy nodded, and I recorded the preliminaries.

"How long had you known Muhamed Subrama?"

"About 18 months. I took a holiday in Bali, and flew with South East. Muhamed had a stop-over there to fly back the next day, and I met him in my hotel. That was where SEA put up their crews. He was clearly attracted to me; I saw him staring at me a lot in the dining room. I'd split up with my last boyfriend a month or so before, and I like men and sex, so I indicated he should come to my table."

"How did that go?"

"As expected. I've never had a man turn me down, and we slept together very little that night." She laughed again, and I knew what she meant. "After that he came to my apartment once or twice a week until soon before he disappeared. He took me to dinner, bought me things, occasionally gave me money. Who am I to refuse?"

"Did you speak to Mrs Subrama?"

"I did. After he vanished. She knew about me, and Muhamed never hid the fact he was married with kids. A few days before he flew away he told me he would not see me again. We'd had a row about something a few weeks before that, so I hadn't seen him for a while. Then he turned up a few days - maybe two or three - before the plane went missing. He said he wouldn't be seeing me anymore, and explained nothing. I wasn't heartbroken, nothing like that, but I liked him, and we'd had a lot of fun together. I thought he would be back, but he didn't turn up, so when his plane disappeared I rang Kadijha to see what she knew."

"What did you have the argument about?"

"Gee, I don't remember that. Maybe I didn't want to go out one night, or told him to go home without his oats, something like that. Not really serious."

"Did you row with Kadijha when you phoned?"

"Not at all. She's a gentle person, and worried about her husband too, as he'd moved out without telling her why."

"Did he tell you about that?"

"It was strange. He told me he was leaving her too, but he did not seem unhappy, just terribly preoccupied."

"What do you think about the media suggestions that he committed suicide?"

Miss Koh laughed again. "Muhamed? No chance. Not the type; not that I know the type. He had a good wife, and children he adored. He was happy getting his rocks off with me, he had a great job and loved flying. I don't understand why he might give it all up and vanish, but suicide? No. Something must have happened, but I can't see him killing himself and murdering - what was it? Over 250 people? Not Muhamed!!"

I went through the routine about the train tracks on the nails, the ring, and the eyebrow stroke, and she said she had noticed those, and joked that the things they used to do together made it difficult not to know every physical detail. She was curiously light-hearted about the whole thing, and clearly regarded Subrama as a pleasant interlude from the past. Then she stood up so I told Matt to stop the camera, and she said: "If that's it, I'd like to call it a day. I have a gentleman friend calling for me in fifteen minutes."

She saw us to the door, and then said: "Say, do I get paid for this?"

I shook my head. "We'd have had to agree that to start with, and then the interview would be dodgy. Spoil the documentary. Sorry"

"Oh well. What the hell!"

On the way down in the lift Matt winked at Greg.

121

Greg said in falsetto: "'I've never had a man turn me down'. It's a bit too much for a bachelor like me."

Noorida told him: "I should give you a slap for that!"

4th August, 2014.

For the last two or three weeks I've been working on other stories, doing some more internet research on SEA439, and getting nowhere fast. I've spoken on the phone a couple of times to Gavin Johnson, to keep in touch and see if he'd heard from his friend in the USA. He said the man might be at sea, and he had no news for me. He reminded me I'd given him my business card, so he had my email and phone numbers, and could contact me if there were a development.

Today I was at Mum and Dad's working on a story on my old lap-top, when a flash in the top right-hand corner of the screen told me that a new email had come in. Saving what I was doing, I went into my email account. The new item was from a chap calling himself Norman, assuming it was a he. It looked liked rubbish, but if so, why didn't it go into Junk?

I transferred it to Junk where I opened it safely without corrupting my system or computer. This is what I read:

Ello Lynn. You don't know me but I know about you. I know you are looking for some information I ave. I sould like to tell you about it. I am a great admirer of Norse mytology, and especially of the god Thor. Do you know about im?

If you are interested, write back and tell me wat you know about Freya, goddess of the afterlife.

Norman.

This was really weird. I was just about to press delete when I realised that this might possibly be trying to tell me something.

I picked up my mobile and phoned the office, and asked to speak to Sid Phillips. He's a magic programmer and former hacker who worked with The Guardian when it collaborated with Julian Assange over the Bradley Manning leaks. Sid was from the East End of London. His cockney accent is almost impenetrable.

"Hello Sid. It's Lynn."

" 'ey Lynn. Ain't seen yer 'round lately. What's going on?"

"This 'n' that. I'm working on a special job a lot of the time so I only come in when I've got some other story ready. Look, Sid, I've got a really weird email from somebody, and I don't understand it. It may be nothing, just junk or spam, but I'm not sure. I don't know how it got to me."

Sid laughed. "You fink it'll mean something to me? Why don't you just forward it ter me and I'll have a butchers?"

"That'd be great Sid, but I'd rather bring it over. If it's important I don't want it floating around the stratosphere again."

"OK Lynn. I'm free at 2.30. See yer then."

I printed off all my recent notes about "The Vulture" for Edna to take to the post, got in my car, and drove to Lancaster Gate. At 2.30 I walked into Sid's room with a copy of the email. He read it carefully. "Well, it's weird alright."

"What makes this bloke think I know anything about Norse gods?"

Sid shook his thick mop of grey curls. "And why's he leave aht all the Hs?"

"He left the one in Thor in, though. I've thought about putting it back in all the other words, but that makes no difference to any of the sense of it."

"Righ' you are." Sid looks puzzled for a couple of seconds. "It wouldn't 'ave made no sense at all. So what gives if we take the H out of Thor?"

"It just becomes TOR. Means nothing to me except outcrops of rock on ..."

"Dartmoor, but bloody hell Lynn, it means more ter me. I fink this person wants to send yer somefink real special. TOR stands for The Onion Route. I' was inven'ed by the US Navy. It's a supposedly one-time secret means of sending and receiving internet stuff so no-one'd know 'ow it came or 'ow yer got it, or where it came from."

"How does it do that?"

"It routes your info through all sorts o' channels where yer can see only the last link, but no' any of the links before that one. This means if anyone is moni'oring your internet usage, they can't find aht where you're getting fings from. If it's sent so it's unattribu'able they can't trace who sent it to yer."

"So what this person wants to send me must be pretty important?"

"I'd say so."

"What do I do now?"

"I reckon I'll 'ave to fix up your system so that you can deal wiv it. Trouble is, TOR ain't so secure since the US

Navy decided to open i' up to the public, but clever hackers go' into it and learnt 'ow to use it 'emselves, mainly for criminal jobs. Assange and Wikileaks and the folks they work wiv got into this years ago. An' o' course, Bradley Manning knew how to use it cos he was in the American Army."

"Thanks Sid. I'll leave this lap top here." It was a good thing it was the old one. I didn't want anyone to know what I was doing on the new one yet, though Sid was always completely trustworthy.

Sid hadn't finished. "There's also PGP. You migh' need that."

"What's PGP when it's at home?"

"It stands for Pretty Good Privacy. That's a system for encrypting yer messages and documents so no-one else can read them 'nless they've got the codes. There's other fings we can do, too. It's 'ow Bradley Manning and Wikileaks worked."

"OK Sid, you're the genius. I hardly know what you're talking about."

"I know tha', don' I? Tha's wha' you go' me for, Lynn."

"There's another thing. I've got another computer I'm doing a hush-hush story on. Can you do something to make it impossible for anyone to get into it?"

"No probs, love. I can hide the story behind a set of passwords, and hide them behind a couple of other sets. Can't say it'll be impossible for anybody to get in, but it'll take 'em a while. Only a genius like me could do i', and your average burglar wouldn't know i' was there, so he wouldn't even look for it."

"Great Sid, but it'd be good if you don't look at the story, and you mustn't tell a soul about it. OK?"

Sid smiled and tapped his forehead. "I've got more secrets than the Vatican up here. What worries me is, can yer remember the passwords I give yer?"

"How about I give you half-a-dozen words to use, and you can do the rest? I should remember my own words."

"Just brill, Lynn. Make sure they're unusual, though."

5th August, 2014.

I had a bad night. It was all very well for Sid to say he'd fix up my system, but I'd still got to reply to 'Norman' and arrange communication with him. I could hardly send him an email saying I knew all about Freya, goddess of death, and then ask him what he knew about Subrama. I lay awake thinking about this for hours. As often happens with this sort of problem an answer came to me as I woke up this morning.

I could send him an email saying: *"Thanks, Norman. I could have a lot of use for Thor, so what you can tell me about him would be great. I can tell you about Freya, too. Did you know she is so important in 'The Ride of the Valkyries'? You must know that piece of music by Wagner. The notes are magic. When you let me know about Thor, remember that in the music it's the fourths that really count for me. They have so much meaning. Lynn."*

I just hoped he would realise what I was getting at.

I threw on some clothes made myself a quick cup of tea, ate some cornflakes, and rushed off out, went into an internet cafe, and fixed up a new hotmail account using a false name, Sylvia_Button53, with 'asp*idistra*8' as the password. Then I collected my laptops from Sid, sent my email from the old address, and went home.

I was now on tenterhooks wondering whether Norman would ever write again.

6th August, 2014.

There was nothing on the old lap-top from Norman. I'd found a tendency to return to my disgusting childhood habit of biting my nails now I was worrying about Norman. I even left my old laptop on all day in case an email came in. Bingo! At 7.45 this evening, there it was:

Hello Lynn. Well, I thank you. I need fairly soon some new Freya info to email my next lecture address the College sent for. If possible can you send it now? Thor info is attached. Will you read it? Be good if you used all of it in your new work. My next speech in reply to students is tomorrow. Norman. PS. Valkiries music is wonderful.

Attached to the email were two extracts from books about Norse Gods. I was sure they were irrelevant. I wrote out his email, underlining every fourth word. This is what I got:

Hello Lynn. Well, <u>I</u> thank you. I <u>need</u> fairly soon some <u>new</u> Freya info to <u>email</u> my next lecture <u>address</u> the College sent <u>for</u>. If possible can <u>you</u> send it now? <u>Thor</u> info is attached. <u>Will</u> you read it? <u>Be</u> good if you <u>used</u> all of it <u>in</u>

127

your new work. My next speech in reply to students is tomorrow.

Norman. PS. Valkiries music is wonderful.

It looks like he understood. He wanted me to send him a new email address straight away. Then he will use TOR and email me tomorrow. I started working out a way to send him 53 year old Sylvia Button's email address using every fourth word without it looking as though that's what I was doing. It took me a while, and I sent it off just before midnight, and collapsed into bed. I was fast asleep in a minute.

8ᵗʰ August, 2014.

I spent the day in the office at meetings with the other members of Malcolm Broadbridge's team bringing them up to date with this 'Norman' development, and then doing some editing on another story I'm working on about the police and criminals, my usual field.

When I got home I looked at the old laptop. Sylvia Button was in luck; Norman had written to her. The email was encrypted as it came through the system, but Sid had installed software that unscrambled it. It told me that Norman was a US Naval seaman. He had served in the place I was interested in, and been there in March 2013. He knew Gavin Johnson, my ex-marine contact whom he had met on an Allied base. The same thing that had upset Gavin had disturbed him too, and without saying what that was, he wanted to get it off his chest. Somebody had to tell the world what had happened.

He did not want to say any more in emails, but wanted to meet me in Atlanta. Could I meet him there? Can a falcon fly? All I needed was to tell Malcolm and the team what was going on. I phoned the office and asked his PA to arrange a meeting of the team as soon as possible.

She phoned half an hour later to say the meeting was fixed for 4.00 pm tomorrow.

11th August, 2015.

The meeting went well two days ago. My trip was approved, but Julian Prentis, the lawyer, was worried about me. He said I should take a bodyguard; if the CIA were aware of me anything might happen. He would contact a good criminal attorney in Atlanta in case I got arrested. He pointed out that this could be some sort of sting.

Today I got on a flight with BA to Atlanta, Georgia. I flew business class, and so did Greg Armstrong, my minder, who sat in the seat behind me; we didn't want to appear to be together. I was sitting next to Matt Gordon, the cameraman. It didn't matter if we were seen together, but it seemed appropriate not to be clocked in the company of a minder. We had arrived at Heathrow separately from Greg. Matt and I had been booked into an Atlanta hotel by different secretaries at Exposure. Greg's firm, Harrington Security, had booked him into the same hotel. Somehow we had to sort out rooms adjoining each other. Fortunately that wasn't hard. Greg went to reception first, so I hung back behind another guest where I could hear his conversation with the concierge. He asked for a quiet room on a floor where not many people were staying. He got one on the fourth floor, and the number was 426. The concierge said it had a nice view of the park. Greg carried his own case to the lift.

After the other guest had been dealt with Matt and I went to the desk. I said: "I don't like to be high up in these tall buildings; just a quirk of mine, really."

"Well, Ma'am, there's rooms on the third and fourth floor, but the third is pretty full." The youngster pointed to a corridor on a plan.

"OK, so let's look at the fourth. Which side of the corridor has the best view, do you think?"

"This one at the back. It looks over the park."

I ran my finger along the plan of the corridor looking as if I was making a choice. "How about that one?"

"OK Ma'am, that's fine. It's 424. All the even numbers are that side and the odds are across the corridor. There is a man next door. I just booked him in. He's a Brit too."

"Well, don't be too hard on us. It's OK as long as he doesn't look like Frankenstein. I'll take 424. Can someone take my luggage up?"

"Sure can." He called a youth over, and told him to take my luggage, and when I'd booked in, he gave me the key card for the room. Matt then spoke. "We're together. Is 422 vacant?"

"Yes, Sir, but there are no communicating doors," the concierge said, blushing.

"That's OK, Sonny. That's not what we're here for, is it Lynn?" I just stopped myself laughing. Much as I like Matt the idea of crawling about over his paunch did not excite me.

In my jeans pocket I had the name, address, and phone number of Julian's attorney friend in Atlanta. Up in my room I got out my laptop and sent 'Norman' an email on Sid's system, telling him where I was, and giving him the number of the hotel. Then I typed out my notes on the other one, and went down to dinner with Matt, where we saw Greg nearby eating his.

12th August 2014.

It was 10.30 in the morning, and a lot cooler in the Church of Christ the King in the Buckhead District of Atlanta than it was outside. I sat at the far end of the fifteenth pew from the front, on the left of the aisle. This was what the email from 'Norman' told me to do. He did not use the phone, saying it was out of order. I'd arrived at 10.15. Greg walked in five minutes later, had a look round like a tourist, took a photo of the altar and something else, and sat on the other side of the church a row behind me. He immediately knelt in prayer. I had no idea whether he was a man of faith, or was just acting a part. I was not praying. I was barely breathing, I was so anxious.

I had left Matt Gordon at the hotel. I did not want to frighten 'Norman' away by turning up mob-handed with a big camera. If he was helpful and willing, we could film later.

Suddenly a voice whispered right behind me. I twitched with fright, but managed not to jump. There had been no-one there when I came in. "Hello, Lynn. Don't say anything. Don't look round. I'm Norman. In three minutes you get up,

131

walk out slowly, go left down the road, and in the cafe on the other side. Get a coffee. In fifteen minutes I shall leave here. I'll come into the cafe, get a take-away coffee and leave. I'm carrying a red brief case. When I've gone a hundred yards leave the cafe and follow me on your side of the road."

I left, and did as he said. Greg stayed where he was. I went to the cafe, got my coffee, and sat at the shelf in the window. I saw Greg exit the Church, and lean against the wall of the church, apparently talking into a mobile. Soon after that a man came out carrying a red brief-case. He was quite tall, may be 5'10," a bit over-weight, wearing a green fleece with the hood up, blue jeans and dark glasses. Greg moved the phone and took a photo. I watched 'Norman' come in, buy a coffee to go, and leave turning to the right. He crossed the road, dumping the coffee cup in a bin. I soon got up and followed him on my side of the road. I glanced back and saw Greg put his phone in his pocket and follow the man on his side of the road. After two or three blocks the red brief case went into a supermarket. I went in too. I picked up a basket, and walked to the vegetables and fruit. 'Norman' and the brief case appeared beside me. He had some shopping in his basket, and added a few oranges.

As I picked up some apples and bananas the man quietly told me where to go next and said: "There's a seat by the trees half-way across. Wait for me there at 2 o'clock." Then he was gone. I went outside and Greg was walking towards me in a leisurely way.

He said: "Could you tell me the time please?"

I looked at my watch. "It's 11.05."

"Thank you. It's a lovely day."

"Just as well. I've got to meet someone in the middle of West Wesley Park at 2 o'clock. Do you know it?"

"No, madam, I'm a stranger here myself. Best of luck."

After a bite to eat back at the hotel I was in the Park on a seat five minutes early. Greg walked by in a track suit and baseball cap. I hardly recognised him, but he winked as he passed. He must have followed me from the hotel, but I didn't see him. He moved off the footpath and started jogging back and forth between two trees a hundred yards away, doing a few press-ups and other exercises, but clearly not exerting himself greatly.

At 2.20 my anxiety was building, when a hand came over the back of the bench and put a battered black case down. 'Norman' followed it and sat down at the other end of the seat. He was fairly casually dressed in a red shirt with no tie, a brown and tan plaid jacket, and jeans, but these were grey. He still wore sunglasses.

"Are you alone?"

"No, I'm not. The man in the track suit back there is my bodyguard. I have to have one. TV Company rules. I'm Lynn Galloway." I held out my hand. He ignored it, looking straight ahead across the park.

"I know. Gavin Johnson sent me a photo. He told me about you – said maybe I'd help you."

"Yes, I've met Gavin. He was very helpful. Look, more company rules. I have to tell you what I'm doing."

"I know what you're doing. Gav sent the photo with a letter telling me that you wanted to know about something

133

went down when we were serving together somewhere. He didn't say what it was, nor where we served. He gave nothing away, but there's only one thing you'd want to know about. You want to know about the plane that went AWOL in March 2013."

I tried hard not to look as excited as that made me feel. "Absolutely. All the passengers and crew died, and no-one knows where they went or what happened to them."

"But you think they got to Diego."

"I think so."

"Well, lady, that's it alright. I saw that fucking plane come in, I saw the pilot get off it, and four armed men guarding three others."

That was a surprise; it was exactly what Gavin had told me. "OK, so you saw the pilot, but you also saw seven others get off the plane?"

"Sure did, lady."

"You can call me Lynn. Am I just to call you Norman?"

"I guess not. I'm Clint Esterhazy. I'm staying at an aunt's in town here. She ain't got no idea why I'm here apart from visiting her. Far as I know the Navy just think I'm on furlough for a week or so."

"Thanks Clint." I took a pen and a note-book out of my pocket. "Is it OK if I make some notes?"

"You ain't got a tape recorder?"

"No, but I could do it with my phone. Here."

"OK, so why don't you just record me?"

"I didn't know if you'd let me. I'll just put some stuff on to introduce what we're up to. OK?"

"Fine. You can use my name, but I don't want you to put it in any articles or programmes on radio or TV unless I say so. Can I trust you?"

"Well, you know who I am, here's my passport to confirm it. I made no bones about the fact that my minder is over there. And you have my photo from Gavin Johnson." Clint nodded. "I'll put on a short intro about who I am, and who you are, the date and time, and where we are." I did that, and then asked: "Now tell me, Clint, why are you prepared to talk to me about the plane that went missing after take-off on 9th March last year?"

"OK. I was stationed on Diego Garcia for a while then. I know what happened to the plane and the folks as was on it. Like I said a minute ago, I saw the pilot get off, and then these four guys take three others off the plane. These three were in handcuffs. And one looked Chinese."

I produced a newspaper cutting with an old photo of Captain Subrama's face. "Is that the pilot?"

Clint took the picture, and studied it carefully. "Well, I never seed him real close up, but that sure looks like the feller." He handed back the paper.

"Were the other four in uniform?"

"Heck, no. They was just in civilian clothes; like tourists, they were."

"What time was this?"

Clint thought a moment. "About 09.00 hours. Morning. I had no duties. I was out jogging on the airfield. About to go and get some breakfast. But I stopped to watch."

"What did the plane look like?"

"Hey, that's a bit of a stupid one if you ask me. There can't be nobody on this here Earth who ain't seen a picture of it in a paper or on TV with its bright green fuselage and the name of the airline on the side in gold. I knew right away what it was because I done an aircraft recognition course. Boeing 777-200ER alright."

"Don't you just have to recognise war planes?"

Clint laughed. "Not anymore. Since we shot down that Iran plane over the Med years ago when we thought it might attack the Vincennes, we gotta be a lot more careful. Not that I got no love for them Muslims, but it sure helps if you know what you're shooting at."

"Of course. So, just for the record, can you tell me what the name on the fuselage was?"

"Right. It was South East Asia Airways."

"You still haven't answered my question why you want to talk to me."

"OK. Well, first up, I know Gav, and he's talked to you. I trust him. He's a hard bastard if ever there was one – haven't seen anyone harder. I ain't that big, and one day at the Brit Club a big army guy objected to me talking to a girl he clearly thought was his for the taking. He dragged me outside, punched me in the head and knocked me down. He picked me up by the shirt. He looked like he was going to give me another one. Now Gav ain't even as big as me. We'd had a couple beers together in there before. He's OK for a Brit. Anyways, he comes out and says to this big guy: 'I think that's enough, don't you?' You know, real quiet like? This bully just drops me straight back on the floor, and says:

"'I don't care a fuck what no Limey thinks'. I haven't heard anyone use that word for years. Then he goes to throw a real hard punch at Gav. He was so smooth an' fast. He moved slightly, grabbed the guy's wrist with his right hand, the front of his shirt with his left, turned further and threw him over his hip at the wall of the Club-house. Jeez, you should have heard the bang. I got up as people came running out. Gav said, 'I think this man tripped over and hit his head badly. Better get him to a doctor.' And strolled off."

"But that can't be your only reason for talking."

"No, ma'am, it sure ain't. Me, I'm a patriot, an' believe in what the US of A stands for, like freedom, free speech, doing the right thing, the rule of law, an' all that, so what I see on DG just ain't right."

"DG. You mean Diego Garcia?"

"I do. See, what happened after these men got off the plane was like this. I started jogging again, a bit puzzled at what I'd seen, and when I got round the other side, near the hangars, I see a whole bunch of guys in fatigues carrying some stuff to the plane. Then they was coming out time after time carrying body-bags with ..."

"With bodies in them?" I'd heard this from Gavin of course, but that hardly made it any the less shocking. I shouldn't have spoken but I was stunned at getting so much more than I'd bargained on.

"That's it, Lynn. There must have been twenty men, and they made about twenty trips each, four guys to a bag. That's about one hundred bodies. Then they went off to rest, I guess, and another twenty or so came out and did the same.

Leastways, I see this second squad start but then I made myself scarce. Lucky no-one seemed to spot me there, but I wasn't that close, and other guys were coming and going between the hangars. The airfield is pretty huge. The runways are 12,000 feet long. That's about two-and-a-half miles.

"Again, Clint, why do you want to tell me this? Why not an American journalist?"

"Ain't sure I trust 'em. Shit scared they'll spill the beans. You Brit journalists are pretty straight, I guess. I mean, look at Bradley Manning. OK, the way he did it, maybe you couldn't find out who he was. If he hadn't blabbed his soul to that other hacker he might still be with Uncle Sam's warriors now. You lot kept the secret until the story was good and ready. No-one ain't trusted anywhere like the BBC and other Brit journalists."

I was almost getting impatient. "You mean Exposure TV." Clint nodded. "But that's not enough to make you talk to me."

"OK. Like I said, I'm a patriot. May not seem like it talking to you, but I'm deep-down ashamed to think the country I love can do something leads to about 250 innocent people dying for nothing. I think most Americans'd feel the same if they knew, and I want you to tell them, not tell the law I told you. I'd get locked up or shot or hanged. I feel guilty. I want to feel good again. Whether I will is something else."

I was staggered. I've seen some brave people reveal terrible secrets but this took the whole tin, not just a biscuit.

"That's great, Clint. Can you tell me what happened to the bodies in the bags?"

"Sure. The troops carried them to one of the biggest sheds. I know there's a food store in there, tins and stuff, and a huge refrigeration room. The bodies went in there. I didn't see that at the time but a few days later I was sent in there with a party to collect supplies for the ship, and as ...."

"The ship?"

"Yep, the one I was serving on. So there we was putting stuff on a fork-lift, the doors to the fridge opened, a couple guys came out, and stood for a moment before they closed and locked it. I could see these huge piles of body bags. They clearly had bodies in.

"A couple days before that different companies and crews were called into the gym, and we were given lectures about not ever talking about what was in the store shed fridge. The officers reminded everyone that we were bound to Uncle Sam by secrecy oaths, and would go to prison if we said anything to anyone. By that time I'd heard several broadcasts on the radio in the dining room, my room, and in the mess on the ship, about this missing plane, so I knew what this was really all about. I wasn't never going to talk to no-one."

"So what changed?'

"Getting the letter from Gav. He must have had some idea I was worried after that day - boy, was I miserable - and like I say, I trusted him, you know? I reckoned he must have spoke to you, and if he could, I could. He was a good buddy.

We often had a drink after that, exercised together. All that kind a' stuff."

"Do you have any proof of all this?"

"Well, I guess Gav must have some idea what this is all about, so that's what-d'yuh-call it, ain't it?"

"Corroboration?" I offered.

"Guess so. Also before the plane disappeared, I took my camera. I went out over the other side of the runway again, so the plane was in front of the hangars. Anyone who knows DG will see what it is and where."

"Wasn't that dangerous?"

"Sure fucking was! But I got interested in the bird-life on the island, like Gav was. We used to do bird-watching together sometimes. If I'd been asked what I was on, I'd have said I was out photographing the wild-life. When I was posted back to the States I had the camera in its case, and hid the film in a pair of socks tucked into some trainers at the bottom of my kit-bag."

"You didn't use a digital camera?"

"No way, cos if they fucking looked, they might see what I'd shot. What I did, I left a film in the camera half used up on social stuff, and a couple of others of the Club, some of the girls and other buddies, and the birds I'd seen, in the camera case. Anyhow, no-one looked."

"Clint, I really need to get this on film to show that you're a real person. I want to come back soon with a camera man, and my producer. I promise we will film you anywhere you like so the location won't be identifiable. We won't use the film itself for our TV show, but an actor who's nothing like you. It'll be a dramatisation. I know this sounds ghastly, but we'd use the film only if something happened to you and it made no difference to you."

Clint almost laughed. "You mean if I'm dead or in prison already. I ain't daft. That's OK. You got it."

"When we come back I'll have it in writing for you, and you can see it. Then we'll send it to your lawyer to hold, or anyone else you like."

Clint Esterhazy said OK again, moved away to the other end of the seat, opened his case, and took out a newspaper. He told me he'd leave the paper behind when he went, and to go and tell my bodyguard to come to the seat in five minutes; there was something inside. He said he didn't want anyone seeing him hand me something, and started to read the newspaper. I walked across the park past Greg, telling him quietly what Clint said, and didn't stop. After a few minutes I looked back and saw Greg leave off touching his toes and stroll to the seat and sit.

I went round the side of the park towards the gate I came in at, and saw Clint fold the paper. He put it on the seat, got up, picked up his black case, and walked off across the park, the opposite way from me.

I waited at the gate where Greg could still see me, and when a cab came, I went back to the hotel. I started writing up my account, to back up the recording in case it got lost. I did not use Clint's name in my notes. I referred to him as Norman. I left out any mention of recording the interview. About thirty minutes later there was a soft thump on my door. There was a slight noise and I looked over from the little desk; there was an envelope jutting under the door into the room. Inside were three different shots of the green and gold plane standing on a runway with hangars and sheds in the background. On one shed the letters 'USAF, DG' could clearly be seen.

15th August, 2014.

Today Matt and I met Clint in a different park, in a village about twenty miles west of Atlanta. The place was deserted, as Clint had said it would be, using a throw-away phone. We sat not far from a boating pond for kids. It was ten in the morning, so no-one would be there until school came out in the afternoon. I stood facing the seat on which Clint was sitting. Matt had his Canon 5 camera recorder and stood so he could swivel between the two faces. For back-up I had a radio mike and recorder in my pocket, and clipped a microphone to the lapel of Clint's jacket. I gave Clint the print-out of the agreement Julian Prentis had emailed to me, which was signed by Marion Gorman.

Greg Armstrong sat on another park bench about 50 yards away, wearing slacks and a windcheater, reading a paper-back. He made it look as though that was what he was doing too; he didn't have the book upside-down, like that film of George W. Bush at a primary school the day of 9/11.

Clint Esterhazy was insistent on one thing. "I seen a bunch of these documentaries where the person don't want to be seen. They film from the back or make 'em a silhouette, but then they film their hands or clothes or jewellery. Then they put that stuff in the program, so anyone really knows the guy can work out who it is. I don't want none of those tricks here."

I pointed to the agreement. "We've done a lot of this before, Clint. This is a dangerous project. The thing you're worried about is in clause 6. The agreement says you're helping us with a film called 'The Vulture'. No-one outside me, Matt and Greg, you, and the team at Exposure knows what that is. This document also promises we won't use this film in any broadcast unless you've passed away, or are incarcerated. There'll be an actor who looks nothing like you using a fictitious name and he'll have learned your words."

We then went over what we had discussed yesterday for the benefit of the film. I got Clint to hold the photos of the plane up to the lens and explain what they showed, especially the writing on the building. Clint told the same story, but he managed not to swear.

He added a detail he hadn't mentioned yesterday. He said he was in the Brit Club one evening with Gavin, talking to some of the girls, when he overheard one of the four guys from the plane say something to one of the others about a man called Zane Pretorius. Pretorius seemed to be connected to the plane, the chap who was speaking and the other three, somehow, but Clint did not know who Pretorius was, and had never met anyone of that name on the island or elsewhere.

"What made you think he was connected to them?"

"They were talking about obeying his orders or whatever."

Then I recalled a question I should have asked previously. "What happened to the plane? Do you know?"

"Sure. It was broke up very rough - looked like it had crashed. Both wings had come off, and the body was busted in two, about two thirds of the way back. One of the horizontal stabilisers had come off, too."

"Stabilisers?"

"Them's the bits like small wings at the rear of the aircraft."

"Who broke it up?"

"Army and Navy engineers on the island."

"And the bodies? What happened to them?"

"Some of the Army guys loaded them onto the plane."

"Did you see this? I can't believe you could just wander about on DG. It's supposed to be high security."

"You better believe it, lady. From outside it's impossible to get in, but once you're in and legit, things get pretty slack, you know what I mean? It's like everyone thinks they're in Fort Knox or something."

My first reaction was that was a bit far-fetched, but then I remembered that Bradley Manning covered his activities by downloading secret documents onto what looked like a pop-singer's CD. I don't suppose the troops get to carry them into the bunkers and the Pentagon any more.

This confirmed what Gavin said Clint had told him. It might not amount to proper corroboration, but it showed Clint had been telling the same tale for some time.

"Is the plane still in bits on the atoll with the bodies inside it?"

"No frigging way. It was loaded, corpses and all, onto a loading dock ship, USS Okinawa. I knew that ship like the back of my hand. I'd been on tours of duty with it in the Western Pacific, helping out islands round Samoa, Kiribati, like that."

"But a 777-200ER is about 210 feet long, and the fuselage is over 20 feet wide. Can you get that onto this Okinawa?"

"Hey, don't forget the fuselage was in two bits, so even if it was exactly in half the bits would only be about 105 feet each. This ship is 610 feet long, and 84 feet wide. It'd be easy to slide the two halves in beside each other."

"What about the tail-plane? The fin is almost 61 feet high."

"You sure have done your homework, Lynn. But remember. One of the horizontal bits of the tail plane had been chopped off too. So if you push the rear section into the hold on the side with the tail-plane snapped off, it'll fit. Have you ever seen a whaling ship?"

"No, but I've seen pictures on the news and documentaries about whaling."

"Now there's a shitty industry, if you like! Well, you know a whaler has this big hole and a ramp at the back, with kind of big hoops across to lift the whales about? The Okinawa is a bit like that. It has a huge hole at the back but it's got a roof on it which is the back, what we sailors call ....""

".. the aft deck of the ship," I threw in.

Clint smiled. "Like I said Lynn, that's good research."

I smiled too. "And the fuselage could fit in there, tail-plane and all?"

"Sure. You can look up pictures of it on the internet. Can't say I know the dimensions of the hole, but if the fin or stabilisers wouldn't fit they'd just break more bits off. Who could say what a plane that crashed into the sea at 550 or more miles an hour and stayed under water for 18 months or more would look like?"

"How deep is the sea-bed in the south Indian Ocean?"

"I'd have to check the charts to be accurate, but if I recall right, it's an average depth of over 8,000 feet."

"Heavens! That's a long way down."

"Sure is. Reminds me, the funniest comment I heard about this plane, but the most accurate, I think it was some British Admiral; he's supposed to 'uv said: 'It's not just looking for a needle in a haystack; they're still trying to find the haystack'."

"Where did the ship go?"

"Dunno. I can only guess it went somewhere unexpected to dump the bits of the plane where nobody ain't likely to find it. Like in the South Indian Ocean, where recovery would be almost impossible. The sea bed can be two or three thousand feet down, and as much as twelve thousand, maybe more, near the roaring forties or someplace. Some of the most dangerous rough sea you can hope to find. Somewhere west and south of Australia would be a good place. The Okinawa left DG about the 18th or 19th of March. It'd be down there in four or five days."

"So if they do ever find it ..."

.".. it'll look like the plane ditched in the sea, and after years in the water amongst the fish an' God knows what, the passengers won't look like nothing on earth, if there's anything left."

"And the black box?"

"Well, I don't know that much about planes, but I reckon if I wanted to do this here crime and get away with it, I'd take out the real black box, put another one in the plane, damage that area, put a hole in the box to let in the salt water, and there'd be nothing on the tape or whatever does the recording."

"What about the wings? What happened to them?"

"Came out of the hangar on a flat-bed trailer; they was loaded into the hold of an aircraft carrier. Like where the fighter planes normally go?"

"You know there're all those reports about bits of wings and stuff being found on beaches on that French island ..."

"Reunion."

"That's the one. And Madagascar and what was it, Tanzania?

Clint smiled: "Well that carrier could just sail about the Indian Ocean chucking bits overboard where the current would be likely to wash it ashore, looking like it came from wherever. God knows where they put the rest of it."

Apart from a couple of women who walked by with a dog, and another pushing a small child in a stroller, we were not bothered by anyone, although they found it difficult not to stare as they went past.

We wrapped up the filming in just under two hours. I assured Clint on film he would not be seen in a dramatisation, and we would be in touch. We all left the park. I had found 'Women on Diego Garcia' hard to swallow. Now Clint had confirmed it. Back at the hotel I typed up my notes with no reference to anyone but Clint's email name, Norman. I put in no mention of Matt or the film, but I phoned Jamie to tell him all was OK and to tell him I loved him always.

20th August, 2014.

Unable to get seats on the plane the next day as it was full, Matt and I got them with our open-ended return tickets the day after that. This time Greg was four rows in front of me.

The plane got in late in the afternoon, and I went straight to Mum and Dad's. Greg and Matt went home. I was dead on my feet, so I went to bed after dining with my parents and phoning Jamie. Today I rose early, printed off the latest stuff for Dad to post to Karen for Niall, and went into the office with Matt. Malcolm, the producer, Julian, the solicitor, and Marion Gorman, my boss from Exposure, who would check my editing of the programme, were there.

I gave them printed copies of the whole of my notes so far, and Matt played them film of the interview with Clint. There was a muted 'Hooray'. Malcolm and Marion leapt up and gave each other high fives, like schoolboys. Julian, much more restrained, just patted me on the shoulder like the older brother he seems to be, and muttered "Well done Lynn," in that lovely voice of his.

Having got over their enthusiasm, Marion, looking more like a model than a schoolboy, took over. "Yes, well done,

Lynn. We heard that Esterhazy agreed to filming, and I agree to what you promised him."

"I hope you do, since I sent him the company's agreement," Julian said, not unkindly. "We're not in the business of betraying him, are we? Of course not," he added as Marion said "no" and Malcolm shook his head emphatically. "I drew up a binding agreement making the promises in return for his being filmed by us. And he doesn't get paid."

"That's great," Malcolm boomed. "So now we hope for something else to break, don't we?"

I lost no opportunity to say: "When it does I want Matt with me again. He's been with me a lot, and he'll be glad to come again." Matt was nodding. "As you know, he can be pretty fussy who he works with, but he seems to be able to put up with me, and he's 100% reliable."

Malcolm agreed.

Marion smiled: "Let's pray that when - if - something turns up it's as good as the Esterhazy interview; then it's worth waiting. That's it folks. Let me know as soon as you've got something more, Lynn. And you must go too, this time Malcolm."

I added: "But I think Nic Stark can handle it. She is very good." Malcolm agreed without taking umbrage.

As the meeting broke up, Julian stood and asked quietly: "What do we know about this American chap Esterhazy mentioned at the end of the film? Zane Pretorius, was it?"

I'm not sure anyone else heard him, and I didn't really take it in.

22nd August, 2014.

In Australia there is a very well-respected government scientific organisation. The experts who work there publish highly valued reports, some of which contradict the views and policies of various governments around the world. For example, they did not endorse the development of Coal Seam Gas favourably, or help governments assert it would have no effect on water supplies, but said it would add escaping methane to the greenhouse gases contributing to global warming.

Yesterday there were items in the media that that institution had issued a report about the most likely disappearance zone for SEA439. It was close to the original southern arc mapped from the signals being sent from and bounced off the plane. That was the arc which ran from Turkmenistan in the northern hemisphere to deep down south in the Indian Ocean. The Institute's Director said that the coordinates for the new area were more or less part of the original southern arc. The map coordinates showed a place in the sea west-south-west of Perth, Australia, way out into the Indian Ocean.

The Australian institution had been plotting this place by timing the Doppler effect of the time it took the plane's 'pings' to bounce to the receiving stations.

I then looked up the map coordinates for Diego Garcia, which were latitude 7 degrees 19 minutes south (of the Equator) by 72 degrees 45 minutes longitude (east of Greenwich, just outside London where GMT starts). As best I could calculate it from my atlas, it seemed that the distance between where it was suggested the plane had ditched and Diego Garcia was about 1,900 miles. As the journey to Beijing and one to DG were roughly of the same length and duration, an additional three-and-a-half hours flying time would be required for the plane to get south west of Perth. Would extra fuel have been loaded to achieve that? There still seemed to be something odd about that, but perhaps the amount of fuel needed to get to Beijing safely could carry the plane so far south. If Clint and Gavin had really seen the pilot maybe he was still alive.

Whatever theory someone came up with there was always some other aspect that didn't fit in with it. These figures from the Australian institute seemed to me to be no exception. There had to be some other explanation. Maybe it was truly Diego, as Gavin and Clint said. Not that I doubted it. It had to be that.

Thinking about the institute's figures I remembered that back at the end of May I intended to write to Rolls-Royce to see what they thought about the handshakes bouncing from the plane to Inmarsat. I'd forgotten to do it. Today I wrote them an email:

I am very interested in what happened to South East Airways Flight SEA 439 which disappeared on 9th March 2013. I understand that: 1) the plane transmitted data periodically to Inmarsat for a couple of hours. They forwarded that data to you and to Boeing about the performance of the engines and of the plane itself. 2) The Satcom system which communicates with Inmarsat then switched off. After that there were eight handshakes (or 'pings'), as I believe they may be called, over a period of approximately seven hours.

3) The last ping was at 9.19 am. That ping must have been when the plane was above water. That is Malaysian time, not GMT.

4) From timing the 'bounce back' of those pings, a more accurate position for the crash site of the plane has been calculated off the coast of Western Australia, somewhere to the south of west of Perth.

Please can you tell me: a) whether the first three points are correct? b) what information all the pings contained? c) whether you agree with the calculations referred to in the fourth point? d) if not, what you think happened to the plane, and where you believe it might have crashed? I tried hard to find this information on your website, but could not even find a reference to SEA439.

23rd August, 2014.

I received a reply from Rolls-Royce:

Thank you for your questions regarding SEA439. I think the simplest answer is that we supplied all the information we have to the official inquiry. The inquiry report is publically (sic) available and we agree with its findings as they relate to Roll-Royce.   *Regards, Rodney Hopkins.*

I thought this a curious response, not just because it didn't really tell me anything: it seemed odd to me to say they agreed with the report's 'findings as they relate to Rolls-Royce'. Did that mean that they didn't agree with the rest of its conclusions? In addition, I had been unable to find any report reaching any conclusion about anything. I tried phoning, but couldn't get anyone to talk about it, and Rodney was never available, so I wrote back:

Dear Rodney,

Thank you very much. I have just looked at the Official Malaysian Reports of May 2013 and 14, and I am no further forward. I could find no reference to Rolls-Royce in the list of abbreviations. I found one to EHM (Engine Health Monitoring), but it gives no clue as to where in the report that might be found, and I could find no proper index. I have found these reports quite unintelligible as I am not in the aircraft or flying industries. I hoped that you or one of your colleagues could tell me in simple language what the answers to my questions are.

Are the Malaysian reports the ones to which you refer? Many countries seem to have had a hand in this. You must know exactly where in a report I should find the bit you mean. Could you tell me that, please? Also, could you please send me the information you gave to the inquiry you refer to? I may be able to find someone who could interpret it for me. Finally, I should be grateful if you would kindly tell me whether you agree with the most recent calculations of the likely position of the wreckage.

Thanks for your help.

Lynn Galloway.

8th September, 2014.

I didn't get any help from Rolls-Royce. I didn't even get an acknowledgement, despite sending a reminder. I had written to Inmarsat, asking them similar questions. I had a reply from them saying they would deal with my enquiry as soon as they could, but heard nothing further. Do I suffer from paranoia, or was there something strange or even suspicious about the failure of these companies, which must know all the answers, to respond? Or did they just not want to be involved? Maybe they thought they'd done enough by giving evidence to the Inquiries.

I was foxed, too, by the fact that the northern arc to Turkmenistan had been so easily abandoned. The southern arc had been concentrated on because some debris had been found in the Indian Ocean, but apart from one identified piece, had it definitely come from SEA439? I knew the plane had gone to Diego Garcia, but no-one in authority was going to say that. In that case the search should be everywhere, not just in the south. The northern route had been discounted, too, because no crash site had been found in Western Asia. But why did it have to be a crash? Why not a landing on an airfield in Turkmenistan or Afghanistan, or Iraq or Iran? The official reasoning was that no terrorist group had claimed responsibility for a hijack. Why did it have to be terrorists? Hadn't Israel hijacked Eichmann from South America and flown him to Israel? Hadn't the US hijacked goodness knows how many alleged terrorists and 'renditioned' them? Was that made transparently public? It seemed to me that abandoning the northern arc was just a mite too convenient, since if the plane could have been landed there somewhere, someone might work out that it really could have gone to DG.

It was almost three weeks since I had seen Clint. Nothing new was happening, but I was getting a lot of new research done. I felt a strange premonition that something would take me back to the States. How was I going to explain another trip to Jamie? He kept pressing me to fix up the wedding.

10th September, 2014.

Today, working at home, I printed off photos of Clint's ship, the Okinawa. My research was further confirmed by articles in the press about 'rendition' and Diego Garcia. A former US General from the Pentagon had made some astounding revelations. He said that interrogation of kidnapped people took place on Diego Garcia. Of course, the politically correct word for this kidnapping is 'rendition'. How can politicians use euphemisms like 'rendition' when they know what the reality is?

It's like 'collateral damage' when what they mean is the slaughter of innocent civilians – usually civilians of the country they say they've gone to help, like Iraq or Afghanistan. In some cases it's civilians of a neighbouring country where they think 'terrorists' may be found, like Pakistan, but they hit a wedding party or school instead, women and children included. Who do they think they're fooling? It's probably only self-deception, and conning those who may be too stupid to know what the politicians are talking about. Or those like former President George H.W. Bush who is alleged to have said: "My country right or wrong." Hitler probably said the same about Nazi Germany! Stalin undoubtedly felt the same about the USSR.

It isn't surprising if the sons and daughters of the people at the wedding, or the fathers or brothers of the kids at the school, don't themselves decide to become 'terrorists' in revenge for the terror inflicted on their families. That way lies eternal conflict.

Even more surprising, while looking for old news about the plane, I read on the internet that on 2nd April 2014, a year and a bit after Subrama went missing with it, the President of the USA announced: "today the United States, with our allies and partners, has reached an historic understanding with Iran, which, if fully implemented, will prevent it from obtaining a nuclear weapon."

Why was that? Was that connected with the missing plane and the two missing Iraqis who were on it, travelling on their false passports? Perhaps. I found that only 15 months before that, on 14th January 2013, two months before SEA439 vanished, a team of experts from the Institute for Science and International Security in the USA reported that Iran could produce enough weapons grade uranium for nuclear bombs by mid 2014. Something had to be done, so they told the President he "should explicitly declare that he will use military force to destroy Iran's nuclear program if Iran takes additional decisive steps toward producing a bomb."

I was glad to realise that the President hadn't gone that far. With Russia heavily involved in the development of Iran's peaceful nuclear capacity, such an attack not too far from Russia itself could have led to us all being wiped out in an atomic holocaust. Perhaps the President had recalled how delighted Kennedy had been when Khrushchev deployed rockets in Castro's Cuba. He might have figured out that Putin would feel exactly the same, only more strongly, about the actual dropping of atom bombs on Tehran.

I think I've got enough ammunition now, so perhaps I should go to the States and see if I can track down that mysterious Mr Pretorius. Maybe not. I'll put that to Marion. I've made a lot less progress than I should have done; I've been wrestling with the enormity of this story. If only I could correctly find and identify Subrama, but even then, cynic that I am, I still struggle with the idea that the USA could do what this tale tells me they did to about 250 people. On the other hand, if I think about the evidence I have from Gavin and Clint on film and on my laptop, why shouldn't I believe it?

Apart from that, sometimes I jerk awake in the night in a sweat after a dream - nightmare really - that some secret network is on to me and will liquidate me for exposing this diabolical crime. I've been in some dangerous situations before where I could get killed, but never one like this where persons unknown may be plotting my death. "OK, that's enough negative thinking," I say to myself. "I just have to get on with it. To hell with the consequences."

I picked up the phone and asked Ellen, Marion's PA to arrange another meeting as soon as possible.

18th December, 2014.

Marion didn't think it was worth sending me back to the States on the off-chance of finding someone we knew so little about, so I was back on the 'police beat', chasing up tips from cops, villains, private eyes, and even scanning the newspapers for stories that looked deeper than the papers made out.

In June I was writing about rendition and torture on Diego Garcia of prisoners taken by the USA in the "War on Terror."

In the end truth does seem to emerge. On 9th December 2014 the US Senate Intelligence Committee released a 6700 page report – top secret, of course – about the CIA's abuse of 'secret' prisoners. A sanitised, 'redacted', or in simple terms, censored, version was issued of around 500 pages. A week or so later the London 'Daily Mail' commented that DG was not mentioned once.

It didn't help me. I had nothing new, and my 'missing plane' tale seemed to be completely dead. At least Marion was finding me other stories to follow and I was chasing down some of my own.

6th May, 2015.

It's curious how a story that seems to be good about one thing turns out to be an even better tale about something almost completely different. The SEA 439 mystery was still just that – a mystery. It was beginning to feel like it had been interred years ago, so I was still on investigations of a much less stunning nature. So what was I doing while waiting for the resurrection of the SEA439 saga, should it ever occur?

Marion was on pretty good terms with a director of one of the major oil companies. Not long after the Subrama SEA 439 story seemed to have died - in December - she told me he had taken her out to lunch and related this case about a filling station manager who had been ripping the company off. Along with the forecourt shop the garage had a car wash. The oil company had very tight procedures for accounting for the sales of oil, petrol, take-away food, crisps, newspapers, and all the other stuff these places sell to motorists. However, in this case they had forgotten to set up any procedure to account for the car wash cash. Where did the money go?

The oil company director told Marion that for months the manager, one Ray Sinclair, must have been banking this money for himself, but they couldn't work out how much was involved or where it had gone. The oil people wanted to make an example of him. They wanted the BBC to run a story about him to deter others from trying the same stunt. They were going to get the Police to prosecute him for theft or embezzlement, and sue him for the money, but they didn't want to do that yet. They hoped we would film the story and Auntie BBC would broadcast something after the prosecution was over. Auntie had already agreed to fund the programme.

Marion had put me onto it. Mr Sinclair lived in a village near Hitchin in Hertfordshire where the filling station was. I decided to go and see him. That was back in February. He hadn't been interviewed by the police yet. The oil man had said the cops did not know about the case yet, as he wanted us to get as much information as we could before the prosecution made investigation by journalists more or less impossible.

I expected a rebuff when I knocked on the old farmhouse door. A lady of about 60 answered my knock, and took me into a typically large farm kitchen after I introduced myself. She made me a cup of tea, saying she expected her husband home pretty soon. It was about 5.45 pm. Just after six, Mr Sinclair came in. He could not have looked more ex-RAF if he were on a film set with a squadron of Spitfires. His fairish hair with a touch of ginger was brushed back from his forehead. Long sideboards joined up with the ends of his luxuriant handlebar moustache. His check sports jacket looked tailored to his broad shoulders, and matched perfectly with his grey slacks and University tie. He looked a bit younger than his wife.

She gave him tea and poured me another cup. I decided beating about the bush was pointless with this very alert man, so I came straight out with it. I expected an outburst. What I got was a surprise. Sinclair looked at me straight for a moment and then burst out laughing. "Look, you wouldn't expect me to tell you all about this if I'm about to be arrested and haven't seen my solicitor, would you, Miss Galloway?"

"I guess not, but if I don't try I never get anywhere."

"Of course not. So I'm going to tell you some stuff about how these filling stations run."

He spent the next two hours letting me into some rather disturbing secrets. The managers of the filling stations carry the can for everything. They are almost a sort of franchise. They have to pay for the petrol as it is delivered. They pay the staff. If customers fill up their tanks and drive off without paying the manager has to make up the money.

Ray Sinclair admitted this was less of a problem once his garage had CCTV cameras installed by the oil men, but it could still be a big drain on his modest margins. He could not stock the shop with goods he could buy cheaper at cash and carry stores. The petrol company made him buy all his stock from them at top whole-sale prices, so he made little profit on sales. On top of that, the company even took 20% of his profits. As all the money, whether in cash or from credit card sales, had to go through the company's till linked to their computers, they were taking all the cream from the business, and he was lucky to be left with the curds and whey. There were many other ways he and his ilk could be penalised by the petrol giant.

He invited me to consider whether there was not a bigger story in the way the managers were treated, than in his own individual narrative. He was very polite, and he and his wife saw me to the door. I said I would think about it, and he offered to help if I wanted to pursue that line. As I got in my car he shouted: "If I don't get arrested I'll even tell you what I did."

Driving away I could not help feeling this was far removed from disappearing planes on the other side of the world and 250 people apparently dying in a crash into the sea, if that was what had occurred.

Even so, I decided that, as I had no better tale to look into, I'd see if what Steve had said added up. Over the next couple of weeks I called in at several filling stations around the Home Counties, and took one or two trips to the Midlands and the West Country. I found there were hardly any independent garage owners, and those usually bought their fuel from smaller independent oil companies. Life could be tough, but at least they didn't feel they were victims. All the multinational filling stations belonged to the giants. 75% of the managers told the same tale as Ray Sinclair: it was a struggle to make a living; the petrol company took a large slice of everything, and any losses of cash or fuel were always down to the manager even when he had no control over what happened; make a fuss and they were out on their ear. Most of the others refused to talk.

Many of them had come into the business after some sort of financial or family disaster when beggars could not be choosers. Quite a few were nevertheless happy for me to record them, but a lot of those wanted no names or identification used. However, around half-a-dozen agreed to be filmed, so I made appointments to go back with a cameraman. I phoned Sinclair and told him what I'd learned. He was pleased, and agreed straight away to a filmed interview. He was prepared to lose the garage.

A few days later I was back at his rented farmhouse. Mrs Sinclair gave me and the man with the camera a good lunch, and then we set about the interview. We recorded all the old stuff, and then I asked: "How did you get into this business?"

"I'd had my own small garage business – fuel, repairs and car sales, but I was a bit silly. I thought I could sit back and let the boys do the repairs and sales and just count the money, but there wasn't enough work. You need a big work force and plenty of work to be able to become just a manager. You still need to get your hands dirty. The business went down the pan and I had to sell it for a song."

Mrs Sinclair said: "We were desperate; we couldn't even pay the rent on this place. Steve applied for the filling station job."

I realised I needed to get more details from all the other managers of the reasons they had gone into this business where all the cards were stacked against them.

The story wasn't about a manager cheating a petrol giant out of sums that to them would barely be noticeable: it was the fact the companies created situations and conditions where men and women were forced to take desperate steps to keep a roof over their head.

I went back to Marion. She agreed to speak to the BBC. Auntie agreed to change the format of the programme, but insisted I go to the director who had given Marion the original story for a comment. When I did, the result was unprintable and certainly not for peak time broadcasting. He wouldn't make a comment on the record anyway. The programme would end with the usual formula: "The petrol company was approached for their side of the story, but declined to comment."

The company did not report the matter to the Police; the adverse publicity would do more harm than good. They did not sue Sinclair for the money, but introduced a rigid system to keep their hands on car-wash cash.

When it was over Mr and Mrs Sinclair asked me to lunch. He told me what had happened. When he realised the car wash money was separate and had been overlooked in their procedures, he started paying it into the bank account every day, and then transferring odd sums, usually in cash, to a bank account his son opened in the name of a company. The amounts transferred did not tally with the sums paid into the filling station account, so it was virtually impossible to reconcile the two.

It was a good story, but I still hankered after finishing the programme about the plane. It didn't seem likely after six months of silence, and then something happened to drive it right out of my head.

***

Today I received a text message from Jamie.

Hi Lynn. Badly wounded. Get here asap. In Instituto Dupuytren Traumatologia Hospital. Avenida Belgrano. Tell editor you have great story. Love Jamie. XX.

A few weeks ago a very happy Jamie told me he was going to Argentina to watch a football match. It was late evening and we were sitting up cuddling in bed. I cannot stand football, but it was the thing he lived for, apart from living with me – or that's what he said. I believed him, as he still wanted to marry me. Although I love him I didn't think I wanted that sort of commitment at the time he asked me - on bended knee in the park - even when he had produced that splendid sapphire and diamond engagement ring.

Jamie is a sport fanatic, which made his job as a researcher at the Meteorological Office in London very useful, as he was wont to put it. "It means I've got just the best idea of any fan which games or competitions are likely to be rained off."

"But why Buenos Aires, Jamie? Why not Athens or Rome or somewhere not so far away? I haven't got time to go South-West across the Atlantic like that. You know how busy I am."

"I do, love, and you know I'd rather you could come too, but I've got some leave due, and I've just got to go this time."

"Got to? What do you mean, got to?"

"Listen, a few years ago 'The Observer' printed a list of 'The 50 Sporting Things You Must Do Before You Die'."

"Don't tell me you're about to die!"

"Don't be daft, woman. It's the Superclassico on 3rd May. It's a Sunday. These two Argentinian teams, Boca Juniors and River Plate, the big ones in Buenos Aires, play a local derby match that day. The paper put it at number one in the list. People say it makes a Glasgow Celtic versus Rangers game or Arsenal v Chelsea match look like a Sunday School picnic. I tell you what: I'll die if I don't go!"

I reached up to put my arms round his neck – not an easy thing to do as he's six foot one to my five foot six. "Jamie, you know I love you, and never say 'no' ..."

"Of course you don't, you sexy beast!"

I clouted his shoulder playfully. "Don't be cheeky, little chap. You really are like a forty-year-old schoolboy, with silly jokes like that, and your football. Well, I'm not going to say 'No you don't' this time either. Just look after yourself, and don't be away too long."

"That's why I love you, too, Lynn," he said as he ran his right index finger slowly, softly, silkily down the side of my face, neck, collar bone and further on down, and then began to run it in increasing small circles around my left breast. "And what is this increasingly firm object I'm finding here, then?"

My left hand began another slow journey down Jamie's chest and abdomen. "I've found this gruesome object down here, too."

Quick as a flash Jamie mimicked a Scots accent. "I know lassie; just keep on doing tha' and it'll grew some more." We kissed at length. "And is it 'aye' or 'nay' tonight, lassie?"

"What do you think?" I slid on top of him.

***

A couple of days later I was working at home on a story about a copper who was alleged to have taken a bribe from a gang boss in the East End. Exposure had had a tip that the accusation was probably untrue; the Exposure Editor, Marion Gorman, asked me to deal with it as I had no other major projects on at the time. Channel 4 had commissioned a documentary about it.

The policeman was to go on trial soon for taking corrupt payments. I called in nearly all the favours I was owed in the Met and the underworld from previous investigations, and found out that he seemed to have been set up for getting a crime boss's son put away for rape three years before. The story was almost complete, and I had a few loose ends to tie up before I could finish it. The plan, agreed with my editor, was that I should go to the cop's solicitor, and offer her the story in return for an exclusive with the officer. He would get a substantial sum from writing a book after the case was over. The solicitor would get the details to acquit her client in any event. Marion made it clear she would not offer the lawyer any kind of blackmail deal, such as: "You'll only get what we have if you agree to our getting the exclusive." That was not how Exposure worked; we could still use the story of the investigation after the trial even if the cop did not want to talk to us. In any case, the editor wanted to see it first.

I rose from my desk to get a cuppa when Jamie came in from work. He kissed me 'hello', put his arms around my waist, and said: "I've got the flights booked. I leave from Heathrow on a late flight on Monday, 20th April, get there on Wednesday the 22nd. That gives me time to have a good look around the city and bits of Argentina - I've always wanted to go there - even chase up the Welsh community in Patagonia - see the match on the 3rd of May, and fly home on the 8th.

"Who're you flying with? Do you want a cuppa?

"KLM and yes, but could I have a coffee instead?"

"Coffee coming up. Is it a long flight?"

"Not half. Thirty-one and a half hours."

"Now that's what I call a long flight!"

"As it's KLM it stops in Amsterdam ..."

"That's one European capital I haven't got to yet."

"It's only a stop, not a stop-over, so I won't see any of it this time. We must go there together soon."

"That's a great idea. I'll try to fix some time off, and book us a trip while you're away."

Jamie laughed. "As long as some other story doesn't take you over in the meantime. I get another stop in Rio, which is why it's such a long journey. Then I fly on to BUE. But I don't get to see much of Rio either. The plane's only there for a few hours."

"What's BUE?"

"That's the code for the airport in Argentina."

That was that, and on 20th April Jamie flew away. I drove him to Heathrow to see him off, and found I was a bit tearful as I drove home. Then two weeks later, having forgotten about Amsterdam, I had this awful text saying he was seriously injured – wounded no less, which sounded worse, a lot worse. I asked the switchboard to get me the number of this 'Instituto', and while I waited I sent a text to Jamie. I noticed his message had not come in from his phone. It was a number I didn't know, and his name was not on the screen on the mobile. I just hoped he'd get this.

I'm praying for you. What happened? When? I'm coming for you at once. All my love, Lynn. Should have married you when you asked me.

I rushed down the corridor to the editor's room, knocked, and went straight in. She wasn't there but her secretary was doing some clearing up and filing.

'Hi, Ellen, where's Marion? And can you give her this, please?' I handed Ellen the police story.

"Sure. She's down in the restaurant."

I ran to the lifts but as there wasn't one available I took the stairs as fast as I could, arriving almost breathless. I quickly picked out Marion Gorman at her usual table. She was a remarkably dynamic fifty year old, with a reputation for fearless media coverage similar to that of editors like Alan Rusbridger of The Guardian, or Ben Bradley of The

Washington Post. Marion was also very popular with the staff. They voted for her appointment. This very intelligent dark haired woman had been in the job about six years. "Hello Lynn," she said. "What's up? Clearly something is."

"I need two or three weeks off, starting now, I'm afraid. It's Jamie. He went to Argentina to watch some bloody football match, and he's in hospital, badly injured."

"Crikey, Lynn, that's awful. How do you know?"

"He sent me a text a few minutes ago."

"You'd better go at once. Keep me posted, won't you?"

"I'll do more than that. If I find a story I'll let you have it. And I've just given Ellen the complete story on the police officer. He should be acquitted. You decide whether to hand it to the Crown Prosecution Service or the defence. Or both. Do you think the prosecution will share it with the defence?"

"Knowing they got it from us, they'd never risk keeping it to themselves and still go ahead with the case. It's a bit of luck, anyway. If we give the police story to the CPS that'll give us back a bit of the credit we lost last year when you put away those two cops taking bribes from a drug dealer. And if you do a story about Jamie or anything over there in Argentina, we'll pay your expenses."

"Thank God for that. I've been expecting to be shot or framed for a murder ever since that drug bust."

"That's a commendable stiff upper lip response, Lynn."

9th May, 2015.

Having gone home to pack a bag and, very luckily, get a flight late the next day, I arrived in Buenos Aires, quite

169

exhausted by two days on the plane. I took a taxi straight to the hospital. It was almost noon. Still toting my bag I went up to the second floor to find Jamie's ward. The nurse at the desk spoke English, and directed me to Jamie's room.

He appeared to be asleep, so I moved a chair quietly to the bedside. He looked very pale, and in pain even though asleep. His eye sockets were dark shadows, what my Dad would call 'piss-holes in the snow'. I kissed Jamie on the forehead, and sat down. After a few minutes he opened his eyes. "Hello darling," he said, very sleepily.

"Oh Jamie, my love, what has happened to you?"

"Look dreadful, don't I." It was a statement, not a question.

"I hate to agree, but yes, you do. So what happened?"

"Too tired now. Long story. Come back tomorrow." He immediately fell asleep. I realised for the first time how much I loved Jamie and had missed him since he left for Argentina.

I continued to hold his hand for half an hour, then kissed him again gently on the forehead, and left the room as softly as I'd come in. I went to the nurse at the desk, and asked what had happened to Jamie.

"We not know exact. He come here in a car, a man come in and asked for help to .... ah .... carry him in here. He say he find Mr Stallard in a street bleeding to death, so he get him in car." Then the man vanished as soon as Jamie was on a stretcher, she said. Jamie had a bad wound in the stomach, and another in his left thigh, and he seemed to have been kicked in the head. It turned out they were knife wounds. He

170

was unconscious. The man was driving past when he saw Jamie, stopped, realising he could not talk or walk. He lifted him into the car to bring him to hospital. The hospital reception did not have a chance to get the man's name.

"The Good Samaritan of Buenos Aires," I thought, in terms of a headline, the way journalists work.

The nurse added: "Mr Stallard, he nearly dead then. He go in .... ah ...."

"Intensive care?"

"Si, for four days."

"So he came in here after El Classico? That means it was after the match."

"Si, Senora." She consulted her notes. "He come out of intensive care on sixth. Then he woke up and we put him in his now room."

"That's when he sent me a text. Did he have his phone?"

"No, Senora. I lend him mine. His stolen, he say."

That explained why I hadn't recognised the phone number on the text. "Thank you. You've been very kind. He's asleep. When can I come back?"

"Any time, Senora."

"Actually it's Senorita, but I wish it were Senora." Too much information, I thought, but it was how I felt.

I went down to reception and asked for directions to a hotel close to the hospital. The three star Hotel Palermo was recommended, and a taxi was called for me.

I booked myself in, dumped my bag in my room, and lay down. After fifteen minutes, tired as I was, I realised I was too hungry and thirsty to sleep, so I went down to the restaurant for lunch and ordered an omelette, a coffee, and some cold water. I looked around. A couple in their sixties sat over in one corner, at the other end of the windows where I sat. On the other side of the room six people were eating and talking rather loudly. Not far from the door a solitary man was eating. There was something familiar about him. Was it the way he ate? Was it the stooped way he hung over his plate?

I couldn't say I recognised him; he just gave me a feeling.

When I was half way through my meal, the man called the waiter in accented English, which was odd, because to me he looked like a well-to-do Native South American, so why didn't he speak Spanish to an Argentinean waiter? He had very black hair, with a little grey, and he appeared to be about fifty. He wore his hair with a plaited pony tail down his back to the bottom of his shoulder-blades.

I looked away. The man asked the waiter for coffee and his bill, again in English with that pretty heavy accent. I knew the voice and the accent, and thought I recognised the set of the eyes, but if it was the man who was beginning to appear in my mind's eye, he must have had plastic surgery. The nose was more slender than that of the chap I was starting to picture, and the lips were thicker. More positive was my recognition of a large ruby ring with an unusual setting. Surely I had seen that before.

I decided to take a closer look risking the possibility he might recognise me, even though I was one of thousands of similar women in this city of beautiful females (vanity, Lynn

– watch it!). I got up to go to the toilet, which meant passing his table. As I did so I kept my face averted until I got closer to him, and glanced down, looking intently at his hands. He was looking down at the table top, on which his hands lay flat.

My glance at the hands told the same story as the voice and accent: there were the train tracks running down the thumb nails. Above all, there was the ring. This was the man I'd met at Nick and Liz Carter's all those years ago. He was the missing pilot of SEA 439. He was Muhamed Subrama, the man in the newspaper photos I had seen. My plane story had come back from the dead.

The man with the pony tail thanked the waiter for his coffee saying he had enjoyed his meal, and put cash on top of the bill. It was definitely the right voice, and apart from the fatter lips, the smile looked the same.

I had eaten most of my omelette, and was drinking my coffee when he got up to leave. I called the waiter and asked for the bill as the man was taking his jacket from the back of his chair and donning it. Subrama left the room.

I had some pesos which I had obtained at a Currency kiosk at Heathrow, so I held up a 100 peso note as the waiter brought the bill, hoping he might think he would get a big tip; the note was rather larger than the bill. "The man who sat over there, is he a regular customer?"

"Si, Senorita, he come here for lunch two or three times a week."

"I think he is someone I have met before, but I have forgotten his name."

"He say he is Senor Ramanos."

"That is kind of you, but do not tell him I was asking about him, will you, please?"

"No, Senorita."

"Thank you. I am staying here and shall see you again." I put the note on the bill, smiled, and told him to keep the change.

Upstairs in my room I collapsed on the bed fully dressed, and my last thoughts as I went to sleep were of the dinner at Nick and Liz's, and the man with the pony tail, whose hair was almost curly then, with no pony-tail, nor botoxed lips and a slim nose. I also thought that no matter how much I wanted Jamie to make love to me, it would be some time before he would be in a fit state to do that. I loved him and adored our sex life. Never had I missed him so much when I was the one who went away, as I so often did on my investigations. How patient he had always been! He must love me very much. I felt tears creep down my cheeks.

Ever since I'd discovered sex at seventeen, I'd revelled in it, but none of the men had given me that special feeling, that extra thrill, which love and making love with Jamie engendered. There had been no other man since Jamie.

***

The next morning I was at Jamie's bedside by nine o'clock; he was awake, and more inclined to talk after I'd kissed and hugged him very gently. He said even that hurt. I told him again I wished I'd agreed to marry him when he asked me years ago.

"So you should, Lynn. I was a wonderful catch, but I'm not sure I'm worth looking *at* now. More like needing looking *after*."

"Can't we get married as soon as you get home from here and feel strong enough? Do you want me to go down on my knees now?"

"Yes, and no. Anyway, I can't sit up."

"Why not?"

"The stomach wound is too painful, and the stitches might part and, well .... I have to stay lying down, so if you kneel I won't even be able to see you over the edge of the bed. Just give me another kiss, but very, very softly this time. That won't hurt, and I shan't get too excited, which would be a complete waste of time, the state I'm in."

We kissed, and he took my hand, and said: "Is that a done deal then?"

"It certainly is. You're looking at the future Mrs Stallard. And we'll have a honeymoon in Holland and Amsterdam." We both laughed, and I asked: "So what actually happened?"

"Are you sitting comfortably? Then I'll begin. It was after the match. Fantastic game by the way. Boca Juniors beat River Plate by two goals to nil. Fantastic goals too; they were scored by ...."

"Bloody hell, Jamie, do you really think I care who scored, with my fiancé lying here half dead, and I don't know why? Just tell me what happened after the match."

***

The Good Samaritan of Buenos Aires.
Jamie Stallard, English tourist, hardly expected to die on

the way back from a football match, but he almost did. He had just seen Boca Juniors beat River Plate 2-0 in the El Classico of Buenos Aires, Argentina on Sunday 3rd May. He was full of the skill of the players and the noise of the crowd as he made his way from the stadium to his hotel. He could not find a taxi in the dense herd of fans leaving with him, so he walked, thinking to find a taxi a bit later. In his euphoria he did not notice that he failed to turn off left towards his hotel; hardly surprising as he had never been in the area before.

He found himself in a strange and rather run down part of town, fairly gloomy and with few people about. As he approached a corner a man in a hoody came round it, and spoke to him in Spanish. Jamie stopped to ask what he wanted, and thought the man punched him hard in the stomach. He punched back at the man's face and connected a bit. His assailant then stooped and hit Jamie on the thigh, and Jamie fell down. He reached out to grab the man's ankle but missed. The man kicked him in the head. Jamie tried to get up but was too shocked to rise or feel much pain. He could feel blood running down his stomach and thigh. Then dreadful pain flooded his mind. He hadn't been punched; he'd been knifed.

He could not resist further, and the thug searched his pockets, taking all his money and mobile phone; he even pulled his watch off his wrist. Jamie was passing out, and did so as the man ran off.

He had no idea how long he lay on the pavement, but came to as someone was lifting him up, and putting him in a car. It was a struggle as Jamie could tell he was a lot larger than his rescuer. "Who are you?" he asked.

The man replied in broken English: "You wounded bad. We go hospital."

By now Jamie was in the car, and fainted again. The next thing he knew was when he was lifted out of the car onto a stretcher and rushed into bright lights at the entrance to a hospital. He passed out completely. He woke up three days later, borrowed a nurse's mobile, and sent his girlfriend (now his fiancée) in London a text asking her to join him as soon as possible.

The nurses and a doctor told Jamie the man who brought him in left no name, phone number, or address, and had vanished as soon as he had explained where he found Jamie and what appeared to have happened to him.

As Jamie puts it now: "There may be a huge stone statue of Jesus overlooking Rio, but Buenos Aires has the real thing, with Jesus himself sending my personal Good Samaritan to care for me!"

That's the story Jamie told, I typed back at the Palermo, and emailed to my boss with a video of Jamie in hospital. Not the usual sort of TV story, but I thought it might make a lighter and less political News item for one of the Channels. "I wonder if Marion will want to edit it to state that I'm the fiancée?" I asked her not to, and fortunately she didn't. I attached copies of photos of Jamie before and after the attack, and suggested to Marion she should find some footage of the stadium.

13th May, 2015.

I did not see the man with the pony tail on the 10th, nor the next two days, but he was in the restaurant when I came back from the hospital at 12.30 on this, the fourth day. He didn't look up as I opened the door, but as soon as I saw him I backed away, and decided to find a cafe elsewhere. I lingered outside the door looking at him through the glass panel as discreetly as possible for a few moments, confirming I was sure I knew him, but as Muhamed Subrama, not Senor Ramanos. I had seen his photo two years ago in the news about SEA439. Then he looked much as he had at Nick and Liz Carter's. Suddenly I saw him do something which, combined with the marks on the nails and the ring, made identification more certain. He put down his knife and fork, rested his elbows on the table, and after licking his middle fingers, used them to brush both his eyebrows simultaneously upwards and outwards towards his ears. It had to be the man from Nick and Liz's. Other people may do it, but it was his way I recalled.

I walked down the Avenida looking for a cafe or restaurant, when a headline on a news-vendor's kiosk caught my eye. I bought a paper, El Independente. It was in Spanish, but it clearly referred to the missing plane from Kuala Lumpur, and next to it was a photo of the man I met at Nick and Liz's. He was the pilot of the missing plane, the one the Aboriginal lady accosted me about in Sydney a year ago. And there was his name: Muhamed Subrama. Everyone said he was dead and the plane was many fathoms deep somewhere in the Southern Indian Ocean. I was now back in full investigative journalist mode. "I'll have to look into this as well as keeping an eye on Jamie!" I told myself.

At last I found an Italian cafe, and ordered a small plate of spaghetti. When the waitress brought it I held out the paper and pointed to the headline. "Please can you tell me what that says?"

"Si, Senorita. It say the look for the plane is wrong area. They look different place now." She looked at me. "Is very sad; all those dead people."

"Yes, very sad." I thought: "If Subrama aka Ramanos is alive and well, what's happened to all the others on the plane? It must be what Gavin Johnson and Clint Esterhazy told me. This is definitely a bigger scoop than Watergate, Bradley Manning, Wikileaks, or Edward Snowden."

***

After lunch I went to the hotel before going back to see Jamie. Up in my room, I dialled reception and asked for the number of El Independente. Then I phoned the paper, and asked for a reporter who dealt with court cases. "Yes, Senora, what can I do for you?"

I gave thanks he spoke English. "You're a court reporter, right?"

"Si."

"I wonder if you could give me the name and address of the most honest and trustworthy lawyer in this city. Not necessarily the cleverest, but the most honest and honourable."

The newsman laughed. "Is a pretty rare animal, Senora."

"I know, but please do your best."

"Very good. You should try Senorita Helena Valladolid." He reeled off a number.

"That's OK. I have it here in the phone book. I'm very grateful to you. Goodbye." I put the phone back, and dialled the lawyer's number straight away. I was offered an appointment at 10.30 the next day. Then I set off for the hospital and Jamie.

14th May, 2015

Having told Jamie yesterday that I would be late today, I went to the lawyers. Senorita Valladolid was very Spanish, with long black hair in a chignon, black eyes, and smooth olive skin. Her English was excellent. After polite formalities, I asked her for the name, address, and phone number of the best, most honest, and most honourable private detective she knew of, and used herself.

"That is an odd request, Miss Galloway. Do you not want my help?"

"Only in that respect at the moment. I came to you because you were recommended in the same honest and honourable terms. That's not odd is it?" I smiled. "I may need your help in the future, but I shall not be in Argentina for long, and I hope I get into no trouble."

"I shall be here if you do. Now here is the card of the man I recommend."

"Thank you. How much do I owe you?"

"Nothing at all. I hope Mr O'Higgins can help you, and that you enjoy my country." She paused: "Who recommended me?"

"Actually, a Court reporter at 'El Independente'."

Helena laughed. "Santa Maria! A reporter finding an honest lawyer! Now that is very odd." I resisted the temptation to tell Senorita Valladolid about Jamie, thanked her again, and departed.

15th May, 2015

I spent the morning with Jamie, and bought a take-away sandwich and coffee for lunch. At 2.00 pm I was sitting on a rather uncomfortable wooden chair in the office of Bernardo O'Higgins, private investigator. He was somewhat shabby, just like his office and furniture, but the place was clean. So was he. He wore a pressed but old grey suit, with a pale blue shirt, clean black shoes, and a non-descript bluish-grey tie. His hair was dark brown with a hint of grey. He was so unobtrusive that if he hadn't been the only other person in the room I might not have noticed him. His only somewhat striking features were bright blue eyes, but they were hidden by spectacles as unobtrusive as his tie.

We introduced ourselves, and I said: "O'Higgins is an unusual name here, and you look Spanish, not Irish."

In perfect but accented English he replied: "Two hundred years ago there was a revolutionary in Chile called Bernardo O'Higgins. He was a Spaniard with Irish ancestors. He fled and lived here for three years before going back to Chile to continue the struggle for independence. Family myth has it that we are his descendants, so I am named after him, but there is no proof. Perhaps that is how I have blue eyes." He smiled. "But let us get on. What can I do for you?"

"I'm told by Senorita Valladolid that you are completely trustworthy, and don't talk about your work. Is that so?"

Bernardo chuckled. "It is very kind of her to say so, but it is also true. If I were not like that, she would give me no work. By the way, I charge 250 pesos an hour, plus all expenses."

"OK. I think I can trust her, so I should be able to trust you." The detective nodded, but said nothing. I continued: "I have seen a man I may know at my hotel. I don't want to approach him, as it is a sensitive matter, and if he is who I think he is, it could be dangerous. This is not matrimonial, just personal. He dines at the hotel two or three times a week. His name is Ramanos. I want you to come there and see him, and then find out where he lives, and whatever you can about him."

"Will you let me know when he is there?"

"Miss Valladolid gave me your card, so I can phone you on your mobile when I see him. If you are free, please come immediately."

"May I give you some advice, Miss Galloway? I infer that you do not want him to realise who you are, or recognise you, at any rate for now, and you tell me there may be danger. You are, if I may say so, a very attractive woman."

I started to bristle. I wasn't there to be told I was lovely or any other chat-up crap. Before I could protest O'Higgins went smoothly on. "If you know him, he may remember you, and your startling red hair is like a beacon. It is very hard for anyone to miss it, let alone a man who might have an eye for women." He smiled and I calmed down. His intentions seemed to be honourable. "And most of us men do. So, if I were you, I'd go straight to the hairdressers. Become mousy, please. I do not like losing clients – at least, not before I have been paid!!"

16th May, 2015

"My God, Lynn, what the hell have you done to yourself? Those black framed student glasses do nothing for you, and as for the hair!! Bloody hell, I hardly recognised you. Are you trying to tell me something, like 'I don't want you to love me anymore, because I don't love you'?"

I had not seen Jamie that agitated or energetic since I arrived in Buenos Aires. Putting my arms around him, I kissed him passionately. "There's the message, Jamie. Of course I love you. We're going to get married, aren't we?"

"OK, so what's this disguise for? It's jolly effective; I hardly recognised you. You look like the most boring woman in the world."

"Thanks, Jamie! Simple really. Remember what it was like on holiday in Rome and Naples? The blokes here are just as bad. I can't take the leering, and the things they say. My bum is for you to fondle, not any old Juan, Ricardo or Hernando. Even more special places sometimes, places reserved only for you." None of this was true in Argentina, since most of the men behaved like gentlemen, but I thought this might put Jamie off the scent. It did, and made him laugh.

In fact I'd gone straight to a salon after leaving Bernardo, where I had great difficulty, not just because the hair artist didn't speak English, but because the man could not bear the thought of 'ruining', as he put it in Spanish, my 'magnificent' auburn hair, which, he said, looked like the tresses in a Titian painting. In the end, with the help of another customer who spoke English, the peso notes in my hand overcame his scruples, he cut my hair and dyed it mouse. Then I went to an optician's where I had more luck with the language, and no trouble buying some spectacles with moderately tinted plain glass in them to conceal the striking green of my eyes. Finally I went into a Catholic charity shop, took two pairs of rather worn black trousers and a dull brown jacket into the fitting room, and as they fitted reasonably but not too well, I came out in them, and paid for them. The shop volunteer put my clothes and one of the pairs of slacks in a black plastic bag for me to take away.

I was delighted at Jamie saying I looked boring, and took it as a compliment. It was exactly the result I had hoped for.

We spent the morning chatting about a lot of fictitious things I said I'd done, and Jamie's slow recovery. I went back to the hotel for lunch; no sign of Mr Ramanos.

22nd May, 2015

There was no sign of Ramanos the next day either. The day after that he was there but unfortunately O'Higgins' phone was switched off. Today I was in luck. I spotted Ramanos in the restaurant, and the investigator came swiftly in answer to my call.

We stood by the door to the dining room, and could see Ramanos at his table. I stood back and watched as O'Higgins went through the door and sat at a table on the far side. He took a paperback from his pocket and appeared to be reading. Then I left.

***

The following morning I met my detective in a cafe. He told me what had happened the day before. "As Ramanos was being served with his lunch and talking to the waiter, I pretended to make a phone call on my mobile, but was in fact taking photos and a video of him, not keying in a number. I then had a telephone conversation in Spanish with no-one on the other end.

"I had a snack lunch, ate it quickly, and paid my bill straight away. I wanted to be ready to leave as soon as Ramanos did. When he called for his bill, I left the restaurant and crossed to the other side of the road, and a few minutes later followed him at a distance when he emerged. I followed him to a house in Moreno. It's not far from the hotel; that's why he eats there. The house is divided into apartments. I walked up the road and waited. After an hour or so he came out, got into a very well maintained Mercedes, ten years old or thereabouts, and drove off. I strolled back towards the house. I had a piece of luck."

"What happened?"

"A woman came out. I told her I was looking for a flat in the area. Were there any empty ones in the house? 'No', she said. She was talkative and told me she was the landlady, and lived on the ground floor. I asked her what sort of people lived there and in the area."

"What did she say?"

"She said it was a good area, and quite prosperous. Her tenants were all quiet and working in good jobs, except - and this was a bonus - Mr Ramanos who lived on the second floor. He seemed to have plenty of money, because he had a very beautiful old car, and didn't go to work. He was no trouble, kept himself to himself, but he had very pretty girls come to the flat about once a week, and she thought that these 'ladies' looked expensive. She actually winked, and added 'if you know what I mean'." O'Higgins handed me a piece of paper with the Moreno address on it.

"The landlady cleans the flat for him, so she knew he had very good furniture, and could see he rarely cooked, but seemed to eat out nearly all the time. That's why she thought he must be well off. He also went to the opera and theatre quite often."

"That's amazing, Bernardo. Do you mind if I call you that? I'm Lynn."

O'Higgins smiled. "That's fine."

"The money fits in with what I'm beginning to think about this man. I'll pay what I owe you now, but I may want your help again."

"We must go back to the office for that. You can pay with your credit card." Then O'Higgins said: "That reminds me. The landlady told me that Ramanos never pays for anything with a card or cheque. It suggests to me he doesn't want anyone to know who he is or where he goes."

"Thank you, Bernardo. That's what it suggests to me, too. I'm grateful. I'll ring you soon." I stood, and went to pay for our coffees. I returned to the table. "One more thing before I go. Can you find out about passports and when people arrive in Argentina? Mr Ramanos in particular. I suppose you'd need to contact the immigration people." I didn't need to tell him about the name Subrama. I was sure a man who was supposed to be dead would not have come here after facial surgery using his own identity.

"Not a problem, Lynn. I have a contact in the Immigration Department. It may mean a small 'gift', but I dare say I shall find out something. I do not know your man's Christian name, or first name. Do you?"

"Sorry, no I don't. Pity you didn't ask the landlady." Bernardo looked resentful at that, as I thought for a moment. "If he is Argentinian, which I believe he is not, then he won't have arrived. If he is foreign, then he will have arrived, and there cannot be that many Ramanos's in this country, and we can eliminate all those who do not live in Moreno, can't we?"

"Of course," he said.

"Very well, make your call, pay if you have to, and let me know what I owe you then. I'll pay you today for what you've done already."

Bernardo got up, too, and escorted me to the door of the cafe, saying he'd make out a bill now, so I went back to his office for it and paid him. He opened the door for me with a slight bow, and we parted.

***

Today O'Higgins phoned. "His first name is Cristobal. He arrived here on an American Airlines Flight from Florida on 18th June 2013. He used a Spanish Passport, which showed he'd started out from Malaga, and had a visa and permanent resident documents, all of which were, as far as anyone could tell, quite genuine."

I was cock-a-hoop. "That's fantastic, Bernardo. Do I owe you a fortune now?"

"Do not worry. You've already paid me for following Ramanos home, and we were lucky. The man I spoke to is quite friendly, and owed me a favour. He didn't want a payment, and as this has only taken three calls, including this one, you owe nothing more." He laughed. "That's on condition you tell people in the UK, or anywhere, come to that, that I am the best investigator."

I signed up to that, smiling, and then added: "Last time we spoke there was one more thing. Now there's another. I'm going back to England now, but I'd like you to keep an eye on Cristobal Ramanos until I come back. If he moves I need to know. You've got my business card, and if you wish you can email your bill for that, or I can settle up when I come back. It may be some time before I get back, so you can bill me monthly if you wish. Just one very important thing."

"Let me guess. I'm not to mention the name Ramanos in my bills?"

"You're on my wavelength, Bernardo. Goodbye."

I phoned Senorita Valladolid. "Mr O'Higgins has done a wonderful job, so thanks for the recommendation. I shall be going back to England in a few days, so I don't think I'll need you again, but if I can do anything to send clients your way, you may rely on me to do it."

"Thank you, Miss Galloway. It was a pleasure to meet you and help you, and I am so glad you are not in any trouble."

10th June, 2015

Back in England I went to see Marion at Exposure and got her to call Julian Prentis in, too. I took a photo out of my brief-case and handed it to her. "This is a photo of Muhamed Subrama, the ..."

"Fucking hell!" She hesitated. "But it doesn't look like him at all. There were photos of him in all the papers a week or so ago when they started a new search for the plane. You're kidding me!"

"No kidding! He's in Buenos Aires. Cross my heart. I saw him in a restaurant in the hotel I stayed at."

"What makes you think it's him. He was curly-haired and this bloke's got a pony-tail. He doesn't even look like him." She passed the picture to Julian, who commented: "It certainly takes a leap of faith."

Then I told them about meeting Subrama at Nick and Liz's, the thumb-nails, the eyebrow stroking, the voice, the accent, the ruby ring, and the general demeanour of the man. The photo was taken by O'Higgins. I explained that and how I had hired him to trace Subrama's address.

"I need to go back to Buenos Aires with Matt and Greg and get an interview."

20th June, 2015.

A few days ago I was wondering how the superpowers

could miss a huge aeroplane that might be filmed on their satellite cameras. Yesterday I found the answer. It was said by an American expert on a broadcast by Document Nation put out recently by the Discovery Channel that these superpowers keep such information secret as they don't want the capabilities (and, in my view, the intrusiveness) of their equipment made public. Surely, with Pine Gap in Australia and an extremely important and highly secret US military base on Diego Garcia in the western Indian Ocean, south of Pakistan, Iran, Iraq, and other major trouble spots, at least the Americans would have filmed something?

It's enough to make you think twice about nude sunbathing or skinny-dipping in your back-garden pool, or on a private beach, if they can spot a cucumber or a couple of pink grapefruit from 50 miles away, or more. The Pentagon could make the porn industry bankrupt! Maybe it has its own porn industry! I remembered some of the things Jamie and I had done on deserted beaches and twice in a cornfield, and blushed.

At 3.30 pm I was at Heathrow waiting for Jamie in the Arrivals Hall. He had emailed me two days before to say he was coming home. He came out of passport control and Customs on a buggy driven by an airline carer, the sort of bloke who usually looks after children travelling alone, or the elderly and disabled. Jamie got off the buggy in a gingerly fashion, and I ran to him and we hugged, but he told me not to be too enthusiastic as he wasn't up to it yet. The carer was about to unload the luggage but I asked him to drive us to my car, which he did.

On the way home Jamie told me he'd been looked after very well in the Argentine hospital, and on the plane. He couldn't walk very far, and his activities would be limited, he said with a wink and a rueful smile.

"Never mind. We'll think of something," I replied, squeezing his hand.

In the car on the way home to Doneraile Street, I joked I was glad his plane hadn't vanished like SEA439. Did he know anything fresh about it? Were the Argentineans interested in it?

"Seems like everyone's interested in it. There was an Air France plane vanished after leaving South America a few years ago, so people there are just as intrigued as in England or anywhere else. Mind you, that one was located pretty quickly considering it went down in the South Atlantic, whereas they haven't detected SEA what's it - at all?"

"439."

The subject just drifted off to more domestic issues, such as how much he could do to look after himself, how much I'd need to do for him, and when he could go back to work. He could stay with Mum and Dad for a while; they had invited him to stay with them for a week or so. They adore him and thought I'd been out of my tiny mind not to have married him when I had the chance. To say they are old-fashioned is to put it mildly. I drove him down to Shere today intending to stay a few days to help look after him.

30th June, 2015.

When I got Jamie home to Doneraile Street I realised just

how frail he still was, so I got a nurse in from an agency to help look after him, and told Marion I could not do anything much except stay at home polishing up the story for a while. I could tell she was pretty frustrated, but she was also sympathetic, and told me to take as long as I liked.

12th July, 2015.

Jamie was making great strides now. The next meeting of the team was fixed for today. My original idea had been to try to meet with Subrama. When I awoke this morning, what Julian had said at the end of one of the earlier meetings came back to me. Just what did we know about Zane Pretorius? That he was American, somehow he knew the men who had been on SEA439, or they knew him, and Clint had seen those men. That was it; that was all we knew. He might be very important. How could I find him? Would he talk to me if I did? Should I see try to see Subrama first?

The more I thought about that the more convinced I was that I needed as much information as possible if I stood any chance of getting admissions - more like a confession, if truth be told - out of the pilot.

When we were all seated in Marion's office, Ellen handed round cups of coffee and put a plate of biscuits on the table. We helped ourselves. Marion asked what this was all about. "We need to get on with this story or put it to sleep. It looks good, the films are good, the evidence seems to add up."

It was my turn, and everyone was staring at me. "That's quite correct, and last meeting we agreed that the next thing

192

would be to try to interview Subrama. However, Julian asked a question at the close of one meeting, and I've been thinking about it."

"What question was that?" Malcolm boomed.

Why does he always boom? Does he think we're all deaf?

"Julian wanted to know what we knew about Zane Pretorius, the man Clint Esterhazy mentioned at the end of the film. We don't know anything much, but it's probable he's important somehow if the men from the plane knew him and were talking about him."

"What are you suggesting?" was Marion's question.

"We spoke about the production team going to Buenos Aires to see Subrama, but I think we should try to find Pretorius and interview him before we see the pilot."

"Look, the figure of 12,000 quid for the trip for all of us to Argentina sounded low to me at the time, but if we all go hunting around America for a bloke we know nothing about, and then head off to Argentina, we're probably looking at nearer 35,000." Everyone nodded in agreement at this comment of Malcolm's, but then Marion spoke: "Do we need to go there to find him, Lynn?"

"I think so. He must be a spook, or a hitman's boss, or something of the sort. He doesn't have a profile or other sort of entry on the internet that I could find. I looked hard. I even phoned the US Embassy and asked to speak to him. They just said no one of that name works for Uncle Sam."

Matt stood up and started walking round the room. "Is it necessary for us all to go? Lynn must go, and she must have

Greg with her. If the CIA don't know she's onto this story already, they will do when we start searching for this Pretorius. I could go if there's a chance of filming an interview, but I can use a camera with a mike, so we don't need a sound engineer. Does Malcolm need to be there for that? No offence intended, Malcolm."

"None taken, Matt. You and Lynn are very experienced and know what works. It may be this fellow won't talk to you, and won't want to be filmed, but at least Matt could set up across the road from Pretorius's front door and knock off some shots if he answers it. Let me know what you get, and when you'll be on the way to Buenos Aires, and I'll send Nic Stark to join you there. We can review the evidence again then, and work out the best way to deal with the pilot."

"Awesome!" was all I could think of.

"It's a lot of money, folks, but this looks like a blockbuster of a story. We'll run with it." Marion was always so decisive. "We'll do what we have to do with this, and let Channel 4 worry about the cost later."

Matt roared with laughter. "Blimey, I've heard everything now!!" We all looked scathingly at him. Not worrying about the money may be a historic development in any TV company, but anyone who roars with laughter in our business is considered an idiot. Can't be true really, as Matt is a genius behind the camera. Hypocrisy rules, OK?

Julian spoke. "I'll ring Channel 4 and clear it with them as soon as we finish here."

Greg said; "When do we leave? I have to warn my old Mum. If I'm away for long I tell her, because I normally try

194

to get up to see her every three weeks." No-one laughed at that. We all need someone to worry about us. Jamie would worry about me, and I'd have to tell him where I was going, but not why it was necessary. No-one needed to remind Greg that he should not tell his mother why and where he was going. "Any idea how we're going to find Pretorius?"

Turning to Marion whilst answering Greg, but addressing them all, I said: "You remember when we were working on that programme a few years ago about Bradley Manning, Edward Snowden and Wikileaks? We were in touch with 'The Guardian' when they broke the Manning story, and one of my contacts there put me in touch with a freelance reporter - Grant Young - who was helping out at 'The Washington Post'. Grant had been in the military and had contacts in the Pentagon and other places, which was why the Post hired him. Pretorius must have some defence connection. Why else would the men from the plane be talking about him? Grant may know something."

Marion said that was good thinking. "He might, unless Pretorius is in intelligence, or something more secretive. Well, we don't know about that, and if we don't go ahead we won't find out. I'll ask Ellen to arrange flights for you, Matt and Greg as soon as possible, and book you into a hotel in Washington for three nights. If you need to extend your stay there it's up to you to fix, but you may be heading off into the countryside to find the man."

"Well, if Grant can't help he may know someone who can, or I'll make more enquiries."

I went to my office, and emailed Grant.

Hi Grant, Long time no see. I'm flying over soon and should like to see you. I need a favour and I'll tell you about it when I get there. Please let me know when and where I can meet you. I shall have an associate with me. Do you mind if he tags along?

Best wishes, Lynn Galloway.

A couple of hours later an email came in from Grant. *Great. I'll see you at home in Georgetown. I'm working all over the place for a while but should be back in a week.* He added his phone number and told me to ring him when we got off the plane.

Having had no success with Rolls Royce or Inmarsat I decided to make some more enquiries. I wrote to a Professor of Aviation at an Australian University with a list of questions about Pine Gap, the US/Australian spy base in the Northern Territories, near Alice Springs. The most important bit said:

I am unable to find out how, at about the same time as the pilot is said to have turned off the transponder which sends identifying signals to secondary radar and Air Traffic Control, the ACARS system also stopped working, as did the transmission of detailed reports to the ground stations linked to Inmarsat. I believe the ACARS and Inmarsat transmissions are on VHF radio, and in the latter case, also via satellite. Could Pine Gap have interfered with these systems, or even sent false messages appearing to have come from the plane?

He replied very quickly with information about ACARS, giving various reasons why he thought Pine Gap would not have done this, and saying:

None of this is to suggest that it was impossible that Pine Gap intercepted a transmission from SEA439, but first, it is unlikely, and secondly impossible to find out without positive evidence about what these installations can and cannot do.

The same might be said about the two other relevant Australian satellite communications monitors at Shoal Bay Receiving Station at Darwin and the Australian Defence Satellite Communications Station near Geraldton.

Ellen had just come in with details of our flights nine days later, the e-Ticket for me, a reservation at the 'The Georgetown Inn', and an open-ended ticket from Washington to Buenos Aires, and a similar one for getting back from there to Heathrow. She said she had fixed Greg and Matt up too.

Immediately I emailed Grant to say I'd see him on the 23rd, as our plane got in quite late.

22nd July, 2015

I had a very good night's sleep after a completely uneventful journey with Matt and Greg. Jamie was not too pleased to learn that I was going away again and I had no real idea how long I'd be gone, but he got over it, and took me out to dinner the night before we flew. That night we indulged three times in a favoured and time honoured way of saying goodbye, so I'd slept well on the plane too. Three times didn't quite make up for what we'd miss while I was away, but some nookie was better than none. And it showed Jamie was his old self again.

I took a taxi with Greg this morning out to Grant's home, an oldish sort of two storey house near the University. We sat in the kitchen with him. His wife, who was willowy and two inches taller than me, with carrot coloured kinky-curled hair, made us really good black coffee, and then went out shopping - for groceries, she said. I thought she probably knew when to make herself scarce.

Before leaving she asked about the hotel, so I said: "It's comfortable, and service is good, but it is huge."

"Sure is. Reminds me of pictures of that monster place at Banff in Canada. Not that I've been there."

"Neither have I, but the Georgetown, with all that grey stone and the pinnacles on the roof, made me think it looked like it'd been brought here piece by piece from Edinburgh."

Grant smiled at her. "Now that's one place we have been, isn't it, Angela?" Maybe I'm mistaken but did the fact that he hadn't introduced her to us mean he took her for granted? He could, with his Brad Pitt good looks, but he saw her to the door, opened it for her, kissed her affectionately a couple of times, waited for her to get in the car, and waved to her as she drove away. "Sorry about that," he muttered as he sat again.

Greg said he didn't expect a man to apologise for saying goodbye to his wife. That made Grant chuckle. "It's not that; it's me - I should have introduced Angela properly. Truth is, I'm a bit obsessed with what sort of favour brings you 3500 miles to see me. So what is it you want, Lynn?"

"Right, Grant. I didn't want to put it in an email, or talk about it on the phone. I think it's a pretty tricky subject, particularly here in Washington ..."

"... Where they're not that keen on independent journos who owe no allegiance to any party, nor to any news baron who prefers to toe the line. That's me, the free thinker!"

"That's me and Exposure TV, too." I paused. "I can't tell you in detail what this is all about. If you don't know you can't tell. If, as I expect, I'm treading on dangerous turf, you don't need to know or be involved."

"OK Lynn, we've all been there, so shoot. I'm all ears, but if there's anything you don't want me to remember, I'm losing my memory as we speak."

"I'm doing a story - or trying to - about an incident some US service men may have been involved in. The name of a man they knew cropped up. I think he's probably related to my story, but I don't know any more about him."

"The name would help." Grant was only pretending to be sarcastic, but it made Greg snort and chuckle. I smiled. "Good one, Grant. Haven't lost your nose for detail, I see. Yes. His name is Zane Pretorius. Have you heard of him?" Grant examined his nails for a few moments, then looked up.

"Can't say I have, but I think a few friends may know something." He fetched a piece of paper and a pen, and scribbled two names, addresses and phone numbers, one at the Washington Post, one at the New York Times. He mentioned another at a magazine I hadn't heard of. Grant explained. "She's a finance journalist at a small but excellent magazine specialising in commercial and business stories.

She gets tips about odd outfits here in town. May be no help at all." I jotted her down but almost discounted her. It didn't seem like a money story to me.

At this point Angela Young came back, so we took them out to lunch at Cafe Milano, about 100 yards from our hotel. We had great Italian food, but stayed very sober. Grant had driven us there. When lunch was finished, I assured him that if ever I could help him with anything, he had only to ask.

When we got back to the hotel I called the reporters, one woman and one man, at the two big papers, but they had no idea at all about Zane Pretorius. It was back to the lady at the magazine. Greg phoned Grant and asked how we could get hold of the lady. Grant picked up the phone: "I'll ring her and see if she's free. Her name's Vivienne Wieniavski." He rang back a few minutes later after speaking to Vivienne. "She said you'd be able to see her at her office in the city not far from the Supreme Court building at 4.30 this afternoon."

Greg and I took a cab to Vivienne's office. It was in a neat small brownstone converted into offices, and was on the top floor of three.

She was a plumpish, fiftyish, homely-looking lady who looked as though she might not be able to add up, but soon showed that she was a fireball of energy and brains. "Don't judge a book by its cover, Lynn," I told myself. She wasted no time either. "Grant told me you wanted some information I might be able to help you with."

"Correct." I repeated what I'd said to Grant about this Pretorius person. "I want to find him and talk to him. I wish I could tell you why, Mrs Wieniavski, but at this stage I can't."

"That's OK, dear, and call me Viv," she said, as she pushed her executive chair away from her desk and rose swiftly from it, crossing the room to a filing cabinet labelled K to N. "I work on a lot of confidential stories too. Makes it hard sometimes, doesn't it, when people won't talk to you unless you tell them exactly why you want the info?"

By this time she'd taken a slim file from the bottom drawer. "I keep most of my stuff in there. OK, someone could break in here and steal it but they'd need to know what they're looking for, and a truck to take it all away." She waved an arm round the room indicating six other cabinets. "There's more of those in my secretary's room, and a room full of old files in a store downstairs. I just don't trust computers. A hacker can break into them and steal everything you've got in an hour, and you don't even know it's gone until they use it, usually against you!"

"You can always keep a computer that's not connected to the internet, type all your sensitive stuff on it, and only connect it up if you want to send it somewhere," I offered.

"Sure, I've thought of that but it could be hacked while you're doing that, or the recipient could be hacked. No. I prefer to get things printed off and deliver 'em. A burglar could just lift the off-line computer, anyway. But that's enough of that dear, and not what you came for." She moved a couple of photos of her husband and family, making room for the file. "This is what you came for."

"What can you tell me?"

"About two years ago I had a tip about a company that didn't seem to do anything commercial, retail, wholesale, financial, industrial, import, export, you name it. It was called Noga Corporation, and it still is. It has offices slam bang in the centre of this city, near all the government buildings. Now, that's expensive, so I figured it must do something. I went there a few times, but no-one would tell me anything, so I got a colleague to keep an eye on the place to see who came and went. After a couple of weeks, he said hardly anyone came or went, but he recognised two or three who did as people from the Pentagon, and the Company."

"That's the CIA?"

"Yes, dear. That's their nick-name."

Viv didn't miss a beat. "Anyhow, that sort going in and out made me think this Noga 'company' " (she raised her hands and made quote marks in the air) "was a sham, and probably a cover for some clandestine government operations, so I lost interest."

Mrs Wieniavski fished around in the file a little and found a sheet of paper and a photo. "This colleague of mine was a bit of a terrier - never let anything go." She was studying the paper as she spoke. "Before I took him off the job he'd seen a guy coming and going from this place quite a bit. He followed him a couple of times, and got lucky once. The man came out, got into a cab, so Kalvin got one straight away and said 'follow that taxi', just like a movie."

Greg and I chuckled politely at that, and she went on. "The guy went into a tailor's. Kalvin went in too, and pretended to look at ties. He actually bought one! Don't think he's ever had a tie before. Anyhow, his quarry went off with an assistant to be measured up for a suit, so Kalvin asked another tailor about cloth and how much a suit would cost, and looked at some patterns until the guy came out, paid a deposit, and left."

Mrs Wieniavski handed me the photo. It showed a tallish, swarthy looking man, early middle age, with a neat beard, very well dressed. His hair was very dark. He looked Middle Eastern. The lady continued. "When this man had left, Kalvin said to his helper he thought the guy was wearing a really nice suit, and he'd maybe like to get one like it. The shop assistant said: 'Ah yes. Mr Pretorius. He dresses very well. A lot of his clothes are very light, for hot countries'. Then the tailor giggles and says: 'He calls himself Zane Pretorius III. Sounds like a king of some place. Bit pompous if you ask me.' Kalvin put it all in this report," she added, flicking the paper with a bright green nail, giving more of a lie to the homely impression I'd formed earlier.

Greg asked: "If you're not working that story any more, could we have a copy of the report and the photo, please?" He doesn't often say anything in such meetings. I'd been just about to ask that myself, so I said: "Yes, please. That would be very helpful."

Mrs Wieniavski rose from her chair again, saying: "Sure," went to a door in the corner of the room, handed over the report to someone and asked them to copy it. Coming back to the desk she handed Greg the photo and told us she had several copies. She wrote something on a note-pad, and tore it off, which she handed to me as a girl brought in our copy report. "That's the address of Noga Corporation. Best of luck. They don't talk at all."

She showed us out, and as we got to the outer door, she stopped and said: "Noga sounds sort of Japanese, but I figure it's just the last four letters of 'Pentagon' put back to front. Is that a clue? Or is it a clue?"

***

That evening Greg and I dined with Matt in the hotel restaurant. Matt had spent the day sight-seeing. We all had an early night, but I typed up my notes on the new lap-top before sleeping, and I decided to write to the Australian Transport Safety Board which had played a big part in the search for the plane. This is what I wrote:

22nd July, 2017.

Dear ATSB people,

Please can you help me? I am trying to understand what happened to SEA439.

I understand the transponder which identifies the plane to ATC and military radar was turned off at about the time it was supposed to cross from Malaysian airspace into Vietnamese airspace. Then the ACARS system ceased to work, and so did the Inmarsat system. SEA439 did not make its usual ACARS transmission at 02.37 am Malaysia time. A couple of pilots tell me that they cannot explain the failure of these systems, since, so far as they are aware, they can't be 'turned off'. **Is that the case? If not, how are they turned off?**

One of them suggested that a circuit breaker could have been pulled. **Is that possible?** *I understand that the device which broadcasts messages to Inmarsat via ground stations and satellites, by VHF radio, is connected to the engines, the* doors, the fin rudder, the tail-planes, and the ailerons, the object being to report the performance of the plane particularly with regard to safety. No-one has said in any report I have seen how it could be 'turned off'. **What sort of device is actually sending the messages? Where on the plane is the broadcasting equipment situated?**

After 2.37 am when the Inmarsat messages stopped there were 'heartbeat' or 'handshake' connections only between the plane and the ground-stations. It was those handshakes which enabled calculations to be made by Inmarsat and the Australian CSIRO indicating the plane may have gone down in the Southern Indian Ocean West-South-West of Perth. There was a mysterious unscheduled partial handshake at 09.19 am, and there were two unanswered mobile phone calls to the plane, but no-one has said what the purpose of those was.

I have been unable to find your report on this matter. I had hoped it might answer my questions. **Perhaps you would be kind enough to email me a copy of it and draw my attention to any passage which explains these points, if any does so.**

I am also very puzzled about this: Once the transponder was off, radar could not identify the plane, and neither could ACARS when that system ceased to function. **There can therefore be no certainty that the plane did turn round above the South China Sea/Gulf of Thailand. There can be no certainty that the plane that was traced by primary radar (just blips on the screen) was in fact SEA439. Are those two statements correct?**

If the answer to that question is "Yes," the following arises. **In that case all the Inmarsat and CSIRO calculations are based on very wild assumptions, are they not? If so, why the conviction that the wreckage is in the South Indian Ocean?**

Inmarsat has a number of satellites permanently orbiting the earth, which can be 'spoken to' by devices ranging from handheld satellite phones to radio equipment fitted to ships and aircraft. This does not say exactly what 'devices' are referred to, nor how or why they can stop working for proper signals but can still perform the 'handshake' function if they receive a heartbeat from the ground station. **Can you please tell me the answer to that?**

I regret the length of this email, but I need to resolve my problems with this disaster and the 'solutions' offered so far.

I look forward to a detailed written reply as soon as possible so that I can study it carefully.

Yours sincerely,

Lynn Galloway, Journalist, Exposure TV, UK.

I also wrote to a Doctor of Philosophy in wireless telecommunications, whose article in a learned magazine I had come across. The article was titled "Interpretation of Inmarsat/SATCOM Signals in the Hunt for SEA439," and said he was at the Australian Department of Science and Defence. In a nutshell my questions to him were directed to the question: *"When the precise turning point (if there was one) of the plane over the South China Sea has not been ascertained, how can you be certain from the subsequent signals where the plane went? After that point, aren't all the calculations based on assumptions?"*

I prefer to get something in writing before trying to set up an interview on something as technical as this.

***

Next morning at ten I went by taxi to Noga's offices. Greg followed separately and stayed close by. He always seemed to carry a book, and sat in a cafe from which he could see the entrance to Noga. We didn't want to make anyone suspicious if two of us went around together. Matt went wandering again.

Noga might be in an expensive area of Washington but inside the place was bleak and utilitarian. I told the receptionist I wanted to see the manager; she said: "You mean the Chief."

I said: "That sounds about it. What's his name?"

"She, not he, and I don't know her name. She's just the Chief to everyone. What do you want to see her about?"

"I'm looking for a man called Zane Pretorius III. I believe he works here. Do you know him?"

"Sorry, no; I've only been here a few days."

The young woman went down a corridor behind her counter, knocked on a door, and entered. When she emerged she was followed by a tall gaunt woman with an unbelievably unfashionable bee-hive hairdo, dressed entirely and severely in dark grey with a black scarf tied round her neck and tucked into the top of a buttoned up white blouse. She was very tall, at least five inches taller than me, and in her fifties. She gave me a very frosty glare, and did not offer to shake hands. "And who might you be?"

I told her who I am and what I do for a living. She turned up her nose and sniffed as if there were an unpleasant odour in the room. "And you want to know about James ... er ... what was it?"

"Zane Pretorius III."

With no pause for thought she said at once: "There is no-one of that name here, and never has been. You may go." And she walked away back down the corridor. As her door closed the receptionist whispered: "She's like that to everyone." As I left I noticed above the reception desk one of those blue hemispheres stuck on the ceiling which have a continuous security camera behind it, and when I went out of the door into the lobby there was another. So I was on film, and if they were CIA they now had my picture, if they didn't have it already. After all, to them investigative journalists are only one step above terrorists and foreign spies, or maybe right below them.

I found Greg in his cafe, and got a coffee. I asked him to go back to Noga, as they did not know him from Adam, and see if he could do any better. He departed, and I went back to the hotel and up to my room to write up more of this story.

***

About half-past five Greg was back. He was smiling. He told me he did not go into the offices, as that was likely to be a waste of time. He waited around nearby, strolled up and down, sat on a bench reading his book and a newspaper he bought, and looked at his watch a lot as though waiting for someone. He had a rucksack with him, containing a complete change of clothes, changed in the toilet of another cafe where he had a bite of lunch, and left the bag with the waitress for $10, to collect later.

He'd seen a young fellow go in and out of Noga's door a couple of times, so he waited up the road a bit for him to emerge a third time. This chap came out again as the office closed and turned in the direction Greg was standing, so he walked towards him, and as they passed Greg said: "I'm Joe Gormley, do you work in that place you came out of?"

The young chap laughed and said: "Hey, Gormley, that's the name of an old Brit trade union leader, ain't it?" Greg agreed. "Coincidence; no relation."

The American said: "Learnt about him when we were doing the evils of socialism at High School. I'm Shaw Bradford. What can I do for you?"

"Like I said, do you work in there, for Noga?" Greg asked, as they shook hands.

"Sure do."

Greg took out the photo Mrs Wieniavksy provided. "This bloke is a friend of mine. He was in the US Army when I was in the British Army and we met in Iraq. I've lost touch with him, but I heard that he worked here. His name is Zane Pretorius..."

"The third," Shaw Bradford added. "He's on leave for a while. Got a place up in Vermont, back of beyond. Near a village called Lowell, I think. I don't have the address, but there's not many folks in Vermont. You'd have to ask around."

Greg leaned back in his chair. "So how did I do Lynn?"

"Bloody marvellous. Odd he spilt the beans so fast, though."

"Maybe not. After all, it's not *supposed* to be a secret organisation, is it?

"True. Now all we've got to do is get from here to Vermont, find a speck of a tiny village, looking for a spy no-one knows. Dead easy."

"Dead right. All the hard work's done. I've got the tickets here." He pulled a travel agent's envelope out of his pocket. "Tickets for Delta Airlines for you, me and Matt from here to Burlington, Vermont at 8.30 am. A hire car from Hertz - actually a Toyota 4 wheel drive - is ready and waiting for us when we get there."

"Why a 4 wheel drive, Greg?"

"It's about 60 or 70 miles over winding roads in the Green Mountains, and I doubt this Pretorius lives right in the village. The travel agent told me it's a great tourist area, so beautiful, only about thirty miles from Lake Champlain, but the village used to be the centre of a huge asbestos mining industry, and people still worry about the health risks, so I reckon a bloke who's not a local but just wants to get away is going to live out of town in a hard-to-find spot. We need a vehicle that'll get us there, Lynn. That's if we find him."

"We'll do our best. You know, I can't help wondering how that young chap could be so indiscrete as to tell you about Pretorius. He didn't even ask to see your ID. He surely won't last long in that job."

"We all need a bit of luck sometime, Lynn. It was my day to get lucky. But him? He'll be very fortunate if his balls aren't being wacked around a golf course if they ever find out that he talked to me."

24th July, 2015.

About 10.15 this morning, having got up at 6.00 am, we walked out of Burlington Airport to our waiting Toyota, Greg got in the driver's seat, and off we went into the most gorgeous mountain scenery. Autumn was under way. The trees and leaves were every colour from fading green through pale yellow to dark reds and browns. If it hadn't been for the sky, it was like a rainbow with the blue and violet part of the spectrum omitted. But the sky was blue with a very few fluffy balls of cotton wool hovering about the tops of the hills, and it got cooler quite fast as we ascended from the valleys. It was stunning. I was glad we had come even if we couldn't find Mr Pretorius. Even Matt, who never seems to be impressed with anything, was gasping at the views.

We drove up through Cambridge and Johnston, where we stopped for lunch. We hadn't intended it to be a slow drive, but we just had to stop every now and again to take in the scenery. The roads were pretty winding; fast driving was only for lunatics, and Greg is no lunatic. Matt took some private photos, some with me and Greg in them, which he said he would share with us later. I could see Matt winning some photo magazine prize such as the Pirelli Tyres calendar was awarded when I was a gleam in Dad's eye. How do I know about that? Dad was very proud of the 1967 copy hanging on his study wall.

At 4.00 pm we arrived in Lowell. We hunted around for a place to stay for a while, but struck lucky at a place in Mountain Drive. We all had a shower, and at six went out to eat at a restaurant on Pope Road. No-one in the B & B, nor anyone in the dining room, knew the name Zane Pretorius, with or without the III. Greg showed them the photo, but they said they'd never seen the man. We went for a stroll feeling a bit down, but Greg cheerfully suggested that if our Zane was really CIA or connected to them, he probably kept himself to himself.

"So we might never find him!" Matt chipped in.

It was getting cold, so we went back to our bedrooms. I'd been sitting up in bed for about an hour reading a John Le Carre novel when there was a knock on my door, so I got up, and just poking my head round it, saw Matt. He said: "Prctorius must eat, so if he doesn't cart all his grub up here from Washington, he must go to the local store."

"Good one, Matt. We'll start there in the morning."

Part 3. Noga and Exposure.

25th July, 2015.

After an early breakfast the three of us walked out of the B & B aiming for the village store. It was a crisp morning and at that altitude our breath misted in the air. The store was on the main road – Highway 100. It was a large shop, with a white sign painted with a rainbow selection of coloured letters spelling out 'Lowell General Store'. Like the emporiums portrayed in cowboy films, the place displayed something of almost everything you could think of from boots and brooms to tea and towels. It had a big section devoted to car and tractor parts, modern things not to be seen in the westerns, but there was a farmer in blue overalls, check shirt, cowboy boots and cowboy hat at one of the counters.

We picked up some pre-packed sandwiches, crisps, apples, bananas, and bottles of water. As Greg went to the till to pay, I saw him take something from a rack. I took the photo over to the farmer. He was tall and thin and very weather beaten. He looked down at me along a very aquiline beak of a nose; he looked like a bird of prey. I asked him if he knew Zane Pretorius III.

He looked me up and down for a few seconds. "Who wants to know?"

"I'm Lynn Galloway. I'm a TV journalist." I held out my hand, and he ignored it.

"What d'yuh want him for?"

"I'm trying to put together a programme in which he might be an important link. Do you know him, please?"

He sniffed loudly and swallowed whatever that effort had brought forth. "Ain't never heard of him, lady."

I showed him the photo. "Nope, and I ain't never see'd him afore, either. And we don't care much for news people in these here parts, nosin' into everyone's bus'ness."

"Thank you. How very kind." Actually I didn't say that, much as I wished to. Instead I said: "I do understand. I'm sure there are lots of secrets up here." I walked over to the till where Greg was collecting his change and the store-keeper was putting our purchases into a cardboard box. Greg asked him about knowing Pretorius.

The shop-keeper, a small, overweight, jolly looking fellow, wearing a baseball cap on back to front, replied: "Can't say I do, Mister, but what does he look like? Most folks round here come in my place for supplies now an' agin."

I held out the photo, which he took and looked at carefully. He looked up and said: "Yep, I know the face. Seen him a few times over the last two years or so. Think he must have a cabin up in the woods on the west side, towards the Lake. In fact I saw him two days ago. He came in for milk and bread and stuff. He's got a black Land Rover Discovery." He turned and shouted across the store: "Hey Nat!"

The surly farmer turned round and strolled across to us. "Where's the guy live who drives that big black Land Rover he keeps so clean? He's up your way somewhere, ain't he?"

The farmer looked down at me. "That who you're looking for? Why didn't yuh say so, lady?"

"Sorry, but I didn't know what sort of vehicle he had or even if he had one." That made Nat and the store-keeper laugh, and the farmer said: "Ain't no-one can survive round these parts without a vehicle, less'n he rides a horse. This guy ain't local so I don't mind telling yuh where he lives. Yuh go north from here a couple miles. There's a dirt road on the left, and yuh drive up there. After half a mile yuh don't take another turn to the right but go straight on for another couple miles. Don't turn right there, neither. That goes to my

214

place. Go straight ahead for another mile or so and there's more turnings but I don't know which one he lives up. I know he lives up there somewheres 'cause I sees him driving up there or back down here past my turning."

Nat turned to the shop-keeper. "Don't think he lives here year round, does he Jude? Just a holiday place?"

"Guess that's right. He don't come in here very often. Never in the winter. Usually spring and this time of year. He sort of looks foreign somehow, don't he Nat?"

"Sure does. Once I heard him talking outside here on his mobile in some foreign language. He talks English like he's from Boston or thereabouts, though. A bit like you, lady. Yuh know what I mean? Kind o' classy."

We thanked them and went outside, where Matt had a camera out shooting the street scene. "Thought it might help set the atmosphere for the programme, Lynn. When we get it."

"Thanks, Matt. I think we'll get it alright. Let's go. Let's see if we can nail Mr Pretorius."

An hour later, having driven past the turning to Nat the farmer's homestead, and explored two turnings on the left and one on the right, we drove on another mile up the main dirt track when it came to an end at a gate. No house was in sight. I got out and opened the gate, and we drove through. Greg was very alert and cautious. He spoke quietly: "Look, we're pretty sure this chap is CIA or something like that, and he almost certainly won't want to talk to us. We'd better walk from here, so he's less likely to hear us approach."

215

"Good thinking." I turned to Matt. "Bring the Canon Camcorder, not the tripod and stuff. When we see the house, sneak into the trees and make your way to a place opposite the front door so you can film him if he comes out. I don't want him to see you. He won't say a thing then."

"Except 'fuck off'. So you're OK with secret filming for this one, Lynn?"

"Got to be. I can't see me asking him if it's OK to do it. He'd just slam the door in my face. Or draw his pistol."

"That'll be fun." Greg was unmoved. "He'll probably do that anyway."

"And use the long-range mike."

"Oh, thanks Lynn. And there I was thinking I'd never done this sort of thing before."

I apologised, Matt pulled the camera from the back of the Toyota, fixed a special mike to it, and we set off. After about a quarter of a mile a sturdy log cabin hove into sight. It was still cold, and a wisp of smoke rose from the chimney. An immaculate black Rover Discovery was parked to the right of the house, and a man who was clearly the chap in our photo was chopping logs with a felling axe in front of the porch steps. Matt had stepped off into the trees as soon as we could see the house, and I was sure the man could not have seen him.

When we were about forty yards away, the man looked round at us, and Greg called "Hello."

Pretorius, for it was clearly him, put down the axe, and took a few steps towards us, brushing his hands together as if to remove dust or wood chips. "And just who might you be?"

He had an educated American accent, almost English, like Franklin D. He smiled disarmingly.

I put out my hand as I advanced and Pretorius shook it. "I'm Lynn Galloway, and this is Greg Armstrong. I'd like to talk to you, Mr Pretorius." The smile vanished.

"What makes you think my name is ... what was it?"

"Pretorius."

"No, I'm Adam Dennis. And what does Lynn Galloway do that brings her up here?"

"To answer your first question, I've been talking to some people I know down in Washington. They told me who you are. As to the second, I'm a reporter with a British TV company, 'Exposure'." Was it my imagination or did he actually flinch slightly at that? He certainly looked hostile suddenly. He started looking around.

"I see. I have nothing to say to you. This is private property and you're trespassing. I want you to leave immediately." He started towards the porch steps and went up them. Greg and I followed, and went up behind him. "I want to talk to you about the disappearance of Flight SEA439 from Kuala Lumpur and ..."

I got no further. As I spoke Pretorius reached through the open front door. I thought he was going to lean on the door-frame to deny us entry, but he brought his arm back with a rifle in it, and fired it expertly and fast into the trees. Before he could fire again Greg grasped the barrel, kicked Pretorius's knee-cap really hard, pulled the gun away and threw it as hard and far as he could out into the yard.

"You're going to meet your maker for that, you mother-fucker," Pretorius groaned.

Greg smiled. "Well, you won't do it without a gun and on your own, Sir."

I was shaking. "What's happened to Matt?"

"If he's the fucker who was using a camera from over there, I hope he's got a bullet hole in his face. Now get the hell out of here." Pretorius moaned a little again as he struggled to his feet.

"You weren't thinking of going out there for your gun, were you, Sir?" Greg kicked him again on the same knee and down he went to have Greg's shoe applied twice violently to his scrotum. Swiftly his hair was cruelly pulled back as a knife appeared in Greg's hand and at Pretorius's throat as if by magic "You just sit there quietly for a while, Sir, and we'll do as you say and leave."

Leaving just then was not what I had in mind. "What did you have to kill all those people for?"

"What makes you think I'll tell you?"

Greg stepped on the man's thumb with his right foot. Pretorius screamed. "Sorry sir; that was an accident. If you help the lady there'll be no more accidents, and you've got four rather nice fingers next to that thumb." As he said this Greg leaned forward putting more weight on his right foot and the thumb, and sliced gently with the knife-blade in the area of the agent's larynx.

Pretorius groaned, almost a scream. "I'm not saying anything, mother-fucker!"

Greg brought his left foot down violently like a guardsman on parade coming to attention at Buckingham Palace. His foot crushed the fingers. This time Pretorius really screamed. Greg smiled again through his hungry tiger expression. "Torture's no fun, is it sir, no matter what President Bush said? What other persuasion would you like?"

"OK. OK. We had to take two scientists from Iran and China prisoner to stop weapons grade uranium getting to Tehran. The passengers and crew were just collateral damage."

That hungry tiger looked came over Greg's face. "Your thumb might be collateral damage. The people on the plane weren't collateral; they were murdered on your say-so. Over 200 of them. Nine of them were British."

"So fucking what? The US of A is the only country that matters."

I took Greg's arm and pulled him back before he could be even more violent. "That'll do, Greg. He's given us what we want. Let's go and find Matt."

We backed down the steps, and as we crossed the yard, Greg retrieved the rifle, fired into the tyres of the Land Rover, emptied the magazine, and threw the bullets into the trees. He picked up the axe and smashed the back of the head down on the barrel of the rifle and threw the kinked weapon back to the porch.

Pretorius's yelling pierced the still, cold air. "You'll learn nothing about that plane, you bastards. That plane has gone for good." He pointed at Greg. "And don't forget, you're dead!"

By now we were close to the trees and could hear what must be Matt fleeing through them. He would not have been able to film or record those last remarks, but he should have the rest.

I laid a hand on Greg's arm. "Where did the knife come from?"

"Bought it in the shop. Really good. Our friend was lucky his head didn't come off."

The Same Day, in the Log Cabin.

Pretorius hobbled to his land-line phone. Mobiles were no use up here in the mountains, surrounded by trees. The nearest connection zone was down by the village store.

"Noga."

"Give me the Chief. It's Pretorius."

"OK Mr Pretorius, sir."

"Just do it fast."

Hardwick came on the line. "Chief."

"Ethel, I've got a couple of English TV people to kill; they just came to my fucking cabin."

"Don't use that sort of talk with me, Zane; you know I can't stand it. A Brit came to the office a few days ago. So why've you got to eliminate them?"

"One of them kicked me, twice. Stamped on my hand too. That's the main reason. And they wanted to talk to me about SEA439."

"Fucking hell!!" She paused. "And don't laugh! Your foul language is catching. Where are they now? Can we catch them?"

"How do I know where they are? Getting away from here as fast as possible, wouldn't you think?" Pretorius thought a moment. "Well, they must be in a car, but I didn't see it. They walked up the track. I couldn't follow them. I couldn't walk, let alone run, and the bastards shot all my tyres out."

"These Brits were *carrying*?"

"Don't think so. The bastard who kicked me grabbed my rifle. I'd just tried to kill their camera-man."

"So they've got you on film? Jesus, what a mess!"

"I guess they flew into Burlington and hired wheels there. They'll take the car back there, so get on to the Police. Have them look for the Brits at the airport. The girl's Lynn Galloway and the thug is Greg Armstrong. She's about 5 foot 6, and maybe 125 or 130 pounds. Dark red hair, and quite a looker. He's about the same height, about 170 pounds, English sport coat. He's very fit, fast and dangerous. There's the camera-man too. Didn't get a good look at him."

"Galloway – she's the one who turned up here. We got onto her details. She flew into Washington a few days ago from London Heathrow, and she's got return tickets back the same way. We'll keep a check on her at Washington Foster Dulles and Ronald Reagan in case they swap flights."

"Better look at Thurgood Marshall, Baltimore, too. Can you get an alert out to all the other international airports? Just in case?"

"I have done this sort of thing before, Pretorius. What about you?"

"I'll get out of here as soon as I can get a ride."

The Same Day, on the Road.

When we got back to the truck a few minutes later, Matt was lying on his back on the ground, breathing fast and heavily. I knelt by his side and felt his chest. "There's no blood, Matt. Are you OK?"

"Just about. Shocked more than anything. Haven't run like that in thirty years." He was panting stertorously between every short sentence. "No-one's ever taken a pot-shot at me before, either. I was looking through the aperture on the camera. Saw him raise the rifle. I'd seen him catch sight of me just before he went up the steps. Managed to dodge behind the tree, but he hit the camera."

"Oh, Matt! Have you lost the film or the sound?"

"Jesus, Lynn. I could've been bloody killed, and you're worried about the film? You can be a nasty piece of work and no mistake."

"OK, sorry, but you say you're just about OK, and you're clearly not dead. It's the film we came for, and I don't want to lose it."

"And I don't want to lose me either. Anyway, the camera's just got a dent in it, so you can sleep easy."

Greg stood by the driver's door, holding it open. "Come on, children. Let's get out of here before that bloke comes down the track with another gun."

There was silence in the car until after we passed the General Store. Greg broke it. "They'll be looking for us at the airport, so we must go somewhere else. If they don't catch us at Burlington in the next few hours they'll put out an alert at all the airports. Pretorius knows we're English. He couldn't mistake Lynn's accent for anything else. Nor mine, perhaps."

Matt was breathing normally by now. "So where do we go?"

"There's another airport down at Bennington. We go there as fast as we can, and hope we see no traffic cops. They'll search the big airports, thinking we'll go straight back to England."

I said: "I want to go to Argentina. I really don't want to go back to see Marion yet. I want to get to Subrama before Pretorius or his people do."

"So what do we do?"

"Here's the plan, Matt." Thank God for Greg. "We get to Bennington and with luck find a private charter, fly to Toronto, get a plane out of there to Jamaica or somewhere they won't be looking, and then fly to Buenos Aires. I don't think they can put out an alert for us internationally. You're a well-known reporter, Lynn. No-one would believe we're terrorists. And Pretorius or whoever he's talking to may not even think of it."

I felt a good bit happier. "That's pretty good. We'll have to chance it." I turned on my mobile. "I don't have a signal here. Should get one in Johnson or Cambridge though. I'll see if I can find a small charter plane at Bennington and hire it now."

26th July, 2015.

Today we flew into Havana, Cuba, getting here at 12.30 in the afternoon. I'd found a small airline in Bennington called 'The Small Airline'. The pilot, who was also the owner, joked that it was called that because his name was Glen Small, but he hoped it would grow to be a big airline one day. He was a big chap, belying his name, with long black hair tied in a bunch of Afro style plats. At first glance he looked as though he'd fill his Cessna on his own, but there was room for us.

He said it would be $1500 to fly us to Toronto, and he wasn't into smuggling so we'd better not have any drugs and things like that. Greg assured him we hadn't, gave him cash, and asked him to fly under any radar until we were over Canada. Small was adamant he couldn't do that. He said he needed to file a flight plan, so we gave him some slightly altered names to enter into the passenger manifest, to throw any Police or Immigration officials looking for us off the scent. We promised another $250 on arrival as he probably realised there was something dodgy about us. He asked no questions, so we told him no lies. We threw all the gear into his machine, and took off.

We slept in Pearson Airport in Toronto all night, Small's Cessna having landed us there really late. Before we tried making ourselves comfortable for hours on the recliner seats in the Business Class lounge, I telephoned Marion Gorman and got her out of bed in the middle of the night. I explained briefly what had been happening, and asked her to get our assistant producer, Nicola Stark, on a plane to Vulture City (our code for Buenos Aires) as soon as possible. I told Marion I'd send an email to tell Nic we would be at the Sarmiento Palace Hotel, which I'd looked up and booked as soon as we got into Toronto Airport. I didn't want to give that away over the phone either. She asked: "What about a fixer? You'll need one." I told her I'd already engaged Bernardo O'Higgins.

I chose the Sarmiento because it was near Avenidas Belgrano and Moreno. I knew the team and I would be within easy reach of Subrama from there, and that it would take Nic at least two days to get there. Marion made no fuss; she would fix it immediately. She added: "Channel 4 have made us another big payment. Still very enthusiastic."

I was speechless, and could barely mutter "Fantastic. Good bye."

Whilst I had not wanted Nic with us for dealing with Pretorius, Subrama was a different proposition. We'd stood little hope of an interview with Pretorius, and the more mob-handed we were when we met him the less chance we stood. As it worked out, there would have been more of us for him to shoot at.

Subrama was the vital piece of my jigsaw; we might get only one chance. We needed as effectively shot an interview as possible. It would be the highlight of the programme and story.

During this call to Marion we called Subrama 'Bader', being a pilot, but not the one in question. For us Pretorius's nickname was 'Purple'. These were the code names we had been using from the outset of this project in emails and phone calls.

I checked my emails. I'd heard nothing from the Phd gentleman, but there was an email from the Department of Science and Defence in Australia, and one from the Malaysian Team dealing with SEA439. The ATSB had sent my email on to them. The Malaysian email gave me some information, but none of it answered my questions. Didn't anyone know the answers?

The one from the Department of S & D was quite peculiar; at the bottom it repeated what I had written to Dr Hazelwood, PhD:

From: *Lynn Galloway*
Sent: *22nd July, 2015.10.56p.m.*
To: *DSD Group Information*
Subject: *Reports. Attention: Dr.Seamus Hazelwood, Phd.*
Importance: *High*

Dear Dr Hazelwood,

I am no sort of scientist, but I have read your article **"The Interpretation of SATCOM/Inmarsat Signals in the Hunt for SEA439."** *I am very interested in what happened to SEA439. I have been unable to find the answers to some basic questions anywhere.*

The questions are:

Bearing in mind that the precise timing and position of the alleged turning of the plane over the Gulf of Thailand/South China Sea is not known, how confident in percentage terms can you or anyone be that the conclusions in your report are really accurate?

You frequently use phrases such as "a high probability," "a prior probability," "a likelihood," "assumed." If any of these assumptions are incorrect, the results must be different from the reality. **If two or more are wrong, the results would gradually become farfetched, would they not?** *You employ the word 'Hypothesis' at the end of the report, but it does not have the same force as the certainty of Pythagoras's theorem.*

The most puzzling phrase of all is in column 3: "... the SDU is believed to have undergone a power cut..." **Is there any proof of that?**

The SDU is the device which sends messages from the plane to the ground station. **Can the SDU or the SATCOM terminal be interfered with, either by the pilot, or, for example, by an external computer system, bearing in mind that it is all computerised?**

Column 1 says: "... at 18.19.30GMT the plane's secondary radar went off-line." Did the pilot turn it off? You make no comment on how it happened. As I understand it the secondary radar is the type which identifies the plane to Air Traffic Control and to the military. Your report goes on: "As evidenced by Malaysian military radar, the plane .... then veered off course unexpectedly, ..." The military radar is the earlier sort which just shows a blip on a screen but does not identify the plane in question. **If that is so, how can anyone**

227

be certain beyond a doubt that SEA439 is the one that was seen flying back across the Malay Peninsula, and out past Penang, where it disappeared from radar altogether?

If they could still identify it from the blips, and see it turn after the transponder was off, they must know exactly where it did so, and at exactly what time. If they do not know that, then the calculations all start from a false premise.

I put these questions to the ATSB. They referred me to the Malaysian SEA439 Investigating Team, which, in a reply headed "Unclassified," referred me to their website and reports, but said nothing relevant to my enquiries. However, I came across your article. It is odd that in a case where the whole world wants to know what happened to the people on the plane, someone may be keeping information 'Classified'. **Do you know the answer to that? Have you seen it?**

I am also puzzled that the Northern Arc towards Turkmenistan was rapidly abandoned because no crash site had been found, and no-one had claimed responsibility for a terrorist hijack. They are not the only explanations for its possible disappearance northwards.

I look forward to hearing from you.

Yours sincerely,

Lynn Galloway, Journalist, Exposure TV, UK.

The reply from the Department said:

From: *DSD Group Information*
<information@dsd.defence.gov.au>
Sent: *25ᵗʰ July, 2015.14:21*
To: *Lynn Galloway.*

228

Subject: *RE: Reports. Attention Dr Seamus Hazelwood, PhD. [SEC=UNCLASSIFIED]*

UNCLASSIFIED

Dear Ms Galloway,

Thank you for your inquiry and attempt to reach Dr Seamus Hazelwood, PhD.

Department of Science and Defence is not the lead investigator into the disappearance of Malaysian Airline flight SEA439.

Please contact the Australian Transport Safety Bureau for more information.

Regards,
DSDG Information Team.
information@dsd.defence.gov.au

I replied at once as follows:

Dear Information Team,

Thank you for your email. If you read the penultimate paragraph of my email of 15th September you will see that I had already been in touch with the ATSB, which told me nothing. They sent my email on to the Malaysian Investigating Team which replied with some information, but did not answer my questions.

The heading "Sec=Unclassified" on your email suggests there is more information - secret information - that is not available to the public.

It is, to say the least, extremely odd, that having written and published a learned paper on this subject, Dr Hazelwood is not allowed to answer questions arising from it. It is very suspicious.

Yours faithfully,

Lynn Galloway, Exposure TV, UK.

The Malaysian reports make it clear that they are interim reports until the plane is found, when a full report will be issued. They don't really tell anyone anything worth knowing. They do not say what they know so far, or what anyone else involved in the investigations knows or may have told them. If the plane is never found, will the relatives of the missing, or the public, ever know the truth? Isn't that on its own incredibly worrying and suspicious?

This morning we found an Air Canada flight to Cuba leaving earlier than the ones to Jamaica, which had been my first idea. We searched around and Matt found the ticket office for Copa Airlines offering tickets for this afternoon from Havana, stopping in Panama, and then making for Buenos Aires. None of us had heard of them, but I looked them up on Wikipedia and elsewhere, found they were quite old, well established, had about one hundred planes in their fleet, and belonged to a big consortium of top airlines. We decided against getting tickets for Argentina there and then in Toronto. I didn't want to give anyone a clue where we were going ultimately. The Americans probably thought we'd use our tickets back to Heathrow, as Greg had said. We definitely weren't going to use tickets from Washington to Buenos Aires.

We took off for Havana. It was an uneventful flight. On arrival, when we were waiting in the Jose Marti International Havana departure lounge, I asked Greg why he thought we had been so lucky. He replied: "I've been thinking about that. I may be wrong, but if you're right about what happened to that plane, let alone two hundred and fifty people on it, the last thing the CIA would want is to have anyone asking why they're looking for us. 'Exposure' would put it out everywhere, and even American news-people would be alarmed about their own safety. The Russians would have a field day."

Meanwhile Matt went to the Copa ticket office and bought three one way tickets to Buenos Aires from Havana. We took off from there in the evening for Panama, where Copa is based. It was almost a three hour flight. We had to wait almost 24 hours for the flight from there to Argentina, so we left the airport for a sleep in an airport hotel, where I typed up my story as usual.

28th July, 2015

The flight to Ezeiza Ministro Pistarini Airport, Buenos Aires, was just over seven hours. By then, despite the sleep-over in Panama, we were all absolutely knackered. We had had no trouble in the airports. No-one queried our passports or identities.

Straight away we checked into a hotel on the fringes of the airport, had a meal, and went to bed.

***

Pretorius had waited in the cabin all day, and heard nothing. He phoned Noga.

"Chief."

"Hi, Ethel, it's Zane."

"Look, we've got nothing on these three Brits yet. We've been waiting for them to use the return tickets to England we know they have, but they must have got on a plane or train going somewhere else. We looked at Burlington Airport and they didn't fly out of there, but they had hired a vehicle there. The FBI got onto it with the Vermont State Police and found the car at Bennington. Where they went from there, no-one knows yet."

"What about little outfits in Bennington?"

"They thought of that, Zane, and asked around, but there's one or two there do smuggling and other illegal flights for cash, and they don't talk. We don't have enough on them to force them to come clean. The passenger manifests were looked at, but none of the names tied up."

"So is someone checking other airline records?"

"Sure, but have you any idea how many airlines there are operating in the US of A? Hundreds. It takes time."

"OK. Keep at it. And check flight plans, too. They should show names of passengers. I can't stay here with nothing to do. I'm coming back to Washington. I got the local garage to fix my tyres."

"Did you say 'Keep at it'? Are you giving me orders, Pretorius?"

"No, Ethel; you're the Chief. I'm just an Indian."

29th July, 2015. Buenos Aires.

When I got up I phoned Bernardo O'Higgins. He said he'd kept Ramanos in his sights, and he was still at the same address. I asked him to meet us there at 11.00 am. If there were any trouble we'd need someone who spoke fluent Spanish, and he could get hold of Senorita Valladolid to represent us legally if necessary. This could end up in Court somewhere. Actually, what worried me more was the thought that if Subrama's English was not as good as I believed we'd have no-one to help us with Malaysian. Maybe Bernardo knew someone.

The three of us - Matt, Greg, and me - were at the airport to meet Nic Stark off the plane at 9.00 am. She said she wasn't tired. "I'm one of those lucky people who just go to sleep as soon as the plane is airborne, wake up for the food, and go back to sleep again. I even slept in the airport when we changed planes in Mexico."

I was glad to hear that. "So we're OK to get going?"

"Yeah. I can put up with being smelly and a bit dirty for a few more hours. I'll clean up when we go to the hotel."

"Right, we'll go to Bader's." In the airport we used his code-name, as we did in any public place.

We got into our hire car, with Matt's gear in the back. Greg drove as always. We got there a bit early, but Bernardo was waiting outside Subrama's in a slightly battered old Seat which would attract little attention – typical O'Higgins anonymity.

I asked Bernardo to go to the door of Subrama's apartment as he could speak to him in Spanish to start with, so he might not be too alarmed. He seemed to be at home because his Mercedes was parked outside. The TV team waited in the lobby and O'Higgins ascended the stairs and knocked on the door. When it opened the detective said: "Buenos Dias, Senor Ramanos." He went on in Spanish to tell Ramanos aka Subrama that he had a lady with him who would like to speak with him. By that time, I had run up the stairs, as the pilot was telling Bernardo in very poor Spanish that he did not welcome visitors without an appointment.

At that moment I arrived on the landing outside Ramanos's door, with Greg following. "Hello, Muhamed, do you remember me?"

"I do not know you. Why should I? My name is not Muhamed, it is Cristobal Ramanos." He tried to slam the door, but Greg already had his foot in the way. One look at Greg was enough to deter Subrama from further resistance, let alone violence.

"I'm sure you remember me. We've met before, years ago, at my friends Nick and Liz Carter. I know you're called Ramanos here, but you were Muhamed Subrama then. You were a long haul pilot, like Nick." I saw him react to Nick Carter's name.

"You are wrong. I am not a pilot. I have never been a pilot."

"I believe you have. Why don't you let us in? It could get embarrassing talking out here where your neighbours might hear. You don't want that."

I took out of my pocket copies of Clint's photos of the plane, and a photo taken by Matt of Pretorius. I held them up.

"I think you know this plane, and this man." Subrama's eyes nearly popped out when he saw Pretorius's picture. He immediately stood back from the door and gestured for us to go in. Greg waved to Matt and Nic to come up and stood in the doorway to make sure they got in. Then he shut the door.

Subrama looked defeated as he dropped like a stone into an armchair in his lounge, which was, as his landlady had told Bernardo, beautifully and expensively furnished.

I sat opposite him. Matt started to set up his tripod and put the camera on it. I asked Subrama: "Do you mind?"

He shook his head despondently. "How much do you know?"

I showed him the photo of Pretorius again, and said: "I've talked to this man." That was true, of course, but only just. "I've talked to two men from Diego Garcia who took the photos of the plane. I showed one of them a newspaper photo of you as you looked before 9th March last year, and he saw you get off the plane. One of them knew a plastic surgeon was brought to the island, and that was for you. I've got films of those two telling me all this." That was perfectly true. I pointed to Matt. "This man took the films and the photo of Mr Pretorius."

"He is not Pretorius. He tell me his name is Mr Dennis."

"He was lying to you, Muhamed. We know his name is Zane Pretorius III. He is with a company that is part of the CIA." Subrama frowned, obviously shaken.

By this time Nic had directed where she wanted Matt to put the camera, so that he could pan between me and Subrama easily. Quietly I told her I did not want her to move

235

our pilot, as he was upset enough, and I wanted nothing to put him off. She agreed, and suggested that if he wanted to get up and move around, she would let him. Nic told Matt that if necessary he should have the shoulder camera handy so he could film with that as well if Subrama did get up.

Surprisingly Matt agreed. He said the content was more important here than artistry, and he'd make the best of it.

"Muhamed, we're going to start filming now. We'll record what you say in answer to my questions. I shall say who you are, and who I am, and that you do not have to talk to me unless you want to. You can stop talking any time. I'll say that into the video too. Is that all OK?"

"Before we do that, tell me: how did you recognise me? I do not look like when you met me at Nick's."

"I tell you what. I'll tell you that after I've put the introduction on the record, and you can ask me that then. You can ask me anything else at any time. OK?" Subrama nodded.

Nic said she would insert some photos of the Captain as he looked 18 months ago to explain the change in his appearance. Our film of Gavin's interview would be put in at different points too, as would an actor representing Clint, but we didn't tell Subrama that. We would also use Clint's photos of the plane on the runway at DG.

We started recording. Nic slapped the clapper board. Off we went. I introduced myself and Subrama. I told the camera that I was about to interview Captain Subrama about the disappearance of South East Airways Flight SEA 439 on 9th

March, 2013, and he was not being paid. He agreed, and asked me how I recognised him.

"I'd met you years ago at dinner at friends of yours and mine, Nick and Liz Carter, in England."

The Captain brightened slightly and clapped his hands, saying: "Ah, my friend Nick. Very nice man." Then he relapsed into his sombre mood.

"I recognised your voice when I saw you at the hotel where you often have lunch here in Buenos Aires. Then I saw you use your middle fingers to brush your eyebrows away like this. I'd seen you do that at Nick's." I demonstrated, and Muhamed almost smiled. Then he licked his middle fingers and did it his way. "I saw the train-track marks running down your thumb-nails. I saw your beautiful ruby ring too. You told Liz it was your grandfather's." He glanced down at it. "I thought no-one else could have all of those characteristics: voice, gesture with the eyebrows, thumb-nails, and the ring. Muhamed, I've told you, you don't need to talk to me; why are you prepared to do so?"

"If I tell you, I not know what will happen to me, or to my family. I do not want to tell you what happened."

"I can understand that, Muhamed. You did something dreadful, and you're worried about getting into big trouble. Do you know why Mr Pretorius - Dennis as you knew him – wanted the plane taken?"

"No. He did not tell me, but he made it clear I had no choice. He always had a gun. I did not want to die. I did not want him to shoot my wife and children. I really believe he would if I did not obey him."

I took a deep breath. This was a point of no return. I was about to get the goods or kill the story stone dead. "But you know that over two hundred people died as a result of what Dennis wanted you to do, don't you?"

Subrama went white despite his brownish skin. He held up both hands, palms towards me, as though in a gesture of surrender, and lowered them as he spoke. As the interview went on I realised his English was almost perfect. His main errors were in tenses of verbs. That was understandable in what was, for him, a very stressful and worrying situation. "As you say, I have did - done a most terrible thing, and the memory of it is driving me mad. I am not seeing my children for over eighteen months, and I miss them terribly. I know I was seeing another woman, but I only left my wife because of what Mr Dennis, or Pretorius, said would happen to my family if I didn't obey him. He is very terrifying man. The first time I saw him he had a gun under his jacket. I want to see them all again – my family."

"Do you think that's likely to happen?"

"I not know. I have to be realistic. I have taken part in a terrible crime. I only say that I did it under terrible pressure and death threats to me and my family. If I am arrested and sent to America I shall probably be killed or sentenced to death. Probably sentenced to death in Malaysia or China if I am sent there. I hope if I tell you the truth and do so in Court, I shall be shown some mercy. At least I may be allowed to see my wife and children while I wait for trial."

"How did you know Pretorius?"

"I met him in the Philippines when I was training to be a pilot. He offered me a small monthly income if I would give him information or do things for his company from time to time. I agreed. For years he ever only asked me for details about crew or people on the plane, if I could find out whether they turned up or missed the flight. That sort of thing. Sometimes he asked me about how systems on the planes worked. Boeing could tell him. None of it seem to matter much."

"How did he contact you?"

"Always came to see me. I never know when he come. This time, a few days before the flight, he came. He say if I didn't do what he wanted I would be killed, and my family, but if I did it, he would move me to a new country with a new identity and a million dollars in the bank."

"Why didn't you go to the Police?"

"Too frightened. Police not always to be trusted. When he told me I had to fly the plane to Diego Garcia I knew the Americans were involved, and that meant the CIA. Although he say his company was Nola Corporation."

"Do you mean Noga?"

"Sorry, yes, that is the name."

"I can see that he organised plastic surgery for you. Did you get the money?"

"Yes, I did, and a new passport and identity papers to enable me to live here. The plastic surgeon came to the place where I landed the plane and operated on me there. Then they flew me secretly to the USA covered in bandages round my head. I was kept in a secret military hospital until my face had recovered, and then they put me on a civilian plane and flew me here to Argentina as Cristobal Ramanos. They already rented this flat for me, but in my name. They still pay the rent."

"What did you do after Pretorius came?"

"I never landed at Diego Garcia before, so I try it out on flight simulator I have at my home. I could only do this because Pretorius give me information about the airfield. You cannot find that sort of thing about the island on the internet or anywhere else. Is a secret place and no-one can go there unless they are from the American or British Forces, or work for them on the island."

"Yes, I read somewhere about the simulator. So what did Pretorius tell you to do?"

"I shall tell you, and it was all the things Pretorius told me to do. When we took off, it was all normal and straightforward. I had a very good co-pilot, First Officer Sirigur, but he had not flown one of these 777s as pilot before. He had only just recently finished his training on them, so I said he should do the take-off. That mean I had to talk to ATC."

"That's Air Traffic Control?"

"Is so. We shared all the pre-flight checks and duties. When we reached our correct altitude of FL350 feet I told ATC we were at the right height."

"What is FL350?"

"Is the pilot's way of saying 35,000 feet." Subrama paused a moment, and then went on. "Sirigur was busy piloting the plane, and had much to do checking all the dials and control systems for the top of climb figures, selecting the auto-pilot, adjusting the auto-throttle for cruising speed and power. And the fuel. That is most important, to see we have no fuel leak. The fuel used in the take-off and fuel in the tank must be same as the fuel we loaded. While he does all this, I get out a special thing that look like a pen which Pretorius gave me. Sirigur is still busy checking instruments and I tell him to look up some figures in the aircraft's technical manual. I hold my handkerchief to my face, hold my breath, and say 'Look at this'. Sirigur, he look round. I press the end of the pen and shoot a cloud of a nerve gas straight into his face. It was a gas like sarin or cyanide, I not sure which, but Pretorius said the Nazis had invented it, and used it to kill Jews."

"What happened to Sirigur?"

"He went like this." Subrama went rigid in his chair with his spine bent backwards, and then he shook violently as if having a fit. I heard Nic mutter to herself: "Awesome!" Out of the corner of my eye I saw Nic smile and give a 'thumbs up' as if to say this was good dramatic stuff. Though I have seen much that is awful in my career I was appalled at this sickening gesture, and found her action very callous. I hoped her whisper had not been picked up by the mike. At the same time, I recognised she was right.

Subrama straightened himself and said: "He died almost instantly. Not so easy to kill him if I been piloting the plane myself." He shook his head in sorrow and a tear rolled down each cheek. "I got out my oxygen mask and put it on until the gas is gone. A little later ground control tell us to contact Ho

Chi Minh City ATC. I replied 'Goodnight, South East Asian 439.'

"Sirigur had a fatal convulsion. What had Pretorius told you to do then?"

"Soon after that I complete all the jobs Sirigur is doing, and I turn off the transponder which sends signals to secondary radar and ATC. Then no-one will know where we go. There is a gap of some miles between one ATC and the next and this is where a plane can seem to vanish. Pretorius, he tell me to turn the plane to port - left - or west, going back almost the way we came. I re-programme the Flight Management System to auto-pilot on my new route. Mr Pretorius give me the coordinates to enter for this route. It flies me back across Malaysia, though further north than Kuala Lumpur, more or less at the top end of the country, and out into the Indian Ocean, between two sets of islands."

"The Andaman and the Nicobar Islands?"

"Is correct. Then I change course again, going West-South-West, which take me to Diego."

"What about the Aircraft Communications Addressing and Reporting System? The authorities say it stopped working, and the SATCOM. How did that happen?"

"I read in newspaper is a mystery. The pilot cannot do this normally, but Pretorius, he tell me how to do it."

"Can you explain it to me?"

"Is tricky. There is a secret switch, maybe only on this plane; maybe fitted by Dennis or his people. Better I do not tell."

"Why?"

"Too helpful to hijackers if it is on other planes. Pilots might say they will fly no more." He paused: "When I turned back from the route to Beijing I was over the Gulf of Thailand, and I tell the passengers to fasten seat belts for turbulence. I press another switch to disable the passengers' oxygen masks. They drop down automatically when pressure in the cabin falls too much as the plane gets higher. Mr Dennis – I mean Pretorius – he tell me to do that. When I push the switch the masks do not drop for the passengers. Then I power up the engines a bit to lift us to 41,500 feet and after climbing for a while I press the switch to depressurise the cabin."

"What does that do?"

"It means there is very little oxygen left in the air and as we get higher the air gets so thin you can't breathe and you go to sleep. It also get very cold, freezing in fact. I was prepared for this as I put my oxygen mask back on, and I had put on two tee shirts under my shirt, and those long pants ...."

"You mean long johns?"

Subrama nodded. "That is the name? Yes, under my trousers, and I had kept my jacket on. I put on the tee-shirts and pants in the toilet at the airport before getting on the plane. I was very hot. Most pilots take their jackets off, and I usually do; not this time. When Sirigur was dead I pulled a beanie over my head and the top of my mask, and put on some sheepskin gloves." I could see that he was getting very agitated telling me this. "By the time we reached 41,500 feet all the passengers and crew would have gone in a coma or dead, so I flew at that altitude for a few minutes. Then I put

243

the plane into a rapid descent to a normal altitude, but lower than the official one of FL350 feet, and turn on the cabin pressure as we went lower."

"Why did you do that?" I was having trouble keeping my hands from shaking and my voice under control. I had never heard a first-hand account of the simultaneous murder of nearly 250 people before. I thought I could hear Bernardo and Greg's breathing getting louder.

"The pilot's oxygen not last all that long, perhaps 70 minutes on full flow, perhaps less. I needed to be able to breathe normally. Also even in extra clothes I would have freezed to death very quick at 41,500 feet. I knew that in the cabin there are some Americans who had some tasks to do for Mr Pretorius, and although they had some oxygen bottles, or could use the passengers' masks, which they could release, these would not last long. Not long enough to fly to Diego."

"And these are all the things Pretorius told you to do?"

"Everything was as he told me." He was really crying now. "I am so ashamed. It is making me a luna .... How do you say?

"Lunatic."

"He must have known the passengers would die if the air was turned off and the cabin depressurised. Very few people have climbed Everest without oxygen supplies."

"Of course, and 41,500 feet is 12,500 feet higher than Everest."

Greg passed me a note so I asked: "Don't planes normally fly at altitudes varying by 1000 feet? Why 41,500?"

"Is correct, but 35,000 or 40,000 or whatever is a height directed by Ground Control. Is a standard altimeter setting. The correct term is Flight Level. You take off the last two zeros, so flying at 38,000 is FL380. No-one knew I was doing this. I went to 41,500. I just needed to get high enough to make sure the passengers all dead."

"Christ!" Matt uttered the rage I felt but dared not express. I hoped that wouldn't be heard on camera either.

"Yes, and The Prophet Mohammed too, may he rest in peace. You must remember Pretorius would kill me and my family if I not do exactly as he said."

I changed tack. "There is a group called Advocate 439."

Subrama nodded. "I have heard of it. Is started by some family and friends of passengers and crew."

"Then you know they were offering a big reward to anyone who would tell them where the plane was or what happened to it. What did you think about that?"

The Captain actually laughed. "I did not think much about it. They offered $2.75 million, but that was a target if they could find the money. They get to about $105,000. Even if they get two point seven five do you think I am mad enough to take it? There is no hope they would keep me a secret. What use would it be that they knew I had killed all those people if they tell no-one? They would tell the police and the world. I never get the money then, but I would hang, or someone kill me. Better they believe I do suicide."

There was a pause. Then I asked: "It's said that one plane communicated with you but could only hear static and garbled talk?"

"What is 'garbled', please?"

"It means it doesn't make sense; lots of radio interference, that sort of thing. They could not understand what was being said."

"Not true. No-one contacted me. I talk to nobody until I was approaching Diego, and then only to get landing directions."

"So those radio contacts would be on the black box."

"Yes. It only keeps the last two hours of conversation. It rewinds and records over the earlier hours. No-one will find out from the black box what happened after we took off."

"But the investigators will hear you getting approach directions from DG air traffic control."

"The black box will never be found. The last thing the CIA want is for anyone to find it."

"Why do you say that?"

"Look, I am sorry but I am tired and need a drink and something to eat. Can we stop for a while?"

Nic immediately called: "Cut!" Matt turned off the camera and mike, and Nic said we should go out to a cafe for lunch. Before I could object Subrama said: "This is not wise, for me to be seen with you. I just want some green tea and I have some food in my fridge and cupboards. I do not cook much but I make some Malaysian dishes."

Matt clapped his hands on his knees enthusiastically. "I love green tea and Asian food. I'll stay here with Captain Subrama, and you lot can go out."

Nic said: "OK folks; two hours."

***

As we walked away from the Captain's flat, looking for a place to eat, I was thinking about Subrama saying that when he turned off the transponder no-one would know where they were. The code Air Traffic Control gives the pilot to enter into the transponder enables the secondary radar systems, as well as ATC, to identify the plane. Once the transponder was turned off, no-one could identify *that* plane for definite, not even the military. It could be any plane which was then seen on radar flying in a generally westerly direction. It would just show up on radar screens as a blip but with no code. If, and I realised it is a big if, that were what happened, SEA439 could have gone anywhere. I had even come across a story that the Israelis had used one plane to fly close below or above another so it was masked by the one radar could identify.

If any of that had occurred, no calculations of the flight path of the plane would mean a thing. At that point I gave up. There was no way I could get evidence to prove that. I didn't need to, anyway, since I knew where the plane had gone, and who had taken it there, and why.

Thirty minutes later Nic, Greg, Bernardo and I were sitting in an Argentinean restaurant, looking rather Spanish with timbered wall linings and wrought iron candle sconces for lighting. We were eating an excellent local version of paella, with a glass of a local Rioja each. Greg had refused to stay with Subrama and Matt, which is what I suggested, as I was worried about the Americans eliminating our pilot, but Greg said he was paid to protect me and Nic. He said it was fascinating, and Bernardo agreed. I was surprised at how glum Nic looked. "What's up, Nic?"

"I'm beginning to have my doubts. I just can't believe the Americans or even the CIA would do this; would murder about 250 people, some of them Americans anyway, just to get three people they wanted. Even if they thought it would stop Iran getting nuclear weapons. It makes no sense."

I could feel myself getting angry. That would do no good. I needed to be persuasive. Or perhaps she would convince me the whole story is fake. Nic is very intelligent. She wouldn't yield to ranting and raving. "That's what I was afraid of when I started, but as I looked into it more, I decided it was just the sort of thing governments will do." I reminded her of the Matrix Churchill case, and how the Tory government conspired to let the company directors go to prison. If they hadn't had such a brilliant defence and the Ministers had not been caught lying about giving the Company licences to sell the arms parts and machines, prison is where they would have gone, for years.

I pointed out that Bradley Manning was sent to prison by a Court Martial, which should be a civilian jury function, with a proper judge, not a bunch of Military personnel who would have no interest in doing the right thing. I said the US could not afford to have him tried by ordinary jurors, who might think that someone who told the truth was a hero.

Nic laughed. "You make it sound like a Stalin show trial."

"Well, what else is it if the object is to get a conviction, not arrive at the truth or justice?"

Bernardo joined in. "My country - Argentina - was a Spanish colony. At college I studied colonization all over the world. I read about the British General Dyer who caused his troops, Gurkhas and Sikhs and others, to fire on an unarmed crowd in a square in India from which there was little chance of escape. At least 370 and maybe 1,200 innocent people were killed or ..."

Nic interrupted. "Yes, it was at Amritsar. But Dyer was forced to resign his commission, and Churchill said it was murder or manslaughter."

Greg now had a go. "Yes Nic, but he wasn't prosecuted. He was made to resign instead of being drummed out of the Army, so he kept his pension and his actual rank of Colonel." Greg paused. "At least there was no cover-up. Although I was in the Army, and proud of it, there are also things to be ashamed of, particularly if you're US Army."

Nic surprised me by beginning to lose her temper. "Why are we keeping on about the Americans?"

I thought she was losing the plot. I tried to be as polite as I could. "It's because we're talking about your suggestion that Subrama's story can't be true. We're looking at the sort of thing governments and armies, and especially American ones, do which may explain why Subrama's tale may be true. That's apart from the fact that the films we have of Gavin Johnson and Clint Esterhazy back him up. And if it's not true, how do you explain that he's not dead, but living here in Buenos Aires."

Nic was agitated, scrubbing her fingers through her short hair. "I can't, but I'm still not sure it's credible."

Very gently Greg came back in. "Let's look at a couple of other things, Nic. In the Korean War, there was a massacre at a place called No-Geun-Ri. About 400 Korean refugees were sheltering in a railway tunnel. The American troops were told that any civilians found in the war zone were to be treated as combatants and shot, so these poor people were strafed by planes and fired on by troops. They were unarmed. No-one tried to find out who they were or why they were there. 210 or so people died or were wounded. Many were children; the rest were women and old men. The US Army made out that the troops had been fired on. The Army knew about it straight away, but no-one made any official report. A Korean bloke fought for years to have the truth revealed; his wife and children had been gunned down there. He got somewhere in Korea but nowhere in America until Associated Press got the story in 1999 – forty-nine years later. The American Forces and Government denied it and the row went on for ages, but eventually AP got all sorts of secret documents telling it as it was.

"The USA never admitted responsibility, and never paid any compensation. President Clinton said it was 'unfortunate', or words to that effect, which was really big of him, but no-one was prosecuted for a war crime."

Nic had calmed down. "Well, it was a long time afterwards, so it would seem a bit hard on the soldiers." She stopped. "On the other hand lapse of time never seems to prevent those suspected of being old Nazis from being hounded and prosecuted."

"That's true," Greg replied. He paused a moment. "You've heard of My Lai?"

"Vietnam, wasn't it? Some sort of a battle?"

Greg smiled with irony. "No battle, Nic. It was March 1968. The Americans had been fighting in South Vietnam for about four years officially, longer in fact. They were there to protect the people from being taken over by the Vietcong and the Communists from the North. At least, that was the official version."

That intrigued me. "What was the unofficial version then?"

"I'm not sure, but I always think the USA goes in for these wars partly because they hate to think that their poor people - a third or more of their population - may get to understand that there are political systems designed, at least theoretically, to create a fairer division of wealth. The other reason is you keep power at home if the voters think there is constantly someone or something to be afraid of, and the defence industries and the oil men make fortunes supplying the Armed Forces ..."

"... while the young soldiers from poor backgrounds go off to die. Sorry Greg, I interrupted you."

"That's OK, Lynn, and true, too. So, Nic, this Company of Yanks was ordered to investigate a village called My Lai where, it was rumoured, the place was full of Vietcong. These soldiers had witnessed their fellows being shot dead, or taken away and tortured by the enemy, and the orders from on high were that anyone in Vietnam could be a Vietcong fighter or supporter. About 700 people lived in My

Lai, but all the young men were out at work, so it was just women, children and a few old men in the village that day. Ironically it was the 13th, not a very lucky day for them. The Americans gunned down somewhere between 340 and 510 of them, depending on which reports you believe. Some of the children had their throats cut, and some of the women had been raped multiple times."

Nic was getting distressed once more. "But these incidents are terrible. If the USA was there to help the Koreans and then the Vietnamese – the ones in the south of both countries – why shoot these people? How can you say that any civilians in a war zone must be treated as the enemy? If you're a refugee, whether you're fleeing from North to South or from South to North, how are you get to safety without crossing the war zone? The Americans never went to fight in North Vietnam, never invaded it, did they? So the civilians in the villages in the South were most likely to be the ones you're supposed to be helping, not shooting."

I had to say something. "You're beginning to get it now, Nic. If you can let your armies do these things, and tacitly approve of them, or worse, defend and deny them, cover them up for decades, you can see that killing 250 more people, most of whom are foreign anyway, may be of no significance to the government at all, as long as it gets what it wants."

Nic was shaken deeply. "Then God help us all." She paused, clearly disturbed. "Maybe this story is worth doing. It'll certainly make people think about it one way or the other." Then she looked up and smiled. "We'd better get back to our Captain and finish filming."

We all had another cup of coffee before departing. Bernardo made a devastating comment. "The best - or worst - of it is that these massacres are just the sort of thing we are supposed to fear from Communists: Stalinist purges of peasants; and the slaughter of Polish officers in the forest at Katin, which was blamed for years on the Nazis."

Greg muttered: "And that's why the West keeps its own outrages secret."

As we walked back to Subrama's flat Nic said something that made me realise just how much more supportive she now felt. "Best of it is, the Australians are still providing the search for the plane. Still, they always do anything the Americans want, no matter what."

***

Back at Subrama's flat Matt and Muhamed had clearly been getting on well. "We talked about our children, my work, his flying, and even had a very sympathetic discussion about Islam and Christianity and their differences and similarities."

"Yes, we didn't even quarrel about that." Subrama smiled slightly as he spoke.

Nic was keen to get going. "You were going to tell us why the black box would never be found, and then we stopped for a break. Can we get back to that, please?"

We all resumed our usual places, Matt signalled that he was switched on and ready to roll, Nic smacked the clapper board, and I started. "Captain, why do you say the black box will never be found, and that the CIA would not want it found?"

"If it was found and had not been altered ... er... how do you say?"

"Tampered with?"

"That is it, tampered with. If it had not been tampered with, you would hear me talking to Air Traffic Control on the island, and them talking to me with American accents telling me how to land. Then the world would know what had happened to the plane, and the Americans could not explain where had gone the passengers."

"What did happen to the passengers?"

"When I left the plane it was about a quarter to nine in the morning. Daylight. Seven men followed me from the plane. Three were in handcuffs, and four were pushing them along. The first three were in ordinary clothing; two of them were dark skinned, almost like me, but more like Arabs, and the third was like a man from China. The other four were all in civilian clothes, not uniforms; they looked European or American.

"I was taken into a building, but soon I was taken out to another building and as we went I could see soldiers in twos or threes moving big black bundles from the aircraft to a huge shed. The bags were heavy, and flopped down in the middle, so I think they were the bodies."

"Do you mean corpses? Whose were they?"

"I mean the passengers, and the crew. I was given food in a second building, and after I eat I was led to the hospital block. I could see bodies still being moved from the plane into the shed."

"What happened to the plane?"

"Still on the tarmac next day, but then something happened to it. It was moved into a hangar. A few days later I saw the wings being taken out of the shed on the back of a big trailer, and they looked broken off, as the ends by the body of the plane were ragged. One wing was longer than the other, like broken off unevenly. Next thing, the wings was driven down to the harbour and lifted by a crane into the hole in an aircraft carrier."

"Do you mean into the hold where the fighter planes go?"

"Is correct. Thank you. Two days later the body of the plane came out of the hangar in the same way. It was broken in half, also very jagged, as if it had been in a crash. Sorry, not in half exactly; the front part was longer than the back, where the tail-planes are. And one of them was snapped off, the starboard one, though the fin was still sticking up. When the bits of the fuselage was out from the hangar many soldiers appeared. They go into the big shed, and bring out the bags with the bodies in. Now they were stiff, as if they had been frozen."

"What did they do with the bodies?"

"Put them into the two bits of the fuselage, which is on two very big trailers. Some soldiers stood on the trailers taking bags from the men carrying them from the shed. They carried them inside the fuselage. Looked like they putting them in the seats. The bags were removed. The windows of the cockpit had been smashed."

"Why?"

"Because they could not put me in my seat dead. I was afraid they might kill me too, but they didn't. If the plane crash into the sea at high speed and broke up, the windows could break and then I might have fallen out in the water."

"And that would explain the missing pilot. I see. These bits of the plane, what happened to them?"

"They were loaded onto a massive grey whaling ship which called into Diego Garcia."

I took the photos of the USS Okinawa out of my lap-top case, and handed them to Subrama. One showed the side view of the whole ship. The other showed the loading bay, the huge access door at the rear of the ship.

He looked at the pictures carefully, and then straight at me. "Yes, this is the ship. It was grey, like this. I think whaling ships are not grey, and the hole at the back is not closed at the top, like this."

"That bit is the deck. How do you know all this? Did you see it all? You surely couldn't have been allowed to wander freely all over the base."

"Sometimes I was taken out for a walk. Also the nurses in the hospital used to talk to me when I was waiting for my face operation, and they used to talk to each other in front of me. Sometimes they talked of things the soldiers and sailors tell them about in a club they used to go to, to dance and drink."

"How did the nurses feel about it?"

"Not sure. Some seemed quite excited about being in a big adventure, but most of them sad. Nurses not glad about dead people."

"What happened to the three prisoners?"

"I do not know. I never see them again, and no-one say anything."

"Thank you, Captain Subrama. You have been very helpful. Just one more question. Apparently there was a SATCOM handshake or ping from the plane to the Inmarsat ground-station at 9.12 am. Is that possible?"

Subrama smiled again for only the second or third time. "Is very interesting. Perhaps the CIA men not know about these handshakes, or not know how to turn them off. Indeed, I do not know if is possible to turn them off. After the SATCOM transmitter on the aircraft is turned off, or stops working, handshakes are sent out by the ground stations, and bounce off the plane. When plane's transmitter is on, it is sending out the messages to those stations. In any case if the transmitter was turned off before the plane took off, Inmarsat should swiftly see something wrong. Also, CIA could only stop the handshakes being sent by Inmarsat to plane by asking them to stop them. Then Inmarsat knows something very strange happening.

"If I crash the plane in the ocean, I do not see how the system could work underwater. The answer for your question, is quite possible that a handshake could have gone back to Inmarsat at 9.12 am. I landed plane at about 8.30am. The engines run for a while after that as I taxi to my berth. Also to keep air-conditioning working for dead bodies;

Diego, it very hot. Aircraft was in open then, not yet in hangar."

With that we wound up the session. We said goodbye to Subrama and told him we would keep in touch through Mr O'Higgins, who gave him his card. He thanked us, and said he was worried about what might happen to him, but felt relief at getting these secrets off his conscience. "I hope I shall now be able to see my wife and children."

I felt rotten. "I cannot promise anything Captain, but I shall see if there is anything I or my TV company can do to help. Take care. I worry about what the CIA may do to all of us."

Once again my notes had to be typed up at the hotel. As with Clint, the notes made no mention of Nic, Matt, his camera, or the film.

29th July, 2015, Noga Corporation.

At 3.00 pm Zane Pretorius III crashed through Ethel Hardwick's door. She looked up with a furious expression on her face; when she saw it was not Shaw Bradford or some other minion but Pretorius she relaxed. She knew he was not afraid of her. She might as well rant at an iceberg.

"Ethel, I've been thinking about what these Brits will do next. The reason they haven't gone to the UK is that they're still this side of the pond somewhere, and I reckon I know where they're headed if they're not there already. Or been and gone."

The chief sat back, locking her fingers behind her head. "Shoot."

"I reckon that's what we've got to do. Shoot people. This female, this Lynn Galloway, she's going to file a story on this, and so much crud will hit the fan we won't be able to see the CIA for mounds of it higher than the Empire State. We've got to eliminate her before she gets the chance to write it."

"OK, we've eliminated people before. That's what Noga is for, so what we do is not easily connected to the agency. Ownership of our little corporation is spread between three of the big six banks, who hold the shares as nominees for other companies who own the shares with the same kind of set up. Some are in the Cayman Islands, Switzerland, places like that, which tell no-one anything. That repeats itself through several structures, making it impossible for anyone to get to the root of it without years of Court filings, and getting past helpful judges here in the States who love their jobs and pay, and won't want to antagonise the government or the voters who put them on the bench, or have the CIA make their peccadilloes public."

Pretorius could barely hide his sarcasm as he replied: "Gee, thanks Chief, I'd never have guessed." Like most of the people at Noga, he was well aware of the Chief's penchant for delivering lectures.

"OK. So where do you think they've gone, these Brits?"

"I've a hunch they've found Subrama, or think they have. If they've found me they've got some very good sources. If they can get Subrama their story is cast-iron; even harder than Watergate after Nixon's tapes came to light."

Ethel's hands descended with a bang onto the top of her desk. "I almost swore then, Zane. We've got to stop her. You'd better get on to our people in Buenos Aires and get them to eliminate her. Find out if she saw Subrama, and deal with him too. But won't she have been filing the story as she goes?"

"Not as far as we can tell. We've been monitoring her emails and we got British intelligence to monitor her phone, but there's never been anything to link her to Subrama. She did go to Argentina earlier this year for a few weeks, but as far as we can tell, it was just to see her guy who got stabbed and robbed there when he went to see a soccer match."

"Right, you deal with her and get on to the Buenos Aires agents, and I'll get more searches done on flights which might have taken them there. Even if she has seen Subrama, no-one else will be able to interview him to confirm the story if he's dead." She grinned. "He couldn't appear in Court, either."

Pretorius nodded. "Cause a bit of a stir if his corpse turned up in the witness box. Better look for flights to London, too. If they've done the business, they may be on their way already. Tell our tough guys in Grosvenor Square as well."

"I hope you mean our gentle, mild mannered agents."

1st **August, 2015.**

Greg, Matt, Nic and I got into Heathrow and grabbed a taxi. Nic caught the tube home. We dropped Matt off at his house in Ealing, and went on to Fulham. I paid the driver off, and with Greg started to cross the road to my home. I was desperate to see Jamie. I was also pursuing a chain of thought that had occupied me on the plane more than once. It seemed unlikely that three men, Gavin Johnson, Clint Esterhazy, and Captain Subrama, should all want to clear their consciences over this matter. I concluded that in fact they all had different reasons and approaches which put paid to what otherwise looked like an odd trio of coincidences.

Gavin had done nothing wrong, but wanted to get the fate of SEA 439 into the open, shouldn't have held his peace for so long, and was willing to face the music. He might be in trouble with the British Army, but he owed no duty of secrecy or loyalty to the USA, and was no longer in the Services. Clint was ashamed of his country's criminal conduct, wanted to get it off his chest. He loved the navy, but was afraid of what the CIA might do to him, so wished to remain anonymous. After Bradley Manning, who could blame him? Subrama was personally ashamed and guilty of what he had been obliged to do under severe duress to himself and his family, let alone the people on the plane. He hoped the revelations might put him in touch with his wife and kids once more.

That was on my mind again as I crossed the road, carrying my lap-top in its padded bag. Suddenly there was a tremendous roar of an engine, and a cloud of smoke from burning tyres as a Jaguar hurtled towards us. I froze, terrified, but Greg, who was following me with my travel-bag, crashed into me with his shoulder, knocking me flying across the road onto the pavement. There was a horrid squelching smash, and as I landed on my back I saw him six feet above the ground, descending head first onto the bonnet of a parked car. Tyres still squealing, the Jaguar vanished up my street towards Fulham Palace Road.

The back of my head hit the ground, and I was a bit groggy, but I got up as fast as I could. Two or three front doors opened and neighbours came out. We all got to Greg at the same time. Blood was running out of both ears and dribbling from his mouth. He wasn't breathing. A woman from a house across the street pulled out a mobile and called for Police and an Ambulance. I didn't think the Paramedics would have much luck with Greg. That was callous, but I was too shocked to understand much except that somehow he was dead and I wasn't.

I was shaking badly and felt sick. The Ambulance arrived first, and quickly confirmed that Greg was no more. That made me feel even worse. I started to cry. I passed out and collapsed. When I came to, the ambulance team - a man and a woman - focussed on me and asked what had happened. They listened to the story, felt my pulse, saw me trembling, told me I was in shock and might be concussed, and put me in the Ambulance. While I was unconscious, Jamie came out to see what the commotion was.

When the paramedics knew who he was they put him in the ambulance with me and took us to Charing Cross Hospital in Fulham Palace Road. I suppose another Ambulance took the lifeless Greg to the morgue, but I was taken to a single room. A young doctor came and I told him I wanted my fiance to stay. Jamie said he was feeling guilty: "I didn't come out when I heard the screaming tyres and the sirens, as I was in the shower. When I got outside there you were on the pavement."

"That's OK, Jamie. You didn't know it was me in the crash." The attempt on my life and the taking of Greg's brought me to tears. I was examined, and told there was nothing seriously wrong with me but I should rest for a few hours, and then go home and rest some more. I had a really bad headache, so the doctor sent a nurse in with a couple of pain-killers, and I went to sleep holding Jamie's hand, and saying: "Being together in hospital is all we seem to get these days."

2nd August, 2015.

Today I was still in bed at 11.00 am when a couple of detectives turned up. Jamie got me up and I went down to the lounge in a dressing gown. They said they were sorry about Greg and what happened to me. I started to cry again; I'd been doing this ever since I woke up this morning. Greg had become a friend, not just a bodyguard. He died to save my life, and I was still tearful at the thought I had nearly been killed. Jamie gave me his hankie, and put his arm round me.

The older detective said he was Detective Inspector Colin Lacey. He gave me his card from SO15, Counter Terrorism Command. He told me most people still think of it as Special Branch. He was about five foot ten, with sandy hair, almost a short back and sides. The officer with him was introduced as Detective Constable Shuttleworth. Lacey said at first blush it looked like a traffic accident, but he'd been called in after Marion Gorman told the Police I had been working on a sensitive international story and it might be something much nastier. I was surprised she had made that call without asking me, but then it was her practice to be concerned for her staff.

I said: "Did she tell you what the story is?"

"No, she didn't. She said she couldn't as it was too sensitive and might affect international relations."

"Too true, so I can't tell you about it either. It certainly looked to me like an attempt on my life, but if I tell you about it, the story will die, and that won't help you to solve this."

"But you seem to be in very great danger Miss Galloway, and we ought to protect you."

"The dead man was a very experienced minder, and he died doing just that. I'm fully aware of the danger, but it goes with the job. The TV company will get me another minder. If I need you I'll let you know. Did anyone see the car or get the number?"

"Afraid not. The taxi driver said it was a green Jag with darkened windows, but that's all, and there are no CCTV cameras focussed on the road in Doneraile Street."

"No-one caught sight of the driver?"

"No. We've no clues at all. Somewhere there's a green Jag with a big dent in the front or the bonnet or both, and we've put out feelers for that. No joy yet." Lacey smiled a very cold smile. "I'm not at all happy with your attitude, Miss Galloway. At the least it's a very serious traffic crime, and at the worst it's a murder and an attempted murder."

"I realise all that, thank you, Mr Lacey, but I'm not lodging a complaint, and did not ask you to call. I could not be more sorry about Mr Armstrong, but my telling you about my story won't do him any good, and will not help you at this stage. What it will do is stop my investigation dead, so that the authors of a much bigger crime, maybe the crime of the century, will get away with it."

"I'll have to consider charging you with obstructing a police investigation and withholding material evidence."

"That's up to you, Mr Lacey. Thanks for the warning. But I'll be in touch as soon as I can tell you what this is all about."

He got up without another word, followed by the totally silent constable, and Jamie showed them out. When he came back, Jamie was cross. "Pardon my French, Lynn, but this is fucking stupid. You won't tell me what this is about, your minder's dead, and you won't even talk to the Police."

"It may sound weird, Jamie, but it's too serious for that. I can get another minder, and I shall be even more careful in future. I want to nail this story if it's the last thing I do."

Jamie swore again, said: "It probably will be," and stormed out, slamming the door, which did my headache no good at all.

I wanted to check another angle I'd meant to look into before. Not long after the plane vanished there was a lot of anti-Malaysian media coverage suggesting that they were hiding something. I'd read during my researches that an ex-Minister in their government claimed he had overseen the building of some state of the art radar system, and that the

Malaysian government and Defence Forces could easily have tracked the plane. This claim puzzled me. Surely, if the Americans, with allegedly the most sophisticated arrays of equipment on the planet, couldn't see where it went the Malaysians wouldn't be able to. After all, unless they had the capacity to build the best stuff, they'd have to buy it, and as far as I knew, the US gadgets were better than anyone's, so where could they get it?

I phoned Nick Carter, who was, luckily, at home and not blowing his trombone at a band practice, his usual pursuit. I put this point to him.

"I don't think it likely the Malaysians have anything to hide. They may have an up-to-date system, but the idea it would beat the Americans is just fanciful. If they were able to do that, the US Defence boys would know all about the plane, and they are saying nothing."

"That's what I've been thinking, Nick. Thanks. Can I quote you?"

"Of course you can. You can film me telling you, if you like, and answering all the other questions you've been bothering me with."

"That's a great idea. I'll get my cousin Spencer to do it too."

"Do you mean Spencer Bunder? He was a First Officer when I was still flying. Get us both in together. Time I caught up with him again. Look, I have a contact in the Air Force. He has a lot to do with air traffic systems, and he'll know more about this than I do."

"If he's prepared to talk, would he talk to me?"

"I'll ask him. If he'll talk to you, I'll give him your number. He's Steve Wharton. He's an Air Commodore."

Nick said goodbye and rang off. An hour later Wharton rang. A real public school voice told me it was Air Commodore Steve Wharton, and that his friend Nick had told him what I wanted. He was brisk and military, speaking in clipped sentences like an officer in an English WW2 film: Kenneth More perhaps.

I told him: "It's very kind of you to ring me. First let me ask this; can I use your name and quote you, or would you prefer it if I say 'I am told by an RAF spokesman'?"

"Don't mind. Name's OK. Not secret info. Just my personal view."

"So what do you think of the allegation that the Malaysians have been hiding something?"

"My opinion? Very unlikely. Any useful information, they'd share it. USA might order them to keep it to themselves. Malaysia's not rich. Couldn't afford such an extensive system it could cover the Indian Ocean. USA is still a massive force in Pacific security and that whole South East Asia region. If anyone has information that's not being shared, it'll be US Defence. Even we don't know everything happening on Diego Garcia, and we still own the bloody place." He chuckled: "In theory." He paused. "Of course, very odd the Malaysian Military didn't reveal immediately that their radar had tracked a plane coming across their peninsula heading west. It was a civil emergency, but perhaps the Air Traffic people hadn't asked them if they'd seen anything. Another thing. If the transponder was turned off, as they say, the military may not have been able to identify it for certain. They say they thought it was a civil plane, they could see it, so maybe they thought it wasn't missing, if they even knew about it. But then I should have expected them to intercept it. All very odd."

I thanked him, and we terminated the call. I put a call through to my cousin Spencer, and put the same questions to him, and got much the same answers as I had from Nick and Wharton. He agreed to be interviewed with Nick.

The allegation that somehow the Malaysian Government or South East Asia Airways had something to answer for seemed more and more fanciful to me. If the Malaysians had kept back information at the request of the USA that was wicked and serious, but it was not the cause of the plane and passengers being lost; it just hampered the search for the wreckage. Marion, Malcolm Broadbridge and I would have to make sure that point was clear in the programme.

I asked Spencer about the accuracy of the recent calculations of the position of the plane crash from the SATCOM Inmarsat data. He said: "There are a couple of points. First, those calculations are based on some assumptions. No-one knows exactly where the plane turned back towards Malaysia, so if the assumptions about that are inaccurate it could throw everything else out. Next, if you look at the official investigation reports, they are full of words like 'assumptions', 'possible', 'probable'. There's nothing very definite you can grab hold of."

"But they say that the calculations are based on the time it takes the handshakes to travel back and forth."

"OK, that's true. But if you do not *know* where the plane was and you just calculate the figures from assumptions, how accurate are your predictions of where it was? For example, there's considerable doubt and speculation about the height at which the plane was flying. If there is an assumption it flew at 35,000 feet over the Ocean, when in fact it was at 25,000, that's a difference of about two miles, which alters the time the handshake takes to travel. What I've read suggests that the plane went up to 40,000 feet or more after it turned, came down to 23,000 feet or so after a while, and may then have flown at about 12,000 feet after that. Those are assumptions too. The difference between 40,000 and 23,000 is more than three miles. Between 40,000 and 12,000 it's about five miles, and between 23,000 and 12,000 it's over two miles, so the calculations can all start and end in the wrong place."

So perhaps my questions to the academics, Inmarsat and Rolls Royce weren't so stupid after all. "Thanks, Spencer. Just one more thing. Do you think the ACARS data could be interfered with?"

"Crikey, Lynn. I don't know, but I guess it's possible. If China can hack into US government stuff and the Russians can hack anybody's phone or computer, it certainly may be possible for someone to use a computer to send false info to a satellite about the position of a plane. After all, the instruments on the planes and the ground stations that send out the SATCOM messages and handshakes are all computerised. They're not state secrets, as all commercial planes have them. And if anyone could do it, do you honestly think they'd tell the rest of the world?"

"So it's just speculation?"

"Afraid so. But do you have a villain for this piece?"

"The Americans could have done it if they wanted the plane to appear to have vanished."

"Well, I suppose if anyone could, they could, but I can't go so far as to say they can or did. You'd need someone from a top university to deal with that, or a college full of them. Or a mole in the Pentagon or CIA. And even if someone says it could be done, or even that it was done, it'll just be denied."

I didn't need experts to prove that. I had the pilot on film. I then entered up my diary on the new computer, and printed off all the new information. I prepared the envelope for Niall.

A couple of hours later Jamie came in. He apologised for slamming out when I wasn't well after all I'd been through. I said I was sorry for holding out on him, but it wouldn't be for much longer, as the story was about to be wrapped up. We had a bit of a cuddle and a kiss, but my head still hurt. He'd walked down to the pub at Walham Green, had a couple of pints, and walked back.

We held each other close and I was beginning to drop off, when I jerked awake. "Jamie, has anyone said anything about Greg's Mum?"

"Don't know Lynn. Do you want me to do something?"

"Yes, love. Please phone Marion straight away. I can't think of the name of Greg's firm at the moment but she'll know. Ask her to tell them about Greg, if they don't know already, and have someone tactful and kind go to see his Mum and break the news."

"OK, Lynn, at once." He started to leave the room but I stopped him. "Jamie, I know you're worried about me. Marion has the address and phone number of Gavin Johnson. Ask her to get hold of Gavin and ask him to be my minder. He's tough and very fit and an ex-Marine. If he hasn't got a job yet, she can ask Greg's old firm to take him on. As he's involved in this thing he might be in danger, too, when we break the story."

"Jesus, Lynn, we're supposed to be getting married, and a secret like this doesn't bode well for our future. Why don't you tell me what it's all about? Why can't we fix the wedding?"

"We shall soon, but not just yet. What I can tell you about the story is I'm on the track of the people responsible for a mass murder, and I think they're now trying to bump me off before Exposure can run the programme."

"Fuck. I guess that's what that cop, Lacey, thinks, too. That's why there was a bobby outside the door when I came home just now. I'll go and make the call now."

I gave Jamie the envelope for Niall, and dragged myself up the stairs to bed. Tense as I was, I fell asleep quickly.

2nd August, 2015. Noga Corporation

"Chief, it's me."

"Yes, Zane."

"I got into London Gatwick last night. This morning on the news they say that yesterday a car tried to run down TV

Journalist Lynn Galloway outside her home, and killed her friend Greg Armstrong who sacrificed himself to throw her out of the way."

"That's bad."

"That is one hell of a big understatement! Mind you, I'm not sorry that bastard's dead. Just wish I'd had a chance to shoot him myself. There's a police officer stationed outside her front door 24/7 now. I've called the Embassy men off, but I want you to get on to them too, and make sure they leave it all up to me. I'm in Grosvenor Square now ordering up their finest to help me. I just hope their finest are better than the jerks who loused the job up yesterday."

"Fine. I'll get onto them immediately."

"And while you're at it, tell them in unmistakeable terms that they are to do exactly as I tell 'em."

"You're ordering me about again, Zane."

"I know, but this isn't your neck on the block. It's mine"

3rd August, 2015

I woke up at 10 am when Jamie brought me a cup of tea and said Marion was downstairs. He brought me a wet flannel, a towel, and a hairbrush. I made myself a bit presentable whilst drinking my tea and told him to bring Marion up. A few moments later she came into the bedroom followed by Jamie carrying a cup for her. He said: "I know you won't want me to hear this so I'll go off to Niall with that envelope. Then I'll be in the kitchen if you want me."

Marion kissed me on the cheek, a thing she had never done before. I was touched.

She told me she had got on to the security firm, Harringtons, and they were sending a director down to Pembrokeshire to see Greg's Mum. She said that Exposure and Greg's firm would split the cost of the funeral when it took place. The autopsy was done and there would be an inquest in due course with a jury as it was clear that what had happened was non-accidental death.

"That's good about the funeral. I'll be up and about in a day or two, and I want to go to the funeral and meet his Mum. He was very good at the job and very good to me. I'm quite shattered Greg is dead."

Marion agreed. "His company are dreadfully upset to have lost him. He was their star employee. They'll all have the day off so his colleagues can go to the funeral if they wish and aren't out on other jobs that can't be avoided. Matt wants to go too, and he can do some filming to go in the programme."

"What did they say about Gavin Johnson?"

"The managing director seemed very impressed you'd recommended the man and would take him on trial as you want him. If he does OK he'll offer him a permanent post. Johnson accepted and will be here later after an interview at the company. His record with the Marines checked out."

"That was fast."

"I told the director that you had to be looked after. He took the very friendly hint that no progress meant no more work for them." Marion paused. "Now, what about the programme?"

"Well, I'm not sure it is just one programme; it might be two, or even three. We've got to remind the viewers what's *known* to have happened to the plane, and all the theories about what *might* have happened to it. Then we need to look at what the experts have been saying, making it clear that they've all been wrong and have just ignored Diego. Then we have to show that that's where the plane went."

Marion nodded. "No problem. We've long interviews with Johnson, Esterhazy, clips of your attempt to speak to Pretorius and of him shooting at Matt, and his little tussle with Greg. We've got a very long meeting with Subrama and interviews with his wife and girlfriend, and ..."

."... we can bring in our own experts, or at least quote them. I've already got my two pilots and an Air Commodore lined up to film. They can also explain the technical stuff. We need an actor to play Clint Esterhazy. And we must kill off any suggestion it's the Malaysians who are to blame in any way, though it is odd that they didn't answer my questions."

Marion nodded. "Certainly. We can refer to the attempts which were made to lay it on them, and say we're satisfied it wasn't their fault, and we get our own experts to confirm it. In any case, that strengthens our argument that the CIA are behind it all. I'll discuss all this with Broadbridge and his assistant."

"Right, Nic Stark. She's very competent, by the way. It should be a good result. I've got to finish typing all this up. I should be able to get back to it today. I'm feeling a lot better.

Good job, as we've got to put all this to the CIA before we can go to air."

"Yes, and you've got to send me the up-to-date reports!"

As soon as Marion left I got up, showered, dressed, had some toast and coffee, kissed Jamie, and got on the lap-top.

At three o'clock Gavin turned up, and Jamie made up a bed for him in the spare room. His interview had gone well. The firm had used up a lot of credit with the Police to rush through a gun licence, and he was carrying a pistol in a shoulder holster. He joked that it spoilt the line of his suit jacket. He'd smartened himself up a lot since I first met him. His shoes shone as though he were back on Parade. He looked more like a successful lawyer than a minder; a very fit and tough looking lawyer, though.

8th August, 2015.

Three days ago Nick Carter and Spencer came into Exposure TV's studios and we did an interview recording all the stuff they'd told me over the last few months.

Today Gavin drove Jamie and me down to St David's for Greg's funeral. His mother was stoical, gave me a hug, and introduced me to her brother and sister and her brother-in law. Their children were there too. So were Matt, and Malcolm Broadbridge. An extremely good-looking well-dressed man introduced himself to me as Alex, Greg's 'partner'. He said that they had been together for some years, but had not 'come out', as they feared it might make life difficult for both of them, as he was a teacher at a boys' school, and Greg's reputation might suffer in the security world. I had had no idea. He laughed and said: "I know you're a journalist. Please treat that as confidential. An item on TV would do me no good at all."

"If it's a secret, it's safe with me, Alex. I took it you didn't mean business partners. Greg saved my life, and I would do nothing you might think would harm his memory, or your reputation." He kissed my cheek.

Greg's boss and Alex delivered very moving eulogies, and after the interment, as we moved away from the grave, I spoke to Mrs Armstrong about Greg in the warmest and frankest terms. In a most dignified way she quietly shed a tear, then held my arm, thanked me for praising her son, and for coming, and gave me another hug. Keeping hold of my arm she asked me who the men near the cemetery gate were. I told her they were Detective Inspector Lacey and a colleague.

"No, dear. I don't mean them. I've spoken to them. I mean the three men standing near that black car outside the gates."

I followed her pointing finger. Two men with crew cuts and black suits looked like they were from some violent Mafia film. The third was in a blue suit with dark glasses and a grey hat with a brim like a trilby or maybe a fedora, but I was sure it was Zane Pretorius III. As soon as they saw us looking they got in a car which started moving off quickly before its doors closed. We did not get the number plate of the Mercedes, but I managed to get a quick photo of it on my phone as they got in, and another as they drove away. I told

Lacey and Gavin. Lacey said the photo could be blown up to see if the number was legible, and to send it to him.

We made our apologies to Mrs Armstrong and left at once. Before we did so Malcolm said he was waiting for me to edit the films and recordings. He was excited.

9th August, 2015.

This morning the phone rang at 9.00 am. Bernardo O'Higgins was on the line. After a few polite enquiries on both sides he let me have both barrels, not in an attack on me, but in the way it made me feel. "Lynn, you need to know that Mr Ramanos, or Subrama, was gunned down outside his home last night."

I sat down with a bang on a kitchen chair. He continued: "I think you're in danger. He was shot six times. No-one saw it. One bullet went into the back of his head to make sure he was dead."

I could not speak. I could hardly breathe.

"Lynn, are you still there? Are you well?"

I managed to grunt that yes, I was still there, not ill, but very shocked. I told him about Greg, and that the event that killed him was really an attempt on my life, so yes, I knew I was in serious danger.

"I had to tell you because this is not likely to get in any English newspaper, and you need to know."

"Thanks, Bernardo. I have a new minder now, and the police have mounted guard outside my house. My fiancé lives here and keeps an eye on me too." I thought for a moment, then asked: "Do the Police there have any idea why Subrama was shot?"

"They cannot work it out. He was not robbed or beaten, just shot very dead. He was still wearing his rather expensive Rolex and that lovely ring. He had a large pile of cash in his wallet, too. For what it's worth I believe he was assassinated to stop him talking. From what you were asking him at the filming, I suspect it was the CIA, and they didn't realise he had already told you everything. I'm surprised they didn't snatch him off the street to make him tell them if you had been in touch. As they shot him like that they'll never know."

"Not until they see the programme! But the Americans always shoot people first, so they never do find out what they could tell them. They shot Bin Laden when he was sitting down watching TV, apparently. They'd already killed his bodyguards. How much might he have told them? Unless they already had him, pumped him for all he was worth, took him to that house in one of the helicopters, and then shot him. I'm sure our SAS would have taken him alive."

The thought they could have kidnapped Muhamed Subrama to get him to talk made my blood run cold. Is that what I'd got to look forward to? I don't go to Church but I have faith, and I prayed silently for God to help Gavin and the Police look after me.

"Are you there, Lynn? It's gone quiet again."

"Thanks, Bernardo, I'm OK. I was just thinking that we didn't get the chance to help Subrama, even if there had been something we could do. He'll never see his wife and children now, and they'll never see him. Sometimes this is a lousy job. People get hurt by it when they don't deserve it."

"Don't punish yourself. Don't forget he helped the CIA murder 250 people. In fact as he flew the plane and turned off the cabin pressure, he actually did the killing. You've got the film to help prove that's what happened. It won't make the victims' relatives happy to learn all that, but many of them hate not knowing."

"It won't make his wife - widow - and kids happy either." We said goodbye and Bernardo rang off.

I went into the lounge. Jamie had gone to work. He'd had a lot of time off because of me. Gavin looked up. "Good Lord, Lynn, you're as white as a sheet."

I sank onto one of the two yellow velvet sofas. Gavin was on the other, holding 'The Guardian'. I told him all about O'Higgins' call. He went to the kitchen and came back with a strong coffee and one for himself. "I'm going to phone Lacey. He needs to raise the alert level here." He left the room. Five minutes later he was back with the phone in his hand.

"Lacey says he can't do any more than he's doing if you won't tell him what this is about."

"Is he still there?"

"Yes."

"OK. Give me the phone. Hello, Inspector." He asked me to talk. A pause. "Look, let me assure you I understand why you don't feel you can do any more. You don't have unlimited budgets, and I'm not a politician, so I don't merit more security. Equally, I can't share the goods with you at

279

the moment. Even if I did, you could do nothing with the information. All the villains in this saga, and believe me, they are villains, enjoy diplomatic immunity. You couldn't arrest them if you tried. They'd be on the next plane, if they haven't fled already, and their government would never, ever, allow extradition."

"Miss Galloway, I can't comment on that. I don't even know what we're discussing, except someone tried to bump you off."

"And not just me. I'm sorry, but that's the way it's got to stay until the story breaks, which will happen any day now."

"I'm not happy, but I'll keep an officer at your door as long as I can."

"Thanks. Did you find out anything about that car at the cemetery?"

"Yes. As you don't share anything with me, I'm not sure why I should tell you anything, but I shall. We enlarged the photo to get the number plate, and traced it to a hire company. They say it was hired on a Russian driver's licence in the name of Brodskovitch. We can't find him, and their Embassy says the licence appears to be a valid one, but no-one can find the man of that name at the address on it."

"Inspector, I'm very grateful. When the story breaks, you'll see how that fits in, but that's all I can say for now. Perhaps you're beginning to see why this may have international ramifications."

"I'll keep working on it, Miss Galloway, in any event." He sounded polite but rather grumpy.

I thanked him, and that was that. I went to the study, typed up my notes, and got Gavin to drive me to Mum and Dad's. I used their printer to print off the notes, and Dad took them to the Post Office in the usual double envelope for Niall.

Just then I realised there was something I could do for Mrs Subrama and her children. I sent an email to Noorida Tiong, the Malaysian fixer who had translated when I met Khadija. I asked her to go and see the widow, tell her what had happened to Muhamed, that he had a lot of money, a flat full of good furniture, and car which should be hers. I even asked Noorida to say that I was so sorry if his death was my fault.

I phoned Jamie and told him I was at my parents', that Gavin was there to protect me, and we would be home in the morning. He'd have to get his own dinner. He joked: "I hope that protecting is all Gavin does." I'm used to that sort of jest, and don't mind too much, since Jamie has been rather sensitive about other men around me ever since I rejected his marriage proposal. The fact we haven't yet got to the altar after our engagement doesn't help him either, but I've just been too busy. Fortunately he doesn't have a problem with Gavin. Jamie finished by telling me he loves me and didn't care about getting his own dinner as long as I was OK. In the light of that, I did not dare tell him about Subrama's death, and in any case, Jamie would not have understood that without my telling him the whole business.

Gavin and I had dinner with Mum and Dad. Afterwards, while Mum and I caught up on family stuff, the two men had a grand time chatting about experiences at sea, as Dad had been in the Royal Navy, and as a marine Gavin had spent a lot of time afloat, too.

Part 4. Revelations

10th August, 2015.

At 6.30 in the morning Mrs Galloway woke Lynn and Gavin up in their respective bedrooms, and they were joined in the dining room for breakfast by Lynn's Father. At 8.30 they all said goodbye before Lynn and Gavin set off for London. He carried the overnight bags to Lynn's Volkswagen Golf, and she had her laptop. She promised to see her parents again soon.

As they drove out of the drive and turned onto the road towards Albury a black Transit van pulled off the verge nearby, and drove along behind them. The passenger in the van took out his mobile, and made a call: "They've just left and are heading your way. We're following."

As the Golf passed round the left hand bend, went under the railway bridge and round the right hand bend the other side of it a large dark red lorry, which was stationary, suddenly reversed towards them, Gavin braked hard, and the van crashed into the back of the Golf, smashing it straight into the back of the lorry. The Golf stopped dead, its airbags exploded and Gavin, who was driving, was trapped between the steering wheel, the back of his seat, and the airbag which covered his face. The impact knocked him out. The same thing happened to Lynn.

Two men got out of the van and one out of the lorry, and ran to the Golf. One opened the driver's door and hit Gavin with a cosh as hard as he could on the top of his head to make sure he stayed completely unconscious for some time.

Because the car did not travel at all after the crash the airbags, which would normally deflate automatically, were only doing so very slowly.

The other one opened Lynn's door, one punctured her airbag with a knife, the other two dragged her out of the car and one of them, seeing she was coming round, knocked her out. The casually dressed men were large and strong, with crew-cuts. One man picked Lynn up and ran to the front of the lorry, jamming her into the seats in the back part of the cabin. The first of the three, using his knife, sliced Lynn's airbag out of the dashboard, and then climbed into the lorry. One man sat in with her, and the other two got in the front. A fourth man, the driver, immediately let in the clutch and roared off down the road. The van and Golf were abandoned where they stood.

Pretorius looked at the airbag. "What the hell are you doing with that?"

"I read somewhere a face leaves an imprint on an airbag, so you can at least see whether the passenger was a chick or a feller. Want to slow the cops down as much as possible, don't we?"

"Good thinking."

At the T junction the lorry turned right and then left into the car park of the village cricket pitch on the heath. It stopped behind some large gorse bushes, next to an elderly non-descript grey Ford Granada, the engine and suspension of which had been 'breathed on' by an expert. It had incredible acceleration and road holding if needed, but looked very ordinary indeed. There was nothing about it to attract attention unless the driver put his foot down. The lorry blocked the view of the car from the club house and grounds, and the bushes cut off the sight of it from the road.

The driver took off his rubber gloves, as did all the other men, and threw them into the lorry. They took new pairs out of their pockets and donned them. The driver took out a key to the Granada and got into it. Two of the men took Lynn out of the back cab of the lorry and put her in the boot of the car. The fourth man was, according to plan, about to torch the lorry, but the driver called to him that a woman walking a dog over by the club house would see the fire and raise the alarm too soon. Number four got in the car, and it drove away at a sedate pace.

Turning right onto the road it drove over the level crossing, down through the tiny hamlet of Brook, and up the hill into Farley Green. The driver turned into the drive of a large 1930s house with a long front garden, well screened from the neighbouring homes, which stood on equally large plots.

Using the remote control as the Granada went up the drive, the driver opened the double garage door and drove straight in, shutting the door behind the car before anyone got out.

The three men lifted Lynn from the boot. One said to the driver: "OK, Mr Pretorius, what do you want us to do with her?"

***

When Lynn came round she had a terrible headache, but she could not move her arms and legs. She thought she was strapped to a plank. She could not see; she was blind-folded. She tried to speak but realised a gag was in her mouth. She was terrified. All she could do was make a grunting sound. A deep voice with an American accent said: "Good, you're awake, so now we can start."

Start what, she thought, but could say nothing, so she grunted again.

"We're going to ask you some questions. The sooner you tell us what we want to know the sooner this will be over, and the less pain you will feel."

Lynn was now so scared she thought she might wet herself. She made a more high-pitched grunt which was really a stifled scream coming through the gag. A hand grabbed the cloth and ripped it from her mouth. She took her first proper breath for what seemed like an age. Her mouth was so dry her tongue stuck to the roof of it. She gasped hoarsely: "I need a drink!"

Water was thrown in her face. "That'll have to do for now lady." She managed to lick some of the water from around her mouth.

"Now get this. We know who you are, and where you work. We know you've been to the States and Buenos Aires, and you've been working on a story about the missing plane,

SEA439. We've got your lap-top, and we think your story is on it. I've tried to get in, but everything is encoded. All you've got to do is tell us the codes to get into the story, and then we'll send you on your way."

"What happens if I don't tell you?"

Immediately the board she was tied to was lifted horizontally into the air; there was a metallic bang as it was rested on something. She couldn't see what it was as the blindfold was still there. Then it was tipped up so Lynn felt her head travelling downwards. Her face disappeared under water. At once she opened her mouth to scream. Her throat flooded with water, making her splutter uncontrollably. As she spluttered some of the water was expelled but more flowed in. She tried to hold her breath. There was hardly any left to hang on to. Her arms and legs convulsed, but could do nothing. Her body heaved, and she was held under water for about twenty seconds, which seemed to her to last a couple of centuries.

She was hauled out of the water. As she came up she realised the plank rested on a bath. The voice spoke again; she recognised it. "That's what happens to people who don't cooperate. You want more, just keep quiet."

After fifteen seconds Lynn recovered her breath and was feeling a little better. She tried to sound brave. "Hello, Mr Pretorius. I recognise your voice from the cabin in Vermont."

A different voice said: "Fucking bitch!" The board rose into the air again, but this time Lynn knew what was about to happen and managed to take a deep breath before the water closed over her head. She held out for 40 seconds but then began to panic and struggle until they lifted her out again. It took longer to recover this time; her breath was ragged and noisy. The men waited.

"Now tell us." It was Pretorius's voice once more.

Between terrible gasping Lynn offered: "That's pretty bad, you know. It's torture."

Another voice replied: "No, it ain't. President George W Bush said so." The men laughed. It sounded as though there were three or four of them.

"Did you know the Nazis used to do this? Is George W a Nazi?" Lynn was amazed that she could be cocky at a time like this.

"Are you gonna share this story with us, or ain't yuh?"

"No."

"Well now, I just think you are." Pretorius leaned down to her, speaking quietly and very menacingly. "Now listen up. We did for your mother-fucker pal who kicked me and stood on my hand, but I didn't have the pleasure of doing that myself, see? So if I tell you I mean to go on enjoying this until you crack, you better believe it."

She went straight back in the water. Lynn knew she could not put up with much more of this. She'd have to tell them how to open her lap-top and access the story. Even if she didn't, they'd have boffins who could eventually, so was she going to die for that? How she managed to think these thoughts as she ran out of breath was incredible, but it helped keep her from panicking again.

As she was lifted out of the water a pair of hands grabbed the top of her jeans, ripped the button, and pulled down the zip. Her pants were ripped off, and her jeans pulled down to the rope around her ankles. A voice said: "Hey, fellers, that's one helluva nice pussy!"

Pretorius said: "OK, guys, forget that, will you? Stick the little electric gadget up her. A dildo it ain't, but it'll certainly send waves of something through her." Someone laughed at the sick joke. A different voice said: "What a fucking waste! Or do I mean what a waste of a good fucking?" Somebody laughed.

This time Lynn screamed in absolute terror. She had read about this. The most sensitive nerve endings in her body would be torn to shreds by increasingly powerful electric currents from the probe until she was a jelly, or died of heart failure.

"I'll tell you! I'll tell you! Just don't do that to me."

Pretorius became soothing. "OK, Lynn, I'm listening. When you've got your breath back tell me nice and slow so I can write it down. It'd better be damn good."

Panting hard, Lynn dictated the codes Sid had told her to use on the new lap-top. A few minutes later Pretorius cheered softly: "Hurrah! We're in, guys. You can send Lynn on her way now."

"Thank God for that. Can I get up now and pull my jeans back up?"

"Sure can, lady," another voice said, as the blindfold was removed from her face. When another had cut the ropes tying her to the plank she stood up but was so shaky she fell over. Two men lifted her roughly and dropped her onto a chair. The ripped pants were useless. Lynn succeeded in struggling her jeans up, but her hands shook so much she could hardly fasten the zip and buttons. She stood up. She found herself staring into the muzzle of a pistol.

"You said you were going to let me go, you bastards!!" She shouted as loudly as she could.

Pretorius looked up from the computer. "You got that wrong, Lynn. I said if you told us, we'd send you on your way. I don't know which way that is, heaven or hell, but you seem like a nice girl, so maybe it's heaven. OK, Jerry."

Jerry Jacobs pulled the trigger, the bullet went straight through Lynn's forehead and exited through a larger hole at the back. Donarski and Hurt caught her before she hit the ground. Peck picked up a sheet and threw it round her and then wrapped her in a blanket of plastic. They picked up the parcel and took it through the house to the internal door to the garage, and put the corpse in the boot of the Granada.

Meanwhile Pretorius made a call on his mobile. "The job's done. We're leaving. Send the cleaners in." Hurt got in the driver's seat, the automatic door opened and the car drove off with its four passengers and a lifeless cargo. The door shut. No-one was worried about the bath full of water, the wet plank, the ropes, the gag and the blind-fold. They weren't even concerned about the blood stains or the bullet in the wall of the bathroom. The highly trained forensic cleaners who would arrive in minutes would obliterate every trace of what had happened in this lovely house.

That was essential. The house belonged to the Embassy in Grosvenor Square, and was used to entertain important guests for weekend house parties, when it wasn't being used for the sort of adventure Lynn had just undergone.

In the driving seat of the Granada Hurt asked: "Where to now boss?"

"I want you to drive slow enough not to attract attention, and fast enough the cops don't think you're pretending not to be drunk. Head for the A3M and go south. That's the road to Portsmouth. When you see the signs for Petersfield, I'll tell you more. It's already getting dark and it'll be pitch black by the time we get there. We're going to park in a pub car park long after it closes, and dump her body. Maybe someone will see it in the morning, but that doesn't matter. We'll be long gone, and you'll be on the plane back to the good ol' US of A."

Jacobs asked: "Won't she have a print-out of the story at home, Mr Pretorius?"

"That's been taken care of. There's nothing there. A team went in when her boyfriend went off to work. Without the computer the story's useless, and we have it right here. She may have been sending bits of the tale to the TV company, but I'm pretty sure they don't have all of it."

11th August, 2015.

The dead body in the gulley spoilt Jane Morgan's day.

Jane always walked through the woods and country paths from her little cottage in Steep Marsh to the primary school where she worked, teaching reception class in Petersfield, Hampshire. She was a pretty girl, with wavy blond hair, but thought herself too much on the cuddly side for five foot five. Her fiancé did not agree. Her route took her down a small road which turned into a farm track after a few hundred yards, and then into a footpath running alongside a gully on her right. Small fields and one or two houses lined the top of a slope rising to her left. The gully looked as though it ought to have a stream in it, but there was no stream, only a puddle or two.

This path ended with a curve to the left, over a little footbridge which crossed a brook, tinkling in the sun, with a very old black and white cottage on her left. However, this morning Jane did not get as far as the cottage. Halfway along the side of the gully she was arrested by the sight of something the like of which she had never seen there before. Down in the bottom of the gully a woman was lying half in and half out of a puddle, face down in the mud, and her feet in the water. Jane was too shocked to move for a minute. She decided at last to see if the lady wanted any help, but her shout went unanswered, so she clambered down the bank, clinging onto branches and foliage, and slithering down when there was nothing to hold.

She spoke to the woman again, but there was no response. Jane could not see the face which was turned towards the other side of the gully, but was sickened by a huge clot of blood on the back of her head, which had been obscured by the dark redness of the dense, thick cloud of hair. The woman was clad in a white blouse and blue jeans.

Jane stepped round the head and still could not see the face properly even from there. Again she felt unable to move for a moment, but plucked up the courage to grasp the left shoulder and roll the woman over a little. Immediately she had to turn aside to vomit into the bank. Recovered, she glanced round again. She had never seen a body in the gully before; she had never seen a bullet hole in anyone's forehead either. How she did not scream she never knew, but clambered back up the bank, mud on her knees and shoes, in no fit state for teaching. She ran across the footbridge past the cottage, as she wasn't sure there was a phone, and headed for the pub a bit further on up the short dead-end road.

The pub was still shut at 8.00 in the morning, but Jane hammered on the door and shouted as loudly as she could. The landlady came to the door. "Hello Jane ..." was all she managed to say before Jane demanded she phone the police at once.

"There's a dead woman in the gully; she's been shot."

"Dead?"

"She's got a bullet hole in her face. I think I'm going to be sick again."

11th August, 2015.

Two detectives from Petersfield Police Station turned up at the pub within 15 minutes of the call from the landlady. Jane Morgan could tell them nothing apart from where she had come from, where she was going, and at what time she had found the body. They could see she was still in a terrible state of shock, and the landlady had given her a cup of tea.

Detective Sergeant Simpson and his side-kick went to the scene in the gulley. He called up the medical adviser from the forensic pathologists, and also a police photographer. Uniformed officers marked off the area as a crime scene. Scenes of Crime experts were going over the ground, taking casts of shoe prints, and measurements of the gulley, the position of the body, taking samples of spots of blood, of which there was very little except on the victim, and searching for anything connected to the murder. All Police personnel had donned white polythene suits and shoes, making it look as though Steep Marsh had been invaded by extra-terrestrials.

Jane was asked to go into the Police Station later so they could take impressions of her shoes to eliminate her from their enquiries. In fact hers were the only footprints going down to and at the bottom of the gulley. Simpson phoned the school to tell the head teacher why Jane would not be in that day. One of the SOC officers found a scrap of white cloth on a spikey branch of a bush halfway down the side of the gulley. He concluded that the corpse had been rolled from the footpath above, where the hard gravelled surface left no trace of walkers or anything else except dog pooh.

The blouse on the body had a tear in one sleeve which probably matched the piece of material. That could be ascertained back at the laboratory.

***

In Fulham Jamie was truly worried. When he got home the previous night from work, he thought it looked as though things had been subtly disturbed, but he dismissed the idea the place had been searched, thinking Lynn must have been looking for something before she left for her parents. However, it was so unlike Lynn not to phone and tell him what was going on that this morning his apprehensions revived, and at 11.00am he phoned her father and asked him if she was still there with Gavin. Mr Galloway said they had left early yesterday, and he thought they should have arrived by now. Jamie phoned Exposure. Marion had heard nothing. She was as concerned as Jamie was, and pointed out that it was only just a fortnight since Lynn had been almost killed outside the house. Jamie snapped: "Do you think I don't know that? Why else would I be so worried?"

"Sorry Jamie, that was thoughtless of me."

"I shouldn't have lost my temper, Miss Gorman. It's that bloody story she's been working on. She won't even tell me what it's about."

"No, she can't, and I won't, not yet. And it seems even more insensitive if I say that we don't even have the whole story yet. She's given us a lot, but I think she must have a lot more to hand over. Let's hope nothing has happened to her."

"You and me both. She's much more important than any bloody story. I'm going to get on to the Police."

***

At about that time Gavin woke up in Hospital in Guildford. The previous day a woman driving from Shere to Albury to work had been unable to pass the Golf and van crushed together just past the railway bridge. She called 999 on her mobile and asked for Police and Ambulance. Gavin, unconscious in the driver's seat, could tell them nothing. The para-medics could see he had had a heavy blow to the top of the head. At the hospital the trauma team feared he had a fractured skull, but could not understand how that could have happened when the air-bag had erupted. He was conveyed straight to Accident and Emergency.

At the scene of the accident an experienced traffic officer looked at the Golf's skid marks, the debris from broken lights and mud from under wheel arches, and the massive damage to the front of the Golf. He formed the opinion that there had been a third vehicle, almost certainly a lorry, into which the Golf had crashed, and the van had driven into the back of the car. The third vehicle had vanished. He could be sure that it was a big vehicle as the damage to the front of the Golf was quite high up. The Golf had some dark red paint in the huge dent in the bonnet. The officer surmised that with luck he would find a big vehicle with some of that paint missing and some of the Golf's on the back of it. The scene was extensively photographed and measured, and the van and car loaded onto a transporter and towed away to a Police compound.

This officer also noticed that both front doors of the Golf had been left open, and the passenger's air-bag had been cut out. The doors had not burst open. The driver could not have opened his door when he was out like a light, so who had? Where was the passenger? And where was the driver of the van? Were the lorry and the van linked somehow? Had the people in the Golf been deliberately targeted?

***

"Is that Detective Inspector Lacey?"

"Speaking."

"This is Jamie Stallard. I'm Lynn Galloway's boyfriend."

"I remember. Hello, Jamie. How are you?"

"Never mind me, Inspector; it's Lynn. I'm very worried about her. She went to her parents two days ago, was supposed to come home last night, and hasn't turned up. She had her new bodyguard, a bloke called Gavin Johnson, with her. She hasn't phoned as she usually does, and I phoned her Dad earlier. He said they left for London yesterday. She should have been here by now."

"OK, Jamie. You're worried because she was nearly run down a couple of weeks ago, right?"

"Absolutely out of my mind. And I think our house may have been searched by someone. It was pretty tidy, but just didn't look right. Can I come in to see you now?"

"Fine. You know the Scotland Yard building?"

"I think so. Didn't I read you've moved to the old building on the Victoria Embankment?"

"Yes, you may have read we're moving, but it hasn't happened yet. I'm working there for a while, and it's still at 10, Broadway, Westminster. It runs off Victoria Street."

"OK, Inspector, I'll get a cab and be with you as soon as possible."

"And I'll send a Scene of Crime team to your house to look for fingerprints and other evidence? Anything stolen? Any signs of a break-in?"

"None at all, except some things had been moved. I didn't notice anything missing, but that doesn't mean it isn't. They must have used a skeleton key or whatever they're called. See you later. They must have come in the back door, as you still have a cop at the front."

***

Just after Jamie rang off, DC Shuttleworth knocked and walked in to Colin Lacey's office. Lacey looked up: "Yes, Peter."

"It's this photo, Gov. It's just come in on the internet from the Hampshire Police. This woman's been shot dead."

"Yes, I see that from the bullet hole in her forehead." Lacey often indulged in black humour rather than goad his juniors. It was invariably his style to be polite to all, whether colleagues, suspects, or members of the public. He was a public servant, so he dedicated himself to serve, not to be a typical film show cop, rather rude and violent at every opportunity. He found it produced results faster most of the time, and didn't upset people he might need as witnesses later on.

Knowing his boss's sense of humour, Shuttleworth smiled and continued: "But they don't know who she is. It's down near Petersfield, some village called Steep Marsh." He pointed to the print-out. "I think it's that lady we went to see in Fulham. You know, the one who almost got killed by a Jag, but it killed her minder instead."

Lacey studied the photo. "You're right, Peter, that's her. Look, I've just had a call from her boyfriend. He's coming in from Fulham by cab, so he'll be here in a short while, but don't tell him about this. Get a car and driver lined up, and we'll take him with us. Find out if there's any point in our going to the scene, or to the mortuary, if they've taken her there."

"Right, guv."

"As soon as he gets here, ask for his keys, give them to SOC, and send them to his house to look for signs of a break-in of some sort, fingerprints, and all that. It sounds like a really professional job if it happened, and it wasn't us. We've got an officer outside the door!!"

Shuttleworth left the room. Lacey got the file on Lynn Galloway and the two week old accident in Fulham from a filing cabinet. He was into it for about twenty minutes when Shuttleworth came back. "There's a car waiting with a driver, guv. Hampshire say to go straight to the mortuary down near Portsmouth, as the pathologist is already on to it, and has more info than the scene can give you. The bloke in charge down there is D. S. Simpson. The body's at Queen Alexandra Hospital in Cosham."

A few minutes after that, a middle aged woman clerical assistant brought Jamie in. The three men shook hands and Lacey asked the assistant: "Could you bring us all some coffee, please Gwen? You got here faster than I thought possible, Jamie."

"I told the taxi-driver I was in a hurry, and promised him an extra twenty for getting here fast. How we didn't get arrested I've no idea, but we were lucky, too. I think we were only halted by one set of lights all the way. If we'd been stopped I was going to tell the cops I was helping Special Branch with some enquiries."

Lacey chuckled. "Smart thinking."

"Have you heard anything?"

"Why don't we sit down?" Lacey took Jamie's arm and led him to a pair of armchairs. Shuttleworth went to a chair by the desk. As they sat the coffee arrived. "I have heard something, Jamie. It seems Lynn has been found down in Hampshire?"

"Hampshire? How? She was in Surrey. What about her bodyguard, Johnson? Have we heard about him? Is he with her?"

Lacey spoke quietly as Jamie was very excited and anxious. "OK. First question; yes, she was found in Hampshire, near Petersfield. We're going to take you down there in a few minutes. Next, we think someone took her there, and it wasn't Johnson. He wasn't with her when she was found. We don't know where he is yet."

Jamie was about to say something when there was a knock at the door and Lacey called "Come in."

Gwen, the female assistant came in. "Excuse me Sir, but I gave DC Shuttleworth a photo a little while ago, and he brought it in for you."

"Yes, Gwen, he did. Have you got something else for me?"

"Yes, Sir. Another photo has come in, and ..."

"OK, Gwen, just step outside with me, please."

Lacey took Gwen out into the corridor and along to another room. She was short and rather dumpy, and her bottom was a good bit bigger than was good for her, but Lacey had lots of time for her. She was very bright, and good at joining the dots. That was why she had the sense to notice the new photo was something he needed to see. He preferred working with older women; less chance of sexual harassment on either side; they worked harder than many of the young ones, too. "Sorry about that, Gwen, but the chap in my office is Mr Stallard, the boyfriend of the woman in that photo. I don't want him to have a bigger shock than the one he's going to get anyway. What have you got there?"

"Two photos, Sir. Surrey Police have distributed them." Gwen handed a picture to Lacey.

"That one's a police photo. There seems to have been a strange accident outside a village called Shere. Three vehicles involved crashed into each other all going the same way. It blocked the road."

"There're only two in this picture."

"Yes Sir. When the Police got there, there was no vehicle at the front; it had driven off. It must have been there because the second vehicle - a Volkswagen Golf - was extensively smashed at the front and there was glass from its lights and windscreen and another vehicle's near-side back lights, in the road. Both front airbags had gone off in the Golf. There was a man sitting in the driver's seat, but there was no passenger. The passenger's airbag had been torn out, and the doors were open. The man was unconscious. The third vehicle - a van - had crashed into the back of the Golf, and there was nobody in the van."

Lacey could see where this was headed. "When was the accident?"

"Yesterday morning. The man in the Golf was taken to Guildford Hospital. He woke up today and told the Police he'd had a woman in the car with him. Her name was Lynn Galloway, and she'd disappeared. He gave them a photo of her."

Gwen handed over the second photo. "That's it, Sir. Hampshire scanned it and sent it out. I thought it looked like the woman in the picture I gave DC Shuttleworth."

"You always get it right, Gwen. What'd I do without you? Thanks. Did the Surrey Police give you the name of the man?"

"They did, Sir. He's Gavin Johnson. He said he's the dead woman's bodyguard."

"Right. I must go back in there. Could you bring us some more coffee? Mr Stallard may need it."

Lacey shut the door softly behind him. He went back to his armchair, and put his hand on Jamie's shoulder as he passed. "I'm afraid I have some very bad news for you, Jamie. The lady who just came in has given me a photo. It's of Lynn. It was given to Surrey Police by Mr Johnson."

"Yes, he'd have been given her photo for ID purposes when he was hired by the TV company. Why wasn't he with Lynn?"

"We don't know. He was found sitting unconscious in her Golf outside the village of Shere yesterday."

"They were staying at her parents. They live in Shere."

"Lynn wasn't in the car." Lacey told him the basics of the 'accident'. "Mr Johnson was found unconscious in the driver's seat. My guess, and it is only a guess at the moment, is that Lynn was kidnapped from the car, and driven off in the vehicle at the front of the pile up."

Jamie reacted sharply and rather aggressively. "Kidnapped? You're kidding me. You just said she'd been found down in Petersfield. So she's OK, isn't she?"

"That's why I said I was afraid I have some bad news for you. You see, Lynn was found in a gulley in a village near Petersfield, and ... There's no easy way to say this, Jamie; she'd been shot dead."

Jamie looked incredulous, looked at Shuttleworth, and back at Lacey. He sat there with his mouth hanging open for two seconds before saying in a bemused fashion, but gradually getting very angry: "What? I don't understand. What do you mean, dead? This is no time for a joke!"

Lacey shook his head sadly. "I wish it were a joke, Jamie. Unfortunately, I regret to say it's true. I can show you a copy of the photo Gavin Johnson gave the Surrey Police, but I don't think you ought to see the last one, after she was found in the gully."

Jamie stood up, went to the desk, and kicked it hard. "Jesus! It must that fucking story she was working on." He shouted: "Just show me the bloody photos, will you?"

Lacey joined him and slid the two photos of Lynn and the one of the accident towards him. Jamie picked up Johnson's ID photo of Lynn and just nodded. Then he picked up the other one; he gasped. "Jesus, Lynn! How could they? They shot her through the face?" He gagged: "I think I'm going to be sick."

"Take him to the toilets, please Peter."

The two men rushed out of the room. Colin Lacey put through a call to Petersfield, and asked to be put on to Detective Sergeant Simpson.

"Hello, Simpson, Hampshire CID. Can I help you?"

"Yes, Mr Simpson, or perhaps I can help you. Colin Lacey here about ..."

"I've heard of you. You're with Counter Terrorism, right?"

"Right. I'm ringing because you've got a dead woman there but haven't ID'd her yet."

"Correct. How do you know?"

"I've seen the photo you sent out. The girl is Lynn Galloway. She's a ... or I should say was, a TV investigative journalist."

"Bloody hell. Thought I recognised her. She does documentaries. I remember one she did on criminal gangs and us lot or something."

"Probably. I shall be coming down and taking this case off you, but I shall need your local help. The reason it's in my bag, not yours, is that she was working on a story which may have serious international consequences. It may be the reason she was killed."

"So it's not the Met horning in on the old country PC Plod this time."

"Far from it. I'm very grateful to you for sending out the photo so fast, and I really do need your help. I have Miss Galloway's boyfriend with me. We'll be setting off to see you in a few minutes, I hope. I understand the pathologist is working on the body now, so I'll go to see him first, and then I'd like you to take me to the scene where she was found."

"OK. I'll meet you at Queen Alexandra's. But if the boyfriend's a suspect you shouldn't bring him with you down here, should you?"

"If he's a suspect I'm Mahatma Ghandi. He can make a formal identification, though I could do that too. No, I think the suspects are probably from a foreign power. I hate to sound accusing, threatening and offensive, but you're the only person in the Force who knows that, so if anyone leaks it to the press, I'd know exactly where to look."

"Don't worry Sir. I'm not offended. I don't do that sort of thing, though I know some as are on a good little earner with the media giving tips. I've always been more interested in catching crims than being one. I'll meet you at the mortuary in Portsmouth in what, an hour an' a half?"

"That's about it, Mr Simpson." Lacey rang off. Two minutes later Shuttleworth ushered a very pasty Jamie back to his chair, and Gwen brought in new mugs of coffee. She spoke tenderly to Jamie. "I heard you'd had to go to the ... er .... been unwell, Sir, so I brought you a glass of water as well. Thought it might be better than coffee."

As she left the room Jamie muttered his thanks and then began to sob.

***

Zane Pretorius III sat at the small desk in his room at the Hyde Park Hotel in Knightsbridge. It was not a grand suite, just a relatively modest room with its own bathroom. The hotel was frequented by a number of American tourists, but was not one of the top flight establishments which attracted the truly rich, famous, or ostentatious. The Hotel did not stand out, and neither did Pretorius. Doing so was the last thing he wanted. He was, as usual, well dressed, but somewhat more downmarket than his usual elegant style. He wished to blend in and be unnoticeable. He had booked in as Adam Dennis a few days ago. He held a genuine US passport in that name.

He took a piece of notepaper out of his pocket, lifted the lid on Lynn's computer, and entered into it the various codes she had been tortured to give him. There were three, and the first two led into files which could only be opened with the next password. Normally rather contemptuous of nearly everybody, he was surprised to find himself thinking that the Brits weren't as dumb as the CIA took them for. The only thing on the screen and list of documents was called "The Vulture." Pretorius opened it and started to read.

At first he was amazed at Lynn's persistence and accurate reporting. Then he realised that she clearly had not written everything she knew in this written record. He was very angry about that. What else did she know? He corrected himself: what else had she known? "We shouldn't have shot her!" he told himself.

She'd identified this bastard Johnson, and even given a pretty good indication of where he lived. Should he be eliminated? Not worth it. He'd obviously been thorough in telling the journalist everything he knew about Diego Garcia. More bodies just meant more trouble. There had been no print-out of these notes in her home where that guy Stallard lived. It may be there was one at the TV offices or studios. Breaking in there would be too obvious. They must have security guards, and if Galloway's body had been found (as it must have been by now), there might even be Police at the studios or offices. Too risky.

He calmed down a lot until he got to the interview with some American sailor. The girl had been clever; this guy did not want to be identified, so she called him Norman in this account called "The Vulture." This geezer needed to be wiped out. The government should have given that Manning shit a final solution instead of locking him up. These traitors who thought it was OK to tell the world of the appalling things his beloved US of A did to people were a cancer in the body of the nation. What did they know of democracy? It could only flourish in the interests of the rich and powerful by deceiving the voters and rarely telling them the truth about anything. Whistle-blowers? He'd like to blow them to hell.

He wanted to kill Lynn all over again. And again. Very slowly and painfully this time. Last time was just playing at it. Did she take films? She didn't up-load them into this lap-top.

However, he had the lap-top, and pretty much the whole story. Pretorius was deep in thought. She could not have given all of it to the TV station. She had had no chance to send off her notes of the last few days, and there were no emails on this thing with which she could have done so. Without the lap-top, they would never know the whole story, and would be unable to make their fucking documentary. "Subrama is dead, so no-one could get him to testify, nor to identify me," Pretorius thought, "apart from her, and she's dead, and the minder's been run over and is dead. There's the guy who was filming me from the trees at my cabin, but without them he can't say who I am. Shame I shot at him if that's on film, but that was Vermont, USA. You can shoot trespassers first and ask questions afterwards back home. That's what I was telling Galloway, that I had nothing to say, and they were trespassing.

"There's the marine, Johnson, but there's no mention of a film of him, he can't identify me, and he doesn't know what we did with the plane and the bodies."

He put through a call to the Chief. When she answered he told her: "I'm all finished here. I've got the jewels from the lady. The price was high, but worth it. There's no story. I'll be on the next flight." Ethel Hardwick just said "Yes, the others are on their way back already."

***

Jamie was feeling better, and Lacey had just proposed that they should leave for Portsmouth and the mortuary when Gwen came waddling in as fast as she could. She looked down kindly at Jamie and then spoke to Lacey. "There's a phone call for you, Sir. A Miss Gorman, she said, and it's about Miss Galloway."

"Put her through. You don't mind, do you, Jamie?"

Jamie shook his head. "No. She's Lynn's boss. She might have some news. It's the story she had Lynn doing that's at the bottom of this. That's about all I'm sure of."

"OK, Gwen, put her through." There was a delay while Gwen went back to her desk and connected Marion Gorman to Lacey. "Hello, Miss Gorman. Can I help you?"

"I hope so. As you know, there are a lot of press and TV people down at a village near Petersfield, where a woman's body was found. I've sent a team down there myself. Talk is that she may be Lynn Galloway. Is it true?"

Colin Lacey thought: "Thank God I didn't put this on speaker-phone. Jamie might hear something to push him over the edge." To Marion Gorman he said: "Normally I'd say 'No comment', but you probably hold the key to this whole business with the story Lynn was working on, so we have equal need of each other. But I need an assurance from you. Do you promise not to publish or broadcast anything about this until I give you the go-ahead? I'll give you permission step by step. This call is recorded."

"It's recorded my end too. You have my word, and this isn't the 'News of the World'."

"OK. It's true. I'm going there shortly with Jamie Stallard to make a formal identification at the hospital, and then visit the scene. Please do not announce it's Lynn yet."

Marion replied in the affirmative.

"Thanks. Now, I'm prepared to tell your station everything I think can be revealed before it goes public, before there's a formal press conference, but I want something in return."

"Try me, Mr Lacey."

"I want a copy of Lynn's story. It'll help me find out why she's dead. She was nearly killed about two weeks ago when Armstrong was run down. It's obvious the story is at the back of it, and she more or less told me so. So did you, but both of you refused to share it with me. Now she's dead."

Marion sounded really serious, and almost distressed. "I'll give you everything I've got in return for the early heads up. I'll go further; I'll give you anything I think might help or anything you ask for, if we've got it. Mr Lacey, you've no idea how much I wish I'd given you the details then. Lynn might still be with us. The trouble is I don't have the complete story. For the last few weeks Lynn didn't send me everything. Maybe she forgot, what with going abroad and nearly being run over. I could scan the stuff she gave me and send it to you, or you could come here, read it, watch the films we have, and ask me any questions."

"Good. I'll come to you as soon as I get back from Petersfield and Portsmouth. What time do you leave the office?"

"I'll stay here until you've been. I feel dreadful about keeping you in the dark before, but honestly, when you see what we think the story is, you'll realise there are terrible international and diplomatic horrors arising out of it. That's what Lynn and I told you before, and I'm sorry to say it's true."

"Give me a clue."

Marion swallowed a slight laugh. "Not on the phone, Mr Lacey. Mine may be tapped or bugged."

"Don't forget I'm SO15, Miss Gorman. If your phone were being tapped or bugged in a case I'm dealing with, I'd know."

"That's the point. It won't be you, or MI5 or 6. I promise I'll tell you all I know when I see you. It may be an ally with whom we are supposed to have a 'special relationship'."

The call ended and Lacey, Jamie and Shuttleworth went down to the Police Jaguar which was waiting for them with a high-level Police driver. On the way to the car Lacey told Jamie: "I'm taking you with me to see Miss Gorman, too."

"You mean I'm not a suspect? That's a relief. I always thought the boyfriend or husband was the prime suspect."

Lacey smiled. "I can't rule anyone out at this stage, Jamie, but if you did it, crashing three vehicles at once, dumping the body fifty miles from there, then getting back to Fulham, and you don't even have a car, you're Superman.

"OK, Baines. We're off to Portsmouth, Queen Alexandra Hospital. Step on it, use your lights and siren when you need to. Get us there as fast as you can. Then we'll be going back to a crime scene near Petersfield. Let's go."

***

Dr Graham Phillips was the forensic pathologist working in the mortuary examining Lynn Galloway's corpse. Her body was laid out naked on a steel gurney connected to running water and the drain. When Lacey, Jamie, and Shuttleworth were announced, he covered her with a sheet. He'd had a lifetime of police officers, who thought they were tough and hardened to everything, being sick in his work-space. Fortunately none of them had actually been sick over the dead, but there was always the possibility.

He told his assistant to let them in. Lacey introduced himself and his two companions. He had not met Phillips before. He saw a short round man with a bald head and round glasses wearing a spotless white coat. Colin Lacey felt he looked more like a chef who ate too much of his own cooking than a man who examined dead people all the time, some of whom would be most nauseatingly mutilated in accidents or acts of frightening mindless violence. His idea of people who did this for a living was that they should be tall, thin, and cadaverous, a bit like the Grim Reaper; even the female pathologists. But they rarely did.

As he shook hands with Jamie, Phillips said: "I'm sorry about this, Mr Stallard. I don't suppose you want to see the whole of Miss Galloway. It's not a pretty sight as a result of the post mortem examination I've been doing."

"No thanks, Doctor. I'd rather remember her as she was - the prettiest sight I've ever seen. I'll just see her face to identify her."

Phillips turned to Lacey. "What about you and Mr ....ah...."

"Shuttleworth. No we'll just see her face too, thanks. I think it's a TV drama thing where the lead detective always goes to see the body. I don't see the point. He can't identify the victim most of the time, though as it happens I could in this instance. And he can't give any useful evidence about the cause of death, which is up to you, Doc."

Phillips agreed, and pulled the sheet back exposing Lynn's lovely face. Shuttleworth actually forgot himself and said: "Gosh, she really was beautiful wasn't she?"

Jamie nodded, groaned at seeing the bullet hole in her forehead, sobbed, bent over her face, and kissed her on the cheek. "That's my fiancée, Lynn Galloway." Then he really started to cry. Phillips handed him a box of tissues. Lacey put his arm round Jamie's shoulders and said: "Sorry, Jamie. Yes, that's Lynn Galloway." Shuttleworth recorded the double identification in his notebook.

The pathologist took them to his office, and they all sat. No-one wanted the coffee that was offered.

"So what are your conclusions, Doctor?"

"Well, it looks at first sight as though she died of a shot to her forehead, and that's in fact what happened. There was just too much blood congealed in her hair for the bullet to have been fired after she was dead."

Jamie stood up. "I'm sorry. I don't think I can listen to this right now," and he made for the door.

Lacey told Shuttleworth to keep an eye on him, and both of them left the room as Lacey said: "Get him a cup of tea, anyway." The door closed, and Phillips continued.

"However, some odd things had clearly happened to her before she was killed. First, there are rope burn marks and scuffing all round her wrists. When victims have been tied up and struggle, the abrasions or bruises usually run all the way round the arm like that."

"What did you make of it?"

"She'd been tied by the wrists and ankles to something, like a board or plank, so tightly that she couldn't turn her wrists over, but she obviously fought hard against her bonds. There were similar marks around her ankles. She has a large bruise on the right side of her face. I'm glad Mr Stallard saw her from the left, so he was spared seeing that. She'd obviously been slapped or punched hard around the face."

"Anything else?"

"Yes, and this is really odd. Her hair was wet, and not from the puddle in the gulley. My assistant says there were traces of chlorine in the water in her hair, meaning it was from a tap. Finally, examination of her lungs showed small amounts of tap water in both."

"Do you mean they'd tried to drown her first?"

"Nothing so simple, Mr Lacey. I did a tour of duty in Iraq and another in Afghanistan. Sometimes I was called in to examine prisoners who'd died. None were drowned, but the lungs of those who'd been water-boarded looked the same. They usually died of heart failure from the strain of repeated submersion. They often had rope burns from the restraints tying them up, too."

"Anything else, Doctor?"

Phillips gave one chuckle. "Sorry, I said 'finally', didn't I? But yes, there was something else. Two things actually. An officer at the scene found a piece of cloth which he thought came out of her blouse. It certainly fits, but I've got my assistant checking it's actually the same sort of cotton. The other thing is the button at the top of her trousers - jeans actually - was torn off, and her panties were missing. Of course, she might not have been wearing any, but I doubt that. I'd speculate that her garments were ripped off with a view to something awful being done to her, probably with an electric shock probe. Or a threat of rape."

"So she was being tortured?"

"Definitely, and the object is usually to extract ...."

."...information; about the story she was working on in this case."

"I see. She was a journalist, was she? You'll be glad to know they didn't get to use the probe, or sexual penetration. There was no evidence of damage to her vagina."

"Mr Stallard'll be relieved to know that, but really upset about the rest of it."

Phillips agreed. "Do you want me to tell him, then?"

"No thanks. We've got a busy day. I'll break it all to him as gently as I can in the car."

"Fine. You'll get my report as soon as it's typed up. By the way, she must have been killed somewhere else, not in the gulley. With that huge wound in the back of her head, she'd have bled all over the place, and the Ambulance crew who brought the body in said there was hardly any blood anywhere."

The two men shook hands, Lacey collected Jamie and Shuttleworth, and after meeting Detective Sergeant Simpson in the reception area, they sped off with him to Petersfield and the gulley near Steep Marsh. There was nothing new to see, and Lacey was content with what the officers on duty told him had been done, and what had been found. He asked them to arrange for Jane Morgan to be brought up to London to see him when she felt well enough. Then he turned to Simpson.

"Look, I know Surrey isn't in your manor, and it's a bit of a cheek my asking you, but would you go to see Mr and Mrs Galloway, the dead woman's parents? They know she went missing, but have no idea what's happened. It needs breaking to them as gently as possible. You know a good bit about it now, and you're clearly a very experienced officer, so ...."

"No problem, Sir. I've had to do that sort of thing a few times before. Got the address?"

***

Jamie could not believe how fast but safely Baines drove them to Lancaster Gate. By now it was just after six, so there was little northbound traffic. Nearly all of it was heading South on the other side of the M3. They walked into Marion Gorman's office at 7.15 pm. She had the TV station's legal adviser, Julian Prentis, with her.

Marion greeted them: "I thought you fellows wouldn't have had anything to eat all day, so I sent out for some pizza. I hope that's OK. Here's a copy of the parts of the story I'd received from Lynn so far. There's a lot of it. You might want to take it away and read it. If you want to do so now, that's OK, but I think you should watch the films we have first."

"Why? Thanks for the pizza, by the way, and can someone get us some water or coffee or something? This is Detective Constable Shuttleworth. And you know Jamie Stallard."

Marion said: "Of course I do, and I'm so sorry about all of this, Jamie." She introduced Julian and picked up the phone. "Thanks for staying late Ellen. Can you please get five cups of coffee, five glasses, a jug of water, and bring in the pizzas?"

She looked at Lacey. "Why the films first? They'll show you very rapidly why this death is so serious. It's linked to the biggest aviation mystery disaster in history. That's what Lynn was investigating."

"You've got to mean SEA439."

"Precisely. The plane didn't disappear. It was taken to Diego Garcia by the CIA. Lynn was pretty sure it was something to do with a Sino-Iranian deal to provide Iran with weapons grade uranium, and two or three weeks ago, a spook called Pretorius admitted it to Lynn and ..... "

"Fucking hell!"

Marion smiled momentarily but was instantly serious. "That's exactly what I said. So you see, the chances of your being able to arrest anyone for this are not just remote; they're pretty well non-existent. My guess is Lynn's murderers are on the plane back to Washington, or already there, and will never be heard of again, buried with new identities in some remote backwater."

Julian said: "Except witnesses in Court is just what they won't be."

Jamie spoke next. "Miss Gorman, you said you don't have all the story. I know she got a new lap-top a while ago. I think she was using it just for this investigation." He turned to Lacey. "Hasn't it been found?"

Lacey shook his head. "Afraid not Jamie. I believe that's what her murderers wanted, and they probably tortured her, as I told you on the way here, to get her to let them into the story."

"You mean to give them the passwords."

"Correct."

Marion started to cry. "You mean that lovely girl was tortured? By the Americans? But they're supposed to be our allies." As Ellen came in with the coffees and glasses, Marion pulled open a drawer in her desk and pulled out a bottle of Glen Morangie. "Anyone need a drink? I know I do."

Jamie and Julian accepted. Shuttleworth looked at Lacey who said: "Thanks, but no thanks, we're on duty and it's likely to be a long night." Then the phone rang and Marion picked up after drying her eyes. "Who is it, Ellen?" She paused briefly to listen, and then said: "It's a Detective Sergeant Simpson for you, Mr Lacey."

Lacey took the phone: "Yes Sergeant." After a minute he said: "Thanks. Goodbye." He turned to Jamie. "That was the Detective from Hampshire. He called on Lynn's parents and broke the news to them. He said he was as gentle as possible, they took it stoically, but he thinks you might go and see them as soon as possible."

Jamie nodded. "I shall. I need to see them anyway. They've always treated me like a son."

"Simpson said he's also liaised with Surrey Police, and they had a report about a stolen lorry being found on the cricket pitch between Shere and Albury. It was damaged at the back, with some of its red paint knocked off, and traces of paint which seemed to be from Lynn's car embedded in it. There were some hairs in the back of the cab which Simpson said look like Lynn's. He'll take them to the pathologist to check."

"Any evidence of who did this?"

"Afraid not. No fingerprints, no hair, nothing that would help. Going back to Lynn being tortured, Miss Gorman, it's only my opinion, but when it boils down to it, I don't think the Americans really have any allies. They act only in their own narrow interests. Now here's what we do. It's 8.00 pm now. I'll watch the films with Jamie and Peter, here, and you prepare a broadcast for the news. It's at ten o'clock, isn't it?"

"Yes, what do you want us to say?"

***

Niall Merrylees sat on the sofa in the lounge, put down his book, and told his wife, who was just off to bed, he was just going to watch the news and then he'd come to bed too.

"Good evening. This is Janice Walsh with a Channel 4 News Flash on 11th August. Today is a very sad day here. Many of our viewers will be familiar with the award-winning work of journalist Lynn Galloway who used to work for the BBC and then for Exposure TV, where she made a lot of programmes for us. Lynn was found dead this morning near Petersfield, in Hampshire. She had been shot. It seems probable that her death is attributable to the story she was working on for Exposure TV and for us. It is extremely unlikely that she committed suicide. The Police are investigating the matter which is in the hands of Detective Superintendent Colin Lacey of Counter-Terrorism who will hold a press conference at Scotland Yard at 10.00 am tomorrow. Channel 4 and Exposure have undertaken to the Police that we shall say nothing further at this stage. When there are further developments we shall make further announcements. Everyone here is shocked and deeply upset by this tragedy, and our thoughts and prayers are with her fiancé, Jamie Stallard, and the Galloway family."

Niall switched off the TV, threw down the remote, and ran up to the bedroom. His wife was reading. "Jenny. Lynn's dead. Shot. Phone Karen and see if she's OK. Lynn was her best friend. I've got to go back to the office and find some papers Lynn was sending me every couple of weeks." He had gone before his wife could say a word. By the time she recovered from the shock and followed him to the top of the staircase, the front door was closing behind him.

***

At his office Niall unlocked the safe and extracted a small pile of A4 envelopes, each fairly thick. Strictly in accordance with the instructions on the outside, he had never opened one of them before. He did so now, and with his practised lawyer's eye swiftly scanned the pages of type, gathering the gist of it; then he sorted the bundles of pages into chronological order. He kept the envelopes in case they were needed for fingerprints or other forensic evidence.

Having locked the safe and his office he sped off to Lancaster Gate in the hope that he'd find someone at Exposure, late though it was. The premises in Lancaster Gate were brightly lit, and although the heavy duty glass doors were locked, he could see a security guard in reception sitting at a desk watching CCTV footage. There were other people about, and it was clear that programmes were still being made. He rang a bell, and the guard came to the door. He spoke through an intercom, and asked what Niall wanted.

"I've just heard the news, that one of Exposure TV's top reporters has been found shot dead. I've got some vital information here that I should pass on to Marion Gorman, one of the editors, at once."

"OK, Sir. Just hang on a moment and I'll check. Who did you say you are?"

"I didn't. I'm Lynn Galloway's – she's the dead reporter – solicitor, Niall Merrylees."

The guard went to the desk, and picked up the phone. Niall could see but not hear him talking. Suddenly he put down the phone, ran to the doors, opened them fast and almost dragged Niall inside. As he shut and locked the door, he said: "Miss Gorman said 'Thank God he's come.' She's got the police here. You can tell them too. You're to go straight up in the lift over there, Sir. Floor three. Turn left and her office is second door down on the left."

Moments later, Niall knocked on Marion Gorman's door and she opened it immediately. She whispered and pointed: "That's Jamie Stallard, that one's Detective Inspector Lacey, and the other one is Detective Constable Shuttleworth. The man over there is Julian Prentis, the company solicitor. We're just showing them films of Lynn's interviews with witnesses in her investigation into SEA 439. Come and sit down and watch the rest. Then we'll talk and look at your offering."

Niall shook hands with them all, and gave Jamie, whom he knew well, a manly hug.

Half an hour later the filmed interview with Captain Subrama finished. The video of Lynn and Greg calling on Pretorius, and of him taking a pot-shot at Matt, followed. The films of Gavin, Esterhazy, Mrs Subrama, and Nancy Koh had already been shown. Marion suggested they put their chairs in a circle so conversation would be easier. This done and everyone seated, Marion introduced Niall. "What have you got for us?"

"Well, first, I just want to tell Jamie here that I'm so sorry for you, and what you must be going through. I haven't had a chance to talk to my wife or my sister Karen about it, but they'll be as devastated as I am." The two men stood and had another manly hug, and sat back down. Jamie was too upset to speak.

Niall opened his briefcase. He pulled out the thick wad of Lynn's notes, and handed them to Marion. "Lynn has been sending these notes to me every few weeks for the last few months. Each envelope told me not to open any of them unless something happened to her, and if it did, to bring them all to you."

"And you just heard the news tonight?"

"I was at home watching TV news when they said Lynn had been found shot dead. I went straight to the office, collected these papers, had a quick shufty at them, and came here at once."

"So you know it's about the missing plane, and is connected to the film you saw just now."

Niall took a deep breath, and shut his eyes for a moment. "Yes. Sorry, but it's a terrible shock. I've known Lynn since I was a teenager; she was at school with my sister. My thoughts don't seem to be my own at the moment."

Lacey stood and said to Niall: "We all understand, Mr Merrylees. I need to see these papers too." He went to take the papers from Marion, but she went to the door with them, and as she went out she said over her shoulder: "I'll get more copies made, so we can all read one."

Niall looked at Lacey. "I may be jumping the gun, but it looks to me as though the CIA had her bumped off to kill the story."

"Yes. I understand Lynn hadn't given the whole thing to Miss Gorman yet, so until you showed up it seemed the story might never be complete."

"I'm new to this case, obviously, and haven't seen all the interviews. I haven't even had the chance to read Lynn's story properly yet, but as a lawyer, it looks to me as though you're never going to be able to lay hands on anyone for this terrible crime, even though it was committed on English soil."

Julian Prentis said: "That's my analysis too."

Lacey held up his hands, palms to the front, as if surrendering to the idea. "That's what Lynn told me, and what Miss Gorman thinks. I've seen the interviews, and haven't read Lynn's story yet, but I'm coming to the same conclusion."

At that moment, Marion returned and handed out copies of Lynn's notes for Jamie, Julian, and the two detectives. "I heard that, Inspector, and that's still my view. Let's read the story, and decide how to proceed."

By the time they finished, it was nearly four o'clock in the morning. Lacey expressed his opinion. "The best way to proceed is to show all this to the Foreign Secretary and ask her to put it to the American Embassy that the four men who took the plane, and this bloke Pretorius, should be extradited and sent back here to help our investigations."

Marion rose and walked round the room. "That sounds like a plan, but what about Lynn's story - our story? I want to put it out there a-s-a-p. Wouldn't it put a lot of pressure on the USA to do the right thing?"

Jamie laughed: "It would, but bear this in mind: although they supported Sweden's attempts to get Julian Assange extradited to Sweden, they won't agree to do the same with their own people. Niall and Prentis are right. They won't even let their people be prosecuted abroad for war crimes. The helicopter crew which assassinated those journalists in Iraq have never been charged. Hypocrisy rules!"

Lacey looked at Marion Gorman. She stopped her perambulations and looked back at him as he told her: "Pressure on the USA is about all we'll get, I think. I must say this: good TV works, like Crimewatch brings in the villains. If you put out a programme soon, it'll help put a rocket up the government to make them send a strong message to Washington. They won't like the adverse public reaction if they're seen to do nothing about Miss Galloway's death. Look how upset people were when Jill Dando was murdered on her own doorstep."

Jamie said: "Christ. That was in Fulham too, just round the corner from us."

Lacey continued: "It might even help me and it might help the relatives of the people on SEA439. I'll support the idea of the programme going out; it might make more evidence and witnesses come to light. Shuttleworth and I must go now, and we'll get Jamie dropped off at his home. I'll see you all at the press conference tomorrow."

The meeting broke up quickly, and everyone made for home and bed.

12th August, 2015.

The press conference hall at Scotland Yard was packed with crime and Court journalists and TV cameras. Lacey sat at the centre of the table on the rostrum, flanked by Mr and Mrs Galloway and Lynn's brother Michael to his left, and Jamie, Marion and Julian to his right. Occasionally glancing at some notes he started.

"Good morning, ladies and gentlemen of the press. As you already know, Lynn Galloway, investigative journalist with Exposure TV, was found dead near Petersfield yesterday morning. I'm sure all of you will know Marion Gorman from that company, and the company solicitor, Julian Prentis, sitting to my right. You will not know Jamie Stallard here, also on my right, nor Mr and Mrs Galloway, to the left of me. Jamie is Lynn's fiancé. He is not a suspect in the case. Mr and Mrs Galloway are Lynn's parents, and the gentleman at the end is their son, Lynn's brother Michael. I'm pleased to say they're not suspects either; please show all four of them the utmost respect at this dreadful time. It was Mr Stallard's unpleasant duty to have to identify the body.

"It seems that Lynn was kidnapped from her car near Shere in Surrey. She appears to have been tortured for some reason ..." (Gasps and mutterings of 'Oh God' and similar expressions ran round the room) "... which I shall not go into at present.

"I'll permit no questions about the investigation I'm pursuing, and if any are asked, this conference will terminate at once. That's because this case has serious international ramifications, it seems. This morning I spoke to the Foreign Secretary and shared the information we have with her. She asked me to give no details of our suspicions until she has had an opportunity to take advice from her Permanent Secretary and Cabinet colleagues.

"You may ask Mr and Mrs Galloway, Mr Stallard, and Miss Gorman, about Lynn Galloway as a person, and as a journalist, and about her highly successful but tragically terminated career.

A journalist spoke: "Will that be it, then?"

"No. When I have been advised by the Foreign Secretary on the approach she wishes to take about the international aspects, it may be possible to hold another conference. I shall arrange for you to be kept informed."

A man's hand went up in the front row and Lacey nodded to him. "Mr Reynolds from *'The Times'*, I think. Yes."

"Thank you, Superintendent Lacey. My question is for Mr Stallard. First, however, I want to thank the parents and Mr Stallard for coming this morning on this dreadful occasion." He swept the room with a gesture. "Nearly all of us have met or worked with Lynn Galloway in the past and we have the greatest respect for her and the quality of her work. The whole of the media and the discerning public lost a great deal when you lost her. You have our deepest sympathy." Murmurs of 'Hear, hear', and 'Well said' echoed round the room. Jamie took out a handkerchief and wiped his face.

"Before I turn to the family, Mr Lacey, you said that Miss Galloway had been tortured. Would it give too much away, or prejudice your investigation to tell us why you believe that?"

"No, Mr Reynolds, I think I can share that with you. In any case, with your resources, or those of your colleagues, you would probably be able to find out that she had been harshly tied up, hit violently in the face at least once, and that the presence of water in her lungs indicated that she ..."

"Had been water-boarded before she was shot?" This was shouted from the middle row.

Several reporters said 'Christ' or 'Jesus', or four letter words under their breath. Mrs Galloway started to cry at the same time as a young woman in the second row. Even Reynolds, a veteran 'crime hack', as he called himself, had turned very pale, removed his spectacles, and wiped his eyes.

"Thank you Mr Lacey, though I'm not sure that 'thanks' is the right word. Some of us may draw some conclusions from the water-boarding. Would we be right?"

"You may well think that, but I cannot possibly comment." Even the hacks laughed, politely.

Mr Reynolds accepted that. "Thank you again. Mr Stallard, please can you tell me ...."

***

Mr and Mrs Galloway had gone home with their son

Michael. They were given a Police escort, and two constables were stationed in their house. Lacey and Shuttleworth stayed at the Yard. Marion and Jamie, with Julian, returned to Lancaster Gate. They were joined by Malcolm Broadbridge, the producer. There was a strong sense of excitement in the room, mixed with some anxiety, as they discussed the future of the programme.

Marion asked Julian: "Do you think the Foreign Secretary intends to issue a D notice against the programme?"

"I very much doubt it. I've been thinking about it ever since she phoned Lacey yesterday. I've looked it up, and confirmed my view that she has no grounds to do that. This is an American embarrassment, and nothing to do with our government, or our national security."

Julian had just finished when the phone rang. Marion rolled her eyes at everyone as she answered it: "Very well, Ellen, put her through." She put the phone on speaker. There was a pause. "Yes, Foreign Secretary, this is Marion Gorman."

"I have been told about the press conference this morning. I want you to join me here at the Foreign Office at 2.00 pm."

Another pause. "I understand, Foreign Secretary. We shall be with you at 2.00 pm."

Marion put down the phone. "Well, you all heard that. We'll get a sandwich and some coffee, and then call some cabs. I want you to come, Jamie. I can't guarantee you'll be admitted to her sanctum, but it'll be difficult for her politically to keep you out."

***

At 2.00 pm precisely Marion, Malcolm Broadbridge, Julian Prentis and Jamie were shown into the Foreign Secretary's grand office. An attempt was made to keep Jamie out, but when Julian pointed out in his most professional manner to the underling to whom this most unpleasant duty had been delegated that the political downside of his exclusion might terminate his minister's career he caved in.

When they entered the Foreign Secretary was standing behind her desk and advanced round it accompanied by an elegant and distinguished silver haired sixty year old man. The Foreign Secretary introduced him as Sir Arthur Napier, her Permanent Secretary. Marion introduced her team and Jamie. Ritual pressing of the flesh took place. The Minister returned to her chair behind the desk, and it was left to Sir Arthur to invite the visitors to sit in a semi-circle of chairs facing her.

"Thank you for coming, Miss Gorman, and for bringing Mr Stallard." She gave a nod of acknowledgement in Jamie's direction. "My stenographer is over there. The first thing I must emphasise is how sorry we in the Cabinet, and here at the FO are about Miss Galloway's death. You have our sincerest condolences, Mr Stallard."

"Thank you Madam." It might be said that he had a tinge of scepticism in his tone of voice.

"That said, let us get down to brass tacks. I am bound by the Cabinet to tell you, Miss Gorman, that you and Channel 4

328

cannot go ahead with a programme focussing on the plane, SEA 439."

Jamie leaned forward. "I'm Jamie Stallard, OK? My girl died pursuing that story in the interests of freedom of speech and freedom of the press and media. And you're telling me these good people can't make a story about it? Is it something the public don't need to know, or just something you don't want them to know? And don't give me any more old cods-wallop about feeling sorry for me! Or about being glad I came. Your slave tried to keep me from seeing you!"

The Foreign Secretary was icy. "I understand your frustration, Mr Stallard. Indeed I do. However, the diplomatic and international consequences of allowing Miss Gorman to tell this story would be catastrophic. I have had a telephone call from the Secretary of State in Washington. He told me that you, Miss Gorman, phoned the Head of the CIA yesterday to ask if the US Government had any comment on the story that the CIA had itself 'hijacked' Flight SEA 439, and had murdered Lynn Galloway for investigating the story."

"It's true. I did. We have to try to be fair, no matter how we feel, so we give the other side of the tale the opportunity to comment. The CIA Chief declined to speak to me, and put me on to a spokesperson. This mouthpiece didn't even deny it. She just kept saying 'No comment', until I put the phone down. I recorded the call."

The anger in the Foreign Secretary's voice was barely disguised. "I hardly need to tell you, Miss Gorman, that this country's special relationship with the USA ...."

Malcolm boomed: "Special relationship my arse! They just murdered Lynn, didn't they? And if the story is right, about 250 other people as well. What's special about that, I'd like to know!"

"Who might you be?"

"Malcolm Broadbridge, Ma'am," Marion said, quietly and calmly.

"I noticed that Mr Broadbridge said 'if the story is right'. If there is any doubt about it you should not be contemplating making it."

Marion was most diplomatic. "We have no doubt. All of us have a great deal invested in this matter, intellectually, emotionally, and financially, and it's hard to swallow that when our friend Lynn has been viciously and violently taken from us you don't want us to do anything about it. Foreign Secretary, I am sure we shall all try to conduct the rest of this discussion in a peaceful fashion."

"Thank you, Miss Gorman. I regret that I have to be the harbinger of bad news, but I too have orders to obey, and mine come from the Cabinet. I repeat what I said at the outset. Exposure TV is not to make and Channel 4 is not to broadcast any programme that focuses on or has as its main theme the fate of SEA 439. Sir Arthur has prepared and I have signed a letter expressing that clearly, and it is being emailed to you as we speak. This is the hard copy. Is what I have said understood?"

Everyone in the room said "Yes." Julian said: "It's not a D notice then."

Sir Arthur reluctantly agreed. Marion took the letter and said: "Good bye," everyone shook hands except Jamie, who looked with contempt at the one the Foreign Secretary extended to him, and said: "You'll be on the BBC boasting about freedom of speech soon, I suppose." He marched out before she could respond.

Outside the minister's refuge there was a prolonged silence. No-one moved. All stood with their hands in their pockets or arms folded across their chests. Excitement tinged with anxiety had been replaced by profound depression.

***

Back at Lancaster Gate everyone sat subdued and quiet in Marion's office. At last Julian rose and walked to the door. He leaned through it and spoke to Ellen. "There's an email on its way from the Foreign Office to Miss Gorman. Could you print off four copies and bring them in, please?"

"It came in just now, Mr Prentis. I'll bring the copies in a sec."

Julian thanked her, shut the door, and strode round the room. "The important thing is what this email and letter actually say. If it's exactly what she said, I have a plan."

"Not one of Baldrick's, I hope, Julian," Marion commented. There were some quiet chuckles. Everyone needed a lighter mood.

"Even so, I hope it's sufficiently cunning. It's just an old lawyer mucking about with the meaning of words. It's what we do."

With a knock on the door Ellen entered and handed each of them a copy of the email.

Julian, having read his copy, waved it in the air. "This is the important bit. 'Her Majesty's Government insists that Exposure TV does not make and Channel 4 does not broadcast a programme or a series of programmes focusing on or having as the main theme the disappearance of the South East Asian Airways Flight SEA439. This embargo applies equally to all other TV and radio channels, and all parts of the press and media. If there is any rumour of such a programme being made, application will immediately be made to the High Court for an Injunction.'"

Jamie was puzzled. "Why do they use this sort of jargon? Why don't they just tell you not to make any programme at all about the plane?"

Julian and Marion started to speak simultaneously. Julian gave way, and Marion explained: "They cannot do that, Jamie. There have been many programmes and news items about the plane, which will continue. After all, it is still the world's greatest tragic air travel mystery. Ordering that no more should be made would be ridiculous. What they do not want is one that focuses on its *disappearance*."

"That is correct." Julian sounded like an oracle. "And that is our answer. We make a programme which doesn't focus on the plane's disappearance, but we tell the story anyway."

"Bloody hell!" Malcolm roared with laughter. Another brilliant idiot in the profession? "How do we do that, for God's sake?"

Julian smiled. "I'm not sure we'd be doing it for His sake, though I'm sure He's as interested in the public getting the truth as we are. Unfortunately it's some while since He made a Divine Revelation to me. How long did you think the old programme idea would take to make?"

"About two weeks from now, and part of it has been done, but we don't have Lynn as presenter." Marion sounded truly anxious. "I'm not sure we want to fall foul of the Government just now, Julian. We've been down that route before."

"Of course we have. What TV station or newspaper worth the name hasn't? But what was the result? Every time it happened our ratings and viewers increased, so adverts poured in to the commercial channels which showed our work, and we received more and more requests to make programmes for them and the BBC." Julian paused. "The partially written script can be redrafted, the stuff Mr Merrylees brought in has to be written up, and I have to go through it with my legal toothcomb and our outside lawyers anyway."

Jamie stood up and went over to Julian, shook his hand, and looked at each of the team in turn. "You all owe it to Lynn. She gave her life for this story, and you could say for Exposure too. We can't just let the Government and the Yanks bury it. The whole thing was evil, and there's no point in fighting evil with evil, and ending up as bad as, or worse than, the people we're supposed to be fighting."

Marion agreed with that, and started walking around the room again, talking as she went. "I think you should still be able to get it finished in two weeks. We have all of Lynn's notes now, thank goodness, plus the films of Johnson,

Esterhazy, and Subrama and his two women, all with Lynn in them. We can make drama reconstructions of the violence, the deaths of Greg Armstrong and Subrama. We need to write a script from Lynn's notes. And we need an actress to read them."

Malcolm interrupted. "Lynn had recorded some of it up to a couple of weeks before she was killed, and didn't Matt get some footage of the Australian woman accosting Lynn in Sydney airport about her husband vanishing with the plane? She barged into the filming. Surely we don't need her permission to use that. Make a stunning start to the programme. And there's Pretorius shooting at Matt."

Julian paused. "Well, we can think about the Australian woman. One thing we can be quite sure of; when this programme goes out, Pretorius and his gang will never be safe outside the USA, and maybe not even in it. I shall see my opposite numbers at Channel 4 to check that they agree the Government can't stop us. If they won't show Lynn's investigation we'd be sunk. However, I strongly doubt that the Government will apply to the Court; the case is far from strong or certain. If it failed our programme would be even more successful than we think it will in any event. Now this is what we'll do."

9.00 pm, 27th August, 2015

For two weeks Channel 4 had been broadcasting trailers of Lynn's story, after their lawyers had agreed with Julian that the programme should go out. Tonight was the night.

The music ended. Sibelius's 'At the Castle Gates' was a dramatic introduction for what was to follow. There was to be no background music. The programme was beautifully filmed, and the story so full of drama and suspense that music would only detract from its power.

"Good evening. I'm Marion Gorman. I am the editor at Exposure TV. It's an unusual role for me to present a programme. It is also a great honour, but one I should rather not have had. I should prefer it to have been presented by my friend and colleague, Lynn Galloway, but as you will be aware, she was shot dead just over two weeks ago. I was working with her on the story she had been pursuing at the time of her murder, the story of the missing plane, SEA429. Our Board of Directors therefore thought it fitting that I should introduce a tribute to Lynn, and Channel 4, who commissioned the story, agreed, despite the fact that we had been told by the Foreign Secretary that the Government did not want such a story aired.

"The programme is in two parts. This part will concentrate on the work Lynn was doing in the last months of her life, and why it resulted in her being killed.

"An actress will read Lynn's own words about that work, and the story behind it, and you will see some film of Lynn recording interviews with witnesses. We should very much have wished to make a programme just about that story, but the United States' Secretary of State and our Foreign Secretary have insisted, in the interests of international relations, that we do not do that. We shall not flout their wishes. This programme will focus on the life and work of

Lynn Galloway. Tonight's episode will focus on the dedication she fearlessly showed in investigating an extremely dangerous, not to say fatal, situation.

"Tonight you will see Lynn's interviews with a former Royal Marine, Gavin Johnson, and an actor playing the part of an American sailor. They will tell you what happened on the British atoll called Diego Garcia, in the Indian Ocean, on 9th March 2013. Many of you will realise that that is the date the ill-fated South East Airways Flight SEA439 took off from Kuala Lumpur and apparently disappeared. A recording of the actor playing the US Navy sailor has been spliced into Lynn's interview with the real sailor. Why have we used an actor? Because there are real fears that the sailor would be murdered if his identity were revealed.

"That those fears are real is illustrated by the fact that Greg Armstrong, a former paratrooper, who was acting as Lynn's bodyguard, was himself killed doing his duty when a violent and deliberate attempt to kill Lynn was made by trying to run her down. A dramatic reconstruction of that hit and run crash will be shown. And of course, Lynn herself was tortured and shot through the forehead. Further evidence is that another of Lynn's interviewees was murdered.

"You will see a film of that interview with the pilot of SEA439 talking to Lynn Galloway a few weeks ago. Yes, she found him, quite by chance, in Argentina. She had met him years ago, and was able to identify him, despite his appearance having been radically changed by plastic surgery. His name, you will recall, was Captain Muhamed Subrama. He was gunned down outside his home a few days after Lynn talked to him. We think that occurred because the CIA did not want Lynn to meet him. They did not know that he had already been interviewed by Lynn and her team. A dramatisation of that assassination will also be shown.

"In another film you will see a CIA agent, who works for a CIA off-shoot called Noga Corporation, take aim and fire a rifle at Matt Gordon. Matt is one of our cameraman who was filming Lynn's attempt to interview the CIA agent, Zane Pretorius III, known as Adam Dennis, about his role in the 'disappearance' of the aeroplane. Fortunately Matt was not hit by the bullet fired by Mr Pretorius. In referring to SEA439 I say 'disappearance' with quotation marks, because, as you will hear, it did not in fact disappear. If it had, naturally Lynn would have been unable to talk to the pilot.

"You will watch an interview between one of Lynn's colleagues, Simon Schaffer, and Dr Graham Phillips, the pathologist in Portsmouth who examined Lynn's body the day after her murder. You will hear him describe the torture to which she was subjected, and the method of her murder. This may be distressing, especially when he shows photos of her wounds. Children under 15 should not watch this programme, and those under 18 only with their parents or a suitable adult.

"The purpose of this broadcast is to show the skill and dedication of serious journalists in general, and of Lynn Galloway in particular. They follow a story fearlessly and at great risk to themselves, to bring you, the public, information about what is done in your name, in the name of your country, and in the name of the USA, allegedly the home of true democracy and freedom of speech and of the press.

"Next week we shall deal with Lynn's earlier life and career, her relationship with her fiancé Jamie, her childhood with her parents, and more of the exciting and risky stories she followed up."

Marion was replaced on screen by an attractive actress who resembled Lynn as far as possible, even to the same halo of auburn hair. She was sitting in one of the burgundy velvet armchairs in the lounge of Jamie and Lynn's Fulham home.

"In April this year my boyfriend, Jamie Stallard, went to watch a football match in Buenos Aires, Argentina. He was mugged and knifed after the game, and nearly died. I went to see him in hospital there. It was all a terrible shock. Not just because of Jamie, but because, by the most amazing chance, I found Captain Muhamed Subrama, the pilot of SEA 439 alive and well. The whole world had been led to believe he probably committed suicide and took all his crew and the passengers, more than 250 people, to the bottom of the ocean with him. This is my story."

Epilogue

In 2016 Jamie Stallard accepted on behalf of Lynn Galloway the Bafta award for the best TV documentary of 2015.

On 23rd November, 2017, the New York Times, under the by-line of Jackie Dent, and the headline "An American Spy Base Hidden in Australia's Outback," published an article about some peace protesters who were prosecuted for getting too close to this highly protected 'Big Brother' monitoring communications for the USA.

The report included this: "From the base known as 'The Joint Defence Facility Pine Gap', the United States controls satellites that gather information used to pinpoint air strikes around the world and target nuclear weapons, among other military and intelligence tasks, according to experts and leaked National Security Agency documents."

At this joint US/Australian facility these 'other military and intelligence tasks' include helping target deadly drone strikes on countries with which neither the US nor Australia are at war. The likelihood is that the public will never be told whether the capability of Pine Gap enables it to intercept and stop aircraft communications, or distort the signals the plane sends out.

Until the Bradley Mannings, Edward Snowdens, Clive Pontings, and Julian Assanges of this world are regarded as heroes, not villains, no-one will ever really know the answer to mysteries like this one, or MH370, except the villains behind them.

Annexe
Aircraft Communications Systems

There are six of these:

1) Primary Radar.

2) Secondary Radar.

3) Aircraft Communication and Recognition System (known as ACARS).

4) Satellite Communication System (known as SATCOM).

5) Inmarsat.

6) VHF radio.

1) Primary radar is the oldest sort, invented in the Second World War to warn a country's Defence Forces of approaching aircraft which might be hostile. It bounces radio waves off an aircraft giving some idea of its approach. It has a limited range of about 200 miles.

2) Secondary Radar was invented soon after the primary. It involves Air Traffic Control (ATC) giving a civilian airline pilot a code to enter into a transponder. The code can be identified by ATC and by military installations when the transponder sends out signals. In effect the transponder is a broadcasting or signalling device. The pilot can turn it off as well as turn it on. Like Primary Radar its range is also limited to about 200 miles. Military aircraft have a separate

transponder and code system, which is not accessible to civilian ATC.

3) Aircraft Communication and Recognition System (ACARS) is similar in some ways to Secondary Radar except that it has a much greater range. The aircraft has an inbuilt code of its own in a VHF broadcasting unit. This code is unique to each aircraft. As far as I can make out it broadcasts information about the position and identity of the plane to receiving stations on the ground so that Air Traffic Control and military installations can be sure of what they are looking at. Over land masses like the five continents it can do this via mobile telephone services or satellites. Over the Oceans it has to do it via satellites. This is part of SATCOM. To the best of my knowledge ACARS cannot be turned off by the pilot. That does not mean it cannot be done, just that I have been unable to find the answer, as no-one answers the question. It is therefore more than just odd that the ACARS system of MH370 stopped working. MH370 was the aircraft which disappeared on 8th March 2014 on its flight from Kuala Lumpur to Beijing. I have based this novel on that tragedy.

4) SATCOM. See 3). This is the satellite communication system through which ACARS messages are sent when over the seas.

5) Inmarsat. This is a real company based in England. It has receiving stations on the ground around the world. The one which is said to have monitored MH370 was situated near Perth in Western Australia. The system uses several satellites orbiting above the Earth in partially fixed positions to give coverage over pretty well the whole of the planet's surface so that most flights can be monitored. The aircraft had a device called a SATCOM terminal which operated on Inmarsat Classic Aero System [5]. a) This terminal broadcasts signals to the ground stations via the satellites. The ground stations then pass the signals on to Inmarsat in London. The signal includes details of the performance of many parts of the plane, including the engines, the control flaps, the 'rudder' on the fin, the doors and more besides, as well as the position of the plane, its altitude, speed, and the amount of fuel on board. Inmarsat passes on the relevant details to the engine manufacturers, and the plane makers. This alerts them and others to possible problems on the plane, and helps with future design for flight safety. The aircraft normally sends a signal at regular intervals. In the case of MH370 they seem to have been intended to be every hour, but they stopped after about a couple of hours of flight, and then the alternative system kicked in.

b) The alternative is that when the plane stops sending the signals, the ground station monitoring the plane sends a signal, known as a heartbeat, to the plane, and if the plane bounces it back it is known as a 'handshake'. It was from these signals and heartbeats that various bodies involved in the investigations into its disappearance have tried to calculate where MH370 went.

6) VHF radio is the means by which the pilot communicates with ground operations on the tarmac, and is also for use with navigation aids. It may well be tuned to the same frequency as the ACARS system.

Acknowledgements

I have received a great deal of help with the aeroplane and technical side of this book from my cousin Winston Bunn, and my old school-friend Nick Carter, both of whom are very experienced commercial pilots. Any technical mistakes are mine, not theirs. In any case, this is a novel, not a flying manual.

What emerged during the course of my trying to understand and get full information about aircraft communications systems was that pilots do not have to know, and are not necessarily told exactly how these things work. That later became very apparent with the crashes of two Boeing 737Max planes where pilots had been given limited information about the way the autopilot computers functioned. Nick approached another commercial pilot with a large airline, a friend of his, who did not know the answers either. What Lynn Galloway says about the emails to and from Inmarsat, Rolls Royce, the Malaysian Investigation Team, the ATSB, and three academics who are apparently experts in fields relevant to this tragedy, is actually what happened to my enquiries. I have not used the correct names, and I have made minor changes to the wording of my emails, in the hope of avoiding embarrassing individuals. I have also altered the dates of those emails to 2015 to coincide with the story. In fact all of them were in 2017. One of the academics replied briefly and said he would write again, but never did; one answered my main question to him, but the answer was not conclusive, as he made clear, because it involves secret defence information to which he had no access; and the third did not even acknowledge my emails, but left it to his department to brush me off. There are three possible reasons for this: first, some addressees did not receive them (but they did not bounce back); secondly, they did not wish to admit they do not know the answers; thirdly, they know the answers, but they are top secret and they are not allowed to tell anyone.

I suppose there is a fourth possibility: my questions were too stupid to warrant any attention. However, if that were so, it is odd that the three pilots did not think so, and the three academics did not say they thought so.

For background on terrorism, political deception, secrecy, and cover-ups I am indebted to David Leigh and Luke Harding's book on Wikileaks and Julian Assange; David Leigh's book 'Betrayed," about the Matrix Churchill case in the UK in 1991-2; and Peter Taylor's "Talking to Terrorists." For a factual account of hijacks, straightforward disasters, mechanical malfunctions, and aircraft disappearances I read, profited from, and enjoyed Nigel Cawthorne's book "Flight MH370 The Mystery," and Geoff Taylor and Ewan Wilson's "The Truth Behind the Loss of Flight MH370" (also known as "Goodnight Malaysian 370").

I have read Christine Negroni's very interesting "The Crash Detectives." It did not, in my opinion, shed any new light on MH370, but it gave examples of government and aircraft industry cover-ups such as the fatal crashes of Arrow Air Flight 1285 in Canada on 12th December, 1985, and Eastern Airlines Flight 980 on 1st January, 1985 near La Paz, Bolivia. She also made the curious point that conspiracy theories help cover-ups by diverting attention from where inquiries should be directed. I find that a circular argument, for if a conspiracy theory happened to be correct, labelling it fanciful or 'far out' may mean no-one ever takes the truth of it seriously. Whether someone is kidnapped for rendition, or a plane is blown up in mid-air by Jihadists, flown into a skyscraper, or shot down by a government anxious to eliminate enemies, people have to conspire together to do it, and conspire to cover it up. Think Watergate, or the Pentagon Papers, or Matrix Churchill.

When I thought this book was ready for submission, I was told about "Someone is Hiding Something" by Belzer, Wayne and Noory. It reaches no conclusion, but, as the title indicates, they, like me, believe we just aren't getting the facts on this plane.

The Youtube film of a plane landing on Diego Garcia is (or was) at www.youtube.com/watch?v=mLmzvF2qkDY.

I have referred extensively to Wikipedia, various newspaper articles, TV reports and programmes, many items on the internet, and a very clear account of the basic facts of the disappearance of MH370 in a documentary on the Discovery Channel made by Document Nation published on 19th June 2015.

Making Lynn Galloway the lead character in the book was helped enormously by a lot of first class but blunt advice from Deborah Davies, a highly respected investigative journalist, formerly with Channel 4 TV and then with al Jazeera in the USA and UK. To the extent that I may have been able to make Lynn's role at all realistic is down to her, but she is not to blame if I have failed.

I am indebted to Dave Gregory, OBE, QPM, Coroner's Officer for Portsmouth, and Steve Jefferies of Hollands, Funeral Directors of Chichester, for making sure I referred to the correct location for the Pathological post mortem examination of Lynn's body.

Whilst the facts of the disappearance of my plane are those of the saga of MH370, the airline "South East Asia Airways" is a figment of my imagination, as are all the characters, apart from two in the following paragraph and my retired pilot friend Nick Carter, and his wife Liz, who are very real and lovely people.

Any resemblance in this novel to a real company - apart from "The Company" (the CIA), Rolls-Royce, and Inmarsat - or real person is entirely unintended, apart from Nick and Liz Carter, the solicitor Julian Prentis, and Detective Inspector Colin Lacey. Julian was my principal when I was an articled clerk in Gray's Inn. He was an old-school solicitor, a gentleman whose word was his bond and his integrity like a fortress. The man in this novel is moulded on the real Julian. Similarly with Colin Lacey, who was a Detective Chief Superintendent, and came to work for me as a litigation assistant in my South Coast solicitor's practice for some years following his retirement from the Police.

This is a work of fiction. It is a possible explanation for what could happen to an aircraft if any of the super-powers - the USA, Russia, China, or even smaller but very sophisticated nations like the United Kingdom, Israel, or

France - organised it. In my tale, Lynn and others give examples of what the first five have done in the past. It must not be forgotten that, in their efforts to preserve their right, with those other countries, to destroy the planet with nuclear weapons, the French Special Forces blew up the Greenpeace ship 'Rainbow Warrior" in Auckland Harbour in July 1985, killing an innocent man on board. The then Prime Minister of New Zealand called it 'an act of state sponsored terrorism'.

My villains did not have to be from the USA. They could have been Russians, anxious to get their hands on the Freescale Semiconductor employees who were on MH370, to find out what the company's work for US Defence industries involved, and maybe how to copy it, or damage it. In that case, a safe landing of MH370 up in, or towards, Turkmenistan on the northern arc would have been very convenient. It could have been the Chinese, after the same people for the same reason, but clever enough not to kidnap them off the plane when it landed in China, thereby provoking a massive international incident, for although most of these technical people were Chinese, the others were Malaysian.

We know that someone hacked National Health Service Records in the UK, and the North Koreans are suspected of hacking much else. Most famously, the Russians are alleged to have used the internet to manipulate the 2016 US Election causing Donald Trump to beat Hillary Clinton. Iranian cyber warfare groups apparently hacked the New York Stock Exchange causing it to malfunction, and the same has been done by others to Banks, and the New York dam control system, which, fortunately, was closed for maintenance. The latter is truly frightening, if true, since if billions of gallons of water were released unexpectedly around a city the size of New York, thousands could die. Is it likely that these hackers are better than the Americans, and have more sophisticated equipment? A BBC interview with an American cyber war consultant about all that was broadcast on ABC Radio 24 hour news on 20th December, 2017.

So where did MH370 go?

It is odd that as I neared finishing this book, three new articles appeared in the media. One in effect advertised Ean Higgins book "The Hunt for MH370." I have now read that book, which does not detract from my fictional solution to the problem. One is a claim by a fisherman to have witnessed the plane go down in the sea and to have entered the coordinates into his GPS (but giving no explanation for waiting almost five years to come forward). The third is an announcement from Cardiff (Wales) and Curtin (Western Australia) Universities that they have plotted a new crash location from seabed data from near Perth and Diego Garcia; the new site is north of Madagascar, where if I read the maps aright, the sea is between 4,000 and 6000 metres deep. This makes it much closer to DG, and need not be inconsistent with my plot. Another odd fact about that story is that apparently the seabed equipment recorded nothing for 25 minutes at the relevant period.

Finally, I must thank my great friends Michael Davies, who formatted and published this for me, and Ron Hindmarsh who designed and painted the book cover. My proof-reader friends did a very thorough job. They are Nick Carter, Winston Bunn, Peter Cocks, Heather Bolstler, Eric Blyth, David Russell, my son Tim, and my wife Christine, who makes all things possible. I dedicate the novel to her.

Terry Stanton.

September, 2019.

Tinonee, Australia.